BROOMS AWAY

AN ARABELLA BLACK MAGICAL COSY MYSTERY

D. A. KELLY

Edited by

REBECCA GRUBB

For Aarjaun.
You helped me to believe.
You led by example.
And your faith in me never wavered despite my self-belief
wobbling around like a tower of poorly stacked blocks.
Built on a house of cards.
And quicksand.
During an earthquake.

A WORD ON SPELLING

Before we start, I thought it best to warn readers that I use Australian English, which is similar to British.

We use 'our' instead of 'or' in words like colour. We use an 'e' instead of 'a' in words like grey. We use 's' instead of 'z' in words like criticise and cosy.

If you find a misspelled word, typo or any issue, I'd love to hear from you. I don't think there's been a book published that hasn't had at least one typo.

Email me at deb@dakellyauthor.com

D. A. Kelly

"*W*here are my stupid keys?" I tossed three red velvet cushions off my couch. They skittered across the floorboards into a wall of potted ferns. I didn't feel bad. They were scatter cushions, after all.

I gathered up my dress's flouncy teal skirt, flipped my long red hair over one shoulder and knelt in front of the couch. Black and faded, it sat centre-stage on my most recent favourite thing: a shaggy grey rug. I resisted the temptation to lie down and make rug angels in the fluffy pile. Twice was enough for one day.

With a flashlight in one hand, I peered under the couch, sweeping the light beam left and right. All I found was an impressive dust bunny. They grew humongous if you allowed them to breed up.

I clambered to my feet and scanned my lounge/dining room. Cat hair floated about like fuzzy grey snow, disturbed by my desperate search. I side-stepped the pile of freshly washed clothes I'd dumped out earlier so I could reuse the basket. The smell of Frangipani fabric softener wafted over me as I hurried past, my skirt swishing against

my army boots. I shoved a wobbly stack of garden magazines aside, causing them to slide across the pine floorboards. Yes, the boards needed vacuuming, and books,
Tarot cards, crystals, and unwashed cups cluttered the
coffee table, but living alone allowed a girl to behave
recklessly.

After coming up empty, I flopped on the couch, leaning
my chin on the flashlight's brightly lit lens.

"Mwah-ha-ha-ha!" My evil villain laugh needed work.

An eerie chill blew through the lounge room, lifting
loose strands of my hair, ruffling the grey rug like wind
through grass. I froze. A primal reaction I could not master
despite years of trying. When I had gathered my courage, I
shot to my feet, preparing for whatever ghosted into the
room.

A translucent female slipped through my bedroom
door into the lounge room, uninvited, and what's more,
unwelcome.

Why do lost souls always find me? "You know you're dead,
don't you?" I sounded rude, but I was late for work, and
my car keys wouldn't find themselves.

Dressed in sodden jeans and an overcoat fastened with
wooden toggles, the spirit had wide, wary eyes. Her feet
were bare, which made no sense considering her heavy
winter coat, but who knew what she'd been up to when
she'd died? Twigs, rotting leaves, and what looked like mud
clung to her clothes, giving me some clue about her place
of death. Long, black hair stuck to her face. She reminded
me of a character from a horror movie: one people paid
good money to see. Maybe if movie-lovers had ghosts and
lost souls visiting them at any tick of the clock, they
wouldn't be so yippie-ki-yay about those things.

"I don't have time for this right now!" I waved the
flashlight, trying to get the spirit's attention. The beam of

light bounced around, illuminating the jungle of potted ferns crowding the lounge and dining room walls. "You're leaking all over my new rug, you know."

The spirit floated a few centimeters above the shaggy mat, water puddling beneath her.

She must've just died!

The newly dead had no clue what to do once they missed their ride to the afterlife.

"Arabella?" The word echoed through my mind. "I'm looking for Arabella."

She knew my name! How did she know my name? I stepped back, my boots catching on the hem of my dress.

"Ding?" She looked left and right, glitchy as an old black-and-white film.

Oh, my shiny stars! No one called me Ding except my sister Rebecca. Still clutching the flashlight, I backed into the couch, and, not looking away, clambered backwards, up and over the saggy velour until it stood between us. Not the best protection considering she had passed through a solid pine door.

"I've come over!" the spirit said, as though dying was something on her to-do list. "She needs you."

"Who needs me?" I knew the answer. The question was a knee-jerk reaction. Gave me time to think.

"I can't remember…" The spirit raised a shaky hand to her head. She winced, whimpered, flickered for a few moments, and vanished.

An icy pressure spidered down my back—she was behind me. I closed my eyes, struggling against fear. I turned, slowly, no sudden movements.

The spirit's translucent face appeared inches from mine, her body ragged, fading to nothing. "She needs you."

A smell of blood and dank, stagnating water washed

over me. I didn't flinch—a first for me. I'd celebrate the milestone later when I could think straight. Perhaps a bottle of bubbly and a party hat.

"Are you talking about Rebecca?" Our faces were so close, my reflection stared back at me from blue-black, fathomless eyes. "Rebecca Black? Did she send you? Is she in trouble?"

Now Rebecca was a globetrotting computer whiz, she always texted or called me to touch base. My big sister, my over-protector. Annoying, but I got worried when she didn't check in on me. Come to think of it, I had heard nothing from her for a few weeks. Sending a message through a ghost, though…

The soul cocked her head. Blinked. Recognition crossed her face. She smiled, triumphant. "Rebecca! You're alive. Why are you here?"

"*I'm* Arabella! I'm Ding! Not Rebecca. You came looking for me. Did Rebecca want you to find me?"

The spirit vibrated, a shudder of washed-out fog. She stilled. Frowned, as though struggling to think. I used the chance to step back and suck in a few calming breaths.

"Your name?" I said. "Do you remember your name?"

She hesitated. Nodded. "Endraya."

I didn't know the name. Not even one that sounded similar.

"Endraya," I said. "Rebecca sent you to get me. Why? Is she in trouble?" Fear and frustration edged my voice. Getting upset would only unsettle this soul further. I slowed my breathing and forced a smile.

"She's hurting," Endraya said. "Alone and scared. You need to find her. Help her before it's too late."

"Where did you see her? In a town, city, forest? Were there people around? Any special landmarks or features that might help me find her?"

After years of trying to help the dead, I'd gathered a list of go-to questions to help narrow down a ghost's final moments.

"It was dark. I heard the water. Little waves on the shore. Frogs or crickets chirping... We were with the protestors. Then someone came with a message."

"Good!" I urged her on. "Anything else?"

"I can't..." she touched her forehead, wincing. "It hurts."

"No, sweetie, it doesn't. You're past pain and fear now."

If Endraya had been alive, I'd make her a cup of English Breakfast tea, sit her down, and we would sort out this carousel of confusion.

"I want to go home now," she said. "It's so dead over here."

For once, I had no smart-aleck reply, despite knowing there was a goody just hanging there. I doubted I would get anything more from this poor soul. I made a decision—stuff work. *Pandora's Box* nightclub could do without me tonight. I'd call in sick as soon as I crossed Endraya over. I was hopelessly late anyway, and I needed to find my sister.

"Thank you," I said. "Thank you, Endraya, for your message. You were very brave. Do you see a light?"

Endraya looked at the flashlight. She blinked. Tilted her head, frowning.

"Oh!" I smiled, fumbled with the flashlight, and switched it off. "Sorry, didn't mean to confuse you. The light you want will be bright. Full of love and people who've come to greet you. You can't miss it! Focus. And try and relax. Think of someone you love who has already passed over. That sometimes works."

"Rebecca?" Endraya asked.

I hope not! "Your mother? Father? Grandparents?"

Endraya turned, a movement too jittery for a living body to perform, a parody of life that never failed to creep me out. I shivered. No matter how many souls I saw, I would never get used to it.

I gasped. What looked like a bone-shafted arrow fletched with blue-black feathers projected from the back of her head. I'd never seen an arrow like that before. The shaft had to be as thick as a pool cue. No wonder she was so confused. She'd probably been shot and tossed in a lake or something. Now I felt rotten for being so rude when she first appeared. I tried not to think of Rebecca with a nasty arrow in her head, but I couldn't help it. Tears filled my eyes, and I scrubbed them away.

I reached forward, my hand trembling as though she was a stray dog. I'd had spirits attack me before and believe me; they're quick.

Her ghostly body strobed as though something was chewing away bits of her movement. Her eyes widened, and her mouth opened in a little 'O' of wonder.

She'd seen the Light.

A slow smile spread on Endraya's face. She really was beautiful in an elfin, ethereal way.

Without warning, she shot forward, knifing straight through my core. I dropped to my knees, clasping my chest as a freezing wind raked my body. My breath fogged the air as I gasped through the pain, and then I burst into tears.

CHAPTER TWO

Still slumped on the rug, I wiped my face with my sleeve. Crying helped no one. I scrambled to my feet. Looked left. Looked right. What should I do? Keys! I needed keys so I could drive to the police—file a missing person report. No! My phone! That'd be faster, and I wouldn't need my car keys.

My gut knotted with fear and grief. I couldn't do this alone. I had to call someone to help me. Tears caught in the back of my throat. I needed Rebecca. She was the strong one. She was my go-to girl when my life spiralled out of control. Sobs shuddered through me. I hugged myself, unable to think. Unable to decide what to do.

I shook myself. Struggled to clear my thoughts. If Rebecca could have contacted me directly, she would have. I needed a place to start searching. A clue. What would a proper detective do? I had watched enough whodunit and real-life forensic shows over the years. According to Rebecca, I had enough knowledge to be dangerous. I smiled, and more tears trickled down my cheeks.

A detective would start at the crime scene.

If only I knew where that was. Darkness, dripping water, and frogs or crickets. Not a lot to go on. Was Becca with Endraya when Endraya died? I squatted, rubbing my fingers through the remains of her puddle. Was this actual water from where she'd been killed, or had she unwittingly created it because it was the last thing she remembered? I sniffed my damp fingers. Slightly dank, earthy. I licked the moisture. Not salty, so it wasn't seawater. So, a river perhaps? Or a lake? Nothing like that existed around here unless you counted the city's four parks. And only one of those had a pond. So, somewhere else? Rivers and lakes were froggy environments, so Endraya had remembered that part accurately. But how many rivers and lakes existed throughout the world? Probably millions. As Rebecca was always travelling on business, there was no telling where she was. I had less than nothing to go on. Tears welled once more. I wiped them away, hurting my eyes.

I had to do something.

Maybe the cards will give me some clue?

Trouble was, I usually got answers I didn't want or need, like, 'Sorry, Arabella. You're being cheated on by your scuzz-bucket boyfriend.'

The break-up with Carl seemed trivial compared to this. If I did a reading now, the cards might reveal information I didn't want to know. But I *needed* to know. Tears pricked my eyes. I grabbed a fistful of Kleenex off the coffee table and blew my nose.

Time to think strong and be strong. My big sister needed me. *No more tears, you hear? You're smart, Arabella Jade Black. Smart because you think sideways. Everybody says so!*

After a few more nose blows, I gathered up my Tarot deck from the coffee table and shuffled, careful not to flick random cards from the deck (which I did more often than not.) That's what happens when you buy a big, fancy Tarot set rather than the Rider-Waite deck that fits in an average human's hands.

I closed my eyes, focusing on my need. "Where is my sister, Rebecca Kerigan Black?" Considering my mood and what I might face, the surname Black seemed appropriate given the turmoil of emotions tumbling through my mind.

I split the deck into three piles, choosing a card from each. One by one, I laid them on the couch.

"Not good!" I stared at my chosen cards. "I should have listened to myself. But, as usual, I never believe me."

First card: The Eagle, Sun, and Stars–An unexpected journey. *Hmmm! I might be short, but I'm not a hobbit! Though a journey could mean searching for Becca. I never expected that when I got up this morning.*

Next card: The Reaper, inverted–Death and upheaval leading to a fresh beginning and happiness. I looked at my messy lounge room. Upheaval was right. I didn't want to think about the death part. Though maybe it meant Endraya? I clung to that interpretation.

The third card was Queen of the Banshee–imminent death of a loved one. One of the worst cards in the deck. My breath caught in my throat. The room seemed to spin and tilt at a sickening angle. Bile filled my mouth, bitter and hot. I ripped out more Kleenex and vomited into them.

When I felt better, I scooped up the Tarot, shoved the cards back in their blue silk pouch, and pulled the draw-cord closed. The whole Tarot reading was rubbish. It hadn't even answered my question about Rebecca's whereabouts. A lazy reading always gave wonky answers. I hadn't drawn a protective circle, invoked the Five Elements, centred myself or anything, so the reading couldn't be accurate.

I only had one loved one in this world. Rebecca. Our

adoptive parents, Jen and Miles Black, were long dead. Goodness knows where our biological parents were. Whenever I'd asked, Rebecca had said she couldn't say. That it was for my own good. Who was she to decide? How was it fair that she had memories of our actual parents, and I didn't? I had nothing. Not even a tatty, faded photo.

I hurled the Tarot cards, shredding ferns as the pouch flew through them. I regretted throwing the deck, and retrieved my cards, placing them on the messy coffee table. It wasn't right to be sulky and petty about something Rebecca had no control over. It wasn't her fault she was five when we were adopted, and I was a few weeks old. I had too many fears and nothing to soothe them. Rebecca hadn't dropped by in weeks. She usually called or messaged me, but I hadn't worried much until now, thinking she was probably working abroad somewhere again. Somewhere with no internet, no phones, no mail. Not even a lousy homing pigeon. Who was I kidding? She worked with computers, installing new systems and stuff.

I grabbed the picture of my sister and me off the TV cabinet. The tarnished silver frame desperately needed polishing, but I liked the patina. Made the interlaced rose pattern look old and mysterious.

We took the photo three years ago, when we were on holiday in Germany. The best part had been the Black Forest. I could have stayed there for weeks, but we'd run out of time and money, so we took this selfie as a keepsake.

I wiped the dust off the glass with my skirt and looked at the photo. Rebecca smiled that warm movie star smile of hers. Some people said we could be twins, but we never believed them. Becca, being five feet nine, was taller than me by a good four inches. She had perfect lips—the type people paid big money to possess. I had pouty lips. I always looked sulky if I didn't smile. Becca's auburn hair sat in perfect waves. My hair was red as well, but it preferred to do its own thing no matter what product I tried. It was our eyes that fooled people. We had the same wide, deep blue-green eyes.

I dragged my fingers through my unruly hair and frowned at the photo. "Where are you, Becs? Where are you when I need you?" She always knew the right thing to say. She was special that way.

I had to call the police. Where had I put my mobile phone? I scanned the lounge room, searching for my mobile's sparkly green case. Why was I so messy and forgetful? What if the cops wanted me to come to the station to make a formal report? I'd need my confounded car keys. I was sure they were in the lounge room–I remembered dropping them on the coffee table. I surveyed the room again. My potted plants filled every nook and cranny, giving it a lovely forest feel. Still, I would need to stop buying them. Soon, I'd need a machete to watch TV. There had to be at least forty ferns and goodness knows how many other plants. What typical twenty-four year old had more plants than shoes?

I couldn't face searching through my plants. It would take ages. Instead, I headed beneath the archway into the kitchen–if you could even call it a kitchen. But then, you could hardly call me a cook, so in the grand scheme of things, the room suited me. I opened the fridge and peered inside. I had been known to leave stuff in there. Keys. The TV remote control. My mobile phone. Some would call this absentminded. I liked to think of it as *selective non-thinking*.

I pulled open the under-bench cupboards. Plates, bowls, and cups, all chipped and mismatched, sat in higgledy-piggledy piles. I really knew how to live! There were no over-bench cupboards, so that limited the search. I opened the oven door even though I wasn't stupid enough to put my keys in there. But I was thorough if nothing else.

Muffled meowing interrupted my thoughts.

"Harvey?" I ducked, looking under the two-seater table. She sometimes slept on one of the chairs, her black and grey fur looking more like a fluffy blanket than that of a Maine coon cat. Nope. I checked for her soft, way-too-expensive cat bed. It wasn't by the back door. She must have dragged it somewhere dark and cozy. Strange, because she was way too lazy to be in the furniture-moving business.

A chilling howl cut through my cottage, coming from my bedroom.

"Harvey!" I ran from the kitchen, bolting diagonally across the lounge, past the couch, to my bedroom door. I flung it open. There was Harvey, black-tufted ears twitching, soot-and-ash-coloured fur licked to perfection, sitting under my crimson quilt, which she'd cat-bulldozed into her own velvet fortress. She slew her amber gaze at me and raised her chin. Aloof and snobby, as usual.

"What's the matter?" I stood at the end of the bed, arms crossed, glaring back. "Why did you howl like that?"

"You were fluffing arrround taking farrr too much time," Harvey answered in a female voice. A human voice. Apart from the rolling, purring quality.

My mind emptied. Totally blank. Then thoughts tumbled through my brain. My eyes boggled. I'm sure I looked like a frog. I had to be dreaming. Or dead!

Maybe Endraya killed me when she blasted through my body!

"Cat got your tongue?" Harvey licked her black paw, then *smiled*. Cross my heart! She actually smiled. "You look like a frog." Harvey stood, arched her back, circled, and sat back down.

Glad I got one thing right today.

"I've made a list," Harvey said. "Come on. You have a lot of packing to do if we hope to help Rebecca."

"How do you know she's in trouble?"

"I got a garbled message."

"From Endraya?"

"Didn't get her name. Enough chit-chat. We've got things to do."

CHAPTER THREE

"First of all!" I waggled my finger at Harvey. "For six years, you have been a regular, everyday Maine coon. No talking. And definitely no list-making."

To be sure, I cast a quick–hopefully surreptitious–look around the room. Nope. No list. Things were looking up.

"First of all." Harvey raised a front paw, waggling it back at me. "It has been twenty-four years. Not six. And I have NEVER been a regular, everyday cat. The very idea is insulting. I've never had fleas, worms, or ticks. I assure you, the only parasite around here resides in the plumbing."

"Is that a fact?"

"Yes, that's a fact. You should watch yourself. You have no idea what I'm capable of. If it weren't for me, you'd probably be composting in a landfill somewhere. I am royalty. A Blood of the oldest family."

"I've fed you fresh fish, top-shelf steak, and heaven knows what else because you turned up your nose at canned food. Now it all makes sense! You think you're a queen! Delusions of grandeur or what? Harvey, queen of the litter box."

"And my name… " Harvey eyed me squarely. "What is with the name Harvey? From all my research, 'Harvey' is a male name. And an old-fashioned one, too."

I shrugged. "When you were a kitten, you used to race around the house, sliding and crashing into walls. Harvey Wall Banger—get it? The cocktail?" I was quite chuffed by the name. Came up with it all by myself.

Harvey wrinkled her nose. "I was never a kitten. And I certainly didn't run into walls."

I raised my chin. "You *were* a kitten. And you *did* run into walls. I saw you. Many times."

"You try acclimatising to a body the size of a fat mouse and see how straight you walk."

I snatched a framed photo from the side table next to my bed and thrust it at Harvey. "See this picture? It's you the morning I brought you home. You couldn't have been more than six weeks old."

"Found me in a soggy box, did you?" Harvey said. "All wet and pathetic looking? Couldn't resist the darling fluff ball of a kitty? And such marvellous timing. You were all broken up because your old cat Chummy had run away. Nowhere to be found despite searching for weeks."

"Now you're just being cruel."

"No, I am educating you. Look here." Harvey shimmered, the light fracturing around her until all I could see was a mosaic of ash-grey and black. When the light reformed, my old ginger cat, Chummy, sat before me. "See, your search has ended. I'm back. Aren't you pleased?"

I sat on the edge of the bed, needing time to think. "Are you saying you were all of my cats? Since I was born?"

"Yes, including the stray tabby your guardian-mother used to feed when she thought your guardian-father wasn't looking. You were a wee babe back then, so you probably won't remember."

"Guardian mother?"

"The female who raised you." Harvey growled low in her throat. "Do you need to know everything now? We can have a lovely chat later. We have things to do. I don't want to return to Grimsmead either." Harvey's tail twitched. "We'll just have to make the best of things."

"Right!" I folded my arms. "Moving on. I need to go to the police—see if they can help me find Rebecca."

Harvey hissed. "A waste of time."

"Not from where I stand."

"The police cannot help us. Not where we have to go."

"We'll be going nowhere if I can't find my car keys."

"You are thinking like a human."

"What? How else would I think? Like a cat?"

"Why do I suffer so?" Harvey buried her face under her paws.

I was confused, rattled, and shaking. But deep down, there was a part of me that was excited—and terrified. Who knew I had a magical cat? I had no clue what she could do. Help me find Rebecca, that's what!

"So, tell me what to do," I said. "How are we going to help Becca?"

"Firstly, we go and prod the drains in your bathroom. It's time Ploggit worked for his soap scum and hair balls."

"Oh, please!" I screwed up my nose and looked out of the doorway as if I could see around corners and through walls into my bathroom. "Who exactly is this Ploggit? Another cat?"

"Not even in his dreams. Come. I'd rather not spoil the surprise. Let us say you are in for a treat." Harvey leaped off the bed, arched her spine, stretched out one back leg then the other, and trotted across the lounge.

"Do you have a nice long stick?" Harvey asked as I opened the bathroom door. "A pointy one? With thorns?"

"Don't tell me," I said. "You're not a fan of this Ploggit character."

"Where did you get that impression?" Harvey raised her tail tall and straight, lifted her nose, and sauntered into the bathroom.

I grinned and followed. This was way better than serving beers, mopping up spilled drinks, and making chit-chat with drunken people at *Pandora's Box*!

CHAPTER FOUR

ou couldn't swing a cat in my bathroom. Believe me, I was tempted to give it a try just to be sure. Curdled-cream tiles covered the tiny area's floor and walls. Not classy, but none of them were cracked. A glass shower cubical stood in the right corner beside a chipped sink, and the toilet sat opposite. The small window between glowed with the light of a street lamp across the road. The room was dated and boring. It didn't even have a towel rack.

After searching my cottage for some kind of stick, I returned with a pool cue that had belonged to my now-ex-boyfriend, Carl. Apparently, it had cost him heaps. More than I make in a month, or so he reckoned. According to him, it was ebony and leopardwood, inlaid with fake pearl and ivory. It had emerald in the tip or something. Whatever. I had planned on using it as kindling at my next barbecue, but jabbing it into questionable drains and plumbing seemed appropriate. Almost poetic. It was probably what he was doing right now, anyway. I chuckled. *Ooh! I am nasty.*

For fun, I chalked the cue tip. Luckily Carl had left a little blue block behind, too. Never know when you might need to rack up a set.

"Oh, Carl, you poor thing," I crowed. "However, will you play with your precious balls now? Smalls, of course." I snickered. "Ooh, I'm wicked."

I plonked the fat end of the cue onto the tiles and banged it up and down a few times. Yep, worth every dollar he wasted. "Now what?"

"Not the stick I wanted," Harvey said. "But it'll do."

I wiggled the cue about in anticipation. "Can I start on the toilet?"

"You can, but I don't see why. Ploggit is a spriggit brownie, not a lowly turgill."

"I'm not going to ask."

"Try the drain in the shower first. That's always been his favourite."

Oh my gob-wobbles! I felt a little sick. "You mean he likes it in my shower? Where I'm naked?"

"Where else would he be—especially when you're showering?" Harvey looked at me as though I was an imbecile. "The water's warm. Nice soapy bubbles. Loose hair slurping down with the water. Perfect for making a winter coat."

"That's disgusting! I hope I don't have to shake his hand when I meet him."

"You'd best hope he didn't sell tickets."

My mouth gaped, and a mortifying chill ran through me.

"Ah!" Harvey chortled–a joyous, rolling purr. "It was worth being mean just to see the look on your face."

I hoped she was joking about the tickets.

With that unsettling image burning in my brain, I spied

my second-most-recent favourite thing on the tiles beside the shower: a soft, spongy white bath mat that turned blood-red when it got wet. Macabre, but fun. How many times had I hopped out of the shower and stomped around on that mat, my wet feet tracking crimson footprints across the fuzzy material? I'd flicked water, and delighted as droplets splattered in a grizzly pattern like blood from a murder, or a terrible accident. If truth be told, I'd secretly danced on the mat, naked, with pure glee.

Heat rushed through my cheeks, down my neck. What if Ploggit had been watching? With paying customers. *Roll up! Roll up! Come to the Freak Show. See the naked human perform her futile mating dance.* And what about Harvey—how many times had she rested on the tiles while I showered? While I danced? No wonder she looked at me with disdain.

Stop thinking of yourself, Ding! Rebecca needs you!

I opened the frosted-glass shower door, bent over and removed the drain cover—or whatever it was called. I decided the chalked end would be best—nice and valuable what with the emerald-in-the-tip-doodad. Smiling broadly, I jabbed the pool cue down the drain and stabbed it around, probably more than was necessary, but what-the-hey? It was a hoot!

"Try enjoying yourself a bit more," Harvey suggested. "You haven't probed China yet."

A defiant squawk bubbled up through the drain.

"One more poke for good luck." Harvey waved a paw, indicating the drain.

"You are dreadful, Harvey Wall Banger!" I withdrew the cue.

"I learned from the master."

Ignoring her, I called down the drain, my voice echoing. "Mr. Ploggit, you have visitors."

"You buying or selling?" Ploggit shouted, his voice sort of gurgling.

"Oh, my gods!" I choked on the words. "You get salesmen as well?"

"Not selling," Harvey said. "Not buying."

"You bought a visitor's pass?"

"Oh! Kill me now!" If only the floor would eat me.

"No." Harvey padded into the shower cubical and called down the drain. "Don't bother wasting time hiding your precious little hoard. No one here wants it."

"Can't be too careful. Made meself a new jacket. Don't want no-one sneaking in while I'm away. These humans— light-fingered as they come."

"Come out *now.*" Harvey scratched at the drain cover. "Or I'll drop a rat down there. One with sharp teeth and a long, flicky tail."

"Hate them tails," Ploggit muttered, his words growing louder. Hollow scraping and grunting drifted up the drain. "Nasty things. All scaly an' pink. It's not natural."

With that, a leathery brown head sporting a red beanie popped through the drain hole, his suction-cupped finger-tips curled over the edge. Ploggit wasn't what I expected at all. I'd pictured a slimy snake-like creature with grabby hands and feet—loads of them. Something that could slither through pipes easily. Ploggit's head looked like an apple-sized walnut with black eyes, a bulbous nose, and dusky green lips. He was sort of cute in an ugly, dripping wet way. I couldn't see his body. Didn't seem fair. He'd probably seen mine.

I pressed my lips together so I wouldn't laugh. At least five blue chalk-dots decorated Ploggit's beanie.

"Nice to see you dressed for a change." Ploggit grinned up at me, revealing sharp teeth that seemed way too large for the size of his mouth.

"Now we have you," Harvey said. "Get a wriggle on. We're going home!"

"To Grimsmead?"

"Grimsmead? Where on earth is that?" I looked from Harvey to Ploggit.

"Rebecca's in trouble," Harvey ignored me "We're going back to help."

"Isn't that a bit…" Ploggit nodded at me, whispering to Harvey, "… dangerous?"

"What are we meant to do?" Harvey snapped. "Forget our oath? We pledged for both sisters. Doesn't matter what we want,"

"Wouldn't be right, would it?" Ploggit dragged off his red beanie. Two bat-wing ears sprung out from his wrinkly head. "I liked Rebecca. Always brought me gifts from her trips away."

"Rebecca knew about you?" I looked at Ploggit, then at Harvey. "About you both? And what's this Grimsmead place? I've never heard of it."

"Of course you haven't!" Ploggit snorted. "It's not of this world. Not even close."

"This should be a fantasy novel." I laughed in disbelief. "I must be dead. Or dreaming. Or nuts! Yes! I've lost the plot. I am crazy—wild hair, drooling, crazy!"

"Get it together, Ding!" Harvey snapped. "Your sister's in trouble. You're not insane. You are not dead. And you're not dreaming. And the sooner you realise the gravity of things, the better."

I was up and down like a frog on a hot griddle. I couldn't keep up. Talking cats. Drain brownies. Other worlds with magic?

"I don't understand!" I threw up my hands, almost knocking Harvey over. "This can't be real!"

"Rebecca brought us all here from our home in

Grimsmead," Harvey wrapped her tail about her body. "Not long after you were born."

Ploggit nodded, his ears flapping like stiff, rubbery wings. "We're your Watchers, Ding. Looked out for you both. Kept your secret, we did."

"Why?"

"That's the question, isn't it?" Ploggit arched a bristly eyebrow. "Only your grandmother and her son—your father—knows. And no one has seen him in years."

"My father? I don't understand! Are you talking about my biological father or Miles Black?"

"Your real father—the dryad one." Ploggit patted my boot, leaving wet suction-cup marks on the leather.

"If it's so dangerous," I said. "Why did Rebecca go back to Grimsmead?"

"She didn't have a choice," Harvey said. "At least she didn't think she had one. I tried to talk her out of going, but she could be so stubborn once she put her mind to something. Nothing could sway her." Harvey eyed me. "Like someone else I won't mention."

"How did she know she had to go?" I pushed, desperate for answers, to make sense of everything.

"She had a visitor." Harvey's tail flicked back and forth. "With news about your family. They needed help, and she chose to go."

"Why didn't she say anything to me?" I pointed at myself. "I could have helped—she might not be in trouble if I'd been there."

Harvey and Ploggit shared a pained look.

"Or…" Ploggit raised his eyebrows, a pleading look that did little to ease my frustration. "You both could be in trouble, and then where'd you be? In trouble, that's where!"

"Least we'd be together."

"Stop being so stubborn," Harvey said. "And listen to us. You're blustering about things you know nothing about."

"Then tell me! You say I'm from another world—a magical world, but you don't elaborate. You say Becca is in this other world, but give me no proof. As far as I know, she's overseas installing a new software system in some international company's computer network. Of course I'm being stubborn!"

"You've just discovered I can change forms and talk," Harvey said. "You have a magical spriggit in your plumbing. Couldn't you take the rest on faith, for now?"

"If I go to Grimsmead without Rebecca ..." My bravado buckled. " ... I won't know what to do. If she's in trouble, what hope have I got?"

"Because you, Arabella Jade Black," Harvey snapped, "have talents that will help us find your sister. *Your* sister!"

"What, growing plants?" I scoffed. "Pulling beers?"

"Seeing the dead," Ploggit said. "Knowing when someone is going to die."

I had never liked that talent. With heaps of effort over the years I'd managed to quieten the visions and the feelings of dread when I was close to someone who was going to die soon.

"Didn't Becca have those talents, too?"

"Not like you do," Harvey said. "I haven't ever met a half breed with your potential."

I'd never known my heritage, but from my red hair and pale skin, I had always fancied I had Irish blood. I definitely had the temper.

"I know you, Ding," Harvey said. "You're only stalling because you're frightened."

"Try terrified," I said.

"So are we. Rebecca is important to all of us." Harvey's voice caught in her throat. Not from sadness. From fear. Harvey, my talking cat, wasn't telling me everything. I was certain of it.

CHAPTER FIVE

"I'll start packing!" Ploggit disappeared down the drain, chatting to himself about his plumbing-gymnasium.

I remained in the shower cubical, numb, my mind racing. Did I have family in Grimsmead? A place to stay? Would I be able to speak their language? Eat their food? What about their culture and customs? For all I knew, they practiced human sacrifice or some other horrendous rite. And what should I pack? Was it hot in Grimsmead? Snowing? Was it a beach town? Or a place in the mountains? How long would we be away? Would Grimsmead have electricity? A way to charge my iPad? My mobile phone? Well, that was stupid, I doubted I'd get a good signal in an entirely different world.

"Why are you still standing in the shower?" Harvey sat outside the glass cubicle, her golden eyes narrowed with what looked like irritation.

"I don't know what to do." Lame, but true.

"Pack your belongings. Like we are."

I pictured Harvey all packed, holding a suitcase and a rolled-up umbrella. In what world did that seem right?

"What clothes shall I pack?" I asked. "Is it cold in Grimsmead? Hot?"

"Depends on the weather."

"Oh, thank you. You're a great help."

"Pack all of your clothes, and you can't go wrong."

"I don't own a suitcase that big."

"No one owns a suitcase that big." Harvey trotted out of the bathroom, leaving me to follow.

In the end, I packed a little of everything, making sure my clothes could mix-and-match. Shoes were harder to choose. I didn't have a walk-in wardrobe stuffed full of them like some people, but I loved them all. I settled on hiking boots, knee-length black leather boots, three pairs of army boots (various colours, of course) and a pair of high-heeled, sage-green sandals. I figured I might need to get all gussied up one day, and they were my gussiest shoes. Though it was silly, I'd packed my mobile phone and iPad along with their chargers. *Candy Crush* wouldn't play itself, you know.

"Is that all you're taking?" Harvey padded into my bedroom and leaped onto my still-cat-messed-up-bed.

"What do you mean?" I glanced from Harvey to my bright-red suitcase. "I think I did rather well."

"You're still thinking like a human."

"I am human. I have blood results, X-rays, and ultrasounds to prove it."

"Hmmm, yes…" Harvey licked her fluffy grey tummy. "Appears that way, doesn't it."

"What do you mean?"

"You'll see. Anyway, gather everything you can't live without, and bring it to the lounge room. Oh! And bring your grandmother's old jewellery box. We'll be needing that."

Whatever I couldn't live without, eh? "And how am I going to carry it all?"

Harvey sighed. "Magic, of course. Now hurry up."

I raced around, grabbing more boots, outfits, jewellery, make-up, and toiletries, heaping them in a jumbled mountain beside my couch. After tossing a few books and magazines on the shag-pile rug, I collected more of my favourite things, including my white shower mat, the photo of me and Rebecca, my crystal collection, and my special plants. I tossed the flashlight onto the pile along with spare batteries.

As an evil afterthought, I propped Carl's pool cue and chalk against my coffee table. The cue wasn't one of my special things, but it would stop Carl from sneaking over and taking it. Petty, I know, but I had my pride to uphold.

Harvey and Ploggit fussed around the rug's perimeter with a leather pouch, Ploggit pouring squiggles onto the floorboards with something that looked like ash and salt, Harvey directing the whole shebang. Where they had stashed that pouch was a mystery. I'd never seen it before even on my most thorough spring cleans.

"Right," Harvey announced. "We're ready to go."

Ploggit, snug in a hairy red coat and blue-chalk-dotted beanie, sat perched high atop a scarred, wooden trunk, its leather straps worn, its buckles rusty. How he had squeezed the beaten up old thing down the drain was beyond me. I was amazed that my bathroom hadn't flooded every time I showered.

He grinned at me, flashing those vicious-looking teeth. "Thanks for my new hat and coat."

Eew! Not knowing what else to say, I settled on, "You're welcome."

Harvey sat beside her fuzzy pink and white way-too-expensive cat bed, in which she had placed a tawny leather satchel, its buckles polished to a warm sheen, its long strap rolled into a neat coil. A bright pink key poked out from under the cat's leather bag.

"*You* stole my car keys?" I snatched them up, sending her satchel flying. I dangled them in her face. "I've been searching for these!"

"Yes, I know. Couldn't have you driving off today."

"So, you knew hours ago? About Rebecca?"

"Who knew what at what time changes little—let's not dwell."

I scooped up Harvey's satchel and plonked it on her bed. "Is that all you're taking?"

Ploggit exploded with laughter. "If you only knew!"

"Open up your jewellery box," Harvey said. "And we'll get started."

"It's just a little old chest. How does it work?" I turned the blackened key in its lock atop the squat, wooden box. The timber was smooth, dark and ancient-looking. I ran a finger over the tarnished copper straps that wove a pattern of offset squares around all four sides. Each corner of the squares sported a simple bronze stud. Interlocking swirls etched each copper strap, some so worn I could hardly make them out. The box sat on four bronze spheres, not unlike tarnished ball-bearings.

The lid was my favourite part. On either side of the keyhole sat two silver bars, each connected to tiny metal workings that disappeared into the lid. The bars were interconnected somehow. I'd never figured out how exactly. But, when I turned the key, both bars lifted slightly and shunted to either side, causing a click within the box. All very mysterious and amazing.

I opened the jewellery box, smiling like I always did as

Rebecca's favourite sandalwood, Chantilly musk and amber perfume wafted out to greet me. We had both sprayed our signature perfumes on silk handkerchiefs, swapping them as keepsakes for when we were apart. I retrieved the neatly folded green silk and buried my nose in it, sniffing deeply. Instantly I felt simultaneously relieved and frightened. All I could do was hope and pray she was all right.

"Now what?" I said, the hanky still clutched in one hand.

"Tip out the contents," Harvey said. "And feel around inside for a small catch. You'll know it when you find it."

"But I want the stuff inside with me when we go."

"Trust me," Harvey snapped. "Everything on your precious rug will make the journey."

I'll believe that when I see it! "All right, if you say so."

"I say so."

I dumped the tangle of chains, earrings, bottle caps and buttons onto the rug. A cobalt-blue marble rolled away. I popped it on top of a drawstring pouch filled with sand and gravel. I had no clue what the pouch was for, but Rebecca had said it was important and to never throw it away. Two locks of red hair, one tied with a jade ribbon, the other with a turquoise one were last to spill out. The small collection seemed sad and worthless. But not to me. Every keepsake held a world of love and memories.

"Oh! I'd forgotten about that!" I wiggled a necklace free of the pile and held up a chain supporting a golden filigree ball. I opened the globe and snapped it closed again, smiling.

"We haven't got time for a trip down memory lane," Harvey said. "You can play dress-up later."

"I'm not playing dress-up," I mumbled, securing the chain around my neck. "My mum gave me this."

"Feel around the inside." Harvey pawed the little chest.

"What am I feeling for?" I ran my fingers across the jewellery box's floor, then around the internal walls. "Is it metal? Wood? Ouch!" I snatched back my hand. "You said a catch, not a sharp point!" A bead of blood formed on my middle finger. I raised my hand toward my mouth—

"Don't!" Harvey pounced, her face so close to mine I smelled the fresh whiting I had served her for dinner. Felt her whiskers tickle my cheek. "We need your blood to open the Gateway to Grimsmead."

I held my hand near my open lips, the blood quivering as it swelled on my fingertip.

"The secret compartment should have opened." Harvey climbed on my lap and inspected the box.

A soft click came from the chest.

"I was worried for a moment," Harvey whispered. "Remove the false bottom. You'll see a runic symbol carved in the base. Open that old pouch, and pour in the contents."

I did as she said, tipping the grey sand and gravel into the jewellery box.

"Trace your blood along the lines of the symbol—be sure not to lose contact with the symbol until you have completed drawing. That's important, Ding."

"What's so important about this bag of dirt?"

"It's from one of the stone markers that border your family estate." Harvey paced by my side. "So many questions."

"I haven't begun to question! Where is this estate? And why haven't I heard about it?"

"On another world." Ploggit squatted by me, his beanie tight on his round, leathery head. "Far away from Earth."

"You mean another planet? Like Jupiter? Or Mars?" I

sat back on my heels. "You mean I'm an alien? Like E.T?" I spat an incredulous laugh. "Or those face-huggers in the movie Alien?"

"Think more fantasy than sci-fi." Harvey stared me down.

"I have to be dreaming, because no one in their right mind would believe any of this."

"Complete the spell, and you'll see I'm speaking the truth," Harvey said. "Come on, before the blood runs off your finger.

"All right! But I'm only doing this so I can see how the dream ends." As I traced the rune, tiny splinters of wood broke away, mixing with my blood and the sand from the pouch. At first, nothing happened. Everything seemed normal. Well, if you can call sitting next to a talking cat while a spriggit brownie dances around atop his travelling trunk normal.

I breathed deep, struggling to focus. My mouth was dry, my palms sweaty. But, if truth be told, exhilaration thrilled through my body. I was about to go on an adventure. A magical adventure just like I read about when I was a kid.

My heart pounded like a war drum, so loud I could barely hear Harvey. Her mouth moved, but her words were muffled. I opened and closed my jaw, trying to relieve the pressure in my ears. The lounge room tilted like a boat in high seas. I clutched the rug, squeezing the soft pile as I struggled to keep upright. Kaleidoscopic colours rushed in and out, swirling like a universe of colourful stars. Pretty, in a nauseating way. I collapsed like a rag doll. Lights sizzled before my eyes. A black veil drew in from the sides, blocking out all colour, all light and sound.

And then nothing.

CHAPTER SIX

"Ithink she's all right," Ploggit's voice floated nearby. "But she's not going to be happy when she wakes up."

"A bit of vomit on transit. Nothing a shower won't fix." Harvey sounded tender, almost caring.

"I'm never showering again!" Pain throbbed through my temples, shooting down the back of my neck. I didn't dare open my eyes. Just the light filtering through my eyelids was enough to make my head ache. "Holy Horseshoes! What happened?"

"It's a bit of a rough ride," Ploggit said. "Must say, you did better when you were a baby."

Soft, rubbery fingers patted my leg. I risked opening my eyes to see Ploggit squatting beside me, his black eyes full of concern, his frog-like hand resting on my thigh. I fumbled for the spriggit brownie's head and patted him in return. "Thanks, Plog."

I imagined him weaving my soggy hair into an outfit, humming away, lounging in an S-bend. His clothes smelled like my new raspberry and vanilla shampoo, so they were either newly woven or he did his laundry in my shower water, too. Revolting! My stomach lurched as a wave of nausea washed through me. I wasn't sure if the feeling was due to the trip or the thought of Ploggit's enthusiastic recycling.

I sat for a few minutes, using my eyelids as blinds against the light. Pain pounded through my head. I rubbed my temples and my neck, as I tried to get a handle on my situation. When I woke up this morning, I had never imagined anything like this. Who would?

"See!" Harvey sounded a bit too smug for my liking. "Not a dream."

"The jury is still out." I disagreed with her out of spite. "You could have warned me about the headache."

"Can you get up?" Harvey asked. "Did you bring any painkillers with you?"

"I didn't think…" I winced. "Just let me lie here for awhile. I'll be fine."

"We really must get organised. But," Harvey said. "We can wait a little while. You're no use to us like that."

"What's going on?" The voice was male, husky, and annoyed. "How did *you* get in?"

"Oh," Harvey said. "Meeks. Still strutting about, I see."

Meeks growled. "You're back."

"Don't get your tail in a fuzz," Ploggit snapped.

Despite my headache, I opened my eyes. There sat a fox. Or was it a raccoon? Meeks had the orange-red colouring of a fox, but the black bandit-mask and white cheek fluff of a raccoon. Definitely more raccoon than fox, if the shape of his head was any indication. A raffox? Foxoon? His auburn-and-black-ringed tail wrapped about his paws, its white tip flicking up and down. Meeks trotted toward me, stood up on his hind legs, and wrinkled his nose.

"Travel sickness?" He wafted one paw about and backed away. "You know that's going to leave a stain."

"Well, you'd know, wouldn't you, Meeks?" Harvey said. "Been on the gin lately? Or have you grown up since I've been away?"

"From what I've heard," Meeks said. "When you weren't such a decrepit old misery-guts, you drank with the worst of them."

"And remained standing."

"Is this Arabella?" Meeks sounded skeptical. "She looks like Rebecca, but…smaller. Frailer. Less impressive somehow."

"This *is* Arabella." Harvey snapped. "And there's no need to be nasty. You're just stroppy because you didn't get the Watcher assignment with Ploggit. Taking out your failings on her shows poor character."

"Now, now," Ploggit said. "Two hundred years since 'the incident' and you're still fighting. Isn't it time you put all that in the past? Think of Rebecca. She needs us."

"You're right." Harvey sighed. "I'll behave if he does."

"Fine!" Meeks said, "But only because I care for Becca."

"It's settled, then." Ploggit clapped, leaping to his froggy feet.

"What are you?" I asked Meeks. "Exactly? Half fox, half raccoon? A Roxoon?"

Meeks stood on his hind legs and rammed his little paw-hands on his hips. Or maybe it was his waist. I wasn't up on veterinary science, so I wasn't sure of the correct terminology.

"I am a raxx," Meeks said proudly. "Half breed indeed! If you want to know a half breed, try looking in a mirror."

"You nasty little beast!" I frowned. "Hey! How come you can understand English? You can't possibly speak the same language as me. This is a whole different world."

"You're not speaking English anymore." Meeks sniffed and looked down his nose at me. "You, my girl, are speaking our tongue, though your accent is woeful."

"That's not possible."

"The jewellery box had a language reversion spell locked in the wood." Ploggit grinned. "My idea. I thought if we got to come home, it'd save you having to learn a whole new tongue."

"Clever." I nodded my appreciation.

"I thought so." Ploggit beamed.

"How you feeling, Ding?" Harvey said. "Better?"

"A little." I sat up, wincing and wobbling, but I was upright. "Oh! My dress! My beautiful grey rug!" Both my green boho dress and my rug were covered with puke.

"I'm certain they'll wash up nicely," Harvey said. "Nothing to be ashamed of. You should've seen Ploggit when he travelled to Earth. Vomit everywhere."

"Not to mention the other end." Meeks' black nose twitched as though he smelled something gross.

"You can talk, Meeks!" Harvey said. "You with your musky stink!"

"No one warned me about travelling on a full belly," Ploggit muttered.

Expecting an argument to fire up, I looked around. My much-loved couch had made the journey along with the coffee table, magazines, Tarot cards, and dirty dishes. Probably because they were within the confines of Harvey and Plog's magic squiggle circle. If I'd realised, I would have piled everything I owned on the rug.

It took a few moments to grasp what lay beyond the remnants of my lounge room. If you could take a forest with all its trees, ferns, moss, and tangled climbing plants and transfer them into an ancient, glass-domed conservatory, then you would get an inkling of this room. No, not a room—a huge greenhouse, with mossy paths weaving past hand-crafted timber chairs, tables, and sculptures. Three mezzanine floors, each level bordered with ornate bronze railings, circled the interior, leaving the central area free and airy all the way to the glass-panelled roof.

Hanging baskets stuffed with white flowers of every shape and size hung on thick, black chains, suspended from beams that supported the mezzanine above. Why there were only white flowers was up for debate, but I'm sure there was a reason.

Three spiral staircases rose between leaves and branches, their filigree framework and steps green with patina. Two coiled upward, passing through the mezzanines like normal staircases. The centre one twisted up to nowhere, stopping just short of the glass dome. A bit stupid, but maybe there had been something there years ago?

The gurgle and splash of running water floated on the warm air, along with trilling birds. I'd never ever dreamed of a place like this.

"I thought *I* had a plant addiction!" I laughed, enchanted. "I don't even recognise most of these."

"This is your great, great, great grandmother's place," Meeks said. "On your father's side."

"I see where I get my love of plants," I said.

"You don't know the half of it." Meeks chuckled, a high-pitched chitter that made me grin.

"Come on. I'll show you around." Meeks trotted towards the central spiral staircase that emptied into nowhere.

"Why don't we take one of the other two?" I asked. "This one seems a bit pointless."

"You'll see."

"Show off," Harvey muttered.

I wobbled to my feet and followed Meeks along a moss-scattered path, leaving Harvey and Ploggit amongst our belongings. Sunlight, tinged green by creepers growing across the milky glass dome above, cast golden pools throughout the dim interior. Candlelight flickered here and there adding a soft, cozy glow to the peaceful gloom.

"You better hold on." Meeks leaped onto the centre staircase and sat down. "Rebecca nearly fell over the handrail first time she rode the steps."

"Do these work for everyone?" I stood on the lowest bronze step. "Or do you have to program them to your voice?"

"Depends on who's asking."

"These stairs have moods?"

"Shhh! You don't want to upset them. You might end up in orbit."

I gripped the railing. "Nice stairs. Good stairs."

"Skyway, level one," Meeks ordered.

The staircase lurched and spiralled upwards like a huge corkscrew, carrying us toward the wide glass dome. As we rose higher, I looked down and noticed a stream bubbling under the greenhouse's glass-panelled wall, wending its way through the forest until it vanished beneath the opposite wall at the far end. Through gaps in the trees I saw Harvey and Ploggit poking though our belongings, probably commenting on my packing technique.

A bronze filigree catwalk magically appeared above us,

growing closer as the stairs wound upward. A hole, obviously created for the spiral staircase, cut through the catwalk's centre.

"Halt!" Meeks called as we arrived at the walkway.

The staircase ground to a stop parallel with the lowest mezzanine.

I pushed open an old bronze gate that blocked us from the skyway, and we disembarked.

"Are the skyways invisible?" I hurried across the walkway, the metal squeaking and groaning with each step.

"Who wants to look up at clunky old skyways when you can have a clear view of the sky?"

"I don't think we have the same ideas about 'clear view'."

Ivy and some other broad-leaf creeper hugged the glass dome, following the support mullions from one side to the other.

Relieved to set foot on solid ground, I opened a thigh-high gate leading from the skyway onto the mezzanine, and scrambled onto the sturdy oak floorboards that stretched left and right, sweeping around to meet on the far side. I leaned over a bronze railing that circled the mezzanine, clutching the filigree metal in both hands. It was like standing in a tree house, with leafy branches overhanging the balcony. I peered upward. Two more mezzanines circled the vast expanse, the dome not far above the top floor.

"I'll show you Rebecca's room first. You can get cleaned up. Maybe after that, you can look for clues. You might find some we missed."

"Oh!" My face flushed with heat. "Sorry. This place is so magical I lost myself for a minute."

"The Forest Room has that effect on people," Meeks said.

Suddenly, muffled shrieks and wailing rang out from somewhere behind the wall, making me jump. Who or what was that? I was about to ask, when Meeks ran along the landing until he reached a closed ebony door, the dark wood arched and strapped with copper.

"Something's in Rebecca's room! The door!" Meeks yipped and cried, pawing at the timber with his claws.

I raised the latch and shoved the door open. Meeks slipped into the room before I could stop him. Anything could be lurking inside.

As I stumbled into the dark room, a cold wind buffeted me, dragging my hair backward, plastering my skirt to my legs. The stench of my vomit engulfed me along with a dank, earthy smell of ancient forests where decaying leaves carpeted the ground, mossy logs mouldered, and mist shrouded the trunks of old, old trees. There had to be an open window in here. And that wailing had to have come from some wild animal hunting outside. Nothing human could have shrieked liked that. I scanned the darkness. Nothing moved.

"Watch your eyes." Meeks switched on the overhead light.

I blinked and peered through the sudden brightness. Meeks stood on his hind legs, one front paw hovering over a small, silver panel next to the open doorway. Must be a touch light. Fancy!

"I can't see anything." Meeks sniffed the air. His hackles spiked. "But I can feel something. Something…"

"Something good?" I could be hopeful. Look at me being glass-half-full.

Meeks shook his head. "I don't know. One moment it feels familiar. The next all I sense is fear and death."

Okay then. My glass just sprung a leak. With every

sense on high alert, I desperately tried to focus on what I could see. What was normal.

So this was Rebecca's bedroom.

"Fancy four-poster bed." I ran my fingers along a smooth timber column. "Looks like something Henry the Eighth would have romped in."

"Henry the who?"

"Never mind." I pulled a face. "Typical Rebecca! Who else could have a white velvet quilt and keep it spotless?"

I picked up one of the forest-green and black silk cushions off the quilt, turned it around, and put it back on the bed. Petty, but I felt a little better.

A door beside an antique dresser stood ajar, revealing a claw-footed bath. My mood lifted.

"Do any of Ploggit's relatives live in this place?" I asked Meeks, not wanting to get naked in front of his extended family.

"Where did it go?" Meeks still padded about the room, sniffing, his ears pricked.

"You are rippling my pond, Meeks." I swallowed and hugged myself as a chill crashed over me.

"The spirit!" Meeks cried and bounded for the mezzanine, shooting through the open door. He yipped and squeaked. "Tell it we're not in the market for new guests."

My desperate need for a shower vanished. The spirit, as if summoned, shot through the timber-panelled wall, crimson and green dress ragged and stretched translucent thin as it whirled around the bedroom. Colours? I saw colours! I had only ever seen spirits as shades of grey.

The spirit howled and wailed. I clapped my hands over my ears, crouching as it swooped down over me, then surged up, hovering above the canopy bed. It snaked around, undulating, wailing, coiled above the head of the bed.

"Talk to it." Meeks peeked around the door frame from out on the landing. "Make it go away."

"Don't you know who it is?"

"No! And I don't want to know."

My first Grimsmead spirit. Banner day.

"Coward," I called to Meeks. "Leaving me here alone."

"Call it your initiation!"

"I'll remember this! You wait 'til you need me."

I blew out a long, slow breath, gathering my wits. Atop the four-poster, the spirit watched me with empty, forlorn eyes, the blue so intense they outshone everything else in the bedroom. Dressed in long, shredded rags, its auburn and silver hair floating on some unholy breeze, I'd never seen a spirit like this one unless you counted the movies.

"Are you all right?" My voice caught in my throat. I breathed in deep and tried again. "My name is Arabella. I won't hurt you, I promise. Can we help you? Can we pass on a message or something for you?"

The spirit shot to the edge of the bed's canopy, peering through hair that cascaded to the carpeted floor. Long, skeletal fingers curled around the railing.

"Arabella?" It said, a haunting, hollow sound. "You shouldn't be here."

"Rebecca—my sister—needed me. I came—"

"No, no. Too dangerous. Can't be you. Can't be you. A trick. They're tricking me."

I hesitated. "Do you know who you are?"

"It's so dark. So cold I can't breathe. I can't see. I can't *see*."

I shivered. The soul's grief and terror flooded me. Her fear sucked my breath away. I gasped for air.

"It's so dark. And I hurt. Burning. It burns." The soul's voice knifed through my mind, the pain reminding me of a toothache. Only worse. So much worse. I clutched my head, hitting my temples. Screwed my eyes closed as I fought for control. When I peeked through slitted lids everything was black.

"It burns!" I cried. "Too dark." My voice sounded as hollow as the spirit's, an echo that rolled through my head, my lips. I gasped, but no breath filled my lungs. Flailing, I staggered, struggling to breathe. Fiery pain raced through my veins. "It hurts!"

A solid thump in my back knocked me to the ground. Fishy breath puffed in my ear.

"Let her go, Ding!" Harvey shouted in my face. "Let her go!"

Where had Harvey come from? Wasn't she poking through our stuff downstairs?

Gasping, my eyes watering, I rolled over. Harvey patted my cheek, her paw warm and soft.

"I'm sorry," I whispered. "She's too strong for me. She possessed me. How did she do that?"

"You'll have to learn how to block," Harvey said. "The spirits in Grimsmead have far more oomph than you're used to. Letting them inside you like that isn't safe."

"You're not kidding! I couldn't stop her." I propped myself up on my elbows, scanning the bedroom. "I didn't do it on purpose. For a moment there, I *was* the spirit. I could feel what she felt. She needed my help. Where is she?"

"On top of Rebecca's bed, watching us."

I had never felt so useless.

"Arabella!" The spirit wailed. She gazed down at me. "Ding? They took it!"

I stared at Harvey. "No. Please. Don't tell me that's Becca up there. Why does she look like that? All blurred and featureless?"

Harvey nodded, her whiskers twitching, her amber eyes wide. "I fear it is Rebecca. But, I don't know why she's so wretched and broken."

"But that means we're too late. She's…" I couldn't say it. She couldn't be dead. She was astral projecting or something. Searching for help.

I scrambled upright. "Rebecca!" I said as kindly as I could, my voice trembling.

The spirit quietened, surveying me with narrowed voids that I presumed were eyes.

"It's me," I said. "Arabella—your little sister. Ding. Remember when you first called me Ding? You shortened my name from Arabella to Bella. Then Ding-dong-bell. Then 'Ding Dong the witch is dead'. You know? From *The Wizard of Oz*. We loved that movie when we were kids. You remember how I hated it when you sang the song and laughed? The more cranky I got, the more you called me Ding. Until that's who I became. It's me. I'm here now. Endraya got through to Earth, to home, like you asked her to. I came to help you."

"No! They're coming back! Leave!"

Was she telling me to leave? Or whoever was there with her?

"I'm so scared," Rebecca whispered, her voice hoarse and brittle with terror. "I told them nothing."

Rebecca spilled over the canopy, pooling a few feet from where I stood. She reached out, her fingers worming toward my face. I cringed. But I didn't run. Tally one up for me. Her fingertips brushed my cheek, her light touch so cold it stung. I staggered backwards, stepping on Harvey's tail. She howled and dashed aside, glaring at me.

An image flashed in my mind's eye of a three-story mansion. Six weather-stained statues supported a wide stone balcony that stretched the width of the second floor.

Every carved-stone window frame sported a pair of rust-red shutters. They were all closed, bar one on the third floor. A figure stood behind the glass silhouetted by flickering gold light. The vision shifted. Running through dark streets. Was she chasing someone or being chased? The vision changed. Hundreds of frowning people jostling one another, waving placards and shouting.

The scene vanished. I stared at Rebecca. She was trying to give me clues.

"Are you trapped at that mansion?" I asked. "Who's that in the window? Have they hurt you?" I couldn't ask if they'd murdered her. I just couldn't.

Rebecca shook her head. "They're powerful. I can't… It's so dark."

"Can you see the Light?" Harvey sat by my side.

I shot Harvey a foul look and immediately felt guilty. She was only trying to help Becca find some peace.

"My heart," she moaned. "It aches."

"Where are you?" I said. "Let me help you."

"They're coming, Ding!" Rebecca spun around, her hands up as though warding off an attack. She turned to me. "I'm scared, Ding. I'm scared. Black. Black and blue shadows. Oh god! Oh god! Please…"

Rebecca hurled herself at me, her arms outstretched as if wanting a hug. She shot through my body. Images of trees, old and twisted, their roots tangled, their branches, withered and leafless, flooded my mind. Howling and wailing filled me, the trees keening, needling through every cell of my body, bitter cold and unforgiving. What sort of forest was that? Poor Rebecca. Those trees frightened me, and I was safe in a house.

I howled. A sound that seemed impossible for a lone human girl to make. All three mirrors in Rebecca's bedroom shattered, crashing to the floor like a thousand jangling bells.

I sagged to the floorboards, panting. I had never been more terrified in my life.

Or more exhilarated.

CHAPTER SEVEN

I refused to accept that Becca had died. She
hadn't said she'd passed away, so I held on to
hope. She could have been astral travelling—her soul
searching for help. Grimsmead had talking animals. They
could use magic and travel to other worlds. Who knew
what else was possible? With that thought fixed in my
mind, I decided to shower and find some clean clothes.

After checking out all of the drains in Becca's bathroom for Ploggit or his friends and family, I showered and
dressed in faded blue jeans, a lacy white off-the-shoulder
blouse, and a pair of hand-painted Doc Martins. One of
my favourite pairs. I loved how the red roses twined up the
sides of the black leather.

Feeling numb and listless, I decided to go back down to
the Forest Room. I should have been tired. I'd been awake
for over twenty-four hours. I don't know if it was the
change of timezone—who was I kidding? change of *entire
planet* zone—or the encounter with my sister's spirit that
had made me so unsettled.

I surveyed the central spiral staircase, still sitting where

Meeks and I had left it. The only problem was the skyway. It had vanished.

Yes, not going to try that one by myself.

Instead, I hurried around the mezzanine until I reached one of the normal staircases. At least I hoped it was normal. I climbed aboard, but, instead of moving down, the stupid thing clattered up to the second floor.

"Just walk down, you fool!" I said to myself.

As fast as I ran down the steps, the confounded thing spiralled upwards. I did a quick feint, running up a few steps. It changed directions, spiralling down.

"Ha!"

Back to running down. Back to spiralling up. Surely it would run out of stairs soon and stop. But they kept coiling upward.

I gasped.

They never went any higher than the third floor. They were like those spiralled metal decorations that seemed to move as they spun around. But it was just an illusion.

"Crud-muffins!" I glanced around, sure Meeks, Harvey, and Ploggit were having the time of their lives watching me make an idiot of myself. I swallowed my pride.

"Harvey!" I leaned over the railing. "Meeks? How do you make this thing go down?"

No one answered.

Maybe this was the 'up' staircase?

It was easy enough getting up to the second floor. Perhaps that's where the stupid stairs felt happy today. I disembarked and hurried around the mezzanine to the other set of stairs, stepped aboard, and said, "Down."

And, the rotten thing spiralled upwards to the third mezzanine. As soon as the stairs connected to the circular access hole in the landing, that rotten staircase clanked to a stop. With nowhere else to go, I disembarked, the rough floorboards squeaking under my weight. No polished floorboards on this level. Dark-green ivy smothered the walls, an invasion that grew down from the glass dome above. Or was it the other way around? It was hard to tell where the creeper originated. The only gaps in the dense growth were around six doors of raw timber with plain bronze latches. Guess these rooms were for guests that you wanted to leave in a hurry. Or prison cells?

Come on, Arabella, get a grip! I leaned over the bronze railing, searching the Forest Room below for movement. The only signs of life were a few tittering birds and the distant gurgle and splash of the indoor stream. A few metres above me, the glass dome didn't look nearly as impressive as it had from below. Murky and spattered with mould and dust, the glass panels appeared ancient. It was amazing any light got in at all. The ivy clung to the metal framework, creeping its way across the rotunda and down the walls.

"How do I get down from here?" I muttered. "What they need here is a slippery-dip. Or a water slide."

A door across the mezzanine creaked open. Then closed. Then open.

Must be a draught from somewhere.

I walked around toward the door, ignoring the little voice of reason in my head. If I was in a horror film, I'd die horribly soon. But that was in the movies. This was real life. A musty breeze wafted out of the open door, ruffling my freshly washed hair. I caught the smell of damp and old books, so perhaps a library? Another of my favourite things.

I peeked around the door. The only light sliced through a pair of external shutters, making thin spears of blue, green, and gold across bare boards. Dusty sheets covered what had to be furniture and, from their height and size, bookcases.

"Arabella…" a breeze whispered–the voice female, soft, and compelling. I ran back to the railing and listened. It had probably been Harvey calling from below.

After listening for a minute and hearing nothing, I headed back into the room. First thing, I pulled open the windows, unlatched the moss-green shutters, and swung them open. I pulled the windows closed, and light streamed in through the stained-glass. The detail was so intricate that only a master could have created such glass-work. Tiny pink climbing roses filled the lower-left corner. Cherry blossoms and delicate spring-green leaves wove across the right top. An aqua sky, dotted with clouds floating above rolling emerald hills, filled the rest of the windows. Talk about art!

The breeze stirred a sheet covering what appeared to be a trunk or crate of some kind.

"Voila!" I pulled back the sheet with the flair of a stage magician.

Beneath sat an old wooden trunk, its sturdy bronze hasp and staple secured by a modern padlock, its tiny screen dark. I tapped the screen, bringing it to life. Four-teen dashes flashed above a qwerty keyboard.

"Great!"

I kneeled, feeling the trunk, searching the bronze strap-ping and corners. My grandmother's jewellery box had a secret compartment, so maybe this did too. I ran my fingers over the trunk's bronze-belly band, and they bumped over a latch. I pressed it, and a door flopped down on my thighs, revealing a narrow shelf and two small drawers.

"Nifty!" I pulled open one drawer. Three yellowed scrolls sealed with old-fashioned wax seals rolled forward with the momentum. I looked through each scroll as though they were telescopes. In two, I noted swoopy writing. Love letters, maybe? The third scroll was a picture. Maybe a map or a painting of a landscape? I rested the scroll on my bottom lip.

Open them or leave them sealed?

I peered at the wax seals, each sporting the same tree. What kind of tree was impossible to say from the simple impression. The rolled parchments weren't mine to open. But they looked so piratey! Curiosity gnawed at my manners.

Mustn't touch, Ding, if it's not yours.

With a sigh, I popped the scrolls back in the drawer. Tapping my thigh, I stared at them, a war raging inside my conscience. I was sure I heard the scrolls calling, "Open us, Ding, we're important."

Well, it'd be extremely rude to ignore them when they sounded so needy.

I pulled out a scroll and cracked open the wax seal, careful not to rip the parchment as I unfurled it. A mouldy-old smell rose from the brittle paper, its surface a mosaic of fine cracks. It looked like a legal document with gilded edges, calligraphy, and a fancy first letter like you see on old illuminated manuscripts. I placed the scroll back in the drawer and took out another.

This one was similar to the first, just as old, just as fragile. The third was, indeed, a map.

So I was right. Piratey! Yo-ho-ho!

But the map wasn't of the ocean or islands. Hundreds of hand-drawn trees formed a forest that edged a mountain range, the hills encircling a lake. An area of the forest was marked out with tiny gold dashes, the words 'Ashmore Holdings' stamped in scarlet ink.

"Like a mining claim or something." I didn't know enough about Grimsmead to fully understand, but I would ask Harvey or Meeks later.

I replaced the scroll and opened the next drawer down and discovered an old key the size of my hand. I picked it up and rust powdered my fingers. Whatever this opened was positively antique and probably forgotten. How mysterious!

Next, I scanned the shelf—nothing but dust and a balled-up scrap of paper right at the back. I reached in, grabbed it, and smoothed the paper out, revealing a hastily scrawled sentence.

"You and the code are not in Kansas anymore," I read aloud. "No kidding!"

I knew the reference was from *The Wizard of Oz*. Only someone from my world would understand that.

"Becca wrote this!" I whispered. "For me!"

What if it had been Rebecca causing the staircases to spiral upward when I wanted to go down? She could have opened the door to this room so I'd notice it. And, she could have stirred the sheet over the trunk. It made perfect sense. Goodness knew what sort of powers she had here in Grimsmead. Remote telekinesis wasn't beyond the realm of possibility.

I grabbed the digital padlock.

You and the code are not in Kansas anymore. I turned the clue over in my mind. You and the *code.* "The *code* isn't in Kansas anymore. *Dorothy*!"

I tapped the screen and the fourteen spaces flashed, awaiting the right code. "Dorothy" was only seven letters. I rocked back on my heels and stared at the blinking dashes.

"You and the *code* aren't in Kansas anymore." I mouthed the clue over and over. It was Dorothy who travelled from Kansas to the Land of Oz. I snorted, disgusted at my dense head. Toto! Toto and Dorothy were no longer in Kansas. I added up the letters. Fourteen! I typed in

Dorothy and Toto and pulled on the padlock. Nothing happened.

"Seriously?" I slumped forward and bumped my head on the trunk's lid a few times.

I sighed. And tried again. "*You* and the *code* aren't in Kansas anymore."

You… if Rebecca had written this for me, then maybe she meant… *Me* and the code.

I entered "Ding and Dorothy." The lock clicked open.

My heart fluttered as I eased it from the metal loop.

"Go, you good thing!" I gave myself a pat on the back, lifted the bronze hasp, and raised the heavy lid. As it creaked open on old leather hinges, I held my breath and peeked inside. A faded blue cloth covered an uneven pile. Rebecca's leather-bound notebook, crimson glass dip-pen, and matching inkwell sat off to one side.

Rebecca had scribbled stories since she could first write. Goodness knows where she got all of her ideas, but she'd managed to write several books over the years. If I tried that, it'd be the size of a pamphlet.

I picked up the glass pen and smiled. This was the first time I'd ever held Becca's special pen. It was magical how ink flowed up the fine, glass grooves when Rebecca dipped the pen's sharp nib in ink. I'd always wanted one of my own, but I knew I'd break it. I'd press too hard and snap off the nib, or knock it off a table. I wasn't graceful, like my sister. A knot tightened in my belly, and I replaced Rebecca's pen in the trunk with shaking fingers.

As I set the pen down, a cloudy, scratched sphere about the size of a Muscat grape rolled from a shadowy corner within the trunk. A rhythmic clicking sounded with each revolution. I picked up the globe and studied the weathered glass. Sealed inside was a wooden molar. Why would Rebecca have a manky wooden tooth hidden with her secret stuff? Maybe she hadn't known it was in there? The sphere looked ancient, the tooth older. I shook it, and the tooth rattled around inside. No flash of magic. No glowing lights. The molar lay there, its bumpy crown worn, its roots slightly curved like a genuine, everyday human tooth.

"Creepy!" I popped the sphere back in the trunk, and it rolled into a corner.

I wiped my hands down my jeans, then removed the pale-blue cloth. Hidden beneath were an iPad, a phone, and a couple of chargers. Two solar panels sat to one side, their spikes coated with crumbling soil. So, Rebecca had figured out how to charge her gadgets without electricity. Go her! I picked up the iPad and pressed the home button. The picture of Becca and me from our Black Forest holiday filled her lock screen.

46% charged.

It seemed these solar doodads actually worked. I pressed the home button again, and the lock-screen needed yet another password. There were six empty spaces. So a word from the *Wizard of Oz* that was six letters long. Scarecrow was too long, so was the Cowardly Lion.

Emerald? No, too long. Who else did Dorothy meet on her journey?

"The Tin Man. Six!"

No cigar.

"Glinda!" I typed the Good Witch's name and cheered as the home-screen appeared revealing a yummy-looking man with messy dark hair. The word *rakish* sprang to mind, but in a boyish, wicked way. He stared out from the screen with intense hazel eyes, his jawline strong and sexy. He wore a black suit, white shirt, and blood-red tie. They must have been going somewhere special.

Oh, Beccs! A cold weight settled deep in my gut. *And now you might never see him again.*

I sat there on the dusty floorboards, tears dropping onto the screen, struggling to think past my grief. Wiping away my tears with the back of one hand, I opened the photo app, and all Rebecca's albums appeared. One was titled Walker and Me. I figured that must be her man's name. I wondered if he knew Becca was missing, maybe…

I couldn't say the 'D' word.

I had to find out what happened. Looking at photos would help, but there were so many of them. Instead, I closed the app and searched the home screen for a journal app or some such thing that Rebecca might use to record her thoughts. I swiped over to the next screen and found a swirly blue quill overlaying a white scroll. It looked journal-y to me.

A part of me felt terribly guilty. This was such an invasion of privacy. I remembered the first and last time I'd sneaked a look at her diary. I was eleven. She was sixteen. If the roof could have blown off our house, it would have. I'm sure she cracked the foundations. Sheesh, she was angry with me. It's not like I'd read much. So what if she'd been kissing some guy and thought she'd found true love. At the time, it had made me gag just thinking about it.

That guilt and the memory of Rebecca's inconsolable rage still lingered. And that surprised me.

"I'm doing this for your own good, Beccs!"

Besides, if Rebecca had created codes that only she and I could crack, then it stood to reason she wanted me to see what was inside. Locking it away in a trunk meant she didn't want it found by anyone else. Made total sense to me. I took a deep breath and tapped the application.

Passworded. Again. Anyone would think she was a secret agent or something. Let's hope Becca had kept to her *Wizard of Oz* theme. Six spaces to fill.

"Aunt Em." I counted out the letters.

Surprised by my own genius, I typed it in. The spaces jiggled and cast my letters away like a dog shaking off water. They vanished.

"Tin Man!" Once more the spaces threw away my answer.

"Hmmm!" I tapped my chin. "It can't be Glinda. We used that one already."

I used only a couple of passwords for heaps of things, even though it was risky. Maybe Becca did, too.

I typed Glinda again anyway with no success.

"*The Wizard of Oz* is way too long. Hang on! What about just 'wizard'—that's six?"

I entered the letters. And they did a happy swill-down-the drain special effect, and I was in.

I hummed the *James Bond* theme as I scanned the various folders, tapping and expanding files looking for anything suspicious.

"Well, M," I said in a posh voice. "What do we have here? By Jove, I think we have something."

I'd found a folder tucked away in a sub-sub file labeled *Surveillance Documents and Stuff.* That definitely sounded hinky to me. I tapped it open, and a bunch of files dropped down. Some were documents, some image files. One was a sound bite.

I made sure the iPad speakers were on, opened the sound bite, and hit play. The first thing I heard was foot-steps—two distinct sets. One lot sounded like hooves. But, not the rhythmic four beats of a horse. These were ... two-footed? The other set was made by boots or shoes —probably Rebecca's. Both were rapid and slightly echoed as though they were running through an empty street. Was she being chased? Or was she chasing someone?

The footfalls slowed. Stopped.

A male said something, but I couldn't make out his words. Hooves clopped once, twice, three times.

"It's not right, you know!" Rebecca shouted, breathing hard. "Hand the wands over and I won't call the F.C.T."

"Mind your business!" the man snarled. "I'm warning you. He knows you're spying on him."

"Who? Who are you talking about?"

"You can't beat him. He's too powerful."

"Hywell Rowlands? Is that who you mean? What does he want? And what's he got to do with contraband wands?"

"Someone's coming." The hooves scraped on the ground, clopped loudly, and faded into the distance.

All I heard then was Rebecca trying to catch her breath.

"You're such a fool, Cael," she muttered. "I've got to tell Walker."

Footsteps. Slow. Rebecca must've been walking. Something that sounded like gravel scraped as though she had turned suddenly.

"What the?" She whispered. "Who's there?"

"Rork-rork-rork," in the distance, followed by a whooshing flap of wings.

"Stupid raven," Rebecca said.

Fumbling sounds. A click. And the sound bite ended.

I played the file again, straining to hear something, some fine detail I had missed the first time. When it ended, I felt numb. What if that was the last thing Rebecca heard? The last thing she said? No. How would she have uploaded the sound file to the iPad and lock it away in the trunk if she'd been attacked and kidnapped then and there?

I had to find this Cael guy—see what he was about. Maybe a more stealthy approach would be the way to go, though. He sounded like a nasty piece of work.

At random, I tapped open a document and started reading.

Found something odd today while out searching in the forest. A carved wooden tooth in a glass sphere. Looks old. Not sure where it came from or why it was in the woods. Looks like a talisman or some morbid keepsake. Anyway, I kept it in case it turns out to be important. After all, I did find it right where the trees are dying. I might show Walker and see what he thinks.

Maybe I should check into this Walker fellow. Seems Becca trusted him.

And what was the F.C.T., for goodness sake? And who was so powerful that he couldn't be beaten? Was it Hywell Rowlands? That had been the first name that had come to Rebecca's mind.

With no answers forthcoming, I opened a file labeled '*Rant Therapy*' and ran a finger down the screen, reading the titles. '*C.A.L.L. Centre Debacle.*' '*Team Unfair Disqualification.*' '*Meeks' Moods.*' That one I understood and I'd only just met the raxx. From what I could see, '*Cadd*' was the most common topic. I scrolled up the screen to the most recent entry and opened the file marked '*Cadd poking her nose into my business. Again!*'

Got into it again with that smart-mouthed Ava Cadwaller. I'm in the woods looking for something to prove there's a smuggler in Grimsmead, when she turns up on that pimped-out ride she calls a broom. Struts up to me, demanding to know what I'm doing. As if I'm going to tell her! Besides the fact I'm trespassing on Old Blood Land, I just don't like her. At all! I don't know why Walker puts up with her. Anyway, I tell her I'm on family business. She watches me for a bit, and then proceeds to cite me for 'environmental cross-contamination'. I'm sure she made it up. She's an F.C.T. agent, so I shouldn't have clocked her one, but I did. Stupid, because she's way stronger and faster than me. She thumped me hard, and had me pinned to the ground gasping for air before I could think straight. So, now I have a fine to pay, and I'm being charged with striking a federal agent. Just what I need at the moment. It was worth it, though! :)

"Go, Beccs!" I fist bumped the screen.

I'd read all the files later. The one labeled *Walker* I would peek at with one eye closed in case the entries were a bit racy. If I saw too much, I'd stop reading. Manners and all that.

Wondering what to do next, I surveyed the room. A dusty white cloth covered what looked like a low bookcase or set of drawers. Atop of the cloth were four circular patches set out in a rectangle: two a hand span apart, two twice that distance. Each patina-green mark was the size of my fingertip. No dust sat within the shape, so whatever had rested there hadn't been gone long.

From the shape, there was a good possibility it had been Rebecca's jewellery box, the pair to mine. Both had marble-sized bronze balls for feet that would leave marks. So, if it was the jewellery box, where was it now? I hadn't seen it in Rebecca's bedroom.

Distant shouts caught my attention. I ran to look over the banister. A man in a long grey overcoat and a black suit stood in the Forest Room. It was difficult to make out his features from this distance, but I was fairly certain he was Rebecca's boyfriend, Walker. Harvey and Meeks stood near him, both blocking his way.

"There are things you must know," Harvey trotted in

front of him, making it difficult to walk without tripping over.

"Is she here?" Walker shouted.

"No, she's not." Meeks, standing on his hind legs, bounded left as Walker dodged right. "We don't know where she is. We're just as worried as you are."

"Look." Walker dragged a hand through his dark, messy hair. "I'm sorry. I didn't mean to say what I said to her. It was a stupid argument."

"I know nothing about your disagreement," Harvey said. "Rebecca is not here. And, frankly, we're concerned about her safety."

Walker glanced up and looked straight at me. "What? Rebecca?"

He shoved Harvey aside and raced to the only spiral staircase that remained on the bottom floor. As the spiral staircase ground and clanked upward, he took three steps at a time, almost flying to the third mezzanine.

Before I could say anything, he swooped me into his arms and planted a big kiss on my lips. He tasted of berries, as if he'd recently drank some juice. Or ate some pie. His breath was warm on my cheek. I tried not to kiss him back. I promise. This was my sister's boyfriend, for goodness sake!

"Um…" I pulled away and looked into his hazel eyes. "I think you've mistaken me for my sister Rebecca."

Awkward.

He let me go. I dropped to the floor, stumbling before I caught my balance.

"You're Arabella? Ding? Rebecca's little sister?"

"The very same."

"I don't know what to say. I saw you leaning over the railing. You know, with your red and silver hair all waves around your face, and I…" He blushed. "Sorry. Is she here? I haven't heard or seen her in a few days, and—"

"An understandable mistake. Hang on! Silver hair?" I grabbed the iPad, tapped in the password and within a few seconds I had the camera on selfie mode. A couple of clicks and there I was, large as life on the screen. Silver-white streaks had invaded my hair. Tons of them. This tripping between worlds was mighty stressful, and definitely overrated.

"My eyes! I look like a racoon!" My fingers hovered over the black … whatever-it-was. Temple to temple, a solid band of black covered my eyes right up to my eyebrows. Black lines, like bare twigs branched out from the bridge of my nose, up and across my forehead. It looked like I'd been crying and my mascara had run. Badly. I mean right down my cheeks! It was as if someone had gone wild with the eyeliner while I wasn't looking. "And…" I stared at myself. My eyes were so blue-green they looked fake. As though I had fancy contact lenses in.

"You look shocked," Walker said. "This is how a banshee is supposed to look."

He reached over, faster than anyone I had ever known, and rubbed his thumb over my forehead.

"What are you doing?" I glared at him, stepping away.

He scrutinised his thumb. "Checking if it's real or makeup."

"I assure you, I might not be a makeup artist, but this is not my day look. Did Rebecca look like this?"

"No." Meeks leaped off the staircase and onto the landing by my side. "She had red across her eyes. A couple of black lines. A few white dots."

"How Halloween of her." I snapped. "Was she happy about it?"

"Not when she first got here, she wasn't. She tried all

sorts of rubbish trying to scrub off her markings. Dyed her hair back to auburn, and within a week, it looked just like yours again."

"What about some hooky-fooky magic?" I spluttered. "Or a potion?"

"Nope!" Meeks flopped onto his belly and gazed up at me. "Welcome home, Ding. Oh, and by the way. Your mother was a banshee, and your father was a dryad—you know, a tree fey."

"You didn't have to tell her like that!" Harvey sat down by my feet and patted my leg. "But, he's right."

"You mean I wail? I can foretell someone's death?"

"Not everyone's," Harvey said. "Just the members of a specific family."

"She's only half banshee," Meeks said. "She might not be bound to the Thornton family at all."

"I have to sit down!" I sputtered.

"You don't have time," Walker said. "I'm taking you to the Federal Crime Taskforce."

"What?" I backed away. "Why? Are you arresting me? I just got here!"

"Rebecca told me that someone planned to clear her family home for a new housing development. Now, she appears to be missing. And you're here. In the family home."

"But I'm family!"

"Not until the F.C.T. says you are. You need to be tested."

"You come near me with needles, and I can't guarantee your safety."

"Are you threatening a federal agent?"

"No. Just warning one."

"I can put you in shackles and drag you down to head-quarters."

"I'd rather you didn't. Why don't you believe I'm Rebecca's sister? Ask Harvey. And Ploggit! He lived in my plumbing for years. They both know who I am."

"Take the word of a spriggit and a mooncat?" Walker snorted. "Look, if you are who you say you are, you have nothing to fear."

"Harvey?" I crouched next to her, pleading. "Can't I claim diplomatic immunity or something?"

"I'm sorry, Ding." She placed her paw on my hand. "Now we're back in Grimsmead we have to follow their laws."

"I want to go home, then."

"What about Rebecca?" Meeks stood on his back paws, pointing a raxx-clawed-finger at me. "I need help finding her. You can't go home."

I was trapped between a puddle and a wet place. I stood up. "Okay. But I'm not happy about this."

"Then, shall we go?" Walker indicated the stairs.

"I suppose."

"Bring that device with you." Walker pointed to the iPad clutched to my chest. "It may hold vital evidence surrounding Rebecca's disappearance."

"Harvey?" I squeaked. "If I'm not back by tomorrow, come and get me, okay?"

"Where's your broom?" Walker escorted me down the spiral staircase to the Forest Room. Of course, the stairs worked for him.

"I hope you're not expecting me to clean for you!"

"Rebecca always said that. She was sure you'd say the same thing." Walker's smile was warm, but he seemed distant, preoccupied. And sad.

I couldn't blame him. Until we found Rebecca, the world seemed darker, more depressing.

"So, *now* you believe I'm Arabella?"

"I'm not convinced. Anyway, what I believe doesn't matter. There are protocols—"

"Yes, I know. Laws, rules, and blah blah."

"Exactly."

"So, why do I need a broom?"

"To fly back to headquarters." He looked at me as though I was an absolute idiot.

I choked. "You're kidding, right?"

"Oh, I forgot. People don't fly everywhere on Earth. They roll around in things called cars."

"Yes, we're primitive like that."

"You could have gained that information from Rebecca."

"And I could have the info because I drive a 1998 Subaru Forester—Canyon Red Pearl Metallic, if you must know!"

"You're fast with details, I'll give you that. But you could've rehearsed."

"You're a complete butt-head!"

Walker stared me down, doubt flickering behind his eyes. "Very quick with details."

I pressed my lips together and growled.

"Let's, for the moment, say you are Arabella," Walker said. "Is Earth as dead as Rebecca says?"

"Dead? You mean with zombies? Or deserted and barren?"

"Dead as in no magic."

"Then yes, Earth is stone-cold-dead and buried."

Walker grimaced. "I can't imagine a world like that."

"How do *you* know about Earth?"

"Rebecca told me that's where she grew up."

"So you believed her? But you won't believe me when I say I'm her sister?"

"Rebecca is missing. You're in her family home. And threats have been made. You do the figures."

"How much did she tell you about Earth? Did she tell you why we were sent there?"

"She dropped a few hints, but nothing specific. What do you know about it?"

"Not a clue. I thought I was human up until today."

Walker stared at me, his eyes narrowed. "Great cover story."

"Do you know anything about my parents," I asked. "The ones here in Grimsmead?"

"Just because you sound sincere, doesn't mean you're Arabella."

"This can't be happening!"

"I'll hire a carpet for you. Might be a little less daunting your first trip."

"Really? Flying carpets? What next? Magic wardrobes?"

We wove our way along the mossy path, ducking under tree branches and overgrown ferns. We crossed a miniature bridge over the stream and followed the path out into a gloomy corridor. Flaming torches, held aloft by blackened sconces upon stone walls, lit the way.

"Medieval or what?" I whispered more to myself than Walker. Unfortunately, my voice echoed about the tunnel.

"Fire keeps turgills away," Walker said. "I can extinguish them if you like. Nothing like a family of turgills moving into the place. They prefer the more … well-seasoned … elements of your plumbing system, if you know what I mean."

Turgills didn't sound hygienic to me at all. "No. I'm happy with the torches."

The tunnel opened up into what only could be called a mausoleum. Creepy! But, maybe that's what people did in Grimsmead. Kept the family close even though they're no longer breathing.

I stepped out of the tunnel onto a black marble floor, the glossy stone veined with silver. Instantly, the air chilled. The sunlight filtering through three round skylights looked golden, but the stark atmosphere seemed to leech away all warmth. We passed between at least twenty life-sized statues, all posed frozen mid-step in some sensuous dance. They held woven branches with leaves carved so perfectly they could have been real and simply encased in creamy, blue-veined marble. Waist-high ceramic pots held soft ferns that draped the floor. Vases of violet lilies and white jasmine stood on plinths, their perfume so sweet and powerful it was cloying.

As we hurried through the mausoleum, our footfalls echoed, chasing us as though the living were not welcome.

"Are these my ancestors?" My hushed words fluttered around long after they were spoken.

"They're Rebecca's. I'll let you know if they're yours after the test."

I chose to ignore the comment. "Where are their bodies?" I couldn't see any coffins or tombs. There were no sealed niches in the walls. No names carved on inlaid panels.

"You don't think they'd be in this place, do you?"

"Isn't that the whole idea of a mausoleum?"

"You really did grow up in a weird world."

"You can talk! What are you, anyway? A werewolf? Elf? Turgill?"

"I'm Special Agent Walker Kane. I work for the F.C.T. Rebecca never spoke of me?"

"No," I smiled. Smug, I know, but it felt great to have a dig back at him. "No, she didn't."

"Oh!" He looked heartbroken.

My smug feelings fell away. "I'd say she couldn't tell me. That would have meant telling me about Grimsmead. From what I can tell, it was all hush-hush."

"You—if you are Arabella—were always her main concern. You and her grandmother."

"I never knew we had a grandmother. I mean, we had grandparents on Earth, but they were human. And they weren't related by blood. More by ink—you know? Documents. Paperwork. Government files?"

"Do you always talk this much?"

"I'm nervous. I always babble stupid things when I'm nervous. Or scared."

"Are you saying you have something to be nervous about? You're admitting you're not Arabella?"

"No! That's not what I'm saying at all. I just travelled goodness knows how many miles to a whole different world. I've found out animals can talk. That my sister's missing and in some sort of trouble. I've gone grey overnight. And it looks like I fell face first in a can of black boot polish. How would you feel?"

"You're defensive."

"And you're offensive!"

"Are you finished?"

"I haven't begun to finish, you, you—not-so-special agent!"

"Just so you know." Walker pointed at my face. "That banshee mask won't stay black."

"It won't?"

"They're newborn markings. When you grow up a bit, they'll settle down—become morphic."

"Hey! I'm not a baby!"

"Compared to me, you are."

I touched my face. My skin felt hot and slightly leathery. Especially around my eyes, cheeks and forehead. Harvey never said anything about this. If she had, I would have packed a bucket-load of concealer. Not to mention moisturiser.

"What about my hair?" I fiddled with the long waves self-consciously. "Will the grey go away?"

"I hope you like wild, silver hair."

"I'm half dryad. That could make a difference."

"So your silver hair will be all wiry with a green tinge."

He had to be joking. I mean, really.

We reached the mausoleum's scarred wooden doors, a

pair of them that stood a hefty ten feet high. Walker pushed them open without even struggling, which disappointed me. A lot. Sunlight haemorrhaged through the dim interior, hot and stifling. How that moron strutted about in a long overcoat in the middle of what had to be summer was a mystery.

No sense, no feelings. I followed him outside, making sure to leave a good distance between us. How Rebecca could like such a clod was beyond me.

The humidity rolled over me, sucking the breath from my lungs. I shielded my eyes from the sun as I adjusted to the sudden glare. When I could see without my eyes watering, my mouth fell open. My family home stood in a cemetery. Weathered statues stretched out in all directions. Not in neat, orderly lines like the cemeteries of earth. No, these statues were higgledy-piggledy. In fact, it looked like we had just gate-crashed an awesome party, and everyone had frozen mid-action. Nothing to see here. No invitation, no dancing, no fun. Admittedly, some of the marble party-goers were missing noses, hands and other bits and pieces. And others looked way too serious, but add a few balloons, a gallon of margaritas, a D. J, and this place would be rocking.

Rock. Statue… I chuckled.

"What's so amusing?"

"Me."

"I'll order you a carpet via C.A.L.L. See what they can scrounge up." Walker headed towards the rear of the stone-walled mausoleum. "There's shade around here. We can wait in the forest."

I peeked around the mausoleum's corner, checking where he'd gone. It paid to be wary in unknown places. He strode toward a wall of hills, their flanks forested with dense, spreading trees.

Walker wasn't wrong about the shade. I don't think one lick of sunlight made it past the first line of trees. I trotted after him, finding it challenging to keep up with his long strides.

We reached the edge of the mausoleum and rounded the corner. I stopped, my mouth agape. The arboretum looked totally different from the outside. And so much bigger! It had been difficult to make out the architecture from the inside because of all the trees and ferns. A sturdy, bronze framework secured hundreds of glass panels, the bottom floor set in arches, their tops crowned with red, green, and blue stained glass. Above, the mezzanine walls appeared to be made from black glass, but it was hard to be certain because they were thick with grime. The windows had their moss-green shutters closed. All except for the ones I opened earlier. The stained-glass window didn't look nearly so impressive from all the way down here.

As we hurried toward the tree line, I scanned the arboretum's interior, looking for Harvey, Meeks and Ploggit. That reminded me. I hadn't seen the spriggit brownie since we'd first arrived. Hope he was all right.

"Too many darn plants in there!" I muttered. "How am I supposed to see anything?"

Walker snorted. "First time I've ever heard someone with dryad blood complain about too many plants. You realise that's another demerit against you? No dryad would ever complain about nature."

I huffed. "Well, according to everyone, I'm half tree fairy. So, it's my grumpy banshee bit that's complaining. Careful, I may be a harbinger of your doom."

"Not amusing, considering your 'sister' is missing."

A slap would have stung less. This was not all fun and games. Rebecca was in trouble. My bad habit of playing one-up-man-ship was childish. He was right. I was a baby.

When we reached the tree line, the shade wrapped around me like a cold compress.

Walker remained in the sun, pulling a black stone the size of a billiard-ball from his pocket. He flipped the stone open as though it was some sort of ancient mobile phone. Sunlight glittered and danced, reflecting off a bed of ice-blue crystals inside the stone. No, not a stone. It was a geode.

"Viggs!" Walker called. "You there?"

A flash of light blinded me. When I could see again, a tiny fairy–or maybe a pixie–hovered before us. Dressed in nothing but silver-blue wings, a buttermilk-coloured tunic, and heavy eye make-up, Viggs drifted toward me, a skeptical look on her tiny face.

"You found her, I see." Viggs didn't sound pleased at all. She drifted back to Walker, her wings flapping so fast they were a blur.

"That's not Rebecca," Walker said. "She claims to be her sister."

"They keep crawling out the cesspit, don't they? Like turgills."

"Hey!" I cried.

"I need a carpet." Walker ignored her rudeness. "She's never flown before."

"I've been in a plane," I protested. "Flew halfway 'round the world. And back!"

"*Plain* seems apt." Viggs sniffed. "Who dressed you? A spriggit brownie?" She laughed, a cruel sound that raised the hair on the back of my neck.

"Order me a carpet," Walker said. "*Now* would be helpful."

"Can't guarantee the quality," Viggs said.

"Just go." Walker snapped, and Viggs vanished, a nasty chuckle fading in her wake.

"If I were you," I said. "I'd trade that one in for a better model. She's got issues."

"Can't be choosy. We get what the Bureau gives us."

"Does everyone have one? I mean other than special agents?"

"How else would we keep in contact?"

"Does Rebecca have one? Her own call-stone? With its own fairy?"

"Ordered her one from C.A.L.L. Signed her up for a personal plan—wider choice of service providers that way."

"Have you tried sending Viggs off to connect with Becca's phone fairy?"

"What sort of agent do you think I am? It was the first thing I did when Rebecca went missing."

"And?"

"Viggs found Rebecca's call-stone, but the fairy was gone."

"Maybe the fairy went searching for Becca."

"We went through her C.A.L.L. logs, and Rebecca's connection had been terminated. And before you ask, not from C.A.L.L.'s end."

"Hmmm!" Their communication system sounded similar to our mobile phone system, only with fairies instead of phones. So…

"Where was her call-stone when it terminated? It would give us a place to start."

"I've searched there. And I found nothing except her stone. There wasn't even residual fairy dust."

"Can you take me there?"

"So, now you're the detective?"

"Fresh eyes couldn't hurt, could they?"

"I'll decide that after your testing's finalised."

"When can I get a stone-fairy?" I asked. "I'd be okay with a basic model. Nothing with the Snarky App included."

Walker frowned. He obviously didn't know what Apps were. "If you're cleared by our experts, I'll help you create an account with C.A.L.L."

"Excellent!"

CHAPTER NINE

A few minutes later, Viggs popped into view, a carpet–well more a rug, really–hovering beside her. Walker opened his call-stone. She glanced at me, sniggered and vanished, a puff of blue light dissipating behind her.

"Does she live in that stone?" I pointed to the black rock as he slipped it back into his pocket.

"I wouldn't say live. More exists. She reverts into her energy form when she's inside. Sort of like glowing dust."

"Tricky!"

"You're eyeing the carpet as though it'll bite."

"Can you prove it won't?"

"Just climb on."

"Does it come with safety belts? Or a harness?"

"Only babies and toddlers need those."

Again with the baby reference.

I stepped up to the floating rug, scrutinising every thread. Well, at least that's what I wanted to do.

"Where did Viggs dredge up this flea-bitten rag?" I ran

my hand over the threadbare carpet. The pattern had long since worn away, leaving nothing but faded blue and brown smudges. The centre had no colour whatsoever. "You sure this is safe?" I poked the rug, worried it would fall apart. The rug recoiled, bobbing downwards. I shoved it sideways. It shoved back, knocking into me with more power than a moth-eaten mat should be able to muster.

"If it's still in service, it's safe."

"Says who?"

"Just get on. Please." Walker whistled and a broom whooshed from somewhere within the forest, stopping by his side. It wasn't what I expected. It did have a wooden handle and a twig and straw-type brushy end. A bit ragged, but that made it look all the more witchy. What surprised me was the padded leather seat, high-gloss timber pannier, stirrups, and fold-out motorbike handles. I'd always wondered how people rode brooms. Surely the traditional way gave the most horrible wedgie.

"Got the beginner's model, eh?" I couldn't help myself.

When Walker ignored me, I tried climbing on the flying carpet. As my knee pressed on the floating rug, it buckled.

I stumbled.

Walker chuckled. "It knows you don't like it. Try saying something sweet."

"Seriously?"

"Couldn't hurt."

Deciding that sweet-talking a mangy old rug would be my last resort, I took a running jump and leaped onto the carpet like a high-jumper. Up, half twist over and onto my back. Not one sugary word needed—and I didn't even drop the iPad. I shot Walker a smug smile.

"Give me that." He indicated the iPad. "I'll look after it from here on."

I hesitated. Then handed it to him.

"Well, now you're aboard," Walker said. "Let's head off, shall we?"

To feel safer on my maiden flight, I rolled onto my tummy, squawking and muttering as I fought to stay on the skittish rug. The whole carpet moved like an under-inflated floaty-air-mattress on water.

Walker laughed, a rich, warm sound that brought a smile to my lips against my will.

"You're hopeless!" Walker said, but there was no malice to the comment. "Even Rebecca did better than you. And she was all arms, legs, and squeals her first time on a flying carpet."

"Yes, well, I expect she couldn't see the ground through her rug."

He opened the pannier, lifted what looked like a winch, and slid the iPad underneath. After clicking the winch back in place, he reeled out a tow-rope that ended with two carabiners.

"For emergency recoveries." Walker hooked them onto brass rings set in the front (or possibly the rear) of the carpet. "In case you decide to try and escape."

"Yes, because I know so many hide-away holes in Grimsmead."

"Exactly."

Walker mounted his hovering broom, slipped his boots in the stirrups, and, without a word, the broom shot upward. As the tow-rope tensed, the carpet lurched, wobbled, and, before I could gasp, we were above the forest.

Holy-moly! I had never gripped anything so tight in my life. I didn't dare move in case the stupid rug tossed me off. Too bad these things didn't come with parachutes.

The wind whipped my hair back from my face. It was

the first time I disliked having waist-length hair. It lashed my shoulders and back so hard it stung. Who knew a broom could fly so fast?

Clutching the rug so hard my fingers ached, I lay my forehead on the rug, eyes squeezed shut. I opened them. Just a crack. And regretted it. I *could* actually see the ground through a threadbare patch. Only a handful of fibres lay between me and death. I was too young to die!

Concentrate on the scenery, Ding! But the landscape was so far below. The forest had given way to a town with meandering roads and a tangle of dark lanes and alleys. It didn't appear to be a modern city with skyscrapers or lots of glass. It looked more old European. It wouldn't surprise me if the streets were cobbled and they still had a set of stocks in the market square.

I glanced right. More town, though the houses grew sparse, the land more rural and fenced with low stone walls. To our left, beyond the dense forest, sunlight reflected off a wide lake. Mountains rose up on the far side of the water, their sides steep and rocky. A spit of land jutted from the mountains, curving into the lake like a great hook fishing for the lone, mountainous island. The landscape reminded me of the map I'd found locked in Rebecca's trunk. High up on the island's craggy ridges, above the tree line, crouched twelve dragon statues.

"Dragons?" I shouted. "You have dragons here?"

Walker glanced at the ridgeline. "Those things? The Hours? They're made of stone."

The Hours? Weird name.

The rug slanted downwards at an alarming angle. Walker's long grey coat flapped wildly as he picked up speed. The 'fasten your seatbelts and put your seats in the upright position' lights would have flashed on by now if I'd been in something that was supposed to fly. Carpets were to make a room cozy. They weren't for carving up the wild-blue yonder.

As we levelled out, we slowed, swooping over a cluster of large, forbidding stone buildings surrounded by a thick rock wall. The shadows seemed darker, deeper within the compound. The windows in the weathered stone appeared to suck in light. None escaped. The word 'fortress' sprung to mind. All it lacked was a moat and dragon.

Walker banked right, and we spiralled downward, my rug swinging wide, the momentum tilting me at a sickening angle. I howled, squeezed my eyes closed and gripped on with all my might.

And then the wind stilled, and the heat smothered me once more.

"I took the scenic route." Walker stood next to the carpet. "Thought you might like a quick trip around the place."

"How thoughtful of you."

"The trip usually takes, maybe two minutes from the cemetery to F.C.T. Headquarters. I'll have to fill in paperwork explaining our circuitous route."

"So bill me."

Walker unhooked the carabiners, reeled them back into the pannier and retrieved the iPad, tucking it under one arm. He whistled, and his broom zoomed off. Probably to a broom parking garage or something. Walker headed toward a squat building with three keyhole arches set in one wall, towing me on the rug as if it was the most normal thing in the world.

"Any new leads, Walker?" a female called.

"Hey, Cadd." Walker waved.

Still sprawled on the floating carpet, I propped myself up on my elbows to see who had spoken.

So this was the infamous Ava Cadwaller Rebecca had

vented about in her *Rant Files*. A woman, perhaps twenty-five years old, with green eyes and a short, cobalt-blue bob sashayed towards us. Strange, grey runes and symbols covered her tanned skin, wavering as I watched. Dressed in a short black leather skirt, knee-high boots studded with pockets, and a simple white blouse, she looked sleek and classy.

"You found her?" She surveyed me, spread-eagled and frumpy on the rug.

Although I felt dowdy next to her, I flashed her my most charming smile. And she ignored me.

"Looks like Rebecca." Her eyes narrowed as she scrutinised me. "But her markings are wrong. She's barely a youngling."

"She doesn't think so." Walker pulled me and the rug into the shade of the building. He shivered and pulled his coat closed.

Cadd followed us. In the shadows, the symbols and runes overlaying her skin glimmered. Not much, but enough that I could see a faint, red glow.

"She claims to be Rebecca's sister," Walker said.

"Sister, eh?" Cadd leaned against the wall, her boots crossed casually, her arms relaxed at her sides.

"That's what she reckons. But there's no mention of her in Rebecca's file." Walker flicked his head in my direction. He shot me a 'keep your mouth shut' glare. "Bringing her in for identification."

"Why isn't she in irons?"

"She couldn't even operate a rug. Where was she going to go anyway? We were high above Grimsmead. Escaping wasn't an issue."

"She could be a changeling or a shifter." Cadd examined me once more. "Had reports of one around here this morning. Talk to Agent Briggs—he's looking into that."

"Henley Briggs?" Walker raised his eyebrow.

"First case since his suspension."

"I bet he's annoyed, getting a Shifter case. A bit of a step down from homicide."

"Haven't heard that much swearing in years." Cadd stared at me, her green eyes icy. "But the day's young."

I flinched uncomfortably beneath her gaze. There was something about her that terrified me. Keeping my mouth shut was easy. And that's saying a lot for me. My admiration for Rebecca sky-rocketed. She hadn't backed down under Cadd's heavy gaze. I would have paid to see my sister clock her one.

"She could be a shifter." Walker nodded at me. "I'll let you know the results once the test is over."

"*I* could question her," Cadd jerked off the wall, her eyes wide and eager.

"Maybe later," Walker said. "If the test goes awry."

"Well, in that case, I'm off," Cadd said. "Protesters by the lake are sooking again."

"Why are they sending you?" Walker asked. "A couple of uniforms could do the job."

"The chief says I might scare the protestors into settling down a bit." Cadd whistled, and a broom flew from the mysterious parking garage. "I don't know why the protestors bother. The development is going ahead whether they like it or not. Hywell Rowlands has the Old Blood Elders believing everything he says. And he has the Thornton clan backing him." Cadd mounted her broom, clasping the leather-wrapped handle. No sissy handlebars for this secret agent. It did have a seat, though. A red leather saddle with studs, its rear fitted with a glossy black pannier. Rebecca was right. Pimped out, indeed!

"Drinks later?" She pulled a set of flying goggles from

a zippered pocket in her right boot and slipped them over her eyes.

"See how we go, eh?" Walker nodded at me as if I was going to interfere in their plans.

With that, Cadd launched into the sky, rocketing upward like a firework on New Year's. No bright sparkles, though.

"Why did you lie to her?" I scrambled off the rug onto what I now realised was a roof. We were atop a large T-shaped building, the squat building with the keyhole arches, the horizontal cross.

"You've got a lot to learn." Walker gave the rug a shake, and it lowered to the ground. Or should I have said rooftop? "That's Ava Cadwaller. She's a verge."

"Never heard of it."

"Powerful fey from across the Smoking Sea. They say the verge came from the centre of the world—rode a pyroclastic flow out of a volcano to freedom, obliterating the land around for leagues. From there, they spread across Arahn."

"Cool story."

"Not so cool for those who died in the fires."

"Is Arahn this world's name?"

"You tell me."

"Seriously? I wouldn't have asked if I knew!"

"You see those markings all over Cadd's skin?" Walker said. "They reveal how she's feeling, *and* if someone is lying."

"But you did lie."

"No, if you recall, I said there was no mention of you in Rebecca's files." He crouched and rolled up the carpet, leaning it against the wall.

"You little sneak!"

"That's what they pay me for." Walker entered the far right arch, and I reluctantly followed.

CHAPTER TEN

We followed a brightly lit corridor that ended at a set of moving stairs, much like our escalators on Earth, only these creaked, rattled, and groaned, and were built of bronze lace-work. I gauged the speed of the steps and hopped onboard. We descended for about thirty feet, veered around a bend, and descended again until we reached a glassed-off landing. Walker led the way, with me trotting close behind, my boots thudding against the marble floor as we wove through a crowd busy boarding the up-escalator. A trio of winged pixies dressed in bright green body-suits and acorn hats stared at Walker, their golden eyes wide. They tittered like teenagers seeing a guy they fancied in the cafeteria.

"How cliché are those three?" I said. "Straight from Fairytale Mode Magazine."

"What are you talking about?"

"Those pixies making goo-goo eyes at you."

"What about them?"

"Almost every storybook has pixies dressed like that."

"Stories have to start somewhere."

That made me think. The implications of this logic were huge. Did Earth fairytales originate from this world, or the other way around? I'd have to chew that conundrum over when I had more time.

We pushed through the glass doors and entered a concourse bustling with people. Well, 'people' wasn't the right word exactly, but calling them creatures or beasts seemed rude and ignorant. I'd never seen a thoroughfare this big. It had to be the length of a football field and half as wide.

"More dragons!" I pointed up at sixteen skylights, eight on either side of the vaulted ceiling, each skylight circled by stone dragons.

"This used to be one of their libraries." Walker snorted with disgust. "They do love looking at themselves."

"When you've got it, flaunt it."

We passed humongous archways, fluted columns, and eight giant robed and crowned statues that supported the roof.

"You're gawking," Walker said, without looking my way.

I closed my mouth and heat filled my cheeks and neck.

"So, Ava is a walking lie detector?" I quickened my pace to keep step with Walker.

"Among other things."

"And she's dangerous?"

"More than you realise."

"Did she know Rebecca? In person? Did she like her?"

"She tolerated her. A favour to me."

"How sweet of her."

We angled right, merging with the ebb and flow of the crowd. To my left plodded what had to be an ogre, or perhaps a troll with leathery, grey skin, horned brows, and a black mop of hair threaded with colourful beads and bones. I tried to keep my eyes front, an amiable expression on my face, but I couldn't help glancing at the hulking creature. It was male. I think. Dressed in mangy furs, boiled leather, and heavy, knee-length boots shod with steel, he looked like a beast straight out of a fantasy role-playing game. A stench of musk and rotting vegetables seeped from him, wafting over me as I scurried along.

"So this test?" I raised my voice so Walker could hear me above the crowd. "Is it painful? Embarrassing?" The thought of taking my clothes off in front of Walker was the last thing I wanted to do.

"If I tell you, it won't be a fair test."

"Well, that's not fair!"

The 'person' in front of me looked like a centaur–top-half man, bottom-half horse–his hooves clopping on the chequered black and white tiles. I wondered if the F.C.T. had a team of pooper-scooper-workers off to the side, all on high alert waiting for big steaming piles of centaur-leavings.

To make the concourse more bizarre, another crowd buzzed and flapped above us, each worker focused on whatever mission they were on for the day.

Walker seemed oblivious, content on weaving his way towards a set of open doors that stood fifty feet high. At least. Dragon library, indeed!

"What happened to the dragons' books?" I asked. "Are they still here somewhere?"

"Some are. Others were burned during the uprising."

"Burning books! That's terrible!"

"So was the uprising."

We passed through the doorway, the ogre-troll turning left, as we turned right. It took a minute or two before the smell faded. Perhaps it was mating season, and he was puffing out smelly pheromones looking for a girlfriend.

We travelled down another escalator, disembarking onto a stone ramp, then hurried down into what looked like the bowels of the building. A long, dimly lit hallway stretched out from the incline—no fancy paintwork on these walls. No windows. No glossy tiles. I followed Walker along the tunnel, my boots echoing on the stone-flagged floor. No sound came from Walker except the rustle of his long overcoat.

"Can't I eat before we start?" It wasn't a ploy to delay the testing. My stomach grumbled so loudly Walker had to have heard it. "See? I'm starving."

"I promise to feed you once this is all over with. Even if you fail the test."

"Bread and water, I suppose."

"Here we are." Walker unlatched and pushed open a plain timber door, ushering me inside a windowless room perhaps ten feet by fifteen. The floor was packed earth, the walls stone. The only furniture was a wooden, ladder-back chair, its arms and legs fitted with iron shackles. A fold-down bench lined with evil-looking pinchers, probes and cutting devices stood nearby. The place screamed dungeon.

Walker closed the door, the thud echoing through the room and down the connecting tunnel.

"What's going on?" I pushed past Walker and backed into the door. "You're not chaining me in that!"

"It's procedure," Walker said. "If you expect us to believe you're Rebecca Ashmore's sister, then you'll sit in the chair and do as you're told."

"Rebecca Black. Her name is Rebecca Kerigan Black."

"Her last name's Ashmore. You'd know that if you were truly her sister."

"Can't you just get Ava Cadwaller to question me?"

"You wouldn't like her methods. Trust me, this will be far less invasive."

I stepped back, bumping into the wooden door. I reached behind, fumbling for the latch, but couldn't get a decent hold without turning around. And, that would make me vulnerable. Who knew what magical powers Walker had?

"I promise this won't hurt." Walker held out one hand, palm outward as if I was a wild animal.

All I read behind his eyes was, 'Trust me, I'm only going to strap you down and do a few experiments. Nothing personal. It's procedure.'

"That's what all the nice boys say." I shuffled right, still trying to get hold of the door handle. "Did you put Rebecca in that stupid chair?"

"There was no need. But, now she's missing after receiving threats about her home. And I found *you* in *her* house. Looking remarkably like her as though you're trying to assume her identity."

"That's ridiculous! I've come looking for Becca. Just like you are."

"What if I promise not to put the shackles on you?" Walker said.

"You think I'm that gullible?"

"No, I can see your fear. It's filling the room like oily smoke."

"I'm *not* sitting in that chair."

Walker called out, "A little assistance, please."

A side door I hadn't noticed opened. In came three burly creatures with red eyes, curled horns and long, braided beards. Their top halves were human, muscled and strapped with chains and leather. From the waist down they were armoured, the silver-plate protecting thick, brown hair that covered goat-like legs.

Satyrs? You had to be kidding me!

They walked towards me, a wall of fur, muscle and horn, their hooves clopping on the hard, packed ground.

My mind fizzed, white lights flashing before my eyes. Everything slowed. All sound disappeared except for the pounding of my heart. All colour faded to shades of grey. My body felt heavy, cumbersome. Every cell pulsed, my blood throbbing past my ears. If the ground swallowed me now, I would cheer and shout, 'Take me anywhere but here'.

The three satyrs rushed me, muscled arms outstretched, reaching for me, every movement, every cruel expression blurred and eerily slow.

I held my breath, closed my eyes and braced myself, ready to bite, claw and kick whatever grabbed me.

A hot, sweaty hand closed around my arm. I lashed out, screaming, the sound muffled as though heard underwater. A hollow, sucking darkness appeared beneath my feet, pulling me down into cold, damp earth. Into the darkness. The heaviness of my body vanished, leaving a light airiness I'd never felt in my life. It was as though I had shed my physical self, and only my spirit remained, leaving me strangely nebulous. I stretched out. Fanned out in all directions. Sensed the roots of old, old trees. Heard wind rushing through leaves, whispers I could almost understand.

"Arabella. Arabella." One voice rose above the others. It wasn't loud. But it was familiar. "Arabella."

Rebecca?

I couldn't shout her name. I had no mouth. No body. No idea what to do.

I strained to hear, but the voices multiplied, so many, so eager they became a deafening roar. I ploughed through the ground, past rocks, up and under tree roots. The soil caressed me, filled me. I had never felt so alive. So free.

The voices cradled me, carrying me along. To where? I didn't know. But I felt safe. And welcome.

One voice sang a lullaby with no words, drawing me towards it. I sensed family, their roots spanning generations, all connected, all waiting.

Buried within the welcome lay a dark, empty hole where no light, no love penetrated. A wall of despair surrounded the void so heavy and desolate I shuddered and backed away.

Rebecca? Could it be her? Scared? Lost? I'd heard her. Sensed her. I braced myself and reached out, my spirit easing through the soil.

Icy tendrils lashed out, forbidding and wary, but giving nothing of itself.

I tried to touch the emptiness with my mind even though it was the last thing I wanted to do. It might not be my sister, but I knew this being needed help.

The tendrils whipped out again, cleaving my spirit like deadly, implacable missiles through cloud.

I took the hint. The rest of this underground family wanted me. I didn't need such pain in my life.

Singing embraced me again, and it was wonderful. It drew me upward, my underground flight slowing.

Soil pressed down on me, filled my mouth and ears, crumbled up my nose. I flailed. Kicked. And exploded out of the ground into a cool, tree-lined glade and landed with a loud 'oomph' flat on my back.

I had no idea where I was, but there was not a hoof or goat horn in sight.

CHAPTER ELEVEN

I lay beneath a shroud of ferns, panting, grit in my eyes, soil in my nose and mouth. I coughed and spluttered, spitting and sneezing mud down the front of my white blouse. What had happened? It'd been terrifying and invigorating. I didn't feel tired, hungry or thirsty. It was as though the very planet had fed and watered me.

My eyes watered and stung, the dirt and grit like grains of glass beneath my lids. After a few blinks, they improved, but not by much. I didn't care. All that mattered right at that moment was I was out of that torture chamber. And, I had heard my sister's call. She was alive. I knew it. I had to find her.

Sunshine bathed the ferns above me, the fronds glowing soft, golden green as they bobbed and shivered, tickling my face. In the distance, birds twittered and cheeped. Water gurgled and splashed. I lay there listening, gathering my thoughts. I felt amazing. I wriggled in delight, grinning like a madwoman. I should have been scared. Any sane person would've been. But, the jury was in. I wasn't human. I didn't know whether to be elated or mortified. I was like a character in the novels I loved to devour. Did that mean I was invincible? No. My enthusiasm died. Rebecca was half banshee and half dryad and goodness knows what had happened to her.

I don't know how long I lay there, but the sun had shifted. All that inner joy had faded, leaving an aching void I'd never felt before. I didn't understand why. After all, I had been through for the last couple of days, no wonder I was so lost and confused. I focused, wrangling my thoughts back to Rebecca. And that lousy F.C.T agent, Walker Kane.

He would be searching for me. Probably had an all-points-bulletin issued the moment the ground had sucked me under. He'd have agents at the mausoleum, waiting for me to sneak home. Probably had his nasty phone-fairy out snooping, too.

Why would Rebecca be with such a creep?

Another part of my mind, the rare, logical part answered with, 'Well, he was searching for your sister. He didn't know who you were. And Rebecca's missing. He was just doing his job.'

Footfalls and rustling drew my attention.

I scrambled to my knees and scanned the forest. Trees encircled me, their grey-brown bark fractured like plate-armour, their leaves vibrant green. In amongst the healthy trees, a few unfortunate ones stood bare of leaf, their bark peeling, revealing axe marks and bore-holes as though someone had been sampling wood to seek what ailed them. Three mossy boulders clustered between one tree's roots, a shallow depression in the top of each stone choked with fallen leaves and dry twigs.

"Can I help you up?" A man with sun-streaked shoulder-length hair walked towards me with the most dazzling smile I had ever seen. Dressed in a crimson collared shirt, black jeans and boots, he should have looked out of place here in the woods. Wherever here was. But he didn't. Behind him, hovered a stout, brown rug stacked with firewood, the small logs neatly piled, trimmed and sorted. By their side sat an axe, its handle bound in stained suede, its blade so shiny it looked brand new.

"Need some help?" He bent over and clasped my hand, pulling me to my feet. His skin was warm, his palm moist and slightly calloused. So not just a pretty boy. A bubbling thrill ran through me. I put it down to my communion with the planet.

"What are you doing in the middle of nowhere?" He smiled. And there went the thrill again. Not the planet then.

"Getting lost." I ran a hand through my messy hair and did my best to brush down my clothes. What a day to swim through miles of dirt and spit mud all over myself.

"I can see that." He flashed me that smile again. "I'm Aylward Thornton. This is my family's estate. But you should know that."

"So, I'm trespassing."

"Yes, sorry, you are. You know what that means?"

"You're going to let me off with a stern warning?"

"No, I have a far worse punishment in mind for you."

"It doesn't involve shackles and burly guards, does it? Because I've done that already, today."

"Well, now you've gone and spoiled the surprise. Looks like you'll have to dine with me sometime. Scary, I know. And there could be dancing. It's cruel, but you did trespass, you know."

"Smooth," I said. "Do you pick up all the trespassers like that?"

"Only the ones I find sprawled on the ground, covered

with dirt and leaves." He picked a leaf from my hair, twirled it between his fingers and offered it to me.

"Seriously, now," he said. "How did you get all the way out here?"

"I'm not entirely sure. I was somewhere. And then I was here."

"Fascinating."

"I was going with 'weird', but fascinating sounds more mysterious. So, Aylward Thornton, if you could point me to the nearest road, I'd be forever grateful."

"Call me Thorn. Only the Elders call me Aylward. Family name." He screwed up his nose. "Firstborn always gets stuck with it."

"Well, Thorn, I'm lost, so if you could help, I'll buy *you* dinner sometime." *As soon as I figure out how money and stuff works here in Grimsmead.*

"You shouldn't be out here alone. There's been some trouble around these parts recently."

"Really?" Any information he had might help me find Rebecca. "What kind of trouble?"

"A girl, very similar to you actually, went missing recently. She owns *Magic, Mystree and Herbals,* a store in town. Lives out in the old mausoleum. She's not native to Grimsmead, so she might have just gotten lost. But that's not what everyone's saying."

"What's everyone saying?" I couldn't keep the eagerness from my voice.

"That she was attacked, taken from her own store. Blood on the floor. Shelves trashed. Stuff everywhere as though someone was searching for something."

"How do they know it was her …" A chill ran through me. I did my best to keep my voice calm, but I was certain distress and fear filled my eyes. "… there was blood?"

"You know how gossip is. People always exaggerate.

Details get skewed. It was probably just a spilled potion or something."

"How do you know so much?"

"I met Rebecca–that was her name, the girl who went missing–a few times when she visited the old-folks home near the lake, Spell Haven. I'm a diversional therapist there. Keep the oldies occupied and happy. Well, at least I try." He shrugged, smiling. "Anyway, Rebecca's grand-mother is a resident there. Staff are being questioned, along with a few of the more dangerous residents."

"And my—her grandmother's out there? At the nursing home?"

"Her last surviving relative, apparently. Not that the poor old thing recognised Rebecca. And when she did, holy-harpstrings, she went off. Screaming and wailing for her to go away."

"What's the matter with the grandmother?"

"Senile. Poor old thing has the memory of an old boot."

"Oh!" My voice caught in my throat. "That's so sad."

"You do look remarkably like Rebecca. You're shorter, though. Prettier."

My cheeks warmed, and I ducked my head. Thorn was easy to talk to, friendly. Nothing like Walker Kane.

"If you must know, Rebecca is my sister."

"She never mentioned she had a sister." Thorn bright-ened, his blue eyes locked on mine.

"The black sheep." I don't know why I lied, but for some reason, I couldn't tell Thorn about Earth. About being exiled from Grimsmead as a newborn. There had obviously been a reason why Rebecca and I were sent away. Even though I didn't know what it was. Yet. Telling someone I had just met would be irresponsible. And maybe dangerous. Until I knew my way around

Grimsmead and who to trust, that was one secret I would not tell.

"Do you know anything else about Rebecca?" I changed the subject. "About her disappearance?"

"Shall we walk?" He placed a hand on the small of my back and nodded at a path through the trees.

"Why not?" I smiled. "We can't stay out in the woods all night."

Thorn gave me a curious look. Puzzled? Amused? I couldn't place it. But, I didn't get danger vibes from him, so I walked beside him along the sun-dappled track. He towed the rug behind him as if it was the most normal thing in the world to do. It probably was.

He saw me glancing over my shoulder, grinning.

"You laughing at the tug-rug? Or my timber splitting technique?"

Hearing the term 'tug-rug' caused me to spit a wicked chuckle.

"You are an odd one." Thorn shook his head.

"Private joke," I said, unable to think of something clever to say. "You take logs for a ride often?"

"Our groundsman didn't come to work this morning. My aunt wouldn't stop pestering me until I went out and collected some wood."

"It pays to stock up. You never know when you're in for a cold snap."

"You're right about that!"

"So, what else can you tell me about Rebecca's disappearance? What happened leading up to it?"

"Rumour is," Thorn said, "that Cael Blightly tried to sell something to Rebecca. Offload it at her store. He's deep in debt—gambling or some such thing. His wife, Knola, she's a real tyrant. She's a cleaner at Spell Haven. I've been at the sharp end of her tongue more than once, so I can see why Cael was in such a bind. Anyway, whatever he said and did upset Rebecca, and she threatened to inform the F.C.T. about him. Apparently, he lost it. A big yelling match in her shop. At least half-a-dozen people witnessed it."

I remembered the recording on Rebecca's iPad. She'd called Cael a fool and was going to tell Walker and the F.C.T. about him. "And then she went missing?"

"Not straight away. A few days later."

"And what did the F.C.T. do? Did they investigate Cael?"

"Yes, but an argument isn't a crime, is it? No weapons were involved. No dark magic. No physical abuse."

"Did the F.C.T. find any leads other than Cael Blightly and Rebecca arguing? Do they have any suspicions?"

"I heard it could be a kidnapping–but don't quote me on that. Definitely foul play. Rebecca wouldn't have trashed her own store and left without a word. Everyone knew *Magic, Mystree and Herbals* was doing well since she took over the business."

"And this Cael character? Would he kidnap someone?"

"I've known Cael for years. In fact, he's our groundsman."

"A bit suspicious, don't you think—him not coming to work today? Maybe he's not who you think he is."

"He's rough around the edges. A no-nonsense type, but I don't think he'd do anything drastic. It's probably a coincidence him not coming to work today. He did have a nasty cut on his arm—maybe it got infected or something."

"If he's that hard up for money, he'd suffer a sore arm for a day's pay."

"You're a feisty little thing, aren't you?"

I studied my boots for a moment as I struggled not to

blush. "What I meant was, people do terrible things when they're desperate."

"Yes, they do.' Thorn sighed. "Your sister had a new boyfriend, you know."

"Yes, I met him. Walker Kane. Special agent extraordinaire."

"You don't like him?"

"I don't know him. Not really."

Thorn frowned. His mind had to be ticking over, putting pieces together.

"I only just arrived in Grimsmead," I added. "I lived overseas for most of my life. With distant relatives." Not a great lie, but a quick one.

"Kane's all right." Thorn smiled and nodded. "Solid. Dependable. I went to Grimsmead Academy with him. We were in the same year."

"Is that a school? Reformatory?" I grinned.

Thorn laughed. And the forest seemed to light up.

"It's a school. Toddlers up to university," he said. "Magic, witchcraft, history, math, reading, flying lessons, biology—you know, stuff about the flora and fauna of the world."

I wanted to ask what this world was called. But, that would give away things I wanted kept secret. For now.

"I know what schools are." I gave him a friendly shove. "So, tell me more about this Cael person."

"His father was our gamekeeper until he died. A hunting accident." Thorn paled, swallowed and continued–his voice soft, distant. "Cael and I played together as children. Like I said, he's our chief groundsman now. Looks after the gardens. Monitors game in our woods. Keeps the poachers away. He's always been reliable, despite his gambling. I don't think he's bad. At least from what I've seen. But who knows what goes on behind closed doors?"

A wicked thought entered my mind about being behind closed doors with Thorn. My cheeks warmed, and I pretended to study the trees as we walked beneath them.

"I wish I had more to tell you," Thorn said. "Cael and Rebecca argued. Then she vanished a few days later. Might just be a coincidence."

"It shows me he had something against Becca. It shows he had motive. Maybe there was more to it?" I thought of the recording again. "Maybe she approached him, gave him a chance to hand himself in to the F.C.T. and he…" I couldn't continue. The possibilities were too horrible.

"True," Thorn said. "I'm just telling you what I know."

A thought came to me. "Who's Hywell Rowlands?"

"You *are* new to town if you don't know who Rowlands is."

"A bigwig, is he?"

"Not sure if he wears a wig." Thorn looked at me with amusement. "But he's big. And powerful. Runs a housing development company. Wants to build a resort by the lake."

"I take it people aren't happy about that?" I know Rebecca would have been furious. She loved nature. Hated conglomerates that bulldozed forests just so they could make a profit.

"About half of Grimsmead aren't happy. A few hundred have set up a camp on The Finger to protest and block any civil works."

I thought about that for a moment. Hywell Rowlands sounded powerful, but I couldn't see him kidnapping Rebecca. There were hundreds of protestors, so why single her out? I wouldn't rule him out, but for now, I'd focus on Cael Blightly.

We walked a while, saying nothing. I was surprised at how comfortable the silence was. I didn't feel the need to fill the quiet with babble like I usually did. The trail rose gradually until we broke free of the forest. Before us hung narrow, wrought iron gates within a high, stone-block wall.

"My family's place." Thorn smiled, blushing. "They're a bit snobby. Don't like Outlings much."

"And, I guess I am an Outling?"

"I wouldn't say you're an Outling. But you won't be the most welcome person to visit."

"Shall I leave?" Not that I knew where to go. Mainly because I didn't have a clue where I was.

"I don't hold to my Elders' antique ways." He dug a key tied to a frayed and knotted strip of leather from his jeans pocket and unlocked the gate.

"You better get a new key ring." I pointed at the old one. "That one has seen better days."

"And worse." He grinned. "After you …I don't even know your name?"

"I'm Arabella, but I'd like it if you call me Ding."

"Ding. Odd name."

"It's what my close friends and family call me."

"Ding it is, then."

Beyond the wall, a rambling garden dotted with wide-spreading oak trees, rose gardens, fountains and meandering paths stretched all the way up to an old mansion.

I sucked in a shocked breath as I took in the three-story mansion with its six weather-stained statues holding up a stone balcony. It ran the width of the second floor. Rust-red shutters covered every window, except one on the third floor. That pair of shutters hung open. No silhouetted figure stood watching, but that was the only difference from the vision I'd received when Rebecca visited me only hours before. What if she was in there somewhere?

Injured? Trapped? I had to get in there.

"What's wrong?" Thorn rested his hand on my arm. "You were pale to start with, but now you're ashen."

"Nothing," I laughed, but it lacked heart. "I'm just surprised by your home."

"It's old, I know. But my Elders refuse to renovate." He shrugged. "They prefer to spend their wealth on land developments, and such. Say they are future-proofing themselves."

"The statues—do they signify anything or anyone?"

"My family. Mainly ancestors. But, see that one on the left, third along? That's modelled on my aunt Rachel. She's still alive. See the one second from the end? On the right? That one is based on her sister Aurelia. My mother. She's in the same nursing home as your grandmother. I'll introduce you if you decide to go visit."

"How old are they? They must be ancient if their statues are any indication."

"We Thorntons are long-lived. A blessing." He gave me a rueful smile. "And a curse depending on the day."

My mind rattled around, trying to find an excuse to get in the mansion. If Rebecca was in there, I had to find out.

"I'm very thirsty." I touched my throat. "It's been a long day. Do you think we could go inside and have a cool drink or something?"

"We have this delicious tea," Thorn said. "Perhaps—"

"Aylward Thornton!" An elderly woman with long silver hair and a scarlet gown hobbled onto the balcony. "Who are you dragging home this time? You know how we feel about your philandering."

"It's all right, Aunt Rachel," Thorn shouted. "I'm rendering help. This poor girl had lost her way in the forest."

"A flimsy excuse! You know how Outlings are—

thieving curse mongers! They'll steal the very words from your mouth."

"You're safe from this one, Aunt Rachel!" Thorn shouted. He looked at me and rolled his eyes.

"And who are you to judge such things?" Aunt Rachel snapped.

"I got the wood you asked for." Thorn jabbed his thumb back at the tug-rug.

"Don't change the subject! Bring the girl so I can see her."

"Just humour her." Thorn looked at me apologetically.

We hurried along a river-stone path, the firewood laden tug-rug hovering behind us as though it was the most normal thing in the world to tow stuff around on a flying carpet. We rounded a fountain depicting a sinking galleon, her masts broken, her sails ragged and frozen in stone. Curtains of water sprayed her moss-caked stern, and men with wild expressions tumbled overboard, their distress captured in crumbling grey marble. A minotaur clutched the ship's wheel, his shoulder muscles taut, his bull head raised, his mouth wide as though shocked by the ferocity of some unseen storm. A bit morbid. But, it probably was a memorial to ancestors or something.

As we drew closer to the balcony, Aunt Rachel screeched and threw up her hands.

I clamped my hands over my ears.

"Curse you, banshee! You'll not howl my death," Aunt Rachel shouted at me. "I'm old, but I've years left. Years, I tell you!"

I guess I'd have the same reaction if I was as old as she looked and a banshee stopped by my place.

"Don't mind her." Thorn laughed, but I could tell he was embarrassed. "She knows we've been looking into placing her in Spell Haven with my mother."

"And she's not happy about it? Gee, I didn't notice."

"Those curse-masked harbingers are like rats—sniffing around, waiting. Never giving good people a chance…" Aunt Rachel wailed and limped back inside. "I've got years left. Years."

"I can hear her mutterings from here," Thorn said. "She'll be ranting for weeks after this."

"I think I'd better head off," I said. Stupid old biddy ruining my plans to check out the house for Rebecca. I'd have to sneak back later.

The garden felt chilly, the flowers wilted and washed out. Even the birds had scattered, leaving the place empty and forlorn. We stood in silence, discomfort settling between us.

Thorn cleared his throat. "I'll call you a—"

"Don't say flying carpet."

"I was going to say a taxi."

"Oh!" Heat prickled my cheeks again.

We walked around the house. It was bigger than it appeared from the back, forming what appeared to be a large, capital E layout, the vacant areas stuffed with statues, ferns and tiny glowing lights that flitted about like iridescent butterflies.

The path, once past the house, led across a stone bridge, branching on the far side. We took the left path, following the stream until we came upon a circular stone-flagged area. Probably a landing pad for whatever vehicles they owned.

Thorn dug in his back pocket and withdrew a slim, polished black stone. It looked like obsidian or onyx. He flicked it open revealing a bed of tiny black crystals.

"Ryll? Can you call *Ding*," he grinned at me, "a taxi?"

Silver smoke puffed from the crystals, forming into a sage-green fairy no taller than my thumb. Tiny white feathers and thread-thick straw crowned her head, running down her back where they wrapped around her waist, forming a brittle tutu. Double wings, alive with opalescent colours hung from her shoulders. She hopped onto Thorn's shoulder, her twig-like legs bent at the knees as she clutched his hair and eyed me warily.

"*Another* female?" She flicked his ear. "You are worse than a satyr on prom night."

"Don't give all my secrets away," he muttered from the side of his mouth while looking at me. His blue eyes sparkled with mischief.

Huffing, Ryll vanished, leaving us alone to wait.

"Do you think your aunt is spying on us?" I asked, not knowing what to say after the stone-fairy's reprimand.

"Probably. Shall we give her something to talk about?"

I laughed nervously. "What did you have in, um, mind?"

"We could have that dance—you were caught trespassing, after all."

"Here?"

"Why not?"

"I'd feel stupid. There's no music."

"Stupid, foolish, kooky-mad." He laughed. "Live a little. It'll be fun. If it helps, I'll hum, but don't blame me if I break your ears. Apparently, my singing should be a form of punishment."

He wrapped one arm around my waist and caught my hand in his.

If there was one thing I had fumble-feet for, it was this up close, waltzy type dancing. If there was a free toe, I trod on it.

Thorn, off-key but enthusiastic, hummed some song I didn't recognise. He spun me around, waltzed a few steps, lifting me as we turned. I'm sure he only lifted me so his toes were safe. But, for some reason, I didn't care. It was fun. It was foolish. And I loved it.

"Are you done?" Ryll had returned. She hovered nearby, her twig-like arms crossed, her pinched little face dark with disapproval.

"For now," Thorn said brightly.

I didn't know which way to look. The ground wobble-spun and my ears buzzed. Spinning around dancing was not something I did often.

As the buzzing grew louder, I realised the whirring and popping emanated from a flying buggy so colourful it made my teeth hurt. Rainbows were miserable, faded things compared to this vehicle.

"Really, Ryll?" Thorn turned to his stone-fairy. "You got those two?"

"I thought you needed to keep your liaison discreet." She raised her nose and turned her back on him.

"You call that discreet?" I watched the taxi land on the paved area. It reminded me of one of those jeepneys that get around in the Philippines. All colour, glitz and gaudy. Think Christmas, a kid's birthday party and a parade all rolled into one vehicle and you'd be close.

Two goblins disembarked and trotted towards us, all bows, smirks and elbowing one another. They both wore cornflower-blue coats, buttoned down the middle with white ruffled shirts exploding from the collars. Stick thin legs dressed in grey hose stuck out below the coats, their knees all bones, their feet decked in stout black boots. They looked like old-fashioned coachmen without the class or genteel manners. One licked his palm and smoothed it over a shock of black hair sprouting from his knobbly green head. As soon as he removed his hand, his hair shot back to attention.

"Sneath," Thorn addressed one goblin, then the one with the disobedient hair. "Clutter."

"Your Highship," Sneath said. "What can we do for you today? It's been a while since we did business."

"This young lady needs a lift back to town."

"Lady, is it?" Sneath shared a grin with Clutter, both flashing mouths crammed with sharp teeth.

"On the quiet, is it?" Clutter winked. "Discretion costs extra, you know that."

"Just take her where she needs to go and put it on my ledger."

"Ledger's growing mighty long, Highship." Sneath shook his head, tutting.

"Look, Mr Sneath." I nodded politely at them. "Mr Clutter. All I want is to go to the cemetery. Nothing underhanded. Nothing sneaky."

"She called us 'Mr'!" Clutter snorted a laugh and elbowed Sneath.

They had to be brothers. The only difference was their hair. Sneath had a crooked part down the centre, so either side stuck out like a thatched roof. Oh, and Clutter had a longer, pointier nose.

"Three silvers." Sneath held out his hand, the frothy lace sprouting from his coat sleeve smeared with suspicious green stains. When no money was forthcoming, he jiggled his hand around in case we hadn't noticed.

Thorn growled and fished some coins from his pocket. He slapped them in Sneath's outstretched palm, then dragged his hand down his black trousers with a look of disgust.

"Pleasure doing business with you." Sneath held the coins up to the sun and turned them over, scrutinising them one by one. "Well, all seems to be in order. Shall we be on our way? My *lady*?"

"You said that like an insult, you know that, don't you?" I followed the two goblins over to the taxi. There were no doors and no windows unless you considered the cracked glass tied to the front roof-struts a windscreen.

"Are you sure that thing is safe?" I whispered to Thorn.

"It might look like an over-decorated bucket, but I'm fairly certain it's magically sound."

"Fairly certain?"

"If anything unfortunate happens." Clutter grinned widely. "We'll return half the travel costs. How's that?"

Sneath glared at Clutter, horrified. "How many times do I have to tell you? Refund is not an option."

I clambered in behind the front bench seat and sat down. Red, green, yellow and orange cushions had been strapped to the wooden seats to make them more comfortable. Bright baubles and streamers hung from the roof, swinging and banging into me as I settled myself. Sneath climbed in behind the long, wooden joystick (well, that's what it looked like to me), and Clutter hopped in beside him.

I waved to Thorn. "Thanks for saving me. Let's hope it wasn't in vain, eh?" I pulled a face and gripped the rough-wooden seat with both hands.

"I'll see you again?" Thorn asked. "Come visit your grandmother at Spell Haven. I'll show you around."

I nodded, smiled and resigned myself to my fate.

CHAPTER TWELVE

Sneath adjusted the bright-orange cushion behind him, pulled back on the joystick, and the taxi shuddered, bumping along the pavers until we got airborne. We rose above the Thornton mansion, flying over the expansive grounds. Their estate resembled a botanical garden, complete with streams and tucked-away ponds. We flew on, over the ancient forest. Aunt Rachel was probably cheering with relief. I hoped I didn't upset every elderly person like that. I was glad Thorn hadn't felt the same way. I remembered his warm hands, swirling me around as he hummed. Terribly. His infectious smile. I shook off my goofy grin. Now wasn't the time to think about such things.

Men are duplicitous beasts. Remember that, and you'll be a lot happier.

"So, to the cemetery, eh?" Sneath turned to face me, one hand on the joystick as though flying a Christmas bauble was the most natural thing in the world. "Meeting anyone *special?*"

Clutter sniggered.

"I live there—in the mausoleum."

"You're remarkably well preserved. For a deader." Sneath winked at me and wiggled his forehead up and down in what I presumed to be a sexy expression.

"I'm not dead!" *Flying around in this psychedelic tin-can could change that, though!*

"You never know who's a deader in Grimsmead." Sneath still hadn't faced the front. "Believe me, we've been caught out a few times ourselves."

"Shouldn't you be watching where you're flying?"

"What am I going to hit up here? Clouds?"

"There was that unfortunate incident with the drag-on." Clutter tapped the cracked windscreen. "Remember."

Dragons? They had real dragons in Grimsmead? Of course. They would have had to base The Hours on something. I really had to do some research on this place. The thought of danger and unknown threats made me think of Cael Blightly. I had to find out more about him. Thorn didn't seem to think he was dangerous, but I couldn't discount anything. Desperation made people do bad things. And it sounded like he was desperate.

"Do you know someone called Cael Blightly?" This pair probably knew every scoundrel in Grimsmead.

"Played *Knees-Up* with him last week. Didn't we, brother?" Clutter said. "Why? He's married, you know, in case you're wondering."

"Do you know where he lives?"

"Down by the showgrounds. Off Livingston Way, in Narrows Run." Sneath focused on driving instead of flirting. The run-in with the dragon must have been nasty.

"What's Cael like?" I made sure to sound casual, friendly. Nothing sneaky going on here. Keep flying—you're doing marvellously so let's keep it that way.

"Why do you wanna know?" Clutter eyed me suspiciously. "He owe you money? You knocked up?"

"No!" I shrank back, disgusted.

"Because we can help," Sneath said brightly. "This taxi flying is our off-hours-job. We're actually private detectives. We specialise in helping damsels in distress."

"For a fee," I said. "A large fee, I'm guessing."

"You want the best, you pay the most." Clutter puffed out his chest, displaying his stained shirt-ruffles like a proud but unimpressive bird.

"I'll bet. I'm just after information."

"Information can be costly." Sneath wriggled his olive-green fingers.

"Would Cael Blightly be capable of kidnapping? Of hurting someone?"

"He has a temper," Sneath said. "But most Satyrs do—testy bunch. Fauns are better—nature-loving, dancing about the forest. Glugging back wine by the flagon."

"Do you think Cael would hurt someone after an argument? Kidnap them, maybe?"

"It's possible," Clutter said. "He's stuck his horns into some pretty shady business over the years."

"Does Thorn—Aylward Thornton know of Cael's shonky dealings?"

"Know about them!" Clutter choked out a belly laugh. "He probably organised them."

"Oh! I got the impression, I mean, I thought Thorn was gentry—you know, of high standing."

"He is. The family line goes back millennia." Sneath waved both hands about for emphasis. "Uppity Blood only keeps fresh so long. Then the taint sets in."

"Yep," Clutter said. "How do you reckon the Thornton family holds so much power?"

"Crime and corruption?"

"I wouldn't go that far, but they don't have the cleanest hands in Grimsmead."

"None of the Old Bloods do." Clutter shrugged. "Though they act all posh and hooty-tilty."

"Don't you mean hoity-toity?"

"Saying still works."

Thinking about Thorn in some mafia-esque family made me ill. I changed tack. "Have you heard any rumours about Rebecca Bla—Ashmore's disappearance?"

"Maybe." The goblins shared a grin.

"I suppose you won't answer until I pay you."

"A goblin's got to eat." Sneath threw me a shrewd look.

Arguing with these two was ridiculous. I decided to start fresh. "Just take me back to the cemetery. I'll be fine by myself."

As soon as I said it I knew it was a stupid idea. F.C.T. agents would be crawling all over the graveyard looking for me. I growled, frustrated and scared. I didn't know what to do. Grimsmead, with all its magic and people, was so far beyond my abilities and knowledge. I needed to talk to Harvey and Meeks. Get their help, their support and advice. Maybe I could send Sneath and Clutter to get them. Bring them to me?

"Do you do pick-ups and deliveries?"

"We do anything," Sneath said. "For a price."

"I'll bet you do. Can you pick up a couple of my friends and bring them to me at the showgrounds? I need to look into a few things."

"You want to go sneak around?" Sneath said with surprise. "And here I was thinking you were a good girl."

"If Cael Blightly had something to do with my sister's disappearance, I want to find out."

"So Rebecca Ashmore is your sister, eh?" Sneath spun

around, his bulbous eyes narrowed. "You two close? Desperate to find her?"

"And if I am?"

"Like my brother said. We're detectives." Clutter grinned, flashing his little yellow fangs in what I assumed was his disarming smile.

"We know people," Sneath added. "Rogues. Scoundrels. Rotten logs of the mouldiest kind. We could sniff around. Pressure folks into talking. Dig up leads, or a few deaders if you're willing to pay for our top classy service."

For a few moments, I considered their offer. These two probably knew all sorts of unsavoury characters. In fact, it wouldn't have surprised me if they were in on the whole kidnapping. My stomach dropped, and I clutched the seat.

"Don't look so worried," Sneath leaned back against his bright orange cushion, one arm over the back of the seat. "It's just an air-pocket. Happens all the time over forests and stuff."

"I'll keep your generous offer in mind." I smiled a friendly smile that I hoped was as disarming as Clutter's. "For now, could you drop me off and then go and pick up my friends from the mausoleum?"

"And your friends can help you?" Sneath asked. "How much do *they* charge?"

"They're my friends! Friends don't expect to be paid."

"Then you have the wrong friends." Clutter crossed his arms. "When coin's on the table, everyone knows where they stand. Common sense."

"Look, drop me off, go collect Harvey and Meeks from the mausoleum and bring them back to the showgrounds. Then wait at the showgrounds until we return from Narrows Run."

"Don't expect us to wait around if we see someone coming," Clutter said. "You'll be on your own."

"You know this will cost you more than Thorn coughed up?" Sneath yanked hard on the joystick and we banked right, making a wide U-turn. "Danger Fee."

"How can it be dangerous if you flee at the first sign of trouble?"

"I didn't make the rules." Sneath waved his skinny arms around.

"What rules?" Clutter frowned. "You never told me there were rules."

"Fine!" I flopped back in my seat. I knew I didn't have the correct currency for Grimsmead anyway. "How about I owe you both a favour?"

"A favour each?" Clutter asked slyly. "Or one shared between us?"

"A shared one."

"How big a favour?" Sneath lurched around on his seat, eyeing me shrewdly. "And we'll want it in writing."

This pair were scoundrels right down to their probably-stolen-boots. If I wasn't careful, I would be bound to them for all eternity or something. "Nothing illegal. Nothing financial. Nothing disgusting or icky. And nothing…" I screwed up my nose. "… sexual."

The brothers thought for a moment, whispering to one another.

"I think we can work with those stipulations." Sneath grinned and elbowed Clutter. "We have an accord–a *binding* accord when you sign the aforementioned contract. I'll have it drawn up as soon as possible. For now, let us seal the deal." He spat on his hand and thrust it at me.

I pulled another disgusted face, spat on my palm and shook Sneath's chilly hand. Think damp frog with bony legs, and that's how it felt.

We flew low over the town, banking right. The land beneath looked like a green sea, its expanse criss-crossed with low, stone walls. Whitewashed houses with thatched roofs of varying shapes and sizes squatted within the stone boundaries, their gardens a riot of green leaves and spindly trellises. This part of Grimsmead had a country feel.

A T-shaped building with creamy yellow walls loomed ahead, the black slate roof tiles streaked with bird droppings.

The birds in Grimsmead must be huge!

Packed earthen paths, grassy ovals, stark outbuildings and stands of semi-circular bleachers left no doubt in my mind where we were.

"Grimsmead's showgrounds." Clutter pointed. "Good place to go after the crowds have packed up and gone home. You can find all sorts of stuff. Coins. Lost jewellery. The occasional lost child. All worth money to someone."

A narrow wood lay beyond the grounds. On its border stood a huge, grey rock, its towering summit shrouded in oily smoke. I had a terrible feeling that was Narrows Run.

We descended, skimming the patchwork of worn grass and empty stables behind the showground pavilions. The smell of manure, popcorn and portable toilets filled the air.

"You better not try charging me for this aromatherapy treatment!" I poked Sneath in the shoulder. He felt like a leathery sack of fish bones.

"Interesting idea!" Clutter sniffed the air. "An aromatherapy day tour. Think of it, brother! Dragon Airlines dung heap would be the highlight of the trip."

"I'm sure it would be a smash hit," I said. "You could serve a picnic of stinky cheeses and three-day-old fish."

"I need to write this down!" Clutter fumbled around under his seat. "This stuff is gold!"

We bumped along the ground, landing alongside a

drystone wall. Weeds and prickle bushes grew up and over the tightly stacked rocks, forming an impenetrable barricade of their own.

"You could have parked on the other side." I searched for the best way over.

"That's Elder Council land," Sneath said.

"You'll hold lost children for ransom, but you won't park on council land?"

"We're not fools, you know!" Clutter spluttered.

"Off you go, then." Sneath waved me off. "We'll get your friends. But, we won't hang around here if anyone comes asking questions."

"If you don't want nosy questions, tone down your taxi. Have you ever heard of camouflage?"

Blank looks all around.

"So, what's Cael's address?" I clambered out of the taxi.

"Four-B Gallows Lane," Sneath said. "Upstairs. Green door."

"How far to walk?"

"Depends on if you need to run or not."

"We've never timed it just walking." Clutter gave me an apologetic look. "Nasty neighbourhood, see."

"Why don't you just fly me there? It sounds safer."

"Not enough gold in Grimsmead will get me to fly into The Narrows." Sneath leaned back in his seat, hands interlocked on his knobbly head and stared at me. His eyes were so dark they looked black. And behind them, I saw fear.

"We're sort of known there, see," Clutter said. "An unfortunate misunderstanding. Not our fault."

"Oh, I'm sure."

"There's a stile a couple of hundred paces in that direction." Sneath jabbed his thumb over his shoulder. "Try crossing the wall there."

Stile. Turnstile? They moved people through walls. Sounded promising.

"All right, then." I headed off, despite wanting to climb back into the taxi and fly in the opposite direction. The one thing that gave me a crumb of courage was that I could always escape underground. I'd done it before. With any luck, I would end up meeting Thorn again.

I hurried alongside the dry-stone wall, and there ahead sat two ladders one on either side, their top rungs and handrails lashed together to form a sort of teepee. Basic, but perfect for the job. I climbed up and over the wall, landing lightly on a path of rough-sawn timber planks. They'd been packed together so tightly that not a stray weed peeked through. I'd expected a road made of bitumen or packed earth, but not this. I supposed when everyone flew on brooms, carpets and gaudy flying vehicles, they didn't really need roads and highways. As if to underscore my reasoning, a broom whooshed overhead, heading in the same direction as me. Only faster. I'd have to get myself a vehicle. Not a broom, though, and definitely not a carpet.

I trotted along the wooden boards, surprised that they didn't budge, squeak or groan under my weight. I rounded a bend and stopped mid-step. Ahead, trees crowded both sides of the path, darkness looming beneath their interlaced canopy. The perfect place for an ambush. Paranoid? Who, me?

I peered into the shadows, searching for movement, straining to hear anything beyond the wind rustling leaves and the occasional bird call. If only I'd brought my flashlight. I'd tossed it on my pile of belongings back on Earth. I had no weapon, not even my over-full handbag, which could probably take out a small troll if swung hard enough. I felt naked. Vulnerable. I was in a strange world. My sister was missing. Grimsmead was full of strange creatures, all familiar with magic and the possible dangers. I had nothing. And no-one. I didn't even have a cranky-fairy-mobile-phone. Who did I think I was? I was no superhero! I pulled beers and mixed cocktails for a living. I grew plants. Played with Tarot cards. The only martial arts I had ever done was mimicking the 'wax on, wax off' hand circles I'd watched in the *Karate Kid* movie.

To top all that, I'd lost my sister's iPad. Well, not lost exactly, but I might as well have now Walker Kane had it in his possession. Who knew what clues it held? I should have handed myself in to Agent Walker Kane instead of blasting about the countryside, thinking I was capable of finding my sister. I could get through whatever horrible tests they'd had planned to check my identity. I was Rebecca's sister, so I wouldn't fail.

Angered and frustrated, I made a pact with myself. I wasn't going to be pushed around anymore. I was on a mission, and no one was going to get in my way.

I dithered about for a few moments before heading back the way I had come. I'd start being brave once Harvey and Meeks arrived. I hadn't walked far when a chill ran down my spine, raising the hairs on the back of my neck and down my arms. Someone was watching. I knew it. I didn't want to turn and look. But, I couldn't keep walking either.

"I know you're there!" I had no plan, but I had to look strong, capable. Nope, no victim here.

I sucked in a deep breath and spun around. There, beneath the trees, sat a huge black leopard, its green eyes fixed. On me.

"Do you talk?" If I'd been back on Earth, that would have been a stupid question. Something like 'nice kitty' would have been more the go.

"Probably better than you do." The leopard's tail flicked, irritably.

I think it was a female, but the voice was so deep, so growly I couldn't be certain.

"Why are you following me?" I asked, stuffing as much confidence into the question as I could.

"I could ask you the same question."

"I'm heading for Narrows Run. I have no issues with you." *Apart from your sharp teeth and claws.*

"As am I."

"We could travel together. Keep each other company. It's safer to travel as a group." I couldn't believe what my mouth was saying.

"Not very educated, are we?"

"What is that supposed to mean?" I had the terrible feeling she meant about dealing with hungry predators.

"If you have to ask…" the leopard raised her head, sniffing the air. Cobalt blue markings shimmered through her black fur.

"You're like that *other* one!" She looked at me, her ears forward, her mouth open as she scented the air. "The half breed. A green-spirit banshee."

"You mean Rebecca?" I stepped forward, eyes wide, eager. When I realised what I'd done, I stepped back, my sight never leaving the big cat.

"Why would I bother learning her name?"

"It's the polite thing to do."

"Do you know what I am?"

"A black leopard?"

"Am I?"

"Well, that's what you look like to me."

The light around the leopard shivered, darkened and sucked in on itself before dissolving. The leopard was now a glossy black raven.

"Shapeshifter!" I whispered.

Ava Cadwaller had mentioned that an Agent Henely Briggs was investigating shapeshifter sightings. I looked around, hoping to see Agent Briggs swooping in to arrest the leopard/raven, but we were alone.

"You're a shapeshifter," I said.

"I've been called worse." Her voice had turned scratchy. Raw.

"What do you want from me?" My bravado was crumbling fast.

"I've been keeping a watch for you. I have a message. From the other one."

"From the green-spirit banshee?" That had to be Rebecca. "What did she say?"

"Guard your heart. Run. Kill if you have to. But guard your heart." The raven hopped towards me, her wings outstretched. She stopped, cocked her head, and eyed me intently. "Her last words were, 'Protect our home'."

"What's all that supposed to mean?"

"What am I? An ask-me-anything hotline? Now I'm off to Narrows Run. I have an appointment, and I can't be late."

"Before you leave—when did the green-spirit banshee give you this message?"

"This morning, as she died. When else?"

CHAPTER THIRTEEN

I crumpled to the ground. Lights fizzed in my head, tiny explosions that shattered my vision. The world muffled, sounds distant, confusing. My heart thudded so loud, so fast I felt it. Heard it pounding. I couldn't breathe. Couldn't think.

Something warm and firm prodded me in the ribs, rolling me onto my back. It took a while to comprehend anything beyond the buzzing in my ears, my head. A shadow hung over me, shifting like liquid velvet. Iridescent blue glimmered, blue fire in impossibly black fur. I tensed, scooting backwards on my heels and elbows. The shadow loomed, a big cat, green eyes unreadable.

"You realise I'm going to be late for my appointment?" The shapeshifter had retaken her leopard form, and her face was inches from mine.

The smell of raw meat and fish floated on the leopard's hot breath. Her jaw looked so broad from this angle, her whiskers so fragile compared to the rest of her.

"Are you going to kill me now? Like you murdered my sister?"

"I was checking you hadn't died. A first for me!"

"So you can kill me?"

"As if I don't have enough to do!" With that, the countryside darkened, chilled. Wind, swarming with hundreds of tiny black wings, rushed over me. And the leopard had vanished.

It had to be a dream. But the faint flapping of wings and *rork-rork-rork* fading into the distance told me the soul-numbing truth.

I don't know how long I lay there. It could have been hours. My body felt numb, heavy. Breathing was exhausting. All I wanted to do was sleep. I wished for the ground to swallow me again, suck me down deep and keep me there. I had heard Rebecca's call when I traveled through soil, rock and root. How could she be dead? I had felt her. She'd visited me not long after I had arrived in Grimsmead. This morning.

This morning…

That's the time when Rebecca had died.

I choked back tears, but my throat was so tight, my chest so tense I could not stop them.

I had been useless. And my sister, my only sister, had been killed. Murdered. There had been nothing natural about her death. There had been nothing natural about our lives. And I knew nothing that could help us. I didn't have the knowledge, or even gut instincts to comprehend the ways of this world. Magic and supernatural creatures changed all reality as I knew it. The leopard had been right. I was uneducated.

A soft paw brushed my face. Whiskers tickled my cheek. Golden eyes peered into mine.

"Harvey?" I wailed. Her soft black and grey face blurred through my tears.

"Move back, Meeks! Give her some breathing room."

Harvey snapped as the raxx's white whiskered face loomed overhead, his brow furrowed.

"What happened?" Harvey's voice, her warm breath puffed into my ear. "It isn't safe here. What are you doing? How did you get here? Where's Agent Kane?"

"Harvey!" I wrapped my arms around her, burying my face in her thick, warm fur.

Through my sobs, I told Harvey and Meeks what had happened.

"We do trauma counselling," shouted a familiar voice. It was Sneath, the goblin. "For a fee. Hourly, of course."

I couldn't help myself. The absurdity of the day's events shoved me over the edge, and I burst into hysterical laughter. It wasn't even funny.

Harvey and Meeks sat beside me on the timber pathway, both saying nothing, both watching me with concern.

"Here!" An off-white bit of rag waggled in front of my face.

I wiped the tears from my eyes with the backs of my hands. Sneath stood in front of me, holding what looked like a handkerchief. Disgusting, and probably used, but I appreciated the gesture.

I took the scrap of cloth with my fingertips, holding it at arm's length. I laughed weakly. "I suppose this will cost me?"

"Can't a goblin do something nice for a lady without aspersions being bandied about?"

"It'd be a first." Meeks gave a haughty sniff.

I turned the handkerchief over a couple of times, looking for the cleanest patch. My nose bubbled and dribbled. Lovely. It was either my white, lacy sleeve or Sneath's handkerchief. I blew my nose a few times on the grubby rag. My face warmed. I knew I was blushing. Nothing like snot and bugle-loud-nose-blows in front of an audience.

"What would you like us to do?" Meeks rested a paw on my leg.

"I need to talk to Cael Blightly. He might be involved in Rebecca's de..." My voice cracked, and my throat ached, it was so tight.

"He'd be at work," Sneath said. "Didn't you see him at Thornton's place? He's the head groundskeeper there."

"I only saw Thorn and his Aunt Rachel."

"And she let you into her home?" Sneath spat a laugh.

"She couldn't wait to be rid of me. Thought I was there to howl her death or some such rubbish."

"Hateful old biddy," Sneath said. "You sell her a couple of fish for her pond, and they take over her garden, and she gets upset. I warned her they were vigorous and bursting with life."

"Back to Cael Blightly." Harvey pawed my arm. "We could have a look around his home. Check his local haunts, see if anyone knows anything."

"Or saw anything," Meeks added. "Some people in the Narrows are happy to talk if you pass a little silver across their palm."

"Some people in the Narrows are happy to do just about anything if you pass silver across their palm," Sneath said. "Anyway, best I get back to Clutter and our taxi. We might be around here when you're done."

"Won't count on it," Meeks muttered.

Sneath trotted back towards the showgrounds. I couldn't help it. I liked him and Clutter. Yes, they were scoundrels, but they made me laugh. I was sure they had good hearts underneath all their bluster.

"I brought you this." Harvey pushed my mobile phone across the ground towards me with her nose. "We can photograph clues and things with it."

"How did you carry it?" I stuffed my mobile into my jeans' back pocket.

"Don't ask," Meeks said, with a look of disgust.

I clambered to my feet, staggering a few steps before gaining my balance. My heart felt heavy, my eyes burned from crying, and all I wanted to do was go home and sleep.

Home? Where exactly was that? Not here in Grimsmead. And what about my world? Could I get back there? No point worrying about that at the moment. We had to find my sister's killer. I wasn't sure if it was Cael Blightly or the shapeshifter. Or even Hywell Rowlands. Maybe they all worked together?

"Have you seen Rebecca's spirit again?" Harvey asked. "Surely, you must have."

I turned in a slow circle. Trees, clouds, timber pathway, but no Rebecca. "I don't see her anywhere."

"Strange." Harvey shook her head. "Why wouldn't she seek you out?"

"You're asking me?" I snapped. "Sorry, Harvey. I didn't mean to sound so nasty."

"I understand. We should head off. It's not safe milling around here."

The three of us entered the tunnel of trees at a run, my mobile phone's torch lighting the way. After what seemed like miles, we burst into sunshine, relieved and panting. No brigands, thieves or spooks to be seen. Maybe I was scary with my banshee mask and grey hairs? Who was I kidding? Today was probably Bad-Guys-Need-Love-Too National Holiday, and they were all in pubs getting sloshed.

"I've never been keen on Narrows Run," Meeks said as we walked along the path.

The imposing grey-stone edifice loomed ahead, stretching left and right for hundreds of metres. It looked more like a bird-limed cliff face than individual buildings.

It reminded me of a fortress but without skirting walls, parapets and towers. As we drew closer, windows pock-marked the battered facade, some dark, some glowing from within.

"Narrows Run," Harvey announced bleakly. "A warren of slop-sucking villainy."

"Lovely!" I wanted to run in the other direction, but I couldn't. I had to do this for Rebecca. Cael Blightly lived in that place, and the shapeshifter had been headed there. What if her appointment had been about Rebecca? About what to do with her body?

I strode along the walkway, the shadow of Narrows Run swallowing me as I neared the broad gateway in the base of the wall. Harvey and Meeks followed—cat on my right, raxx on my left.

"Perhaps you both should have remained with the goblins." It wasn't right to drag them into this scary town. But I was terrified. I just couldn't bring myself to go in alone. All my earlier bravado seemed childish, desperate, now I saw the Narrows.

"And leave you to run the Narrows alone?" Meeks said. "What kind of friends do you think we are?"

People hustled around the gateway—some dressed in rags and begging, some hawking odds-and-bods from straw mats, and some surveying the scene with shifty eyes and tight lips. Now I thought of it, 'people' was a broad term.

"What term do you use?" I asked, my voice low enough not to carry. I didn't want to insult anyone if I could help it. "For all the different races as a whole? Like 'people' or 'citizens'? You can't exactly use 'humans'."

"Depends." Harvey dodged a stream of pixies carrying baskets zipping towards us like a string of birds. "For a town, we'd say 'folk' or 'community', but as a whole, I suppose we'd say 'people'."

"Each race has its own term, really," Meeks said. "Herd of Centaurs. Swarm of nippers. Horde of trolls. Troop of fairies."

I studied the crowd. Satyrs, with their curved horns bound in leather or strapped with studded bronze, their beards strung with gold, teeth and neatly tied ribbons. They would definitely be a 'herd' or a 'riot'. Yes, 'riot' was a great name for them.

A few goblins in garish clothing flashed gold rings, bangles and necklaces to anyone who'd stop to listen. 'Rabble' sounded good for them. Or, now that I'd met Sneath and Clutter, a 'dodge' or a 'racket' seemed appropriate.

Soon there were so many races surrounding us, I couldn't think fast enough to categorise them.

Pixies flitted about, wings buzzing so fast they sounded as though they sizzled. Several people looked as human as I did—as I used to before the banshee markings. They could have been anything: witches, vampires, shapeshifters, mermaids taking a stroll on the wild side. I had no way of telling because I had no frame of reference. Just because I'd read fantasy books and seen movies and TV shows about magical creatures didn't mean they'd been accurate.

We pushed our way through the noisy crowd, under the soaring gateway, and entered a barrel-roofed tunnel. The gloom stunk of sweat, damp and unwashed bodies. Water pooled where cobbles had either been dislodged or had eroded away. This place felt older than time. Magic, chilly and oozing with malice snaked around me. I couldn't see it, but I felt it. I shivered. Kept my eyes neutral, my stance relaxed.

Yes, I've passed this way before. Hundreds of times. Nothing to see here. It took all my will not to look at the ground. I met the gaze of a satyr. She glared; I put on my meanest sneer and strode along the tunnel.

A figure wrapped in a cloak of burnished green scales bumped into me, sending me sprawling into the tunnel wall. I caught myself, slapping my hands back on the slimy stonework. As I regained my footing, I fought the urge to wipe my hands down my jeans.

"Watch it!" I shouted after him. "Or I'll be coming for you. Drag your miserable soul through fire and back."

Harvey nipped my heel, glowering at me, her whiskers twitching with disapproval.

Scale Cloak glanced over his shoulder and ripped back his hood. Sorry. *Her* hood. Stunning, amber eyes raked me over. She laughed. Beautiful didn't begin to describe her. Snow-pale skin, high cheekbones, aquiline nose, slender body draped in sheer moonlight-silver. Even her moss-green eyebrows and tangled lichen hair looked amazing. If I strutted about wearing lichen hair, I'd look like I had lost a battle with a compost mound. Slender twin horns spiralled from her high forehead, their sharp tips wrapped with gold chains, bells and beads.

"You don't frighten me, half breed," Scale Cloak murmured. "I battled trollops like you before you were born."

"Ding!" Harvey clawed my jean leg. "She didn't mean it, Highness!" Harvey addressed Scale Cloak in a pandering tone. "Did you, Arabella? Tell her you didn't mean it."

I growled. Averted my gaze. "I'm tired, is all. Hungry."

Why I affected an uneducated tone, I didn't know, but it seemed to calm Scale Cloak. She raised her hood, grunted and continued along the tunnel and out of Narrows Run.

"What is wrong with you?" Harvey stood on her hind legs, her front paws resting on my thighs. "Don't anger a dragon!"

"That wasn't a dragon!"

"Just because she's walking around all woman-like doesn't mean she isn't a dragon," Meeks said. "They're not scales, songs and claws all of the time, you know."

Ha! I had just faced down a dragon. Until I didn't. How was I supposed to know?

Deciding to remain alive, I kept my mouth closed and followed Harvey and Meeks through the tunnel and out into a rectangular area the size of a basketball court. The only feature seemed to be a circular well beneath a slate roof. Narrow alleys branched off the courtyard in all directions, dark fissures carving through towering rock walls.

"We need to find Gallows Lane." I squatted between Harvey and Meeks. "Any clue where it is?"

"That way." Meeks flicked his head, indicating a dingy little alley to our left. "It's where they used to hang the Dead."

"Don't you mean criminals? Alive ones. Until they weren't?"

"Convicted felons lost citizenship," Harvey said. "They lost everything. They were locked away 'til they were hanged. Until then, they were known as the Dead."

"No wonder this place is called Grimsmead. Seriously, this town freaks me out."

CHAPTER FOURTEEN

The name Narrows Run made more sense now as I scurried along the town's cramped alleyways. I dodged left to avoid rough-cut steps jutting from a towering rock wall, the stairs no more than two feet wide. They had no railings, no landings and were impossibly high. Doors–many only drab curtains–opened directly onto the stairway.

"Carrying shopping, kids or furniture up and down those skinny steps must be a nightmare," I called to Harvey and Meeks.

"Most people have portable winches," Meeks said. "With baskets or hammock devices. They seem to work."

Harrows Run would have been a more appropriate name for the maze. I was reasonably certain no town planning had gone into the design of this place.

"Do they have a sewer system?" I wrinkled my nose.

The reek of sewerage, rancid cooking oil, sweat, damp and animals mixed with a miasma of smoke and dank air. I'd have to shower for a week just to rid my hair of the smell of mutton and onions.

"Not exactly," Harvey said. "But a good storm works a treat."

"Lovely!"

Most of the alleys weren't paved. Planks laid end to end barely kept my boots above the mud. Please let it be mud.

Every alley existed in perpetual gloom, sunlight bleeding away to darkness. Lamps, atop bronze posts, were havens of murky-gold, the ground beneath eroded from constant use.

"Who built this place?" I glanced up at brightly-coloured washing sagging from makeshift lines strung between the walls. How the clothes dried without sunshine was beyond me.

"Not entirely certain." Meeks ran along a plank on his hind legs, his front paws held up for balance. "The whole place is quarried from a single rock monolith. Homes carved into the superstructure, burrow deep inside connected by tunnels, stairs and air shafts."

"Ingenious."

"And old," Harvey added, bounding along the plank.

Despite the depressing gloom, children's giggles and squeals rose above the hum of broken conversation. Kids played in whatever gap or vacant spot they could find, laughing, taunting and play-fighting like human children. They were kind of cute. Satyrs with little nub horns, short hairy legs and cloppity hooves. Pixies the size of bumble bees squabbling over a yellow flower they had found.

"Here! Miss!" A goblin sang out from his impromptu shop within a doorway. He flashed me a grin, indicating his wares spread on a blue and white striped blanket. "Fresh bread—only three days old. A dob of strawberry jam, and you'll think you're in heaven."

"No, thank you," I called. "Not hungry."

"Ignore them." Meeks glared at another goblin squatting on some stairs, bowls of pungent cider at his feet.

"Easier said than done!" I muttered.

Another goblin jumped up from his strip of green cloth, waving a fist-full of jewellery at me. "Pretties for lovely lady!"

Goblins! Entrepreneurs, the lot of them. I could see where Sneath and Clutter got their 'skills'.

Eventually, we turned into Gallows Lane. No dead bodies swung from ropes. No corpses rotted in gibbets– thank goodness for that. The lane was nowhere near as crowded as the previous streets, but it was far from empty. Beggars slumped on faded rugs, holding up small dishes and chipped cups they'd chained to their wrists, a vain attempt at making them thief-proof. Fey folk hurried past them, avoiding the hollow stares of the homeless. Every jingle and jiggle of a chain broke my heart.

"What was the number?" Harvey padded along blackened planks of wood.

"Four B." I couldn't see numbers anywhere.

They didn't seem to use mailboxes in Grimsmead. There were no numbers beside doors and curtains either.

"Down this way." Meeks ran ahead, his black and auburn ringed tail streaming behind.

He stopped at the bottom of some stairs on the right of the walkway. When we caught him, he bounded up the steps until he reached the second doorway. He nosed his way beneath the faded, red curtain and disappeared. Harvey and I followed close behind. Well, Harvey did. I cringed and prayed with every step, one hand clasping the rough stone wall, the other clutched to my chest.

"How did you know where to go?" I lifted the curtain and looked into a dim passageway.

Meeks stood waiting, looking at me expectantly. "Didn't you see the number?"

"No, and believe me, I was searching."

"You need to learn how to look," Meeks said. "Stop using your eyes."

"Then how am I supposed to see?"

I peered into the darkness. A cloaked figure rushed at me, a voluminous hood covering the being's face. All I could see were narrow black braids tipped with blue beads dangling over one shoulder.

The stranger barrelled past me, knocking me sideways. I grappled for their cloak to stop myself from toppling down the stairs and caught hold of something prickly and rolled up hidden in the folds. I let go and stumbled hard, falling on my knees. The bristly object tumbled over the side of the stairs. A splash told me it had landed in water.

Rude-Cloak-Person shoved me aside and fled down the stairs, black cloak billowing behind, boots silent on the stone as though they were flying.

"Hey!" I shouted, but Rude-Cloak-Person kept running.

I turned to Harvey. "Did you see that?"

"Barely. I was too busy getting out of their way."

I snatched my mobile phone from my jeans pocket and took a few photos of 'Rude-Cloak's' back as they raced through the milling crowd. I peered over the edge of the staircase. A coir doormat lay half submerged in a puddle.

Seriously? Someone had stolen a rotten old welcome mat? Narrows Run really was a town of villainy. Without much thought, I snapped a photo as muddy water flowed over the mat, obscuring whatever welcome message it held. Probably, *Wipe Your Feet Before Stealing.*

As I turned back to the doorway, another cloaked figure shoved by me and ran down the stairs. I caught myself one-handed on the red curtain, praying it wouldn't give way. The sounds of clopping, like hooves on stone, echoed along the laneway as the second stranger fled the scene. When I gained my balance, I added another photo to my collection.

"You smell that?" Harvey twitched her nose.

"Blood!" Meeks licked his muzzle, saw my look of disgust and added, "Sorry. Instinct."

'Oh! Eew!" I winced. Blood smeared my white blouse. "That person was bleeding! On me!"

Meeks darted down the cheerless passage. Thin beams of light leaked through air vents in the roof but did nothing to lift the gloom. Archways carved from the rock stood every fifteen paces, stark formations coated with mildew, peeling whitewash and graffiti.

I gagged. I'd thought the stench was bad out in the alleyways. It took all my will to follow Meeks past a series of coloured doors. Red, yellow, blue, and finally green.

"Here we are," Harvey said. "If we go in, we'll be breaking the law. You're sure you need to do this, Ding?"

"Someone killed Rebecca. I know Cael had motive. He had debts *and* Rebecca threatened him with the F.C.T."

"It might have been that shapeshifter," Harvey pointed out. "You said she was there when Rebecca died."

"Maybe it was a coincidence she was with Rebecca. The shifter could have murdered me then and there. I was alone. Vulnerable. She just gave me the message."

"Maybe it was Blightly and the shifter," Meeks said.

"And maybe neither." I stomped my foot, my voice growing louder. "I have to start somewhere."

"Let's break and enter, then." Meeks stood on his hind paws and clapped his paw-hands.

"Hang on a moment!" I said. "Look at the dust by the door. It forms a rectangle. The inside's clean, sort of."

"This is where the doormat came from!" Meeks pawed the evidence.

"You haven't done this before," I said. "Have you?"

"I got excited." Meeks shrugged, his chuckle weak and a little too high pitched.

"Why steal a grungy old doormat?" I frowned. "Doesn't make sense to me."

"Unless it was incriminating them in some way!" Harvey bolted back down the corridor, Meeks and I right behind.

I burst through the doorway, flapping clear of the red curtain.

"It's gone," Harvey said.

"Already!" I couldn't believe it. "This place is stuffed with thieves!"

"One of the cloaked strangers probably came back for it once we'd gone inside." Meeks stood on his back paws, looking left and right.

"We should hurry." Harvey followed Meeks under the curtain. "Before someone gets suspicious."

When we reached Cael Blightly's front door, Meeks dissolved into fiery mist, slipping under the door.

"That was so cool!" I looked down at Harvey. "Can you do that?"

Harvey raised her nose. "No."

She didn't elaborate or regale me with her amazing powers, so either she couldn't do anything impressive—except change into different cats—or she wouldn't tell me. Cat-shifting was awesome, but nothing like turning into golden mist.

The door swung inward, its hinges creaking. It sagged alarmingly. I propped it straight and looked inside Cael's home. Meeks waited inside the doorway, staring at what had once been a comfortable sitting room.

"This isn't a good sign." I walked in, stepping over a crumpled up forest-green rug. Three gold-fringed lamps hung from the ceiling by chains, their light cheery even though the middle one flickered on and off.

"No, it's not!" Harvey wove her way between two pink and green floral couches that laid upside down, their backs slashed, cushions shredded, their feathers scattered across a patchwork quilt.

I crouched, tracing the quilt's perfect stitching. "Who would do this?"

"Someone desperate to find something." Harvey sniffed a low, pine dresser, its three cupboards open, its draws flung among the chaos.

"Look!" I pointed at a door in the left-hand wall. "Blood smears on that doorknob!"

I snapped a few photos of the room with my mobile phone to study later, then squatted in front of the dresser. One plate painted with yellow wildflowers sat alone on a shelf. The rest of the dinner service lay smashed on the stone floor. The other cupboards were empty, their contents strewn across the ground.

Unsure what else to do, I foraged through the mess, stopping to examine slips of paper when I found them. Most were receipts, a few bills for services rendered. No jobs were specified, so what the services were was anybody's guess.

I rifled though a few more until I got to a receipt from a shop called *Good Hunting* for a new bow and a quiver of handmade arrows. Twelve of them. 'Special Order' was stamped across the top. Three hundred and thirty-five somethings was the total cost. Pricey. But, Cael was a groundsman. He guarded Thorn's land from poachers. A bow and arrows would be standard equipment.

I couldn't help thinking about the soul, Endraya, and

the bone-shafted arrow sticking from the back of her head. Another demerit to Cael Blightly.

The receipt didn't specify what the arrows were made from. Just that they were handmade. All I had was more questions.

I pocketed the receipt, stood up and spotted an axe near one of the couches. It wasn't large. More like a throwing axe than one to chop wood. I wrapped a bit of paper around the haft and picked it up. The blade appeared clean, but particulates could've gotten caught between the handle and the axehead. I took a sniff. Smelled earthy, woodsy. I took more photos.

I picked my way through the mess and looked through the open doorway. Blood smeared the ivory-coloured floor tiles and the matching bathroom sink. Even the toilet bowl was splashed and smudged with fresh blood. Possibly from that person who had bled all over my favourite white blouse. The person with clopping hooves. Like a horse. Or a goat. Or a satyr!

"Not good," Meeks murmured. We shared a worried look.

"What's in there?" I pointed at the closed door beside the dresser.

"Probably the bedroom." Meeks walked toward it. "You want to look?"

"No." I wrapped the scrap of paper around the handle and opened the door.

The bedroom was tidy compared to the lounge room. Long, wild gashes ran the length of the bed, the feathered stuffing strewn across the entire room. A bright red comforter sat in tatters on the floor. Matching pillows lay in shreds amongst white feathers like blood on snow. The stone walls had been freshly painted lavender; I could still smell the paint.

I walked around the bed. Stopped. And backed away. A body was sprawled on a fluffy, crimson rug. No. It wasn't crimson. It had been white. A satyr lay on his stomach, his left arm by his side, the right stretched forward alongside his head. I took a couple of photos, my eyes half-closed so I wouldn't have to look.

"Is that Cael Blightly?" I glanced at Meeks. Then Harvey. Then back at the body. "Or his wife?"

"It's a male. Larger horns. Darker skin—more brown than tan. Muscular." Meeks poked the satyr's goat-like leg with his paw. "Think he's dead?"

Cringing, I bent down and felt for a pulse in his neck. His skin was still warm, but there was no pulse.

"Am I feeling in the right place?" I asked. "I've never done this before. Especially not on a satyr."

"You're feeling the right place." Harvey stood next to me, examining Cael's face. "He looks dead. No life in those eyes."

I shrank back. "Must have just happened. You think it was his wife? She's said to be a tyrant. And that second person who nearly knocked me down the stairs had hooves, I'm certain of it."

"Why would she trash her own home?" Harvey said.

"To throw off suspicion. Make it look like a burglary gone wrong."

I looked around for Cael's spirit, my brain rattling through excuses for being in his home if he got all huffy about us being here. Usually, after a violent death, the soul was confused and lost so I could pretty much make up anything, and he'd still be muddled.

"You see his spirit anywhere?" Harvey tilted her head expectantly.

"Nothing. No chills, no voices. I sense nothing. Just like

Rebecca." My lower lip trembled, and tears filled my eyes before I had a chance to brace myself.

"Don't jump to conclusions," Harvey said. "Their souls have probably already crossed over. Rebecca knew what to do—what to expect."

"Without saying goodbye?"

"We should examine Blightly's injuries," Meeks cleared his throat. "Satyrs like arrows. Daggers."

Harvey and I shared a pain-filled look. I nodded and wiped my eyes.

"Do I have to?" I really didn't want to roll the body over. "We're disturbing a crime scene. That's the last thing we should be doing. I'm already in enough trouble with the F.C.T."

"I thought we were looking for clues," Meeks snapped.

"How's looking at his wounds going to prove if he had anything to do with Rebecca's death?"

"Perhaps whoever killed your sister also killed Blightly. Any clues we find may help us establish a pattern," Harvey said. "What type of weapon was used —if the killing was in anger or methodical. That may give us a profile of the murderer. A clue to who it might be."

"How many forensic shows did you watch back home?"

"Same as you."

I went to roll over the body.

Hesitated.

Gasped.

"Look!" I pointed at a message scrawled in what looked like blood.

Harvey and Meeks leaped on the bed, both leaning over the side, scrutinising several spidery letters drawn on the stone floor.

"Is that blood?" I asked. "He wrote in his own blood before he died?"

"Looks that way," Meeks sniffed. "Very fresh."

"What if the killer wrote it?" I said. "To divert the F.C.T. It's possible, you know."

"Anything's possible," Harvey said. "But we've got to follow all clues regardless."

I stashed the thought away in my, *'To Be Obsessed Over When I Have Time'* file.

"I can make out the word 'spell'," Harvey said. "And what looks like an 'H' or an 'A'. But his arm has smeared the rest of the word."

I scrutinised every shaky letter. "I think that next part says, 'Ward 1'. And then a 'K' or an 'R' or 'B'."

"Spell H or Spell A and ward 1," Meeks tried out the words a few times.

"Spell Haven!" I almost clapped at my own cleverness. "The nursing home. Ward 1 in the home?"

"That's where his wife Knola works. She's a cleaner. And her name starts with the letter 'K'." Meeks and I shared a collaborative smile.

"But why would he use his dying breath to scrawl where his wife worked?" I frowned. "Surely, that's public knowledge."

"Maybe something's going on at Spell Haven?" Meeks said. "Knola might have told him something? Or hid something at the nursing home—a clue or proof of something? Or maybe she killed him over something that's going on at Spell Haven?"

"Then who is the message for?" I said. "Unless he was trying to warn his wife—alert her to watch her back at work? Or maybe *he* hid something there, and he was telling her where to look?"

"That second cloaked stranger," Meeks said. "The one

who almost knocked Arabella down the stairs—that could have been Knola."

"Well, they had hooves," I said. "Maybe she was rushing to Spell Haven after seeing the message?"

"Or," Harvey leaned in close to us. "She was leaving the scene of the crime and didn't even know Cael had written the message?"

"We need to head over to the Spell Haven," Meeks said. "See what we can find."

"And soon." I lifted the body's right hand and examined the fingers. They were coated with blood, and his body wasn't stiff with rigour mortis yet. Another sign that Cael had not been dead for long. Even though we'd found some clues, he could have been murdered by anyone. Who knew how many dangerous people skulked around Narrows Run? It could just as easily have been a loan shark looking for his money. Someone had been searching for something. The suspect pool had more and more swimmers.

"Do you see a weapon anywhere?" I took a photo of Cael's dying message.

"No," Harvey said. "But have a look at this."

"Someone cleaned a blade off on here." I bent over the quilt cover. Smears and the impression of a long-bladed dagger stained the linen.

"Step away from the body."

I knew that voice. Special Agent Walker Kane.

I glanced at the open bedroom door. Walker and Ava Cadwaller entered the room, their gaze fixed on me.

"We've been hunting for you," Walker said. "Quite a trick you did back at headquarters."

"You came for a repeat performance?"

"Funny." Ava said cooly. She looked at Walker. "She's funny."

"The stand-up comedy routine costs extra." I edged backwards. My boot caught on Cael's body, and I fell into the wall, jarring my shoulder.

"And then she blunders all over the death scene." Ava rammed her hands on her hips, glaring at me. "Get out of this apartment. Now."

"What else have you touched?" Walker asked. "I should arrest you three for contaminating a crime scene as well as murder."

"We didn't kill him!" I spluttered. "We found him this way."

"Move away now." The markings on Ava Cadwaller's skin darkened, throbbing crimson in her tanned skin. She pulled a wand from a holster strapped to her thigh like a gun-slinger. Ten-inch selenite crystal, leather binding, and from the looks of it, fluorite handle. It even had a cross-guard of clear quartz. You can't say I don't know my crystals.

"Gee, if I had a wand, we could have a duel. Wands at high-noon. Thirty paces, ready, turn and fire." Why oh why did I crack such lame jokes at the worst possible times?

When no one laughed, I sighed. Nursing my shoulder, I walked around the bed and stood before the two F.C.T. agents.

"Where's *your* wand hiding?" I raised my chin, eyeing Walker wryly. "Or aren't you glad to see me?"

Again with the stupid jokes. I really had a problem. Seems nerves always got the better of me, and my mouth would spout the most foolish things.

"I'm not going back to that torture chair," I muttered. "Can't you do a DNA test instead? That'll tell you I'm Rebecca's sister."

"We'll deal with that later," Walker said. "Why are you here? Did you murder Blightly?"

I hoped later meant never. "We're here because he argued with Rebecca. I wanted to find out if he had anything to do with her death."

"What?" Ava snorted a laugh. "You were just going to waltz up to a satyr and accuse him of murder?"

Walker grabbed me by the arm. Pain shot through my shoulder. I yelped, but he didn't let go.

"Are you saying Rebecca's dead?" His voice broke, his eyes wide, pleading. "How do you know? We haven't found her body. Tell me!"

"A black leopard told me. Well, she was also a raven. She liked to change shapes."

"Were her markings blue?" Walker shook me. Not hard, but enough to make me wince.

"Cobalt blue."

Walker and Ava exchanged concerned looks but said nothing. He let me go.

"What?" I rubbed my shoulder, glancing from one agent to the other. "Do you know this shapeshifter person?"

"She gets around," Ava said.

"Is she dangerous?"

"Let's say you don't want her coming for you."

"She's already found me. Not far down the way from here."

"Either you're lucky, or she isn't after you," Walker said.

"Yet." Ava crossed her arms. "But we can hope."

"Shouldn't you tell Agent Henley Briggs?" I said. "He's the one looking into the shapeshifter sightings."

"Isn't she cute." Ava crossed her arms and laughed. "Telling us our job like she knows what she's talking about."

"Did Rebecca tell you about Cael Blightly?" I ignored

Ava and focused on Walker. "She said she was going to. About the argument, the illegal wands he was trying to unload? How she chased him, trying to get him to hand them over?"

Walker narrowed his hazel eyes. "You say you only arrived in Grimsmead this morning. How could you know all that?"

"For one thing, I could have asked Meeks." I met Walker's cold glare with one of my own. "But, I got most of the info from Becca's iPad—that glassed screen device you confiscated."

"That thing?" Ava scowled. "It's useless—nothing can make that cursed thing work."

"Maybe it's not the iPad that's useless." I smiled at Ava.

Walker stepped between us and addressed me. "Explain."

"She has …" I dragged in a shuddering breath. "She had a journal on there." I turned my glare on Ava. "Some fascinating information stored in the memory if you're smart enough to use it."

Walker chewed the inside of one cheek. Until that second, I didn't realise how tall he was. Easily six feet five or six inches. How could I have missed that? His presence, or was it his power flooded the room. Fiery electric shocks raced across my skin. I shuddered and stepped back. A weighted silence loomed as we let him think.

"We need to get a forensics team over here." Ava touched his forearm gently, and he blinked a couple of times, as though returning from some dark, private place. "We have to salvage what we can now that Miss Clueless and her team have stomped all over our crime scene."

"Cordon off the site," Walker said. "The whole of Gallows Lane. Call in all available agents—I want them door to door questioning everyone. Tell headquarters it's Priority Level Two."

"An L-Two?" Ava frowned, pointing at the crime scene. "For this?"

"For Rebecca and anyone involved in her murder." He looked down at me, his lips pressed in a hard line. "Anyone."

I flinched and kept my mouth closed. Harvey and Meeks cowered at his feet.

Ava flicked her wand. "Valarr Portalis!"

Within moments, Ava's broom swooshed into the apartment, stopping by her side. I really had to get me a wand. She opened the glossy black pannier and took out a wooden box packed with crystals, many in the shape of pyramids. She placed them at various positions around the apartment. When she put a fist-sized Herkimer diamond down on the ground, a translucent curtain shot from floor to ceiling with the words '*F.C.T. Crime Scene Do Not Cross*' strobing across it. Distant yelps, curses and squawks told me that the cordoned off area had surprised many of the folk out in the laneway.

"What brings you here? Now?" I asked Walker. "Did someone alert the F.C.T.?"

"Taking down a fully grown male satyr tends to get people's attention," Walker said. "Someone called it in."

"Anonymously, I guess?" I raised an eyebrow. "On a burner stone. All nice and untraceable."

"And here I was, thinking she was stupid." Ava picked through her box of crystals. "It's as though she grew up in Narrows Run."

"You're right," Walker said. "Rebecca had told me about her fight with Blightly, and that he was trafficking illegal wands."

"Then why didn't you arrest him before Rebecca went

missing?" I scowled at them both. "Probable cause and all that."

"Rebecca wasn't missing at that point," Walker said coldly.

I grumbled to myself. "What took you so long to get here, then?"

"A manhunt for a certain fugitive who'd escaped my custody." Walker's words were a cruel hard slap to my ego. Here I was feeling all smug about escaping, and all I'd really done was drag him away from Rebecca's case.

"My guess is, Blightly needed money fast." I tried to mend the demolished bridge between us. "He had gambling debts, you know."

"We're aware."

"Isn't she adorable?" Ava smiled sweetly. "All pumped up with information we already know."

"Turn around and put your hands behind your back." Walker whirled his finger in a little circle as though I needed a visual cue.

"I'll turn, but good luck with getting my hands behind my back."

"Are you resisting arrest?" Ava said.

"No. I hurt my shoulder when I fell into the wall."

"Hands in front then." Walker pulled a pair of bulky handcuffs from a pouch attached to his belt. "Iron. Special for your kind," he said. "In case you decide to use magic again."

"You call flying through the ground magic?" I asked. Then I thought for a moment. "Yes, I suppose I can see your point."

Wow! I did magic! Something I always wanted to be able to do. And, here I was getting arrested for it. Be careful what you wish for, indeed.

Walker clapped me in irons as though I was an actual

prisoner. When the cold metal settled on my wrists, my skin began to burn. It didn't sizzle like bacon, but the sensation wasn't pleasant. Sort of like thousands of pins and needles.

"You two should know better," Ava said to Harvey and Meeks. "If this one wasn't such a baby," she nodded at me, "I'd think she was a siren."

"Hardly." Harvey sat by my feet, no longer cowed, now that Walker had stopped brooding. "You've never heard her singing in the shower." She shot me a haughty look. "Or seen her dancing."

Meeks sat by the foot of the bed, tail curled tightly about his paws, glaring at anyone who looked his way.

"Are these really necessary?" I lifted my hands, shaking the cuffs, making the chain jangle.

"I'm not having you escape again," Walker said. "This place is natural stone and earth. Easy for you to shoot through."

"What if I promise not to?"

"Oh well," Ava said. "Seeing as you promise ..."

"You really are a sarcastic so-and-so, aren't you?" I didn't know whether I hated her or liked her.

Truth be told, I had no clue how I'd travelled through the ground the first time. It might have been instinct, or possibly just desperation fueled by terror. Doing it again was far from a done deal, so I shut my mouth.

Ava fished a polished green stone not much wider than her thumb from a pocket in her boot and walked into the lounge room. I heard her deploy a forensic team to Narrows Run.

"You want backup too?" A jingly voice answered. Probably her mobile-stone fairy.

"Any extra agents available would be great," Ava said. "Walker's declared an L-Two."

"Ooh! Exciting," Jingly-Voice replied.

"Not really," Ava said. "Apparently Rebecca Ashmore has been murdered."

"So no loss then."

I wanted to rush in the lounge room and throttle both of them.

Walker glanced at the bedroom door, then at me. "I know you're Rebecca's sister."

"How? You never did the testing."

"Taking you to the room with the chair and the armed guards *was* the test."

"Oookay…" I backed back a step.

"The only other person I've ever known who could travel through the ground like that was Rebecca. At first, the only way she could do it was through fear. Real fear. The need to flee. Or falling from a great height fear."

"… so you terrorised me?"

"It was necessary."

"What if I couldn't do it? What if I'd frozen in panic? People do that, you know."

"I had back-up plans. Just be happy you did it the first time."

"Why all this then?" I flashed my handcuffs at him.

He indicated the murder scene. "Are you kidding me? You're our primary suspect. We caught you leaning over a fresh kill. You think Blightly could have killed your sister. That's plenty of motive. I'm unsure of means yet, but I'll know the truth soon."

"Oh, great!"

"What about the two cloaked suspects we saw running from the scene?" Harvey said. "Almost knocked Ding down the stairs."

I nodded vigorously. "Twice! Yes! Very suspicious all that running. Kept their faces hidden under hoods and everything."

"So, no description? Convenient."

"I have photos!" I twisted my hip, so he could see my mobile phone in my back pocket.

Walker withdrew the phone. "Show me. And no, I am not taking off the cuffs."

"Fine!" It wasn't that difficult to swipe in my pattern code on the lock screen, but I made sure the chains clanked and rattled as much as possible. I tapped on the photo gallery and shoved the screen at him. "There!"

"A blurry black cloak. Well, you just broke this case wide open."

"Scroll through the pictures." I motioned with my finger as though swiping an invisible phone screen. "There might be one that's good."

Walker didn't need to be shown twice. He frowned. Scrolled. And frowned some more.

"I'm fairly certain the second suspect is a satyr. I can just make out the hooves." He handed me my phone with an unexpected half-smirk. "By the way, nice legs!"

I looked at my phone. Walker had scrolled too far back and right there on the screen was a photo of me in a pair of denim shorts and an aqua, boho top. My cheeks warmed. "Thank you! I grew them myself."

Walker pulled a palm-sized sheet of clear crystal from his coat pocket and tapped it twice. "Can you recall *any* details?"

"Very long, narrow black braids," I said. "Blue beads on the ends."

"I see," Walker said.

"Why aren't you writing this down?" I asked.

He showed me the crystal sheet. And, there were words. My words. My physical description right down to the ash-leaf-shaped birthmark on my upper left thigh. How rude! Was nothing private?

"Anything else?" Walker watched me patiently, but I could see the desperation–or was it fear in his hazel eyes?

"The other one had hooves," I said. "They clopped as they ran away."

"Yes, I saw the picture."

"They had something to do with Cael's death," Meeks said bitterly. "Why aren't you out chasing them?"

Walker ignored the raxx and called through the bedroom door. "How long 'til forensics get here, Cadd?"

"Half an hour. An hour." Ava walked back in the room and nodded at my 'accomplices' and me. "They say anything?"

He gave her the crystal note-recording-sheet. Her green eyes flicked back and forth as she read. She grunted and handed it back.

"Let's go," Walker said.

"Please don't make me fly on a carpet again," I said. "I still haven't recovered from the last trip."

"How else am I going to get you back to headquarters?" Walker smiled, but there was no mischief in his eyes. All I saw there were grief and pain.

CHAPTER FIFTEEN

This jaunting around town on a mortally wounded flying carpet had to be some sort of hazing. If that was the case, then gods help me on initiation day. At least this time, I had Harvey and Meeks clinging on beside me. I shouldn't be so mean, but it was hilarious. Both were spread-eagled, claws buried in the rug, furry cheeks wobbling in the wind. I laughed. They scowled and moaned, and I laughed some more. A bug buzzed into my mouth and down my throat. I coughed and spluttered, then Harvey and Meeks laughed. I'm sure they would have high-fived if they'd not been hanging on for their lives. At least my shoulder didn't hurt as much. And Walker had had the decency to remove the handcuffs before towing us away.

My mind wandered to the shapeshifter with the blue markings I'd met on the way to Cael's place. Black leopard. Raven. She'd been on her way to Narrows Run for an appointment. I thought of the hooded figure running from Cael's building. It had been dressed in black: black hair and blue beads.

What if they're one and the same?

The shapeshifter's appointment could have been with Cael. But was it to murder him? Was it to keep him quiet? To extract information? Did they fight over gambling debts? Maybe she was a nasty debt collector that worked for the mob? Her leopard claws would certainly be able to shred furniture. And kill! Whoever had killed him had been looking for something. But what? And did it have something to do with Rebecca's death? Or, the two murders could be totally unrelated.

Too much information. I needed to write all this stuff down. Make a mind-map linking clues together.

As we walked through the F.C.T. hallways, escorted by Ava Cadwaller and Walker, I couldn't help but notice how people avoided eye contact with her. She walked with a confidence that I envied. And, despite her short leather skirt, gothy boots (Which I loved, by the way!) and her bright blue bob, she commanded attention, and from what I saw, fear.

Maybe I should be a bit more careful around her!

I suddenly glanced back at Ava, at her black clothes and blue hair, and sucked in a shocked breath. Seriously! Why hadn't I noticed before? She was obviously dangerous and powerful. Why hadn't Walker noticed? And the big bosses of the F.C.T.? No! I had to be wrong. The whole F.C.T. wouldn't let a murderer roam about freely.

"We're here." Walker pushed open a door and ushered us into a comfortable room, softly lit by floating 'snow globes'. Blizzards swirled in the glass domes, making life miserable for the tiny figures and towns inside. There had to be thirty globes, all different sizes, all hovering at various levels below the ceiling. How awesome! I needed to buy myself a few of them. I'd have to ask where they got them.

I breathed a sigh of relief. "A bit more comfortable than the last dump you took me to."

Four three-seater couches finished in sapphire-blue velvet furnished the room. Not the cheap stuff, either. I couldn't help myself. I sat down on the closest couch and ran my hands over it—soft, luxurious, and way outside of my personal furniture budget. Eight ladder-back chairs lined the far wall, their padded seats covered in grey material. A table centred the room, draped in white linen and laden with cups, steaming teapots and plates of pies, tarts, cakes and biscuits. How civilised.

The worrywart in me whispered, *They're probably poisoned. Or laced with truth serum or something.*

"How thoughtful to make us such a lovely lunch." I watched the two F.C.T. agents' reactions to see if they looked guilty or devious. Nothing.

"I am starving, you know." I nodded at the table. "This being detained business really builds up a girl's hunger."

"I can imagine," Walker said. "But you'll have to wait."

"If this is your interrogation room—" My voice caught in my throat. Darn! And I had been trying so hard to remain strong. I cleared my throat and affected a charming smile. "I might take up a life of crime."

"Bit late for that." Ava stood in front of me. "This room isn't for you. You're coming with me."

"Wait? What?"

"She's a joker, this one. Nothing like Rebecca." She gave Walker a questioning look. "You're certain they're sisters?"

"Positive," Walker said. "Doesn't mean she didn't kill Rebecca, though. Or Cael."

"I did not kill Becca *or* Cael!" I remained seated—a small protest. One I was sure I'd pay for later.

"And yet, we found you leaning over Cael's body."

Walker crossed his arms. "His corpse still warm, his blood fresh."

I felt the full weight of his gaze crushing me from above. Memories of blood, the coppery smell, the tackiness, filled my mind. I held forth my sleeve, the blood now brown and beginning to powder. "This came off the suspect—the one with the hooves that almost knocked me down the stairs. It got on me when they pushed passed. You should have it tested."

"And it could be the victim's blood. Murder is a messy business." Ava shrugged, dismissing my brilliant detectiveness with a few words.

"Get her a clean top and bag her blouse," Walker said. "Couldn't hurt to get the blood tested."

I tossed Ava a triumphant glare.

"We'll soon find out the truth," Ava said. "My interrogations never take long." She glowered down at me. "And yours will probably be quicker than most."

"Was that an insult?" I glanced at Walker. "Is she going to do her *thing* on me? That thing you warned me about?"

"She interrogates all murder suspects."

"Call it my hobby." Ava grinned at me, wicked and brimming with anticipation.

A glass wall stood directly across from where I sat. Probably a two-way mirror so people could be comfortable while they watched people suffer. Watched me suffer.

"If she sucks my brains out, I'll sue the lot of you." I stood and faced her. She was taller than me, but only by an inch or so. Somehow though, she filled the room, her presence overshadowing us all.

"I doubt you use your brain often. So not much of a loss, really." The runes and symbols adorning Ava's tanned skin glowed, lit with inner red fire. She shoved me through the doorway, back into the hall.

"You get off on this, don't you?" I stumbled into the next room along.

The wall on this side was mirrored, so I was right about it being two-way. There were no ominous-looking chairs. No table. No bright lights. And no torture equipment. I puffed out a sigh, my shoulders relaxing a little.

"Why are Meeks and Harvey allowed to watch?" I turned to Ava. "Won't that compromise our statements?"

"Not the way I do things."

"I suppose you've got thumbscrews in one of your boot pockets?"

"I wish."

"Are you mean to everyone? Or just me?"

"Just you."

"Figures."

"Stand still and look into my eyes."

"On our first date?" My words were cheeky, but I wasn't fooling anyone.

"Please—resist me. It'll be so much more enjoyable."

"And terrible for me."

"Exactly."

I checked the floor—iron panels by the look of them. Rust, or it could have been blood crusted the flooring in suspicious patches. No fresh dirt to plough through to a safe forest somewhere. Plus, I was in a building full of F.C.T. agents. They probably all had superpowers. And what was I? A bulldozer with no instruction manual. There was no getting out of this.

"Okay." I braced myself. "Let's get this over with. I *am* innocent. You can apologise to me when it's over."

Ava stepped so close her breath ruffled loose strands of my hair. She gazed into my eyes. Green to green, only her eyes had an otherworldly glow.

A giggle bubbled up inside me. I couldn't stop it. Was this what historians called a gallows laugh?

She grabbed my face between her hands. I froze. Deer caught in headlights was an understatement. Her hands were cool, clammy. Sweat trickled down my spine, my forehead and neck. She didn't say anything, she just stared into my eyes.

Was it going to hurt? Was I going to be sick? (Hopefully all over Ava.) Spill every secret I'd ever had?

The blue-grey runes on Ava's skin glowed soft, buttercup yellow. Low vibrations resonated through her body, shooting into me until every one of my cells quaked like I was a living tuning fork. The radiance pulsing along her skin evolved to luminous orange. Then candy apple red. Scarlet. Lapis blue. Then pure, blazing white so bright I could no longer see her. The pressure of her hands on my face diminished. Feather light. But her power throbbed between us, a living force so powerful I buckled under the weight of it. Her green eyes flared fiery white. A shiver ripped through my body, but not from cold. Ava merged into my body like two drops of mercury becoming one.

Remorseless, unrelenting vibrations snaked and wormed through my mind, dredging every shadow, every recess, every secret. Even ones I never knew I had. And I could do nothing to stop it. Flashes of memory came and went, so fast they barely registered. And yet, I relived every one of them. Felt what I had felt. Saw what I had seen. Heard what I had heard.

The time I was forced to apologise to my entire third-grade class for insisting a ghost was mimicking Miss Carlton. The shame I felt for being the only kid who could see spirits.

My first kiss with Dean Ambrose, a boy three years older than me. I had been nine. At the time, it was the most disgusting thing I'd ever experienced. I'd run into Dean years later. Believe me, the kiss would have been far more pleasant if we'd waited.

My lonely years as a teenager. I didn't fit in. Not really. Everywhere I'd gone, I had seen ghosts, spirits and lost souls. It had made socialising awkward and strained, especially when I didn't know if I was talking to the dead or the living. Things had improved as I learned to block and fend off the spirits, but my reputation had stuck.

Ava sliced my life, layer by layer, memory by memory, leaving every detail bare. Naked for her scrutiny.

I tumbled from a great height, landing hard on a cold iron floor. Needles of pain sizzled and stabbed my exposed skin, but I could do nothing to help myself.

As darkness sucked away all light, I heard Ava call, "Next!"

CHAPTER SIXTEEN

Globes of whirling light swam above me, their brilliance smeared and flaring as they glided through a murky haze. I blinked, peering upwards.

Pretty.

I'd like a few of those. The balls swam through the fuzziness giving no hint as to where I was or how I'd arrived there.

"What happened?" I mumbled, my tongue thick, numb like I'd been to the dentist and had a mouth full of novocaine.

Cold water dribbled between my lips, catching in my throat. I coughed, struggling to sit up. Once I could breathe without wheezing and gasping, I realised I was back in the observation room. Meeks lay beside me on the couch, snoring softly. He kicked, whimpering and squeaking in his sleep.

"Cadd wanted to put you in chains." Walker crouched beside us, a glass of water held in one hand. "But I figured you wouldn't escape. Unconsciousness is better than shackles."

"Chains? But I didn't do anything wrong!" I rubbed the tears from coughing away with the back of my hand. "If my innocence is still locked away in my brain, get Ava back in here. She can merge with me again."

"Not many suspects offer to do that after Cadd has interrogated them."

"Then they're hiding something." I searched the room for Harvey. "Is Harvey in there now? With her?"

"Has been for a while."

I moved Meeks so he was comfortable on the couch and sat up. My bloodied white blouse had been replaced with a plain black one scrawled with the words *Kill Me, and I'm Yours for Life* across the front.

"A gift from Ava?" I tugged on the soft shirt.

"One of her very own. It's actually quite amusing if you know the saying's origin."

"No doubt." I stagger-lurched across the viewing room. Graceful as a cat, that's me.

I leaned against the two-way mirror, resting my forehead and hands on the cool glass. On the other side, Ava kneeled on the iron-panelled floor. Either she was immune to the metal, or she could withstand the pain without flinching. Harvey gazed up into Ava's eyes, shivering, her black and grey fur on end, her eyes impossibly wide. Harvey's tail flicked and swished.

"You wonderful cat," I said. "You resist that upstart cow."

Ava never moved. Never blinked. Her runes and symbols shimmered, drifting across her skin, pulsing cobalt blue. Then pure white. Suddenly, Ava's eyes shone with scintillating light. She grinned, triumphant. Her body rippled, oscillating until it became incorporeal, a wash of pure light. Her runes reeled, whirling across her skin as though someone had stirred them with an invisible spoon. Ava's spirit, or whatever it was, melded with Harvey's shuddering body. Her fur took on Ava's runes. They shifted and merged within Harvey's fluffy coat.

"Did that happen to me?" I didn't turn around. I knew Walker was behind me. He had a presence all of his own, weighted, predatory. But it was restrained. Controlled. And far more potent than Ava Cadwaller's magical abilities.

"You lit up like a miniature sun," Walker said. "You have great power, you know."

"Didn't help me get out of this."

"You need schooling."

"Me? Go to Grimsmead Academy?" I remained leaning against the two-way glass, my breath forming foggy patches. I laughed. "I'm twenty-four years old. I'm not going back to school now."

"I'm still learning, and I'm over eighteen hundred years old."

"Seriously?" I glanced over my shoulder. He didn't look a day over thirty. "Did Rebecca know she was dating a geriatric?"

"You're to the point, as usual." Walker smiled, but it was full of sorrow and grief. "She even met my grand-mother. Now there's a geriatric. I wouldn't say that to her, though. Very sensitive about her age."

"I can imagine."

I turned back to watch poor Harvey. She lay on the ground, a sad bundle of black and grey fur. Ava was nowhere to be seen, at least until she shoved her way into the waiting room and strode towards us.

A look of disbelief crossed her face when she saw me standing with Walker, but she quickly masked her shock.

She glared at me, addressing Walker. "They didn't kill Cael Blightly."

"You sound disappointed." I crossed my arms. "I told you we didn't do it."

"Oh, I have a treasure vault of secrets about you, dear." Ava smiled, but her green eyes were cold.

"Firstly," I said. "You know for a fact I didn't kill Rebecca. Tell Agent Kane here." I thrust my thumb in Walker's direction. "Tell him I had nothing to do with it."

"I can't do that," Ava said.

"Why not? It's true!"

"Your sister died because she was protecting you. You and your precious family secrets."

"What? What secrets? Up until today, I didn't even know I *had* a family. Besides Rebecca and my adopted parents, that is. How did you get that from me if I didn't know about these unsubstantiated secrets?"

Ava tapped on the two-way glass and pointed at Harvey. "Because she knows. As does the raxx."

I stared at Harvey, all limp and helpless in the middle of the iron floor. My cat. My lifelong friend had known about my family secrets? I felt betrayed. Betrayed and alone. Now who could I trust?

CHAPTER SEVENTEEN

I had never seen a more sorry bunch than Harvey, Meeks and me. Ava, on the other hand, was all smiles. She knew something I didn't, and she found every opportunity to remind me. Why she had taken an instant dislike to me, I didn't know. Maybe she was mean to everyone. Everyone except Walker. For some reason, she deferred to him. Respected him, even. Perhaps she respected her elders. Walker was after all over eighteen hundred years old.

We had been escorted down to what Ava lovingly termed, 'the dungeons'. A series of spartan rooms reserved for travelling F.C.T. agents and former suspects awaiting processing and discharge. The walls were white, the floorboards bare. I sat on a single bed beside a pile of folded blankets, sheets and a pillow. Reminded me of a prison bunk.

"Some food and drink would be nice," I said to Ava. "What about that food in the waiting room? I'm sure no one would miss a few biscuits and a pie?"

"That's for staff." Ava sat on a table next to the wall, her legs swinging back and forth.

Walker had gone to fill out paperwork so we could go home. He'd left over an hour ago. He was probably in the observation room, scoffing a plate of cakes or something.

"I was just thinking of scoffing a plate of cakes myself." Ava smirked at me.

"How did?" I slung her a nasty glare. "Get out of my head."

"But it's *so* roomy."

"That's an invasion of privacy."

"You gave up that right when you withheld evidence."

"I did no such thing."

"You grew up on a planet called Earth, but you were born here. You *and* Rebecca." Ava nodded at Harvey, who lay curled near my feet, licking her paws, her expression forlorn and hopeless. "She knows. She was sent as your Watcher. Keeping you alive until it was safe to come home."

"Wasn't so safe for Rebecca," I snarled. "Was it?"

"Rebecca came back to help your family—to save your home. Harvey couldn't stop her."

Harvey looked up at me, her eyes moist. She lowered her head onto her paws. My chest twinged with pity, but it quickly shifted to anger. I'd deal with Harvey later.

"You're *those* girls," Ava said suddenly. "*Those* two sisters who vanished over one hundred years ago. The F.C.T. hunted you for years."

"I'm twenty-four years old, so how could I have possibly vanished over one hundred years ago?"

"My guess is that time moved more slowly on Earth. No wonder you're so backward."

"What have I done to make you hate me so much?"

"You look like your sister," her voice was sharp with venom. "You could almost be twins."

"You're jealous! You're in love with Walker, aren't you?"

"You don't know what you're talking about."

"Rebecca stole his heart, and you hated her for it. And now you're taking it out on me because I look like her."

Ava grunted and crossed her arms. "Think what you like."

"How do I know you didn't kill Rebecca? Jealousy makes people do horrible things."

"I'm not people."

Well, she had me there.

Meeks whimpered. He sat on one of the chairs pulled out from the table, his muzzle resting on his front paws, his eyes closed.

"Their heads ache." Ava glared at me accusingly. "Why doesn't yours?"

"I don't know."

She muttered something that was probably a nasty insult and looked at the closed door.

"Missing him, are we?" I couldn't help myself.

"No! I was wishing he'd hurry back so I can be rid of you."

"I won't say anything else if you tell me about my family secrets. About why Rebecca and I were sent to Earth."

Harvey looked up at me, held my gaze for a moment before lowering her head onto her paws. Crying.

"A clue then," I urged Ava. "Something. Anything."

"Apparently, your father tried to kill you and your sister." Ava smiled, watching me for a reaction. "Murder you for your powers after your mother disappeared. Many agents believed he'd killed her. Many cited his love for her and refused to believe that he'd do such a thing. Others sat on the fence, allowing the evidence to guide them. See, your parents were the first-ever banshee/dryad pairing. The F.C.T. had no clear frame of reference to base the case around. Whatever happened, the F.C.T. never found out the truth."

"Wow!" My dad was a criminal—maybe even a murderer? My blood was half his. A chill ran through me. Was I capable of such evil? I didn't think I was, but who knew what the future would dredge up?

"Is that all you can say? Wow?"

I nodded, fearing my voice would betray my feelings. No point in giving Cadd further ammunition.

An uncomfortable silence filled the room. Ava sat on the table, her legs swinging impatiently. Meeks snored gently. Harvey lay in a desolate heap. I sat on the bed, trying to get my head around the fact that my father had tried to kill Rebecca and me. Surely Ava was lying? It would be just like her to do something so cruel.

My thoughts flicked to my biological mother. A banshee. Did she foretell her own death? How weird would that have been? Maybe that's why she vanished weeks after giving birth. To me. Had she been trying to escape her own death? Was that even possible?

But what if she *had* been killed? By my father? What if he'd killed Rebecca too? Years apart, their deaths could be connected. I'd only been a baby—five weeks or so. Rebecca had been five years old. With our mother gone, we would have been vulnerable. Easy prey for a killer. But had the murderer been a stranger? Or my father? What parent tries to kill their children? What if my mother was still alive? What if she had started a new life–far from Grimsmead? Away from my father? She could've up and left him. He didn't sound very nice. But why would she leave Rebecca and me behind knowing our lives were in danger?

"Your mind doesn't shut up, does it?" Ava circled one hand beside her head.

"Stop it!"

"It's not like I can catch every word or image rattling around in that skull of yours. Thank goodness! Your brain is more like river rapids gushing over rocks. A lot of useless noise. But, occasionally, I grab onto something juicy."

"How wonderful for you. What happened to my father?" I asked abruptly. "Was he caught?"

Ava shrugged. "He left town. No one ever saw him again."

"Did the F.C.T. search for him?"

"Of course they did—biggest manhunt in years. You and your sister had mysteriously disappeared without a trace. Your mother was nowhere to be found, presumed dead. Possibly murdered. Your grandmother had a nervous breakdown—lost her mind overnight. Grief, I expect. Did you know your mother's name means 'Weeping Mother' in the old tongue? Now I've met you, I can see why."

"You are hilarious. A living, breathing, walking comic book."

"I do try."

My shoulders drooped. She didn't even wince. I'd have to brush up on my insults.

"All F.C.T. agents," Ava went on, "are required to familiarise themselves with cold cases, yours included."

"So glad my family history is required reading. Did you verify anything by digging around our brains?"

"Not just your brains."

"I hate to think where else you probed."

"When I scoured your mind and soul, impenetrable warding walls blocked me from seeing everything. Powerful magic. Not a run-of-the-mill mental lockdown. Same for the mooncat and raxx."

"What can I say? I know nothing about that." I had my suspicions, though. Ava had said nothing about the jewellery box's role as a portal between worlds. Whoever had set those mental walls in our minds must have warded information about the box too. A safeguard of sorts. But who had set the walls? Whoever it was had to be connected to the jewellery box somehow.

"Finally!" Ava closed her eyes and leaned backwards. "A moment's peace and quiet from that brain of yours."

Ah! So the jewellery box *was* warded from prying minds. I watched Ava closely. *Jewellery box! Jewellery box! Jewellery box! And all my junk inside it!* Her expression remained calm, her eyes shut. *Excellent!*

As soon as I got back to the mausoleum, I'd grill Harvey, and get as many facts about why Rebecca and I had been shipped off to earth.

'And there you go again." Ava glared at me.

She hadn't made many snarky digs at me since I'd found out about her secret love for Walker. I sort of missed her feisty attitude.

"I suppose you'll be sneaking around Spell Haven Nursing Home next," Ava said. "Causing trouble. Getting in people's way."

And she was back.

"How do you know we were going to investigate Spell —? Never mind."

"I also saw the message Cael had left in blood. Saw it in real life and your memories."

I decided to do some mind-prying of my own. "What do you know of the Thorntons?"

"Old Blood. Rich and powerful. I wouldn't want to go up against them."

I'd already worked that much out for myself. "What about Aylward Thornton?"

Ava narrowed her eyes. "How do you know Thorn?"

"I met him."

"When? I didn't see anything in your mind about him."

Really! Now that was strange. Had I blocked that from my mind? Or had he? Or Aunt Rachel?

"Just in passing," I said casually. "He seemed pleasant enough."

"Hmmm." Ava eyed me shrewdly. "Pleasant is one word for him, I suppose."

Deciding to change tact, I said, "What else happened when Rebecca and I disappeared?"

"It was on all the news. I remember how Grimsmead Academy added security spells to the grounds. I remember my parents talking about it."

I'd made the news and hadn't even realised. I wondered if my return would be just as newsworthy. No, that would be dangerous. What if the bad guys found out and came after me? I needed a disguise. A new name. The ramifications of my situation hit me full on.

My mother.

My sister.

Me.

"Do you guys have a witness protection program?" I asked.

"You're joking."

"What if whoever killed my mother and sister finds out about me?"

"I'd lead them straight to your door."

"Well, that's not very nice."

"We could use you as bait. Draw them out."

"You'd love that, wouldn't you?"

"I'm serious."

"What if it's my dad? Was there ever any proof he tried to kill Rebecca and me? Was there evidence he had something to do with my mother's disappearance?"

"There were witnesses." She glanced down at Harvey. "And a spriggit."

"You mean Ploggit?" That reminded me. Plog had vanished not long after we got to Grimsmead. What if he was in trouble? The sooner we returned to the mausoleum, the better. I hadn't known the spriggit long, but he seemed like a lovely little thing, dressed in his beanie and jacket. I was even getting used to the idea that he slopped up any hair I lost in the shower. His recycling saved on plumbing bills, for one thing.

"You are really sitting there thinking about a spriggit brownie?" Ava looked revolted.

"This mind-reading thing better not be permanent!"

"The link between us will pass in an hour or so. But at the moment, I'm revelling in all that open space between your ears. Does it echo when you babble away to yourself?"

"Can you read anyone's thoughts anytime you feel like it?" Fear edged my voice. There'd be no hiding stuff from her if she could. Unless everything I ever thought while I was around her was bookended by 'jewellery box'. That would get tiresome fast.

"No, thank heavens. I have to prepare. Establish a physical connection. The connection fades eventually."

The tension in my shoulders eased a little. "My mum was a banshee. Was she a pureblood?"

"Pure as they come. Bound to one of the Old Blood Families."

"Which one?"

"The *Thorntons*." Ava studied me, watching for my reaction.

My stomach dropped. Thorn had been the best thing that had happened to me since I got to this world.

"Funny that, eh?" I tried to make it sound casual. "My mum was bound to the Thornton family."

"I just said she was."

"What do you mean by 'bound'?"

"Don't you know anything? A banshee senses when death approaches a member of the family she's bound to. She wails for them. Gives them notice so they can prepare."

"I'd run in the other direction." *Just like my mother might have?*

"You can't flee death. When it's your time, it's your time."

"I'd give it a darn good try."

"I'd pay to see that."

"Does that mean *I'm* bound to this Thornton family?" I wondered if Thorn had recognised anything about me? Sensed my mother's bond to his family?

"You're a mixed breed—half banshee, half dryad. A banshad. The Thortons wouldn't associate with you if you were the last banshee on the planet. If anything, you're probably bound to some wingless harlot down on Flash Street."

"You should visit Flash Street. Get a little loving. You're more prickly than a grouchy hedgehog."

Ava looked at me, her mouth agape. She rocked backward, resting her head on the wall and exploded with laugher, a rib-tickling belly laugh.

"What's so funny?" Walker entered the room, a folder of papers under one arm.

"I told you she was a funny one!" Ava choked between laughs.

Walker glanced at me, eyebrows raised.

"What can I say?" I said. "I'm a laugh a minute."

"Let's see how much you joke after you complete all these forms." Walker patted the folder. "In triplicate."

"I'd rather let Cadwaller dig through my mind again."

Ava snorted and laughed even harder.

Either she was loosening up, or the jokey fun part of my mind had found a comfy home in her brain somewhere. If that were the case, she'd be so much more pleasant to be around.

A more sinister thought emerged. What if Ava was laughing at me? Not with me. She knew things about my past I couldn't even begin to imagine. And one of the details was my mother's bond to Thorn's family. And, what if Ava was in league with whoever killed my sister? Jealousy could make people do the most heinous things.

Arg! What if Ava had left her unpleasant, suspicious part of herself in my brain? What a horrible thought!

I played along. As soon as I could get out of here, I was going to find out the truth about my family, even if it landed me in prison. No one was going to mess with me anymore.

CHAPTER EIGHTEEN

alker waved farewell, mounted his broom and flew up and over the forest behind the mausoleum. The moment he was out of sight, I puffed out a sigh, closed my eyes and tried to relax. After a couple of deep breaths, I walked towards my new home. At this point, I had to face reality. Grimsmead was home, and I lived in a graveyard. Funny how your life could change so rapidly. Whether or not it was for the better, I couldn't say. So far, the jury was out—*way* out, deliberating. Still, I had never been so glad to walk through a cemetery in my life. Harvey and Meeks stayed on the threadbare rug as I towed it along behind me. Ava's interrogation had really taken its toll on them.

"Are there dead bodies buried in this cemetery?" I glanced over my shoulder at Harvey and Meeks.

"This is more a memorial garden than a cemetery." Harvey remained curled up, her face hidden by her front paws. "There are a few burial plots for keepsakes, locks of hair, baby teeth and Rest in Peace talismans—that sort of thing."

"So no rotting corpses or prospective zombies living on our doorstep."

"Not on our doorstep, no."

I went to ask Harvey to elaborate, but decided I'd rather not know exactly where the bodies and zombies lived.

"How are you both feeling?" I knew the answer, but it seemed right to ask. "Terrible?"

Harvey and Meeks moaned their answers.

We entered the mausoleum, my boots sending soft echoes through the silence. The statues loomed over me with their widespread arms and sinewy bodies. Now I had time to look at them, I could see they were dryads. Dryads transforming into their human form, or perhaps transforming back into trees. I couldn't be sure, because I knew so little about their ways and customs–my ways and customs.

I wondered if I could turn into a tree. Would it hurt? Would I get splinters? And if I could morph into a tree, would I be able to shift back into my everyday body? A dog would probably wee on me if I were a tree. An image formed in my mind, and I spluttered a laugh. I would never have the elegance and timelessness my ancestors possessed. Perhaps they took deportment classes at Grimsmead Academy.

I hurried through the torch-lit tunnel and entered the glass arboretum. My heartbeat slowed, my breathing calmed and my mind grew clear. The gurgle and splash of the indoor streams and the fresh scent of trees and flowers infused every cell of my body. I could almost hear them. Maybe one day I could understand their language. Grimsmead Academy probably had classes like *How to Chat With Weeds 101* and *Talking Philosophy With Ancient Oaks and Fungus.* I'd have to look into taking a few lessons.

I towed the rug through the indoor garden until we reached my favourite shaggy grey rug piled with my belongings—an island of home in a sea of magic and strangers. The faded black couch and the messy coffee table had made the journey from Earth, along with some of my plants. The ferns, orchids and palms were the only things that seemed to belong in Grimsmead. The ramshackle heap, remnants of my life, looked sad and lost. Or maybe that was just me.

I lifted Harvey and then Meeks onto the overstuffed couch. They flopped into miserable piles of fur and refused to talk.

"Journey complete," I said, and the flying carpet plonked to the ground just as Walker had said it would. I rolled it up and stashed it by the glass wall.

"Is there another bathroom besides Becca's, Meeks?" I couldn't face going into Rebecca's bedroom to shower.

"All the bedrooms have an ensuite," Meeks grumbled. "Pick one."

"There's a bathroom off the Forest Room," Harvey said. "It'll save you taking the stairs."

"Excellent point!"

My stomach grumbled, gnawing on emptiness, the feelings of rest and repleteness I'd gained from my trip through the ground long since worn off. I wondered if they had fast-food deliveries in Grimsmead.

"Is there a kitchen here somewhere?" I called out.

When no one answered, I went looking myself. It took a bit of finding, but I finally stumbled upon it. I couldn't see an oven or a refrigerator, but there was a double sink with hot and cold running water. An empty bowl sat beside a range of pottery canisters, each containing cooking essentials such as flour, sugar, salt and rice.

All ingredients and no food! Great!

Benches wrapped around three walls, the fourth sporting the door. The upper cupboards sat so high I'd need a ladder to inspect them. Either they'd been built for seven-foot-tall trolls, or that's where they stashed all the yummy stuff. Finding no ladder or box to climb on, I searched the cupboards and drawers lowest to the ground. One, with a pull-twist-and-pull handle revealed the mother lode—a fridge, of sorts. I didn't know how it remained cold, but I didn't care. Among other things, it held grapes, cherries, plums, and chilled lemonade. Not the shop-bought stuff, either. This was homemade. I glanced behind me to see if anyone was watching and downed half the jug. Marvellous. So tangy and cold.

I rifled through the 'fridge' and withdrew a pat of butter, a loaf of uncut bread, and a pot of blackberry jam. Seedless. Bonus.

An hour later, I was full. Bread crumbs and sticky smears covered the bench-top, and the lemonade jug stood empty. I found the bathroom Harvey had suggested, which was awesome. Arguing with those rude and disrespectful spiral stairs would have topped off my day. The bathroom was dusty, cold and empty of all personality. Creepy but perfect. I showered, brushed my hair and teeth and changed into a flouncy peacock-green dress. Very boho and nice and loose. I slipped on my oldest pair of walnut-brown knee-high boots and headed into the Forest Room.

Harvey and Meeks snored on the couch. I didn't have the heart to wake them, even though I wanted to question Harvey about all the secrets she'd kept from me. I glanced up at the mezzanine levels. All the doors were closed; the one to Rebecca's bedroom seemed darker, more ominous. There was a chance her spirit could manifest in there again, but I couldn't face venturing into her room. Not alone.

I spotted my Tarot cards on the coffee table. I could check them for a clue. Not a full reading, just a one-card draw.

I cleared a space on my rug, sat cross-legged and shuffled my Tarot, concentrating on what I needed to know. "Who murdered Rebecca Kerrigan Black—I mean Ashmore?"

With my eyes closed, I repeated my question over and over as I shuffled. When I felt ready, I withdrew a single card from the deck and laid it on the rug in front of me. Breathing deep, I braced myself and opened my eyes.

"*The Gorgon*—reversed. *The Medusa card!*" I'd never drawn that card before. No one I'd done a reading for had drawn *The Gorgon* before. Especially reversed. I turned the card around and stared at the snake-haired woman dressed in a black, scaled bodysuit. A full moon hung to her right, highlighting the daggers in her hands. Every snake writhing on her head had a different face, a different expression. I must have drawn the wrong card because I was tired. That was it. I hadn't focused enough. Or long enough. I chewed my bottom lip and shoved the card back in the deck. I'd try again later. If I pulled *The Gorgon* again, I couldn't deny it. Then I'd tell Harvey. See what she reckoned.

I turned my attention to the crime-scene photos I'd snapped with my mobile phone, searching for some clue, something I may have missed. After the day I'd had, I couldn't think straight, so I slipped my phone down one boot, vowing to look at the photos again later.

I needed to sleep, but I couldn't bring myself to stay in Rebecca's bedroom. I didn't want to battle the stairs or go through all the rooms upstairs searching for a bed. Instead, I took a cushion from my old couch and lay down on a bed of moss by the stream.

As I lay there, listening to the water bubble and murmur over stones, swishing through turns and around boulders, my thoughts meandered with the sounds. I had tried to get Walker to return Rebecca's iPad, but he'd said it was evidence. I really did need to go through all of the files, but I couldn't exactly do that with Ava Cadwaller and Walker staring over my shoulder. I had, however, managed to get him to give it to me for a few minutes so I could show him the sound-file of Rebecca chasing Cael. Walker and Ava had made me play it over and over, both straining to listen to every single sound. Walker had asked me how he could unlock the iPad so he could investigate further. I'd told him it was locked with Earth magic, and I was the only one who could access it. Call it insurance so I could get into it at some point if I really needed to.

I smiled.

And drifted off to sleep.

"DING!" Fishy breath wafted across my face. I flapped my hands, feeling around, my eyes still closed.

"I'm having a lovely dream. Go away."

A heavy fur-ball jumped on my chest, and a warm paw swatted my cheek. "Ding, wake up. Ploggit is back."

It took a few moments for Harvey's words to filter through my sleep-addled mind.

"Ploggit?" I rolled over and wobbled to my knees. Any closer to the edge of the stream and I would have tumbled in.

"Where is he?" I blinked, trying to see straight. "Is he all right?"

"No. He needs a physician."

"What? Oh?" I staggered to my feet. "Where is he?"

I chased Harvey as she ran through the arboretum, dodging trees and fountains I hadn't realised were there yesterday. We hurried into a hallway opposite the torch-lit tunnel that led to the mausoleum. Doors fed off the hall, all closed, so I had no clue what lay within them.

"This place is bigger than I thought!" I shouted, my voice echoing, my boots slapping on the slate tiles.

"I still don't know the entire place myself," Harvey called as she slid left around a corner.

We burst into a room that was filled with a tangle of pipes, taps and plumbing. A jungle gym for spriggit brownies. Who would have guessed?

Meeks sat beside a bundle of blood-soaked rags. I crouched beside him to get a better look.

"Oh, Plog!" I went to stroke his head but stopped. His little face was swollen and bruised. A cut ran through his eyebrow, and blood crusted his nose.

"What happened?" Harvey asked. "Who did this to you?"

"Don't know," Ploggit said through swollen lips. "I came in here—to check if everything was still all-special-like. There was this glorious singing. So wafty and sweet. And wham! Someone plugged ol' Ploggit from behind. Next thing, I got this masked maniac hurling questions and punches while someone sung songs with no words."

"What questions?" I sat crossed-legged as close to Ploggit as I could so I could hear him. "What about?"

He cocked his head and peered out of his good eye. "You. Wanted to know why you're here, and where you've been. If you and Rebecca were family. Where your jewellery box was. And somethin' about an old tooth and your family map."

The wooden molar in the old glass sphere flashed though my mind, along with the parchment map. My gut tightened. I hadn't relocked the trunk when I'd finished snooping. The scrolls and wooden tooth would be easy pickings if someone searched the place.

"They want 'em bad." Ploggit whimpered. "I told them nothin' 'cos I knew nothin'."

With that, poor Ploggit's little body sagged, and his eye closed.

"Is he dead?" I cried. "Please don't tell me he's dead."

"He's unconscious." Meeks looked up at me. "We need to get him medical help."

"I've got to check something first! Come with me!" I leaped up and bolted for the stairs, Meeks by my side.

"I need to go to the top floor," I said. "Make the stupid stairs work."

"Bossy!" Meeks said.

"Sorry, Meeks. This is important."

Meeks called the stairs down and then ordered them up to the top floor. I exited onto the landing and ran into the room with the old trunk. The drawers were on the floor, empty, surrounded by Rebecca's solar chargers and wires. Two scrolls lay discarded, the third was missing. I searched around and couldn't find the tooth or the map.

"This is my fault!" I grabbed a drawer, running my fingers around the inside, not believing that it was empty. "I should have locked the trunk back up. Thrown the cloth over it."

"What's your fault?" Meeks asked, sniffing the scrolls.

"Whoever interrogated Ploggit has the wooden tooth and the map." I waved the drawer around, showing him how empty it was.

"Nothing we can do about it now," Meeks said. "We'll have to deal with that after we get Ploggit help."

"Of course," I said. "You're right."

"I really don't want to fly the carpet by myself," I said. "But I could get those goblin brothers and their taxi."

"I've got a safer idea." Harvey patted my leg. "You carry Ploggit and follow me."

I did as instructed, cradling Ploggit as gently as I could. I trailed after Harvey and Meeks further along the hallway, and in a few minutes we came to a set of bright-red double doors. I pushed them open using my shoulder, and followed the cat and raxx into what looked like a storage shed or garage filled with dusty trunks, cupboards and boxes. It smelled musty, damp and a little sour, as though there were rat droppings scattered around the place.

I sneezed.

"Sorry, Plog," I said, cradling his limp body.

A space had been cleared between the junk for a fluorescent pink golf cart. Three of what *had* to be this world's version of golf-clubs stood in a rear luggage recess, their tops—or was it bottoms?—protected by colourful socks.

"Are you serious?" I squawked. "A golf cart?"

Meeks looked at me as if I was stupid. "Croquet buggy. Rebecca was in the *Hi-Flyers*—top team in Grimsmead."

"Since when do you need a cart to play croquet?"

"When you play it the *right* way, like us. Check the cart's side panels—you'll see the team logo."

I took a quick squiz at the crossed croquet mallets crowned by the words Hi-Flyers. "Nice! Really fancy. Anyway, we've got to get going. I assume the cart flies?"

"Of course it flies!" Meeks leaped onboard and patted the orange, green and pink floral, cushioned seat. "Put Ploggit here next to me. Harvey can ride in the back with the croquet mallets."

"It'll be simple," Harvey said. "Just like driving a car on Earth."

I placed Ploggit next to Meeks and climbed in behind the steering wheel. At least that was familiar. How hard could it be anyway? I searched for a start button, or a key.

"Rebecca always used to say, 'Beam me up, Scotty' and that seemed to get it flying," Meeks said.

"No key?"

"What is this, the dark ages?" Meeks said.

Harvey jumped into the luggage recess and stood on her hind legs, her front paws resting on the seatback. "Meeks will tell you where to fly."

"What we need is a G.P.S system," I said. "Then I could fly anywhere."

"You mean a G.P.N system," Meeks said. "Guided Pixie Navigation. Rebecca bought a unit, but she hadn't got around to installing it before …"

"We don't have time for that now." Harvey poked me with her paw.

Here I was, sitting in a flying croquet cart, taking instructions from talking animals. Oh! And don't forget the spriggit brownie that lived in drains and had been kidnapped and roughed up. I had to be dreaming. No one would believe me back home.

"How do we get out of the garage?" I glanced over my shoulder to see if there was a roller-door, but all I saw was a stone wall.

"You hold the steering wheel and say 'Beam me up, Scotty!' and the roof sort of vanishes."

"Really? How cool!"

"Beam me up, Scotty." I gripped the steering wheel expecting the cart to shudder or wobble around as it rose in the air.

Nothing happened.

"Maybe it doesn't recognise my voice," I said, both disappointed and relieved we were not careening through the sky.

"Rebecca did program the crystals to her voice," Meeks said. "Try saying it like her."

My sister's voice was deeper than mine, more mellow and sexy. I used to try imitating her, but that had only been to embarrass her in front of guys.

I cleared my throat and used my best sultry voice, "Beam me up, Scotty."

"She used to use more emphasis on 'up,' and a little deeper on 'Scotty'." Meeks shrugged. "She thought it was amusing."

I tried again doing as Meeks suggested, and the car rose into the air. No motor, no fumes and what was a bit off-putting, no doors. At least this vehicle had a windscreen. Not like the cracked glass the goblins had on their taxi.

As we got airborne, the stone roof wavered and went translucent. I cringed, expecting to bang into it, but we flew straight through, sailing above the cemetery.

I pressed what looked like an accelerator with my right foot, and we flew forwards. Then I tried the other floor pedal … just a tap. We slowed, hovering like a leaf in an updraft. I gave the steering wheel a slow turn, and the cart banked left and started turning. I tried the same to the right. And off we went to the right.

"How cool is this!" I shouted. "Put your brooms away, guys! And your ratty old carpets. This girl is ready to fly!"

"Just don't turn the wheel too hard," Meeks said. "You want to throw us out?"

"Check that attitude, buddy," I said. "Or you'll be wishing this thing came with parachutes."

He gave me a confused glare. "Head that way." He lifted his right paw, indicating the direction.

I turned right, just a little, and away we went.

"We're being followed," Harvey said.

"We only just took off!" I couldn't believe it. I'd probably lose my licence before I even got one.

"Looks like an F.C.T. agent," Harvey said. "We're under surveillance."

"Of course we are," I muttered, pressing the accelerator to the floor. "How fast can this jalopy go?"

"Not very," Meeks said. "It's for playing croquet, not high-speed racing."

"I know which sport I'm taking up if I have to remain in this place."

"Just keep flying," Harvey said. "We can't waste time answering some F.C.T. agent's questions."

I followed Meek's directions, rising high above the forest, the lake glistening beyond the forest to our left, the twelve stone dragons looming high upon their island precipice like grim sentinels.

Without warning, the closest dragon opened its mouth, and flames roared forth like a blast furnace. A faint smell of smoke and sulphur drifted on the breeze. The next dragon along opened its mouth, stone fangs gleaming as a great tongue of flame blazed long and loud. Three more dragons, one after the other did the same. And then there was silence except for the faint hum of Grimsmead going about its business as though nothing had happened.

"Five o'clock," Meeks said. "We still have a few hours before dark."

"The Hours!" I remembered what Walker had called them. "Those stone dragons are like a clock?"

"The dragons flame on the hour," Harvey said. "Five Hours doing their thing means it's five o'clock."

"Like an over-the-top cuckoo clock?"

Harvey nodded. "I'd forgotten how annoying The Hours are."

"And they do that every hour? Even during the night?"

"Unfortunately," Meeks said. "But you get used to it."

"Oh, I'm sure."

We flew over Grimsmead's town centre, the narrow back streets cobbled and winding, the main streets smooth, wide and paved in sand-coloured stone, their length teaming with people, some of them more animal than human.

"Park it down there." Meeks pointed at an open area behind a pitched, slate-roofed building. "Behind the Apothecarium."

"Isn't an apothecary like a chemist?" I asked. "A pharmacist? They're not doctors."

"Our medical system works a bit different here," Harvey said. "Try not to be too alarmed."

My mind boggled at the possibilities.

"You do know how to land this vehicle, right?" Harvey shuffled along and rested her front paws on my shoulders, her head alongside mine.

"Is there a special landing button?" I scanned the dashboard. All it held was the steering wheel. The floor sported the go pedal and the stop pedal. Maybe if I pressed them down at the same time? "What did Becca do?"

"She aimed the cart where she wanted to land and pressed the brake," Meeks said. "Softly and slowly. I think."

"You think!" Both Harvey and I spluttered.

We couldn't fly around forever. I mean, how long did flying crystals last before they needed refuelling?

Ploggit moaned.

I made a decision. At least we were near medical help

if anything bad happened. Thoughts of leeches, hot-cupping and blood-letting popped into my head. Surely Grimsmead wasn't that medieval?

I pressed the brake pedal. Not much, but enough to slow us to a wobbly hover as I steered the cart toward the open area behind the Apothecarium. The closer we got, the firmer I pressed. Cringing, closing my eyes, I planted my foot flat to the floor.

Harvey yowled. Meeks yelped as he toppled into me, his soft fur and warmth filling my lap. With a satisfying yet painful thud we landed, the front half of the croquet cart nestled in a bush, the rear end nice and straight on the stone-flagged parking area. Or was it a tarmac? From what I could see, there were no other car-like vehicles. A few brooms sat propped in something resembling a bicycle rack next to the Apothecarium's back wall, but that was it.

"We made it," I said. "Safe and sound."

"Barely." Meeks clambered out of my lap and jumped from the cart. "Can't say the bushes look pleased about it."

"Look at them as acceptable losses." I surveyed the bushes' snapped and shredded branches. "A quick prune, and they'll be up and growing in no time."

"You're not like any dryad I've ever known," Meeks grumbled. "They'd be all crying and hugging the thing, trying to love it back to health."

"I'm not like any dryad *I've* ever known." Since the only dryad I'd ever known was Rebecca, I wasn't kidding. A sharp ache blossomed in my chest, lodging in my throat. I'd never see Becca again. Given everything that had happened in the last couple of days, I hadn't had time to process her loss. The lump in my throat was so tight and painful I couldn't breathe. Tears filled my eyes. The parking area seemed to tilt. I grabbed the steering wheel, something solid and real.

"I didn't mean to offend you, Ding." Meeks sat by me, one paw resting on my arm.

"It's all right, sweetie." My voice broke. "I was thinking about Rebecca. I can't believe she's gone."

"As soon as we get Ploggit some help, we will find out what happened," Meeks said. "I'll rip the sod's gizzards out and make him eat them—would that make you feel better?"

"It's the thought that counts." I stroked his head. "But maybe we should leave the punishment to the F.C.T."

The words were hardly out of my mouth when a man on a broom landed a few feet away. Cropped black hair, long jacket, flying goggles and boots a bikie would be proud of. He didn't glance our way, but I was fairly certain it was the agent who'd been tailing us.

"Nice landing," I called. See I was no bad guy. Friendly, that's me.

"Can't say the same for yours." The man nodded at our cart, which was sitting half in and half out of the garden.

"I sneezed at the last moment." *Ooh good answer, Ding.*

"Happens." He dismounted and locked his broom into the parking rack beside the others. Without another word, he strode down a narrow lane between the Apothecarium and an adjacent building.

"Perhaps he wasn't following us." I got out of the croquet cart and picked up Ploggit.

"Perhaps." Harvey stared at the vacant laneway, her whiskers twitching, her tail flicking. "And perhaps that's who broke into our home, hurt Ploggit and stole the map and wooden tooth."

CHAPTER NINETEEN

The laneway was cobbled, dark and wonderfully cool as we hurried towards what looked like an open marketplace. Voices hawking wares rose and fell, carried on the murmured roar of conversation, laughter and hundreds of footfalls. Exotic spices, cooking meat and fragrant wood smoke wafted along the lane, making my mouth water.

The Apothecarium's wall to our right consisted of tightly stacked limestone blocks criss-crossed with forest-green moss. Three arched, stained glass windows sat head-high, the panes alive with flickering, gold firelight.

We exited the laneway. Squinting, blinded by the glare, I turned, searching for Harvey and Meeks. That was when I bumped into a tall, cloaked figure.

"Sorry." I peered upward, blinking, trying to focus. "Didn't see you there."

"You again."

It's that queen dragon lady! Despite the heat, I shivered. A pale face loomed above mine, amber eyes hard and cold as chips of sunlit ice. Her breath smelled of brimstone and roses. Weird combo for a toothpaste, but who was I to judge?

Her translucent skin glowed as though lit from within. She radiated heat that couldn't possibly be healthy. Probably had a raging furnace where her heart should be. Dragons breathed fire, so it had to smoulder somewhere inside. What baffled me was, where did they store the fire when prancing about in human form?

"Sorry. Sorry, your majesty." I held forth Ploggit, his battered and bruised body limp and forlorn. "We're in a hurry."

"You offering up a sacrifice?" The queen-dragon-lady laughed, a curl of sulphurous smoke escaping her lips. "I pick more appetising things from between my teeth. Where did you dredge up the vile creature?"

You really are horrible! "We need to go." I glanced at the Apothecarium's grimy front window. *Dalford Hrimm's Apothecarium - Established 287. Original Physician Still in Attendance. Enter and Ring the Bell for Service* arched across the glass in chipped gold lettering.

"If I were you," Dragon Queen said. "I'd feed the little beast to a griffon. Save yourself a lot of bother."

"Well, you are *not* me. And I *am* going to help my friend."

"Just like your sister. Rude, ignorant and arrogant."

"You can tell the difference between Rebecca and me?"

"You taste different."

I stepped backwards before I could stop myself.

Dragon Queen laughed again, a golden, fiery glow painting the inside of her mouth. "Better not follow her path, eh, or you might meet the same mysterious end."

"What do you mean by that?"

Meeks tugged my jeans, but I ignored his silent plea.

"What do you think I mean?" Dragon Queen eyed me

sourly and tossed her head, the golden bells wrapped about her horns tinkling. She stalked off, her green, scaled cloak billowing behind her as she wove between the rainbow of canvas stalls. Grimsmeadians (or were they Grimlings?) scrambled out of her way, their eyes wary and their mouths closed.

When she was out of sight, I gasped, my vision spinning a little. Threatened by the queen of the dragons— could this day get any worse?

I pushed open the Apothecarium's heavy wooden door, holding it ajar as Harvey and Meeks trotted inside. As the door closed behind us, darkness fell as if dropped from above. My eyes were certainly getting a workout today. I stood for a few moments, allowing my sight to adjust to the gloom. Details slowly emerged around me, shadowy and many of them unrecognisable. A bright scent of flowers, perhaps jonquils or freesias laced the darkness, a sweet smell compared to the musty air.

Hundreds of candles flared to life, some overhead in soot-stained chandeliers, others sitting in puddly wax nests that must have taken years and hundreds of candles to build. A sturdy counter stood halfway into the room, its rich, dark wood gleaming in the smokey, gold light. A bank of drawers, eight rows across and six drawers down, made up the side of the counter facing me. On top sat a polished slab of golden timber, easily ten feet long and four feet wide. As I walked closer, I noticed the drawer handles were iron reef knots. Or granny knots. I always got them muddled up.

"Ring the bell." Meeks flicked his tail, indicating a hangman's noose dangling from… nothing.

A magical noose. Nice touch for a place of healing and health. I tugged the frayed rope, and a bell clanged in the distance.

My fingers fizzed with tiny magical shocks. I scrubbed my hand down my dress and shivered.

"Death," Meeks said.

"What?" I frowned at the raxx.

"You're feeling the death sucked up by that rope."

"That's disgusting!" I rubbed my palm on my skirt again. I'd need a three-day-long shower by the end of today.

"Where are all the patients?" I looked around. "Or are we the only ones here?"

"Behind locked doors, I'd imagine," Harvey said cheerfully. "Safer that way."

When no one answered the bell, I cringed and pulled the noose again. The noose tugged back. How lovely! I was playing tug-o-war with a petulant hangman's noose. How many necks had it squeezed? Or broken? My palm prickled with icy pins and needles. I shook my hand, but the residue of death remained.

"How many times do I have to say it?" A nasally male voice shouted. "Can't you read? There are enough bleeding signs about!"

A squat shadow waddled toward us, his features clearing as he entered the light. Perhaps three feet tall and dressed like a Victorian funeral director in a black tuxedo with tails that swept the floor behind him, came what could only be a gnome. Twin sprays of ginger hair sprouted from the sides of his broad, wrinkled forehead. He stopped by a low, round table crowded with glass bottles and domes, reefed up a sign and hurried over to stand between Harvey and Meeks.

"**Don't** upset the fairies!" The apothecary shoved the sign up at me, waggling it about to make his point. "Can't you read?"

"The words on your sign are a tad more colourful than 'Don't Upset the Fairies'," I said.

He eyed me with annoyance over his wire-rimmed glasses. "I don't talk bold and brittle language when a lady is about."

As far as I could see, I was the only female in the place. I'd hardly call myself a lady.

"In my defence, the sign in the front window said to 'Ring the Bell for Service'."

"And you believed it?"

"Look, we need medical help for our friend here." I kneeled down and showed him Ploggit, who lay limp and moaning in my arms. "Are you Dalford Hrimm, the physician?"

"Are you stupid as well as blind, girl?"

"Can we save the attitude until after you fix Ploggit?" I kept my tone as polite as I could for Plog's sake.

"Snippy, this one is, eh?" Dalford nodded at me then looked at Harvey and Meeks, rolling eyes that were barely visible under his bushy ginger brows. "Well then," he said. "You better follow me. And mind how you go. I don't want my walking loaches and thistle fairies getting into another fist-strumping ruckus because you can't keep your voices down. Took me weeks to get the slime balls and ratchet burrs off the ceiling last time."

"Slime balls and ratchet burrs?" I whispered to Harvey with a look of disbelief.

The Apothecarium was far larger than I expected. From the outside structure, I had pictured a narrow, cluttered inte-rior, perhaps with a basement, or attic-room nestled beneath the pitched roof. Now I was inside, my mind boggled. Corridors led off in four directions like outstretched arms and legs, all stemming from this central chamber.

I peeked down the hallway to my left. Two life-size mummified figures flanked the corridor's arched entrance, each staring straight at me with glittering, green eyes.

"I hate how those mummies watch everything I do," Meeks muttered. "It's creepy."

Harvey nodded and shuffled around, so her back faced the mummies.

Dalford waved away Meek's words. "Prevents thievery."

I pulled my gaze from the mummies and noticed a vase of freesias, daffodils and jonquils on a shelf. So that's where the wonderful scent came from.

"Beautiful flowers," I said to Dalford. "They smell glorious."

"For my lady friend." He grinned, his eyes sparking, his thin-lipped mouth wider than I'd expected. "She loves perfume and flowers."

"You chose well."

"You'd expect anything less?" And Dalford was back to his grumpy self.

I glanced down the hallway again to see what other mysteries lurked there. Smokey lanterns jutted from the walls, their glass scratched and blackened, their washed-out light making shadows dance and lurch. Shelves, trunks and dusty, glass display cabinets lined either wall. This place was huge. There had to be magic at work. It was the only reasonable explanation.

"Just like the arboretum at the mausoleum," I whispered. "Rebecca lives in a magical house. Lived…"

I lowered my head and dragged in a ragged breath.

"Are you ill?" Dalford tugged on my skirt, peering up at me. "Your aura is all a-wish-wash. All muddy and locked to your body. Snaking around, like."

"Funny that," I said. "Because that's exactly how I

feel."

"She just found out her sister died." Meeks nipped at Dalford's tuxedo tails.

"Yes … Rebecca Ashford. Twins were you?" Dalford looked me up and down. "Hope not."

"What's that supposed to mean?" I rushed at the sour-faced little gnome.

Harvey and Meeks jumped between us, their front paws outstretched, blocking my attack.

Dalford Hrimm didn't flinch. He looked me over again and sniffed. "Definitely related. I suppose you'll be my herbal dealer now, girl?"

"You're joking!" I looked at Harvey, then Meeks. "He's joking, right?"

"I never jest about a physician's simples," Dalford said. "I hope you know your herbals?"

"I know mint goes in a Mojito and a Mint Julep. So, call me when it's cocktail hour."

"How do *you* know about Rebecca's death?" Harvey rose on her hind legs, so she stood eye to eye with the gnome.

"Her soul came to me," he said abruptly. "Needed to oomph her power so she could visit her sister–you," he pointed a fat little finger at me, "–so she could pass on a message."

"She came to me," I said. "But she didn't make sense."

"Was it her banshee soul or her dryad soul? Or were they still woven together?"

"How would I know? She looked like a banshee, but when she blasted through me, I smelled old-forest smells."

"Hmmm." Dalford tapped his pointy chin. "Sounds like she got through just in time."

I suddenly remembered the colours black and blue. They kept popping up everywhere I went. The leopard's fur. The stranger running from Cael's place with black and blue beads in their hair. The colours had to be clues about Rebecca's death.

"What do you know of shapeshifters?" I asked the gnome.

"Crafty blighters. Greedy. Hard to detect. For all I know, you could be one."

"Well, I'm not."

His answer didn't help me at all. "What about black and blue?" I asked.

"Like a bruise?"

"No, as a feature like hair, or fur or feathers? Or even beads?"

"No clue. Not my colours. I'm more of a chartreuse-and-green kind of gnome. According to the ladies, they bring out the colour of my eyes."

"Ooow!" Ploggit groaned.

"Sorry, Plog," I said. "We should be concentrating on you, not me."

With that, Dalford Hrimm trundled off again.

My boots scraped and scuffed on the dusty tiles as I followed him past shelves, drawers, cabinets and milky glass terrariums, all stuffed full of bottles, crystals, urns and dried, leathery wings, paws, ears and tails. *Pin the Tail on the Donkey* must be a real hoot at birthdays here in Grimsmead.

We stopped at a gap in the wall, the breach flanked by two ceiling-high bookshelves. A broad, square hole yawned in the floor, its pink inner edges spiked with what could only be called teeth. A stairwell? Or a mouth?

"I don't see any danger signs." Meeks glanced around. "Anyone could topple down that hole if they didn't know it was there."

I had to agree with Meeks. The only signs displayed warned not to disturb the fairies.

"I wouldn't have to feed Stepps if someone fell in, would I? A bright side to everything, I always say." Dalford flapped away Meek's comment.

"Not for the poor wretch who ends up as stair kibble." I edged closer to Stepps. I had to give Dalford credit. It was the perfect name for a set of stairs that had a mouth for an entrance, but it wasn't very imaginative. Clear liquid oozed over Stepps' fangs, dripping into the darkness below.

"Stepps' mouth is watering, you know!"

"What do you expect?" Dalford said. "You lot are a four-course banquet. Don't worry—Stepps has wonderful table manners. He won't start chewing until we say 'Grace.'"

"Wonderful!" I backed away. Better to be safe than dinner.

"You are indeed fortunate," Dalford said. "I just realigned and tuned my resonance chamber, so it's all ready for healing. Last case was simple but nasty—festering splinter. Dreadful things when they have a mind of their own. Worse when fools try to cut them out themselves. Just makes the splinter cranky."

I focused on the stairwell, rather than Stepps' teeth. Concave grey stone stairs descended into darkness. How many people had used those stairs to wear them down like that? Next to Stepps' open maw, in the bottom shelf of the right-hand bookcase, sat an open-top wooden crate, its insides padded with crimson cushions.

"Down we go, then." Dalford dragged the crate out, unlatched the front panel and hopped inside, nestling himself on the pillows. He grinned at me, his mouth alarmingly wide for his nobbly little head. "Give me the spriggit." He flapped his hands and nodded at his lap.

I placed Ploggit in with Dalford and stepped back while the gnome closed the front panel.

"See you at the other end."

"But it's dark," Harvey said. "How will Ding be able to see?"

"Not my problem." Dalford clicked his fingers, and the crate shot off down the stairs like a roller-coaster whooshing on nothing but air.

The 'Woohoo!' floated up Stepps' throat, along with a suspicious rumble of a hungry belly.

"At least if I fall I'll get a ride in his crate," I muttered.

CHAPTER TWENTY

The journey down the winding stairs wasn't as bad as I'd expected. With Harvey and Meeks guiding me and a firm grip on the handrail, I had managed the descent with only a few stumbles and no broken bones. Even better, Stepps had behaved himself, though drool did festoon the stairs and stone walls, and the stench of rancid meat hung heavy in the dank air. Disgusting, but not digesting. I had wondered where Stepps' stomach was located, but decided it was better not to know.

We found Dalford Hrimm bustling about a large stone chamber illuminated by hundreds of glowing crystals, some embedded in the rough-hewn walls, some floating free, clinking into one another, bowing and then moving on. Crystal etiquette, how enlightened. Shadows shrouded the ceiling. I don't know how I knew, but hidden within the gloom, eyes watched my every move. I shivered and fought the urge to look up.

Instead, I focused on what could only be called a cave. It had no fancy panelling, paint or adornment, but I had never seen a place so pretty.

Silver bird cages bobbed amongst the crystals, some basic enclosures and others filigree masterpieces, all with knotted hair and dried herbs tied will-nilly on the bars. Wisps of light zipped around inside some of the cages, crystals bobbed about in others.

"Why are some of the crystals caged?" I whispered to Harvey. My skin tingled and the hairs on my arms stood on end as though electrically-charged-air filled the cavern.

"Troublemakers, obviously." Dalford Hrimm dragged a three-stepped box out from under a scarred timber workbench.

"Obviously," I murmured, fascinated by the magical light show.

Why the wisps and crystals didn't slip between the bars was beyond me. One cage was more iron box than cage, its battered sides rusted and punctured with random holes which glowed a faint crimson in the gloom. Goodness knows what was trapped in that one.

Groaning with effort, the gnome knelt on the ground where the steps had been. He tapped the packed-earth with his stumpy little fingers. I heard a click, then a grinding sound, and he raised a trapdoor. I peered into the dark hole, but couldn't see anything. Dalford fished around inside, grunted with relief and lifted free an iron chest the size of a loaf of bread, its sides braided in silver, its lid carved with symbols. He got up, closed the trapdoor with one foot, tucked the chest under one arm and shuffled up the three steps. He jumped onto the workbench, set the chest down and huddled over it.

"Turn away!" Dalford snapped. "Can't have you lot seeing my unlocking spell."

Harvey and Meeks turned their backs, but I could tell from their swishing tails they were as pleased about it as I was.

"What could you have stuffed in there that's so valuable?" I turned away. On impulse, I grabbed my mobile phone, tapped the camera app and chose video mode, recording discreetly under my arm. A little rude, but I needed every clue I could find.

"None of your never mind," Dalford said. He murmured under his breath. A flash of lime green light bloomed around us along with the smell of brimstone. A series of clicks and clacks followed that had to be the magical locking mechanism.

"You can turn back now," Dalford said. "I have what I need."

"All that for a stick?" I regarded him with disbelief.

"And you a dryad!" Dalford glared at me. "Have you no schooling whatsoever?"

"Half dryad," I said. "And I've had plenty of schooling, just not here in Grimsmead."

"No! I'd never have guessed!" He jiggled the stick in the air and green sparks zapped from the tip. A twenty-foot-high crystal pyramid shimmered into view, its side joins capped in what looked like silver, its top crowned with swirling cobalt-blue light. Occasionally, as the light misted and swam around the pyramid's summit, I saw a golden cap-stone. Ploggit lay on a soft and squashy mattress inside the crystal edifice, his poor little body barely visible behind the mattress mounds.

"You okay in there, Plog?" I shouted.

The spriggit brownie raised a skinny arm and gave us a feeble wave.

Dalford harrumphed. He pointed his precious stick up at the floating crystals. "You six, time for work!"

They zipped down, hovering in front of him, bumping one another out of the way, their inner glow flickering excitedly.

"Seems they're eager to get started," I said.

"Where did you get that idea?"

"The crystals—look at them. They all want to be first."

"You're not very bright, girl." Dalford grabbed for the blue lace agate, but it dodged, knocking the rose quartz into Dalford's fat little hand.

And you're just plain rude! "Wait! Those crystals really are alive?"

"What do you think makes them so medicinal?" Dalford looked at me as though I was an imbecile.

"Are they sentient? Do they know what's happening?"

"Why else do you think they don't want to be first into the glory-box?" He stomped a foot three times on the workbench, waggled his stick and an ornate silver trunk ghosted up through the stone floor and bench to hover next to Dalford. He tapped the chest, and instantly, it solidified.

"So, you murder the crystals to heal someone else."

"A bit harsh, but you could say that."

"It's not murder, Ding," Harvey said. "Not as you know it. Their energy is released and harnessed. It still exists, just in a new form."

"How nice for them." I cast a sidelong glance at the six crystals. It felt rude to stare. Their glow had dimmed. Sulking, most probably. I recognised the crystals—or at least I thought I did. Rhodonite, amethyst, fluorite, a fist-sized piece of viviante, rose quartz and blue lace agate. Although, they could've been totally different than those we had on Earth.

"What have you heard about Rebecca's disappearance?" Harvey leaped up onto the workbench.

"Last time I saw her, she was in a tizzy about Cael Blightly," Dalford flipped open the glory-box, revealing empty slots and a jumble of leather straps. All six crystals, now clutched under his arm, wiggled as though trying to escape. "She said he was dealing in protected antiquities and illegal magical paraphernalia."

"How long ago was that?" Meeks asked.

"Maybe a week. She came to deliver an order of simples."

"What about a shapeshifter?" Meeks added.

"No. Heard nothing about that. But, Rebecca was concerned about her grandmother—"

"The one in the nursing home?" I had only heard of one. Perhaps I had other grandparents getting about.

"The very same," Dalford said. "Rebecca was worried someone was upsetting her—pushing her for information about the family home."

"Do you know whom?"

"Knola—Cael's wife. Offering the old girl gifts and things. Taking her for walks into the forest. Knola reckoned the nature strolls were helping your grandmother regain her memories, being she's a dryad. But all it really did was get her all fidgety and stroppalised."

I assumed that meant cranky.

"So maybe Cael and his wife were working together." Meeks trotted back and forth beside me, his bushy, ringed tail flicking in irritation. "She works in Ward One at the nursing home. We *need* to check her out as soon as possible."

"One more thing," I said. "What did *you* think of Rebecca?"

"Everyone loved her," Dalford said.

"You didn't answer my question."

"I did."

"You said, 'Everyone loved her,' nothing about how you felt."

"If you must know, I thought she was uppity and

condescending—always looking down on us wee folk. A little like you." Dalford scowled at me over the top of his glasses.

"You're three feet tall."

"You know what I mean."

"Maybe that stems from your issues, not mine."

"Dalford," Harvey said. "Where were you at the time Rebecca disappeared? Exactly."

"Can't say."

"Can't or won't?" Meeks lowered his head, watching Dalford suspiciously.

"Can't. Don't know exactly when that was. You tell me the exact time, and I'll check my diary."

Harvey caught my gaze and sighed, shaking her fluffy head.

The snippy little gnome had vexed Harvey's attempt to narrow down the time of Rebecca's disappearance. A fact we were still unclear about.

I glanced at Ploggit, half-swallowed by the puffy mattress. "How long does this healing thing take?" I felt bad for asking, but desperation boiled inside me. I had to get to that nursing home as soon as possible.

"Oh, a day or so." Dalford shuffled through the crystals, scrutinising each one.

"A day!"

"Or so." Dalford tapped the fluorite and licked it, smacking his lips as if checking the magical seasoning trapped within.

"We have to get to the nursing home," Meeks said. "Before something happens to your grandmother."

"Surely Knola wouldn't hurt her." I struggled not to pace the floor. "I mean, everyone working at the home would suspect her. Out in the woods alone together. And after my sister's…" I drew in a shuddering breath. The healing room suddenly felt hot, stuffy and confining.

"What if Knola isn't really Knola?" Harvey said. "What if she's the shapeshifter?"

"For all I know *you* could be the shapeshifter." Meeks stopped pacing and looked at Harvey, one eye narrowed. He turned his gaze on me. "Or you! Or maybe even Ploggit."

We all stared at the spriggit brownie lying inside the pyramid. He had been off somewhere after we returned to Grimsmead. Could shapeshifters make themselves look all bruised and broken? Black and blue…Made sense that they could. If it could change shape, colouring and size it could be Ploggit.

No, surely not! I pushed the horrible thought away. I couldn't allow paranoia to cloud my thinking. Besides, I knew the shapeshifter was female. Ploggit was a male. But, could shapeshifters change gender?

"What about that developer?" Harvey's question interrupted my thoughts. "We heard he was at odds with Rebecca about the land development by the lake."

"Hywell Rowlands?" Dalford snorted. "I'd say he's capable of anything. He's an 'end-justifies-the-means' sort of ogre. A scapper of the worst kind. Funded by an Old Blood family to develop some land by Lake Mead."

"He's an actual ogre?" My eyes widened. Going up against him suddenly seemed a lot more scary than I had imagined. But, if I was going to find Rebeca's murderer, I would have to scope him out. I couldn't count on the cops to do a thorough job, not if Ava Cadwaller was involved with the investigation. She could have killed Rebecca so she could have Walker to herself.

"Unless Hywell Rowlands is the shapeshifter," Harvey said.

"I'm pretty sure the shapeshifter is female," I said. "So how could it be Hywell Rowlands?"

"Shapeshifters can be anything they choose. Male or female makes no never mind to them," Meeks said. "It doesn't take much to put on a fake voice."

I slumped against the workbench. All those years wishing I could live in a fantasy world now seemed stupid. I wasn't ready for Grimsmead and all its mysteries and magic. What I would give to go home to plain old Earth.

CHAPTER TWENTY-ONE

The Apothecarium's front doorbell clanged, echoing down through Stepps into the healing cave. The crystals swanning around above jerked to a stop, trembling, their inner glow shrinking into pinpricks of dull light.

"Blast and blow it!" Dalford Hrimm scowled. "You go and see who it is, girl. Tell them to come back later."

"What if they're really sick? Or injured?"

"Then tell them to come back sooner."

"Hrimm!" A voice roared from above. "Where are you, you sly little bog-trotter?"

Dalford tutted and rolled his eyes as he struggled to shove the rose quartz into a slot in the glory-box. He fumbled for the leather strap, the silver buckle jingling between his knobbly fingers.

"It's Hywell Rowlands," Dalford snapped. "Curse the leathery old rotter. He'll want his belly medicinals. They're in a black stone box under my service counter. Give him three vials and no more. If he grumbles, give him two."

I froze. Me tending an ogre. Serve him a drink maybe,

but nurse him? Still, it would give me a chance to question him about my sister. I looked at Harvey for support, and she padded toward the stairs, stopping to look back at me. "Come on then." She wasn't fazed at all.

I wanted to grab her and smush my face into hers like I used to. But, now I knew she was no ordinary cat, I felt uncomfortable even thinking such a thing.

"What are you waiting for, girl?" Dalford jabbed a thumb at the stairs. "You want him to punch a hole in my floor?"

"He couldn't do that!" I looked at Harvey and Meeks. "Could he do that?"

"He's a rock ogre." Meeks shrugged. "It's what they do."

I imagined Hywell Rowlands with fists of dynamite and flaming breath to ignite them. Cripes!

Meeks nudged my leg with his nose. "You go. I'll watch this one." He scowled at the gnome. "To make sure he doesn't change out the crystals for used ones."

Dalford squawked as the stubborn rose quartz wriggled free of the half-buckled straps and shot into the air, trying to lose itself in amongst its comrades. They formed ranks, blocking its escape. Comrades my foot!

The gnome leaped a good seven feet into the air, arm outstretched, grabbing the crystal before it had a chance to dash into the darkness.

What on earth? But I wasn't on Earth, so a high-vaulting gnome seemed quite reasonable.

"Why don't the crystals escape if they're so miserable?" I headed up Stepps, Harvey by my side.

"Net trap," Harvey said, her voice fluttering in soft echoes.

"I can't see any net."

"You're not a crystal."

"Can't argue with that."

Stepps' mouth loomed above as we mounted the worn stairs, drool dripping down the walls like ewwwy rain. Once we neared the exit, Harvey and I shared a worried glance and bolted out of Stepps into the Apothecarium's storefront.

Hywell Rowlands bellowed, "Dalford! Get your stumpy waddle-butt out here!"

"What an insolent, arrogant…" I stared. "Mountain."

The rock ogre had to be twelve feet tall, his hide the colour of weathered grey granite, his muddy-brown hair braided and studded with bones and rainbow crystals, each plait tied with a bright red ribbon. How cheery!

Greasy furs draped his hunched shoulders, beneath which lay a simple green tunic laced at the neck. Yellowed tusks spiked through the shoulder-furs, three on each side. Whether they were part of the furs or grew from his shoulders was unclear. Ankle length leather breeches clad his thick, stocky legs, the bottoms lashed tight with dried sinew.

He turned to face me, his heavy black boots sending little sparks as they scraped metal on stone tiles. How the rock ogre had managed to fit into the Apothecarium was beyond me. But, there he was jammed between the old timber counter and shelves of wax-sealed ceramic pots.

Soft, agitated, "shushing," floated through the shop. Probably from Dalford Hrimm's high-strung fairies. I almost hoped for a flurry of ratchet-burrs to rain down on the ogre, but the fairies kept their missiles to themselves. I guess they knew better than to upset him. Pity. I really wanted to know what ratchet-burrs were.

"You!" Hywell Rowlands rumbled, pointing at me. "Aren't you supposed to be dead?"

"You sound disappointed." Harvey stalked to within pounding-distance of the ogre.

Brave kitty! Reckless kitty.

"Enormous kitty!" I whispered, my eyes widening as Harvey morphed into a tawny, sabre tooth tiger complete with black stripes, shaggy fur and neatly folded wings. Way to level up, Harvey!

How did something so big fit into a cat? There had to be some pretty nifty folding and tucking involved.

"I'd mind your manners, Rowlands." Harvey leaped onto the timber countertop and flopped down onto her side. She sounded like Harvey, only deeper, more velvety. Her purr vibrated through my chest. The counter seemed smaller, less impressive with Harvey draped over it.

"I might have guessed." Hywell squared himself, the wax-sealed pots wobbling and knocking together on their shelves behind him. He raised his stone-like chin. "A mooncat. Always sticking their wet, slimy noses into other peoples' affairs. You don't scare me—you with your black blood and ill-gotten powers."

Harvey arched her back, every muscle rippling beneath her fur. "I could have you arrested for those words alone."

"Threats, is it? I know how you Old Ones stick together."

"What ails you, ogre?" Harvey asked. "Why are you here?"

"Got me pains again." Hywell Rowlands rubbed his stomach. "Need my special medicinals to settle it. Where's Hrimm? He knows what I like."

I scuttled around the serving counter, looking in drawer after drawer for the black stone box. I found bundled feathers, vials of iridescent green slime, dragonfly (or were they fairy?) wings pinned in velvet boxes, jewel-like and shimmering in the candlelight. There were gnarly roots bound in threes by braided leather, dried frogs, their mouths agape with a hairy-looking stone wedged between their gums.

Hope I never get sick in this town!

I pulled out another drawer and discovered wax-sealed glass bottles filled with yellowish liquid. Each bottle contained an eyeball, the green-blue blood vessels and pink tendrils still attached. As I peered at them, the eyes swivelled around and glared at me. I slammed the drawer shut.

I am going to have nightmares for months!

Out of the corner of my eye, I could see the ogre squinting at me. "How did you rise, banshad?" Hywell's deep, gravely voice thrummed though my whole body.

I glanced at Harvey, unsure what the ogre meant. How did I rise? I pulled open more drawers—still no black stone box. I wished Dalford had been more specific with his directions.

"What's it to you?" Harvey's green-gold eyes flashed shrewdly in the candlelight.

"Curious is all. Why have a whole troop of F.C.T. agents poking about the forest looking for your body if you're alive?"

"Have they found anything?" I looked directly at the ogre. Brave, no. Desperate, yes. "Do you know anything about Rebecca's death?"

He cocked his head. "Who are you, banshad? If you're not that mouthy Rebecca, then you gotta be kin. Close kin. Sister? Ah yes! I see it now."

"My sister is not mouthy."

"Really? She led the protesters down by the lake. Trying to stop my development, curse her. Got most of Grimsmead behind her, including two of the Old Blood families. Delays are costing a fortune in holding costs."

"I heard you were funded by a rich Old Blood family."

"I have partners in the venture—equal partners. We sunk a fortune into environmental studies, council fees and the like. Pulling out of the deal now would mean financial disaster."

"Seems to me," I said, "you have more than enough motive to kill my sister. And the means. And, no doubt the opportunity." The room began to spin. I toppled to one side, catching myself on the counter before I fell over. I don't know if it was anger, fear, grief or exhaustion that caused me to feel so wonky. Probably the whole lot.

A heavy paw rested on my shoulder, heat rolling through me. The dizziness passed.

"So now you know who I am," I said each word carefully, trying to calm down. "Do you know anything—anything at all that could help me find my sister's killer? Please."

"Hmmph." The ogre looked me over, his lipless mouth twitching. He scratched his chin. "Seems as you said please … I saw her arguing with that blue-haired verge—the one who works for the F.C.T." He spat a laugh. "Nasty little thing when she gets cranky. Clobbered your sister so hard she fell over."

"Did you tell the F.C.T. this?" I stepped forward, all fear replaced with the need to know.

"Are you joking?" Hywell's eyes widened. "I'm not a fool. I like my head where it is."

"Are you saying F.C.T. agents are in on this?"

"Could be." He shrugged, the furs across his shoulders rippling as though they were still alive. "But I'm more concerned the verge will track me down if she knows I was spying on them when she cracked your sister across the jaw."

I'd figured Ava Cadwaller was powerful, but I'd never imagined a rock ogre quaking in his furs about her.

"Why were you spying on them?" I asked.

"A good developer keeps his enemies close. Saves a lot of time when you can counter their ploys and legal injunctions."

"Killing off enemies would also save you time and money."

"I like how you think, banshad. But I'm a law-abiding citizen, despite the rumours flying about Grimsmead."

"And your partners in this venture?"

"The Thorntons?"

There was that name again. "Yes, the Thorntons. Would they kill to bring in a business deal?"

"Centuries ago, they would have done whatever it took. Wouldn't have flinched. But times have changed. Especially since they set up the F.C.T. Ah, I miss the good ol' days. A bit of blood-play was how you knew you were alive. Now, it's all about laws and rules. And I abide by them. More or less."

"From your mouth to god's ears. Where were you when Rebecca disappeared?"

"Same place I always am. At work."

"Your work could take you anywhere." Harvey admired her huge paws. I suppose I would too if I had claws like small curved daggers.

"I was in my office." Hywell crossed his arms. "Doing paperwork."

"And do you have witnesses to verify your claim?"

"Yes. But don't think I'm narking on them to a lowly banshad. You ain't the law."

"Have you found Hywell Rowland's medicinals yet?" Harvey caught my eye, nodding slightly. A subtle push to hurry up.

After a few more drawers, I finally found the black stone box. With a triumphant grin, I placed it on the countertop and flipped the lid open, showing off rows of vials, each sealed by turquoise wax.

The ogre let out a grunt of approval. Or it could have been relief. It was hard to read him. Not surprising, considering he was the first rock ogre I'd ever met. I dispensed three vials and held them out. My hand hardly shook at all. Look at me go!

"Only three?"

I took one away, hiding it behind my back.

"Blast and bodkins!" Hywell snatched the two vials from my palm. "Did that gnat of an apothecary tell you how many to give me?"

"He's the boss." I cringed, waiting for the ogre to throw a tantrum. He seemed the type. An idea popped into my head. "If I give you more medicine, will you tell me where the F.C.T. are searching in the woods, and where Ava Cadwaller attacked my sister?"

Harvey stayed quiet, her tail twitching, her ears pricked.

"How many we talking?" Hywell's murky brown eyes sparkled with excitement.

"Double your regular dose."

"Add two more, and I'll draw you a map."

"Make it a map of the forest with all the Old Bloods' estates marked and any mining claims, and you've got a deal."

"Can't say it'll be accurate. I'm not privy to their exact locale."

"A big shot like you?" I fluttered my eyelashes. Not my usual mode-of-operation, but I somehow knew this fellow responded well to flattery and flirtation. "I was sure you'd be their go-to ogre for such sensitive information." I almost gagged.

"I'll do my utmost, but just so's you know—there are no

mining claims in the forest." Hywell's clay-like lips split into a grin. His fangs glinted in the candlelight, the top middle two boasting a pair of diamonds. A bit garish for my taste, but they were sparkly.

"Then we have a deal?" I wiggled the box.

"Indeed we do!"

CHAPTER TWENTY-TWO

I flew the pink croquet cart above the forest, looking for the easiest place to land. A large open area would have been great, but all I saw were trees, Lake Mead's shimmering waters and more trees.

Harvey sat beside me on the bench seat. She was once again a Maine Coon. I'd asked her why she didn't fly beside the cart, you know, stretch her wings a little, but she had just growled and said that would be showing off. Perhaps she just needed some encouragement.

"Why don't you grow your wings and tow me down to the ground? Just a quick flight. There's no one around, so you wouldn't be showing off." I prodded Harvey in the ribs, grinning widely. "Come on! It'd be fun."

"And then you'll never learn how to fly."

"Spoilsport."

"Look!" Harvey pointed to the right with her tail. "There's the nursing home."

Spell Haven Nursing Home, when viewed from above, was a confusion of grey-slate peaks and valleys, round towers with conical roofs and awkward-looking outcroppings fashioned of white stone and dark-timber frames. I was no architect, unless you counted my famous sandcastles, but this place looked like it had evolved over time, all to accomodate a humongous sequoia tree that rose through the jumbled roof. It looked like enthusiastic five-year-olds had built the home from Legos, scraps of wood and piled pebbles.

Stone gargoyles perched in pairs on the eaves, all fangs, talons and moss-covered wings. One sat apart from the others, his wings droopy, his head bowed, his expression bleak. Who knew what had happened to its partner. Off on an errand? Divorced?

I pulled Hywell Rowland's map from under my backside and spread the rumpled paper across the steering wheel. Yep, there was the nursing home: a bunch of squares and circles with a stick tree in the centre. So where was the Thornton Estate? I didn't see anything that I remembered from my last appearance in the woods.

"I wish you could just tell me where the estate is." I gave Harvey a grumpy look.

"I can only show you where it was before I left for Earth."

"Building houses that roam the woods is just plain stupid."

"They don't roam the woods. You make it sound like they meander around every other day. It takes years. Houses don't scroll through every mood in a few hours like you do. You're like a slot machine some days, Ding."

"Now you're being rude."

"And you're being unreasonable. These houses are ancient. Sentient. They feel emotions, draw them in from the families that dwell within. From the very bedrock beneath their foundations."

"Well, changing locations seems rather drastic to me."

"You like going on vacations—a change of scenery now and then."

I thought of Rebecca and I on our last holiday together. Harvey had a point. "Fine, you're right."

Harvey sat a little taller, her chin a little higher.

"I saw that eye roll," I said without looking at her. "Pride's a sin you know."

"So is a smart mouth."

Ouch.

"Landing might be a good idea," Harvey said sweetly.

"I can think of a few good ideas—none you'd enjoy, though."

"There!" Harvey pointed her tail at a patch of grass on the banks of Lake Mead. "You can set down there, can't you?"

"And if I overshoot?"

"Then there's lots of room in the lake. Come on, you're wasting time."

"Time we don't have. I know. I still haven't figured out a plan for when we get to the Thornton place. Any ideas?"

"They're Old Blood. I don't think it's wise to go up against them. Not until we know more."

"You're Old Blood. Didn't you have fancy get-togethers? Soirees for the rich and snooty? Can't you say you're just coming for a cup of tea to catch up?"

"The Thorntons are Old Blood. We're Ancient. It wouldn't be seemly."

"Prehistoric ancient?"

Harvey sniffed. She stared ahead, quiet, every strand of fur still despite the wind rushing through the cart.

"Yes," she said finally. "As old as that."

"Then how did you end up looking after Rebecca and me? What did you do wrong?" I made it a joke.

"I'll not speak of it. Ever."

Once again, my big mouth, working its destructive magic.

"I think we should go to Spell Haven first," Harvey said. "Look into Cael's wife. Check out Ward One. Meet your grandmother."

"But we'd planned to go there after the Thornton place."

"The little voice in my head said to change our plans. And my little voice is rarely wrong."

I almost said 'her little voice' had to be wrong sometimes, or she wouldn't have been put on babysitting duty, but I held my tongue. See, I could learn from my mistakes.

"You're nervous about meeting your grandmother," Harvey said. "Aren't you?"

"Oh, cripes!" With everything that'd gone on, I hadn't given the actual meeting of my grandmother much thought. What a rotten granddaughter I was. "Well *now* I'm worried. Thanks a bunch."

I settled upon Harvey's suggested lakeside landing site. It was the only area suitable for someone with my marvellous fly-driving skills. I eased on the brake, steering the cart toward the shoreline, one eye open, the other squeezed closed in apprehension.

"Yes, because one-eyed flying is the perfect way to land safely," Harvey said with a sniff.

"All back-seat drivers should vacate the vehicle immediately. Especially those who refuse to grow wings."

We hit the ground with a thump, bounced three times and ended up with water lapping my boots. All things considered, I declared it a first-class landing.

With my skirt swashing about in the water, I dragged the cart out of the lake onto the grassy bank, chocking the wheels with a couple of hefty stones in case it rolled away.

"Should I anchor it?" I placed my hands on my hips, frowning at the cart. "It might take off without us."

"You think a lemur will pop into the driver's seat and say, 'Beam me up, Scotty'?"

I pulled a face. "Stop looking at me like that. I'm learning as fast as I can, here!"

A heavily wooded spit of land protruded out into the lake about one hundred paces away. Thin curls of smoke broke through the treetops, torn away by the breeze. I folded Hywell Rowlands' hand-drawn map and tucked it down my boot.

"So, everyone, remember where we parked." I flicked a hand indicating the weeping willows, a fallen log that was more moss than bark, and the finger of land.

Harvey looked at me as if I was a total dimwit. "Come on, let's get going before you start putting up signs and direction arrows."

As soon as we entered the tree line, I shivered. Every cell in my body fizzed and my mind cleared. I felt like I had dived into a glass of champagne, and it had infused every bit of my body.

"This forest is old," I whispered. "I can feel the weight of it. Almost hear its memories."

"Older than you can imagine."

"Is this near where Hywell Rowlands wants to build his little empire?"

"From what I've heard, you'd be standing waist-deep in his swimming pool."

"How could you possibly know that? We only just arrived back in Grimsmead."

Harvey ignored me. Again. So, I continued on, regardless.

"Why have a pool when the lake is right there?"

"Yes, and the bar is just there." Harvey nodded toward a patch of soft, green ferns.

"In the middle of the pool—figures."

"Apparently, it's considered 'upmarket' and lures in the holiday-makers."

"I prefer the lake to a pool. I'm obviously down-market."

"You wouldn't want to swim in Lake Mead." Harvey's whiskers bristled. "Not a place for the young and unlived."

"Unlived?"

"Not enough years under their belt, so to speak."

"Rebecca?" A woman of silver light and swirling mist drifted between the trees, floating towards me.

Ghost? No. She radiated a vibrancy and sensuality no ghost could muster. The only other creature I could think of formed of iridescent air was a sylph, one of the five elementals that make up the natural world. In all the fantasy books I'd read, Air, Fire, Earth, Water and Spirit all had their own elemental race.

"I'm not Rebecca." My reply was harsher than I intended. "I'm her younger sister. Arabella."

"My apologies. Have you come to join us?"

"Join?"

"The protest."

"Against Hywell Rowlands?"

"I refuse to speak his name."

"Fair enough. Were you friends with Rebecca?"

"She's one of my closest."

"She is dead, you know. Murdered."

The sylph's silvery light dimmed, her misty body falling still. No one could fake such a reaction.

"You didn't know." I felt rotten for springing the terrible news on her, but I'd wanted to gauge her reaction. Her involvement, if any.

Shame and anger ripped though me and my face flushed with heat. I'd become so suspicious since arriving in Grimsmead. "I'm sorry. I thought you knew." I lied, and my shame swelled.

"What's your name?" Harvey asked, her tone soft and caring.

"Issalsyr."

"Did anyone threaten Rebecca, Issalsyr?" Harvey asked softly.

"She got a note that upset her terribly. It wasn't signed, but we all suspected that… resort developer."

"What did this note say?" I suddenly wished I'd laced Hywell Rowland's belly medicine with belladonna and nightshade.

"To back off or face the consequences."

"Back off Rowlands' development?"

"I'm not sure. But that's what we all thought. Rebecca wasn't convinced. She thought the writing had more of a woman's touch."

"Hywell's secretary, perhaps," Harvey said, but from her expression, she wasn't convinced.

"Ava Cadwaller!" I said. "I bet it was her. She's got a thing for Walker Kane, you know."

"Would she kill to keep him?" Harvey said, skeptical. "*If* she ever had him."

I didn't know if Harvey sounded bitter or dubious, but I had a feeling there was something in her past that coloured her opinion.

"That verge turned up at our camp a few times," Issalsyr said. "Arrested Rebecca more than once—even when she wasn't manning the picket line. Said she was the ring-leader."

"There you go! Misusing her position in the F.C.T.!" I said. "Even Hywell was frightened of her. Said verges are really powerful. I reckon she is up to her blue-bob-haircut in Rebecca's murder. *And* she could steer the investigation any way she wanted to. She could do that mind-melding thing with suspects and tell Walker a heap of rubbish—put the blame on anyone. I don't recall what she saw in my memories—lost all recollection of the verge-merge within a few hours. She had plenty of opportunity to plant evidence and pass the blame. Do you remember what she saw in your mind, Harvey?"

"Not anymore."

"There you go, then."

"Would you like to come and meet the rest of us?" Issalsyr said.

"Maybe later, if that's all right?" I said. "We have to visit my grandmother in Spell Haven first. Then we have a few other errands to run."

"She's a lovely dryad," Issalsyr said. "Confused, but when you get her out in the woods, she really comes to life. A shame she lost her son and daughter-in-law like she did. It destroyed her heart and mind."

"My real mother and father," I whispered, a dull ache rising in my chest.

"Such a tragedy," the sylph said. "And so unexpected. They were in glorious love, you know. Didn't care what anyone said about their union. Banshee and dryad—a first in our world. For him to kill her and then try and murder you and Rebecca—it never made sense. It's good he's gone, if you ask me."

It suddenly dawned on me that I didn't know my parents' names. How could I not know their names? I turned to Harvey. "What were they called?"

"Your mother was Vanara. And your father was Druash."

I remembered what Ava Cadwaller said about my

mother's name. "Does Vanara really mean 'Weeping Mother'?"

Harvey nodded. "Unfortunately."

I sighed. "Figures. I suppose we should go, now. We still have a lot to do. Oh!" I remembered Endraya, the ghost that had visited me on Earth. "I'm sorry to tell you this, but did you know that Endraya is also dead? I guess you knew her, too?"

"I knew her." The sylph, frowned sending tiny ripples across her forehead. "But she died over a year ago."

"That's not possible!" Harvey said.

"It's the truth. A horrible hunting accident. Her body was found days after she went missing by the lake near Willows, not far from the Finger.

"Who found her body?" I asked.

"Hywell Rowlands. He was surveying our land for his dreadful resort."

Harvey and I shared a worried look. If Endraya had died more than a year ago, then how was it she'd been with Rebecca only a few days ago? Perhaps she hadn't crossed over and was drawn to Becca? Lost souls often trailed after those of us who can see them. But, Endraya had seemed like she was Becca's friend. It didn't make any sense. Unless you factored in the time difference between Earth and this world?

"We think Endraya was murdered by Rowlands because she stumbled on him doing something shifty," Issalsyr said, interrupting my troubled thoughts. "But we could never prove it."

"Wouldn't surprise me," I muttered. "Money and power can buy silence."

"So can many things." Issalsyr shook her head sadly. "Mayhap we will see you later? Our headquarters is on the

Finger. A few of us remain there each night in case that nasty Rowlands tries to murder more trees."

"Thanks, Issy," I said. "Do you mind if I call you that?"

Issalsyr laughed, a haunting sound that raised goose-bumps along my skin. "That's what Rebecca calls me. Called me…" The joy in her ethereal face vanished, and then she shot off into the forest.

"I think we should investigate Spell Haven undercover," I said. "Say we're there to visit my granny—it's the truth after all. That way, we can ask questions without arousing suspicion."

"Sounds reasonable."

"Why do you sound so surprised?"

"Because you are rarely reasonable."

I grumped along a narrow winding track, ducking under branches and stepping around fallen logs and knee-high mushrooms. I could almost set up house in those things they were so big. I didn't notice any windows, doors or miniature mail-boxes decorating the mushrooms, so I figured they were your every day, blue-capped, gold-speck-led, cream-stalked, foot-tall fungi. Suddenly, I accidentally bumped into a mushroom and luminescent blue spores showered my boot, making it glow in the dark. Every time I ventured out into Grimsmead I found some new surprise.

"Wish Meeks was here," I said, more to myself than Harvey.

I had only known the raxx a couple of days, but I missed him trotting along beside us, nose to the ground, snarky comments at the ready. He had agreed to stay with Ploggit and watch out for any suspicious shapeshifter behaviour. Better him than me, I suppose. A shapeshifter could walk right past me and I'd be none the wiser. Meeks had also agreed to check out *Good Hunting*, the store where

Cael had bought that bow and quiver of twelve handmade arrows. I was fairly sure one of those fancy arrows had ended up in poor Endraya's head.

We walked along a path edged by low-growing ferns, the packed soil giving way to herringbone pavers splashed with broken shadow and sunlight.

"Well, here we are," Harvey said. "Spell Haven."

Ahead, squatting amongst the trees, sat the facility. Four stories tall, more glass than wall, the higgledy-piggledy white-stone building spread in all directions like an immense, broken spider. The only sections that looked as though an architect had been involved were the entrance porch and the four floors directly above. From the amount of ivy growing on the walls, it must have been the original building.

"They really like their windows here in Grimsmead," I said. "Style comes before privacy, I guess."

"Bespelled glass lets light in and keeps prying eyes out."

"Neat! I've never seen trees bursting out of a roof before. What if a bushfire rages through here? Spell Haven would be toast."

"You're thinking like a human again, Ding."

"I don't know any other way to think."

I saw no signage announcing Spell Haven. No information about the place at all.

"See that black, pitched roof behind Spell Haven?" Harvey said. "That's Grimsmead's mental health facility. And over there in that mushroom-shaped building–" she twitched her tail, the tip pointing to the right of the nursing home. "–that's the beauty spa, *As You Wish*. I've never needed their expertise." She raised her head regally and strode toward Spell Haven.

"How about the loony bin?" I followed her along the path. "Ever needed their expertise?"

Harvey glared at me. I couldn't tell if she was mortified, or if I had touched a raw nerve.

I'd have to ask Meeks if he knew anything. I hated it when I didn't know a secret. Curiosity always chewed me up.

At the end of the pathway, we mounted five cream-tiled stairs flanked by two white marble columns and stepped onto an entrance porch, the expanse lit by two flaming sconces. How medieval! A pair of twelve-feet-high ebony-dark timber doors loomed before us, the polished wood decorated with bronze strapping and fist-sized bolts. A doormat as long as the doors were wide lay in the fluttering shadows. Creepy as well as medieval.

"Ring the bell," Harvey said. "That chain with the handle, give it a pull."

I stepped forward, reaching for the handle–thankfully not noose-shaped this time–and heard a yelp from below my boots. I stumbled back, gathering up my skirt as I stared down at the doormat.

"Oy! Gee! One at a time, please!" A brusque woman's voice snapped, her words flashing across the mat in a wonky, black text.

Of course! A self-narrating welcome mat.

"Well, that was rude!" I nudged the mat with my boot. I really wanted to stomp on it, so I was impressed by my restraint. "I'm only 112 pounds–the size of one perfectly normal woman."

"You're neither normal nor a woman." Doormat guffawed and a large laughing emoticon pulsed on its bristly coir surface.

My mind flashed back to Cael Blightly's stolen welcome mat. If only we had managed to retrieve it, we might have known who had killed him.

"Do you know who I am?" I asked the mat.

"Should I?"

"Maybe. I don't know."

"It's not as though you're important."

"This coming from a doormat who gets up close and personal with the bottom of everyone's feet."

"I don't know who you are. But I know what you are. You're like the *other* one. Too uppity to wipe her feet. Too snooty to say hello."

"Rebecca was none of those things," I said. "You probably insulted her. Or curled up one edge and tripped her over."

"You play a joke a couple of times—"

"When did Rebecca last step over you?"

"Six days ago. Came to visit her grandmother. Didn't stay long. Must have been upset because she stepped right on me. Both feet." Two cartoon emoticon feet danced across her, their little faces grinning.

Hope Becca's shoes were muddy! "And did you notice anything? Anything odd?"

"Apart from that old bronze-strapped wooden box she had clutched in her hands, nothing."

An old wooden box strapped with bronze? Maybe Rebecca's jewellery box? But why bring it here?

"Are you done interrogating me?" Doormat sniffed with disdain as a cranky face flashed across her coir bristles. "I had enough of that earlier. Nosy F.C.T. agents."

"You know you really are the most unwelcoming welcome mat I've ever met."

"At least I don't associate with pariahs."

"I know a raxx that would love to mark his territory on you," Harvey said. "I can get him here before you flash a shocked and disgusted face."

"I'd expect nothing less from *you*," Doormat said. "What do you want?"

"Entry without insults." Harvey sat on the mat and licked her backside.

I wanted to cheer, point and say, 'Yeah! What she said!'

The doors swung open, flooding us in rich, yellow light. I gasped and headed inside, making sure not to stand on the mat in case she flung more insults my way.

Harvey scuffed her back paws a few times on Doormat as though covering up something smelly and followed me into the vestibule.

The entrance hall was tiled in pale strawberries-and-cream slate. Pretty, but that was nothing compared to the rest of the place. Smack-bang in the middle of the vestibule grew a sequoia tree, its lower branches woven and braided into banisters that swept upwards, enclosing two matching curved staircases that led to the second floor. The tree trunk grew straight through the plasterwork ceiling, its crown somewhere above the roof. It had to be the tree I'd seen as we'd flown over Spell Haven.

When I could pull my attention from the sequoia, I noticed three trolls clustered near the bottom of the left-hand staircase. They stood there grinning, large as life, one with his hands raised, his mouth wide as though cheering. A group of gnomes and fairies gathered about the base of the tree, all with wild-eyed joy etched on their tiny faces. Not one moved. At all. I wasn't that scary, was I?

"Oh, you dip-stick!" I snorted with disgust at myself for not realising sooner. "They're statues!"

"They're not statues," Harvey said.

"I think I know something made of stone when I see it."

Harvey nodded. "On Earth, yes."

"So tell me, what are they then?" I scrutinised the not-statues. Grey stone flecked with what looked like silver glitter. Remarkable detail right down to the trolls' fountainous eyebrows.

"About two hundred years ago, the Spell Haven staff organised a surprise party by the lake for a resident's six-hundredth birthday. Her name was Ursula, a frail, slip of a thing. Spell Haven and Ursula's family invited half the town. Trees were decorated, barges, lit by all manner of fairy lights, floated in the shallows, tables laden with food and drink ready for the celebration. When the time came, everyone hid as Ursula's daughter led her to the lakeshore. When the pair reached the shadowy, silent clearing, hundreds of folk jumped up and bellowed 'Surprise!'. It was quite tragic, really."

"And…?"

"Well, you see, Ursula had early onset dementia and had quite forgotten it was her birthday. A tragedy in itself. But worse still for many of the guests. No one had considered what a gorgon with dementia would do if half the town flew out of the woods cheering, clapping and hollering."

I spat out a laugh, a great raspberry of a noise. I couldn't help it.

"Those poor folk can hear you, you know." Harvey scowled.

"Sorry. I—" I choked back another laugh. "Where are the rest of the *stoned* guests?"

"Seriously? You went there?"

"Someone had to."

"In the town's botanical gardens."

"So, they are basically bird roosts now?"

"Pretty much. Shall we move on?"

An information sign hung from one of the sequoia's sturdy branches, swinging slightly on two chains. Fancy but functional, the gold lettering was a bit curly for my liking. I was used to fonts like Times New Roman, not Medieval Frills and Froth. It took a moment to decipher the sign and find the directions to Ward One.

By the time I nodded to myself in triumph at reading the sign, Harvey was already trotting past the tree, towards an archway opposite the front doors.

"Ward One is on this level in the Long Gallery," Harvey called back. "Are you coming?"

I fished my mobile phone from down the side of my boot and snapped a photo of the sign. I'd study that later in case we had more sneaky snooping to do.

CHAPTER TWENTY-THREE

Harvey and I walked under the timber-framed archway and into Ward One, an intermittent expanse of glass, ferneries and cozy private rooms. Each of the residents' quarters had unique doors, some twelve feet tall and made to withstand a siege, others three inches at most and hand-painted with daisies, pansies, bluebells and snowdrops. And they were just the flowers I recognised. Think greenhouse, castle, fairy town and hotel all rolled into one.

As we entered the ward, I whispered to Harvey, "What are we looking for, exactly?"

"No idea. Let's hope we know it when we see it."

"Wish Cael had been a little more clear with his dying message. Spell H Ward 1 is pretty vague. And who knows what the next bit meant–K or a B or an R—"

"Yes, the dying are so inconsiderate."

"Smart Alek!"

"Best we look in hidey holes, cupboards, pot-plants—"

"Have you seen this place? There are thousands of

places to hide something. It would make it so much easier if we knew *what* we were looking for."

"I can't imagine it would be big and bulky."

"That makes sense. So how are we going to snoop around without attracting attention?"

"Let's start with visiting your grandmother," Harvey said. "Then we have a reason for being here."

"And we can say she lost something and we're helping her look for it. People have been saying she's not all there, so it sounds plausible." My voice wobbled enough to show I was more nervous than I thought. Visiting an ageing relative with dementia you didn't even know existed until a couple of days ago. What could go wrong?

A rhythmic thudding and muffled music echoed through the ceiling. Powdery grit rained onto the slate tiles as heavy thumps joined the music.

"Spell Haven has a nightclub?" I brushed a sprinkling of white plaster from my shoulder.

"Obviously." Harvey shook her whole body, her ears twitching, a cloud of powder lifting from her body.

I followed Harvey, striding along the timber floorboards, weaving around plants and tinkling ponds as though I owned the place. Nothing to see here, madam. Move along, sir.

About halfway through the ward, Harvey stopped in front of an open door. "This is her room."

I braced myself, fashioned the best here-I-am-Grandma-smile I could, and entered the room. I expected it to look like a hospital room: a couple of steel beds with crisp white sheets, a pile of rock-hard pillows and a commode chair tucked behind pale-blue privacy curtains.

"Where are the beds?" I stared at two patches of rich, loamy soil bordered by ferns and mossy rocks. Between the garden beds, a narrow stream gurgled over stones, the water disappearing under the floor. Probably a reticulated system that fed back into itself. A conveyor belt of crisp, clear water. Nice!

"This isn't a human facility, Ding. Your grandmother is a dryad–she rests with her roots deep in the soil."

"Doesn't she have any feet?"

"Not when she's in her tree form."

"What is her tree form, exactly? Oak? Rowan? Maple?"

"Silver Ash."

"Is that where the name Ashmore comes from?"

"And people say you're not very bright."

"People don't say that! Do they?"

Light, quick footfalls caught my attention. A chubby pixie dressed in pink ankle boots, a lime green bodice with a spray of pink petals that reminded me of a knee-length tutu hurried toward us.

She ran her finger down a clipboard of paper, peering over wire-rimmed spectacles. She shook her head and the lenses wobbled within the metal frames. How amazing! Liquid lenses instead of glass. If I had a pair, I'd add a few drops of food-colouring–a different colour every day.

"Aren't you supposed to be dead?" The pixie adjusted her spectacles, causing the liquid-lenses to jiggle. She scrutinised me from head to toe, her nose wrinkled as though I was something distasteful.

A bit rude! No hello, no nothing.

I glared at the pixie. "Are you a nurse?"

"Hardly! I am Spell Haven's resident physician Urdula Pring."

"This is Arabella, Meduil's other granddaughter," Harvey said. "She's been travelling."

"It's all right for some," Urdula said with a sniff. "Are you here on business?" She looked at me with disgust, pushed her glasses up her snub nose and consulted her clipboard again.

I stared at her blankly.

"You *do* shriek for the Thornton Family, don't you?"

Harvey stepped between the rude pixie and me. "She's half-banshee. I doubt she has a death-herald connection with the Thorntons."

"Pity!" Urdula Pring pursed her lips. "Those Thornton sisters will be the death of me. I've been hoping one of them would drop dead."

Ooh! A bit of gossip that might shed some light on Thorn's mysterious family. I went to ask her why she wished them dead, but the glare I received made me shut my mouth like a mousetrap.

"Are you here to see Meduil Ashmore, then?" The pixie scanned her clipboard.

"We are." Harvey's tail swished with irritation. "Where is everyone? This place is usually bustling."

"In the Activity Room." Urdula Pring pointed at the ceiling. "It's Music and Movement hour."

"Dance class!" I did a little jig. "This should be a hoot!"

Physician Pring glowered at me over her spectacles. "There will be no hooting in Spell Haven."

"No hooting. Understood." I felt like saluting. "While you're here, can you tell us where Knola Blightly is please?"

"She failed to attend work today. Again."

"Do you know why?" Harvey asked.

"She never called in. It's very unlike her not to let us know. Oh, and you, girl," Urdula pointed at me. "I'd appreciate it if you'd go to your sister's herbal establishment and fetch our monthly medicinal order. It's late. Don't think her demise breaks our supply and demand contract. Blood is blood when you sign on the dotted line."

"Are you serious?" I wanted to wrench her tutu up over her head and tie it in a knot.

"Deadly." She spun on her boot heel and marched off.

"What a horrible little pip-squeak!" I muttered.

"I heard that!" She called, striding the length of Ward 1. "I'll expect our order delivered by the morning."

"Like that will happen!" I glared after her.

Urdula Pring walked through an open doorway at the end of the ward, stopped and looked up. A tall human-shaped shadow fell across her, but I couldn't see who it belonged to. Pring's lips moved, but her words were muffled. A male answered, his voice hushed. The only bit I heard clearly was, 'shifter nearby.'

Harvey and I stared at each other. Her hackles rose and she shivered. If I had hackles I'm sure they'd be standing at attention, too.

"So," Harvey's voice cracked. She cleared her throat. "Knola didn't turn up for work. Maybe she's on the run? Maybe she did kill Cael, after all."

"And Rebecca? The only connection I know of between her and Cael is illegal wands. Unless Knola's involved with the wands too. Maybe she ran things and Cael ripped her off? He did have a gambling problem. Or so Thorn said."

"Possibly. Maybe she found out Rebecca was onto them and needed to silence her."

"Why are wands illegal, anyway? Seems stupid to me."

"They aren't illegal, you just need a licence to own a wand. There are strict laws regarding their use. Everything from age restrictions to what materials they're made from."

"So kids can't use them? Not even at school? How do they learn to wave a wand if they're not instructed?"

"Yes, they are taught how to wield a wand at Grimsmead Academy. But, only within the school grounds and only under strict supervision. To do otherwise is punishable by Binding."

"Binding? Sounds painful."

"Someone from C.A.R.M.A. Binds the child's power while they're being rehabilitated."

"Remind me not to break the law here."

"Grimsmead isn't a Disney fairytale land, Ding."

"I'm starting to realise that." I decided to take our conversation in a different direction. "How does Ava Cadwaller fit in with Rebecca's murder?"

"I wouldn't believe everything Hywell Rowlands said about her. He probably strung you along to get more of his medication."

"Or he murdered Rebecca and was trying to divert suspicion." I growled my frustration. "And how is that shapeshifter involved? We are going in circles. For all we know, they all could be involved. Or none of them."

"We've watched enough crime shows to know that clues are like puzzle pieces. Some pieces look like others, and some don't fit at all. I'm sure it will make sense by the time the credits roll." Harvey laughed, a deep purring chortle.

"Let's hope so." I curtsied to Harvey and said in my most prim and proper voice, "Will you accompany me to the dance?"

"I don't dance." She padded through Ward 1, leaving me to catch up.

"I bet you'd dance if you were a dog."

Silence.

The thudding music faded, as though dampened or sucked away by some unseen force.

A frigid pressure surged from Harvey, rolling over me

like an invisible wind. I gasped. Where had Harvey's amiable mood gone?

The hairs on the back of my neck stood on end, and I shivered.

Harvey turned, her gaze brimming with rage, her fur bristling. The tip of her tail slashed the air.

Left.

Right.

Left.

Right.

The air around her shimmered, peppered with scintillating gold light, swelling until it brushed the vaulted ceiling. When the light faded, Harvey loomed over me with the body of a lion and the face of an eagle. A griffin! Where had she stuffed that extravaganza in her cat body? She ruffled her wings, great feathered sails folded at her flanks.

She cast me a long, icy stare and then launched into a run, her paws silent on the flagstones. The only sound was the whup-whup-whup of Harvey's outstretched wings.

And the rapid thudding of my heart.

CHAPTER TWENTY-FOUR

I stood in my grandmother's room beside the doorway, mouth agape, staring at the archway to the entrance hall. The last place I'd seen Harvey before she'd left me standing breathless and alone. The archway seemed tiny after watching her bound under it, her wingtips brushing the dark timber framework. Once again, the thumping music from upstairs shook Spell Haven, raining puffs of plaster and dust onto the strawberries-and-cream slate.

If I could turn back time, I'd go and stop myself blurting out the dog comment. A good slap and I might have kept my mouth shut. I had no idea Harvey was so sensitive. Then again, up until recently, I didn't know she could understand everything I said. Some of the things she must have heard over the years. Some of things she must have seen. Oh my! It didn't bear thinking about.

There was no use worrying over all that now. I had other things to figure out. I searched my brain for answers. Nothing sprang to mind. I had no frame of reference to base a plan on. I'd grown up in a brick three-bedroom house with a double lock-up garage, a shed in the backyard storing a lawnmower and enough tools for basic repairs. In the middle of suburbia, what's more. There were no fairies in my garden then. No trolls waltzing down the street. No dragons with snotty attitudes.

What was I supposed to do now? Alone! There I was, surrounded by ferns and babbling water, bathed in that earthy, damp forest smell I loved so much—my grandmother's home. I didn't even know what she looked like. Would she recognise me? Talk to me without Harvey there to introduce us? There was no point fretting. I'd promised myself I'd be strong now, that I would stand my ground. Such a wonderful, loamy ground. Stuffed with old leaves and rich, compost…

Even though my grandmother was nowhere to be found, I sensed her essence radiating through her room. A feeling of oneness and connection to all living things embraced me, soaking through every cell in my body. I had never felt this on Earth. I'd loved forests, yes, but this innate connection to nature, to the earth itself was on a whole new level. It was as though my perception of the world had shifted, and I had more than the five senses I'd relied upon growing up. Maybe because *this* was my world. Magic lived here. Who knew what that would do to a girl's bits and pieces?

I am half dryad, after all.

The earthen beds in my grandmother's room called to me. Not in words. That would be stupid. It was more like a pulling sensation deep within my mind, my chest. Like knowing there was a freshly made chocolate cake sitting in the kitchen. Unguarded. But this craving was so much stronger. All consuming.

My feet tingled, itched to bury themselves in the soil. I imagined doing soil angels, lying in the dirt, moving my arms and legs up and down like I did on my grey lounge-room rug. Now that was just creepy.

If this is how my dryad part feels towards dirt, what will my banshee part find exciting? The thought scared me.

I shook myself. I was wasting time.

Well, it's easier than venturing out on my own!

"Nope," I said firmly. "You have more important things to take care of. There'll be time for rolling around in dirt later. Followed by cake!"

CHAPTER TWENTY-FIVE

Rifling through a bunch of senior citizens' cupboards, shelves and drawers was not something I'd ever imagined myself doing. But there I was in some poor old man's room digging through his wardrobe. I figured he had to be a gnome or something because all his clothes were small and in immaculate repair. Especially his boots. All fifteen pairs of them. Perhaps he was a magical cobbler, like from the fairytales back on Earth. The stories had to start somewhere. His belts were carefully rolled up and cinched with perfectly tied bows. His socks were rolled into balls, all with smiley folds at both ends. I couldn't help myself. I turned one upside down so it looked like a sad face. Life was about balance and no one could possibly be this perfect.

"What you doing with my things?"

I spun around, shoving the wardrobe closed behind me. I smiled, trying to look as innocent as I could, which wasn't easy considering the circumstances.

There stood a gnome, and he was nothing like the

apothecary Dalford Hrimm who favoured undertaker attire. This fellow stood a head taller than Hrimm, his body thinner, his face more angular, and he wore a black glittery jumpsuit decked out with chains and sharp-looking studs. Peeking out the bottom of his flared pants, were wide, sallow-skinned feet in strappy, black-leather sandals, his toenails painted black to match his ensemble. Even his heavy-lidded, yellow eyes were lined with black make-up.

Seriously? A goth gnome! I would have giggled if I hadn't been caught digging through his belongings.

"I lost my way," I said in the most matter of fact tone I could.

"And you think you'll find it in my wardrobe?"

"Secret panel?"

"Nope. I know 'cos I already looked."

"So, no escape routes?"

"No secret tunnels either. If you need one of those, there's an entrance way under the beauty place down the road."

"And you know this how?"

"'Cos I helped build them passages—leagues of the things. Back during the dragon wars. It's like a maze down there."

"So you're not a cobbler?"

"Whatever gave you that idea?

"All of your boots."

"They're not mine."

"They're in *your* wardrobe."

"I'm looking after them." He tugged the neck to groin zipper on his jumpsuit and dropped his gaze.

"You stole them, didn't you?"

"Never know when you might need a new pair. In fact, that's why I've come back to my room. I need a good clomping pair. These sandals don't thump loud enough.

When you got such jiggy music playing, you need a good pair of sturdy-stompers."

"I see," I said. "I imagine you're a wonderful dancer."

"I pride myself on knowing all the steps and wiggles." He did a little twist and a few jaunty kicks.

"Very nice," I said. "I bet all the ladies love you. What's your name?"

"Galivonn Smargett." His face flushed. "The ladies think I'm something, all right. In fact, it was a lady's suggestion I came down to get my foot-stompers."

"Was she gorgeous? This lady?"

"Ravishing." He blushed again, his sallow cheeks rosy, his long skinny neck bright red. "She told me to hurry up and change my shoes before the band played the Cods-Waddle-Strut."

"Is she a lovely gnome like you?"

"Nope. She's a long-legged lady. An Old Blood to boot!"

Suspicion niggled through my mind. Funny how the gnome arrived just as I was going through his stuff.

"What's this long-legged lovely's name? I might know her."

"Rachel Thornton."

"Thorn's aunt?"

Galivonn nodded. "Sister to Aurelia the Second. Daughter to Estellia the Third and High Blood Kalion the Fourteenth."

"Of course she is. Can you hang on for a moment?" I glanced over my shoulder, then hurried out of his bedroom, scouring Ward 1 for the old biddy. The ward was empty, almost too empty. Water splashed and gurgled, a soothing counterpoint to the thudding music coming from the upper floor.

How had Aunt Rachel known I was here? I'd bet

almost anything she was paranoid enough to keep me under surveillance. Wouldn't want a banshee sneaking up on you when you weren't looking. Then again, maybe I was the paranoid one. Coincidences like this one happened every day, and no one thought anything of them. Synchronicity—that's what it was called when coincidences happened unexpectedly. Apparently, it meant you were on the right path to complete your life's purpose. Scared me a little now to consider what that might be. I didn't have time to ponder. I'd have to keep a lookout for Aunt Rachel in the future.

I hurriedly retraced my steps and popped my head back into Galivonn's room. "You wouldn't happen to know my sister Rebecca? We look alike. Red hair–banshee mask."

"Thought you was her. Figured I must a grown on account of how short you look today." His shoulders slumped. "But I was wrong."

"So, about Rebecca. Did she ever spend time with anyone other than our grandmother?"

"Well, there was that satyr cleaner, Knola. And Thorn our fun and activities feller. He's putting on one terrific dance upstairs."

"I bet!" My heart quickened. Thorn was right upstairs. "I can hear the music from here."

"Would you care to come shake a leg with an old gnome?"

"I'd love to. Maybe a bit later I'll meet you upstairs. How about that?"

He eyed my brown knee-high boots. "Got some fancy stompers right there."

"I do love me a good pair of stomping boots." I did a bit of a soft shoe shuffle, silently thanking my mother for all the dance lessons she'd paid for when I was growing up. But she wasn't my birth mother. I growled at myself, ashamed. She had been a good mum. There was more to being a mum than blood and birth.

"Mind if I choose a pair of boots?" He pulled open the wardrobe door. "The Cods-Waddle-Strut is on the playlist, and I don't want to miss it."

"Is there a utility room for Ward 1?" I asked. "A place for all the cleaning equipment? Or a tea-room for the cleaners? Something like that?"

"By the laundry, out the western door at the end of the ward. Why? You thinking of cleaning?" He shot me a doubtful look and went back to choosing his stompers.

Another shower of dust rained from the ceiling. I smiled.

"With all the dancing and thumping up in the Activities Room, there's a growing pile of plaster and dust on the floor." I shrugged. "Thought I'd sweep it up for Knola. Apparently, she didn't come in to work the last couple of days. She'd probably appreciate the help. Especially if she's sick."

He tugged off his sandals without undoing the buckles and pulled on a pair of black patent-leather platform boots that came up to his thighs. He did a few knee bends, shuffle-tapped in a circle while making 'jazz hands' and finished off by hopping from foot to foot. He grinned up at me. "I'll see you on the dance floor. Oh, and by the way, there's nothing worth stealing here. I keep the good stuff somewhere secret." He winked and thumped off, out of his room and through Ward 1, his footsteps fading into the muffled lively music.

I exited his room and looked left and right. I headed west—at least I hoped it was west, through Ward 1 towards the cleaners' room, repeatedly glancing over my shoulder for signs of surveillance. I'd need a neck massage after tonight with all this spinning and turning.

Once through the ward and standing in the doorway of the cleaners' utility room, I congratulated myself. I'd guessed which way was west the first time. Usually, my sense of direction worked best in shopping malls. It was easy to find your way using favourite shops as signposts. That seemed weird now that I knew my heritage. You'd think a half dryad half banshee would instinctively know cardinal directions and stuff.

I hurried into the cleaners' storeroom and opened every cupboard and drawer. Brooms, mops, cloths and rags, wooden buckets, bottles of liquid, some marked with a skull and cross-bones, others with a bouquet of flowers, tubs and pots sealed with cork or wax or both crammed all the cupboards and shelves. I grumped to myself and stood up, stretching the kinks from my lower back and noticed a closed door at the far end of the room. I opened it, cringing as the leather hinges creaked in protest. I peered around the door. A wooden table with four ladder-back chairs sat on a floral rug in the centre of the room. Hip-high cupboards flanked three walls, supporting a blue-stone counter on top of which sat a pile of china plates, stacked glasses, a mountain of magazines and a blue vase of wilted yellow daisies.

Above the blue stone bench, in the wall opposite the door, a sash window had been propped open using a chunk of wood. Some kind of glowing green bug buzzed and bumped into the diamond-patterned window panes, its huge bulbous eyes shining in the light. Its wings moved so fast they hummed rather than flapped.

A breeze ballooned the cream-coloured curtains out

over the sink, lifting strands of my hair and cooling my skin. I could have stayed there for ages enjoying the sensation, but I didn't have time to mess around.

I scanned the cupboard doors. Six had name plaques, the writing scrolled in pen over smears and faded letters of previous workers. I almost cheered when I found Knola's. I bent down and flung open the cupboard. Not wanting to waste time, I dragged out a chipped sky-blue teacup, hairbrush, empty hip flask and a novel. I snatched up the book and fanned through the pages, shaking it until a bookmark fluttered to the ground. The image on the bookmark matched the novel's cover: a scantily clad satyr male looking fiercely into the eyes of a female sylph, her lips parted, her eyes wide and innocent.

Oh, Knola, you naughty thing!

Chuckling, I dropped the book and searched the cupboard. One thing remained. I withdrew a neatly folded orange jacket with a torn pocket. Inside was a journal, bound around the middle with a leather thong. After a hasty look over my shoulder at the door, I unwound the binding and flipped through the pages. Handwritten notes, all in a clumsy, almost childlike script filled page after page. I opened the last page. There were three entries:

Took her out for another walk when my shift finished. She seems better when in the forest. Feel bad taking her back to the home after our walks, but I have my orders. I told Cael it'd be better to keep her in the forest because the longer she's out there, the clearer she thinks, but he just shrugged and gave me that, 'Not my problem,' look he uses when he's too stressed to think straight.

I'm getting close. She trusts me more. She showed me a stand of ash trees. But wouldn't say anything more than, 'I was an ash once.'

I keep telling them. You can't rush old people.

She drew me a map. Kept tapping the X and begging me to take her home. I'm going there once I get off work. If I find anything important, I'll take Cael and see what he reckons.

I RIFFLED the journal's pages and out fluttered a scrap of paper with a quivery drawing that had to be the map. I dug Hywell Rowlands' map from my back pocket and held it alongside the one that my grandmother must have drawn. I gasped. From what I could see, my grandmother's 'X' was in the same place that Hywell had noted that Rebecca and Ava Cadwaller had fought.

Laughter and heavy footfalls caught my attention. I stuffed Knola's belongings back in her cupboard, closed the door and rammed her journal under one arm. Voices grew louder, so loud that they had to be in the Cleaner's Utility Room next door. The only escape for me was the window. I scrambled up on the bench and thrust the wooden frame up as high as it would go–about one foot. I strained, trying to open it further, but that was its limit.

Cripes! Headfirst? Or feet first?

"See Mr Liggit dancing with Miss Popply?" One of the cleaners–I assumed they were cleaners–said with a snorting laugh just outside the closed door. "Thought he was going to have a heart spasm, he was trying so hard to impress her."

The doorknob jiggled.

I shoved my head and shoulders out of the window, wriggled and slithered over the window sill and flop-rolled into a low, spreading bush, sending a cloud of fluffy seeds skyward with the impact. The light from the window glinted off a golden orb and chain by my leg. My necklace had fallen over my head during my escape. I would have hated to lose that. I slipped it around my neck, tucking the filigree ball under the bodice of my dress.

The humming glow bug bumped into my shoulder, then my neck and I batted it away, wincing as the buzzy wings vibrated along the back of my hand. The window thudded closed, and the block of wood that had been holding it open fell to the ground missing my head by inches. A scent of something like lilacs floated around me. My nose tickled as a sneeze built, ready to blast my covert investigation right out of the water. I scrambled away on hands and knees, Knola's journal clasped in one fist as I struggled not to sneeze.

The window scraped open again.

"Where's the bit of wood?" The voice was female, deep and rumbly. "Must've fallen out. Reckon that's why the window banged closed."

"Told Pring to get it fixed, but she never listens to us." Light, tinkly and fairy-like, the second voice couldn't have been more opposite to the first speaker.

"Where'd they be without us, eh?" Answered Deep-and-rumbly.

"Waist deep in you-know-what, that's where."

The sneeze tickling the back of my nose felt like a squadron of ants hard at work with feathers strapped to their feet. Holding my nose, I squashed into the shadows, the cold stone wall hard at my back as a large, horned head poked outside. The glow bug bashed into my chin. I didn't dare swat it away in case the movement caught the cleaner's eye. I squeezed my eyes closed and hoped like mad the bug's glow didn't illuminate my face.

The window slid shut, muffling the voices within.

I couldn't hold back my sneeze any longer. I think I blew out every ant, their rotten feathers and half of my brain.

As I wiped my nose and mouth with the back of my hand, I waited for the window to shoot up. But the voices continued, melting into the music pounding from the second floor. Plates and cutlery clinked and clanked; cupboards opened and closed.

I sagged against the wall, sucked in a few deep breaths and closed my eyes for a moment. The bug flew a low bombing run, smacked me fair and square in the forehead and spiralled to the ground. It buzzed once, twice, rattled around and zipped away.

Finally! I lay in the bush for a moment, catching my breath.

I crawled out of the foliage and brushed the seeds and dead leaves from my dress. What idiot decided a flouncy dress was the correct attire for snooping? I needed to work on my strategy and planning skills.

I wiggled the golden chain and filigree ball so they hung straight and hurried back to the front entrance of Spell Haven. Once out in the open, I felt a niggle of paranoia and glanced upward to see a dark figure watching from a window on the second floor. I couldn't tell if it was male or female because shadows surrounding the figure jumped, wobbled and blurred, dancing to the ominous, thumping music. The shadowy figure reminded me of the vision I'd seen when Rebecca's souls had rushed through my body in her bedroom. The location was different from that in the vision, but the uneasiness and foreboding felt the same.

I knew right then that however tonight ended, it wouldn't be pleasant. Especially for me.

CHAPTER TWENTY-SIX

As I raced up the front steps onto the entrance porch, I tried to think up something smart and witty to fire at Doormat. Something so scathing she wouldn't have a comeback. My mind was a tangle of thoughts, none of them clever or cutting. Torchlight and shadow licked Doormat and writhed across the massive ebony-dark doors, gleaming on the bronze strapping, ominous and primal, as though the power of the ancient forest had come knocking. Strange. Spell Haven hadn't seemed so threatening when Harvey was with me.

"You again," Doormat snapped, red words scrolling across her coir bristles in a large blocky font. She flashed me a sour emoticon face.

"You know what?" I nudged her with my toe. "How would you like to go for a nice, deep swim in the lake? Picture this: You rolled up tight and stuffed in a sack filled with heavy rocks. Me singing enthusiastically as I fly a bright pink croquet car up into the sky. You falling overboard in the centre of the lake. Splash. Glug, gurgle, gurgle, cough."

"You wouldn't!"

"Try me."

Doormat grumbled into silence, a series of disgusted and cranky emoticons scrolling across her surface. I jumped on her, did a couple of knee bends, a nifty soft shoe shuffle and shoved open the door.

I burst into the vestibule. Nothing had changed. The tree, the gorgon-turned-to-stone people, the thumping music from upstairs, they were all exactly as they'd been when I first arrived with Harvey.

I didn't have a plan.

Or back up.

Or even an idea what my grandmother looked like. But, I had one advantage. Well, two if you counted Thorn and the boot-stomping gnome. They could introduce me to her. Hopefully, she would be able to tell me something about Rebecca. Or Knola and their jaunts through the forest.

I scanned the information board suspended from the tree branch. The activity room was on the third floor. With my heart pounding and my mouth dry, I ran up the right-hand staircase, my boots thudding on the pale pink and cream slate tiles. As I moved upward, sounds of music, singing and pounding feet rang through the warm air, intensifying until I had to put my hands over my ears. Music and Movement Hour was obviously a favourite of the Spell Haven residents.

I burst onto the third-floor landing, turning left to follow the shouts, singing, rhythmic thumps and raucous laughter. Sounded like Mardi Gras on steroids. Thick, forest green carpet lined the length of the gallery, the external wall set with huge, arched windows allowing the setting sun to bathe the long, hall-like expanse.

A pair of twenty-foot-tall, iron-strapped oak doors

stood closed, blocking my way. I hurried over to them and placed one hand on a doorknob. Vibrations and thudding pulsed though the handle in time with the music. The doors shuddered with the ruckus. Who knew old people had so much enthusiasm and energy?

I sucked in a deep breath, braced myself, pushed open the doors and entered the Activity Room. Mouth gaping, I stepped into the huge, dimly lit hall crowded with dancing figures. The floorboards shook underfoot, the reverberations shooting up my legs. I'd been to rock concerts more sedate than this place. I'd been to live bands in pubs and taverns with less enthusiastic patrons. Of course, there had been no iron-shod trolls, ogres and centaurs bounding around in the gigs I'd attended.

Fairies dressed in dainty flower-petal tutus and tight bodices of all colours, flitted about the big guys, their wings a blur of golden-white light. If it wasn't for their silver-grey hair and bony little elbows and knees, I'd never have guessed they were oldies. Whatever 'oldie' was in fairy years? Thousands? More?

Holy-bun-raisins! How long will I *live now I'm here in Grimsmead?*

Given what happened to Rebecca…

Could be centuries! Or I could be murdered like Becca! Determination swept through me. I had to find out what happened to my sister—*and make sure it did not happen to me!*

I couldn't tell if the music was recorded or belted out by a live band, but I was fairly certain it emanated from the other end of the room. Solid, throbbing drumbeats, wild fiddle playing, haunting pan-pipes, sonorous organ music and some kind of bass pulsed through my chest.

"Ding!" Thorn's rich tenor voice rose above the din.

I couldn't help myself. I shivered with delight.

I scanned the dancing fey-folk cavorting around the

place, their arms flapping, legs kicking, knees bending, feet pounding. Thorn waved madly at me.

"Over here!" He ducked a troll's arm that swung too close to his head. We shared a grin, my smile all dopey and foolish, but I couldn't help myself. I waved back and launched myself into the crowd.

Thorn grabbed my hands and spun me around.

"What are you doing here?" He shouted close to my ear. "You're a bit young for Music and Movement Hour."

"I'm here to see my grandmother," I bellowed back. I caught my breath as he twirled me like a ballet dancer in a child's music box.

"She's up near the band."

"Dancing?"

"Of course!"

"I thought she was frail and poorly."

"I get everyone up." He grinned. "It's good for the spirit."

"Yes! Everyone is very lively."

Thorn half-danced, half-thrust me through the crowd. It was like fighting through some crazy dream, a mash-up of fairytales, biker gangs and a rock concert. With fiddles and pipes. And fey of all kinds. Even a fire elemental whipped around the ceiling, her fiery body sinuous and graceful as her flames charred the plaster moulding. We dodged and weaved wildly swung walking canes and iron-shod boots pounding dangerously close to my toes. The heat radiating off the crowd hung heavy and suffocating, making it difficult to breathe. I stumbled on, elbowing between a leathery old troll and a wobbling tower of pixies standing on one another's shoulders. A fairy loop-de-looped, her wings fluttering so fast, a cool breeze wafted across my face, bringing with it a scent of jasmine and damp grass. I wanted to take her with me as a portable fan, but decided that would be a bit rude.

At last, I stumbled free of the dancers, gasping for breath, sagging to my knees. My head buzzed as if it was filled with hundreds of hummingbirds, their energy thrilling through my entire body.

I clambered to my feet, swaying a moment, a little dizzy and disoriented. These oldies had more stamina than a college football team on spring break.

"My band!" Thorn steadied me from behind, one hand on each of my shoulders. "We're called BullHorn."

"How very appropriate!" I shouted over the music, still wobbling, but at least I could stand without help.

The six-piece band played upon a floating wooden stage, above which hovered bobbing snow-globes flickering with bright, pulsing lights. What a hodgepodge of musicians! An ogre with an impressively horned brow-ridge bounced around the stage playing the pan-pipes. He wore pin-striped red trousers and silver-threaded-leather suspenders that strained over his chest with every movement. Two fairies no bigger than my hand played the double bass, strumming and plucking the strings. How the instrument remained standing was a mystery, especially with the ogre bounding around. A goblin played the wildest set of drums I'd ever seen. Think a ring of drums, symbols and wooden xylophones, all different shapes and sizes, with a goblin in silk emerald-green hot-pants dashing about them with drumsticks that resembled hammers. Another goblin, dressed the same, but in hot pink, pounded away on what looked like an organ with silver pipes sprouting out the top and sides like metallic snakes, coiling around one another.

I took a few calming breaths and remembered why I'd braved Music and Movement Hour. My grandmother,

Meduil Ashmore. Cael's dying message and Knola's unexplained absence just made the mystery deeper.

Thorn leaped on stage and started singing. I prepared to smile politely and cringe with embarrassment, but his voice was warm and rich, every note true. So he was just pretending he couldn't hold a tune when he hummed and danced with me at the Thornton Estate. Probably didn't want to show off. Or maybe BullHorn was magical and could make anyone sound gifted.

The crowd cheered and sang along with him. I shook my head and laughed, did a little wiggle and hummed along. Badly. I didn't even care what people thought, which wasn't like me at all. If I had to retire in Grimsmead, I wanted to retire here at Spell Haven.

A small hot hand slipped into mine, gave it a squeeze, and before I knew it, Galivonn Smargett was jigging about beside me.

"You came!" he bellowed, bopping to the music.

"I said I would." I hadn't really meant it when I agreed to come and dance with the boot-loving gnome, but what could I do? Here he was grinning, his sharp teeth gleaming in the flickering snow-globe lights, his boots stamping and kicking like a mad thing.

"Come on, girl!" he shouted. "Knees up. Wave your arms. Give that backside a wriggle. That's it! That's it!"

Laughing, blushing, I danced about like a wild creature. I had never had such fun. The energy of the dancers swept around me, through me and I bounced around the dance floor.

When the song ended, I bent down and asked Galivonn, "Was that the Cods-Waddle-Strut?"

Galivonn threw up one hand. "Nah! That song was tame compared to the Strut."

"I didn't think music could get boppier."

As the music fired up once again, I smiled at the gnome, made my excuses and turned to Thorn who was still on the stage singing, his rather attractive hips swinging, his boots stomping. My heart fluttered and I fanned my hot cheeks.

Steady girl! I caught Thorn's eye and shouted, "My grandmother?"

Thorn pointed, directing my attention to a shadowy area left of the stage that was hugged by potted elephant ear plants, their huge green leaves fanning out and up. Between them, fountained maidenhair ferns so dainty and fragile they seemed like soft green mist. Moss blanketed the pots, spreading across the floorboards.

With all the bedlam and noise, I hadn't noticed eight floor-to-ceiling stripper poles, set in timber-framed beds of soil. A tall, slender woman with floor-length green hair woven with ivy, red berries and bright turquoise feathers, whizzed around the pole closest to the band.

I glanced back at Thorn, my mouth wide in disbelief.

He grinned and nodded.

My grandmother. Meduil Ashmore. Pole-dancing in a gauzy, silver-grey dress so sheer I momentarily averted my eyes. This was not what I'd expected at all. I'd pictured her elderly and frail. She didn't look any older than Rebecca did. A chill daggered my heart. Than Rebecca had…

My sight adjusted to the dim light surrounding the poles. Her feet changed into twin roots revelling, snakelike, in the soil. I shuddered. The thought of being able to do that myself made me queasy.

Hang on, Ding! She's a full dryad. I'm a bitsa—a banshad. Maybe it won't be the same for me.

But, then, I had bulldozed my way underground to escape Walker Kane and his test. And I had felt fantastic after I'd recovered from the shock of underground flying.

I straightened my posture, dragged my hand through my messy hair and marched toward my grandmother with the kindest smile I had in my smile-file. I tapped her on the shoulder, not a demanding tap, just a tentative one to get her attention. Energy sizzled through my fingertips, the tingle hot and cold and buzzing with unfathomable powers I somehow recognised, but were so alien to me. I reeled backwards and fell. Bony hands caught me, lowering me to the ground, so I didn't lose all dignity. That was a bonus.

My grandmother looked at me, blinked and looked again. She frowned and wailed, a shrill howl that cut through BullHorn's music, which shuddered to a whining silence. Everyone turned and looked at us, me on the floor, my grandmother huddled in amongst the potted elephant ears, eyeing me with horror.

"Why are you here?" she screamed. "You're gone! Where's my son? Where's Druash?"

Unsure what to do, I searched for Thorn. He stood between two elderly women dressed in matching, flowing gowns, the hems shredded, the handkerchief sleeves so long they brushed the ground. The only difference was the colour. Aunt Rachel's was crimson. The other lady's was a deep, royal purple. She had to be Rachel's sister, Thorn's mother, Aurelia. The resemblance between the women was remarkable. Tall with finely boned faces, grey hair twisted atop their heads with silver and mother-of-pearl clasps and clear, blue eyes beneath perfectly arched eyebrows. Despite their age, they appeared regal, classy as though they'd always known elevated standing in Grimsmead.

Blurred movement above the Thornton family caught my eye. Ghosts, so many ghosts with the same finely boned features as the sisters. The spirits swirled around Rachel, Aurelia and Thorn like shredded shirts in a washing machine. A chill wind filled the room. No one seemed to notice the spirits, or their rush of energy. No one saw them except me. The ghosts saw no one but me. I shuddered, my gaze darting across the crowd, around the room, searching for help.

Standing beside Rachel, Galivonn Smargett refused to meet my eye, his gaze on the floorboards, his hand tight in his long-legged lovely's.

"Galivonn?" I pleaded. "What's wrong? Why won't you look at me?"

He scuffed the floor with his stomping-boot and kept his gaze low.

"How dare you address Galivonn when I'm standing right here!" Rachel scowled at me. "You're not welcome here!"

"Why?" I scanned the crowd, but everyone looked away. "Thorn? Galivonn? What's going on?"

No answer.

I stared at Thorn in disbelief and confusion. Surely his aunt didn't have that much power over him. Over every resident of Spell Haven?

"Leave," Aunt Rachel snarled. "You'll not wail my death. Not today. Not ever."

"Leave," Aurelia echoed. "You'll not wail my death. Not today. Not ever."

"I'm not here for you!" I shouted, frustration and tears breaking my voice. "I don't understand. I'm only a half-banshee, a banshad. I don't even know you."

"You have your mother's blood." Rachel sneered. "I can smell it. I can feel the bond between our blood even if you can't."

"That's not my fault!"

"Fault has nothing to do with it," Aurelia added, her eyes wide with fear. "You are what you are." She fiddled with her high, lace collar and withdrew a small glass ball suspended on a silver chain. She held it forth like a charm to ward off evil.

I gasped. There, in the sphere, was a wooden molar just like the one I'd found with Rebecca's stuff. Was it the one that had been stolen along with the map? It looked the same, with its milky, weathered glass. No, surely not… I couldn't believe Aurelia had escaped Spell Haven and bashed up poor old Ploggit. But she could have paid someone to torture the spriggit brownie and search the mausoleum. Cael perhaps? Or Knola? I looked at Thorn. He wouldn't meet my eye. Surely *he* wouldn't have done such a horrible thing to Ploggit?

Rachel glared at me, her wrinkled, elegant face hard, her gaze cold. Now she would definitely hurt a helpless brownie, especially if she believed it was necessary. My mind flew to Hywell Rowland's and the land development by the lake. The construction delays. The lost money. All good motives. But who was the real threat? The Thorntons were rich, the sisters elderly. How would developing land serve them? Rowlands was a greedy power monger who would do anything to get his resort built, of that I was certain.

I shot Rachel and Aurelia a vicious look. They didn't flinch.

Murmurs and whispers trickled through the crowd. The floor opened up in a circle around us as creatures backed away.

A pixie pointed at me, then cowered into the leg of an old female ogre. Or was it ogre-ess?

I didn't understand. Everyone had been smiling and dancing before the sisters had ruined everything. Had Rachel and Aurelia that much power over the residents that they'd all follow their lead rather than stand up to them? Apparently the Thorntons were a powerful family, but how powerful?

"Go back to whatever hell spawned you." Rachel fumbled for her sister's hand across Thorn.

Aurelia looked at me with horror and disgust as she dangled the glass ball in front of her like a shield. I felt unclean and repulsive. I had never been reviled before. Disliked at times, but never despised.

I stepped back, closer to my grandmother. She howled and shoved me away. I stumbled to my knees, the fizzing heat from her hand still burning where she'd pushed my shoulder. I scrambled away from her and rushed toward the crowd of Spell Haven residents. They shuffled out of my way, stumbling over one another in their haste. Once at a safe distance, they all stared at me, terror etched onto every wrinkled face. The silence was solid, deafening after the rowdy dancing and music only minutes earlier.

"Thorn?" My voice broke as tears welled and my throat tightened.

He looked at me with a bleak expression, but didn't move to help me. Didn't explain to everyone that I meant no harm. That I hadn't come to howl someone's death. I'd only come to visit my grandmother. And snoop around— but they didn't know that. Unless Galivonn had told them how I'd been going through his belongings. But he'd been so friendly when I got up here. I'd felt no danger or animosity from him. Unless he'd used our dance as a way to delay me? But for what reason?

Tears streamed down my cheeks. I threw Thorn the most hurt, nasty expression I could and ran to the door, shoved my way through and bolted for the stairs.

CHAPTER TWENTY-SEVEN

$\mathcal{I}$ careened down the stairs three at a time. The lights of Spell Haven refracted through my tear-filled eyes, looking like hazy stars, making it difficult to see. I didn't care. So what if I fell? I'd just get to the bottom faster.

"Ding!" Thorn's shout chased me down the steps. I didn't slow or turn to see if he followed me. He hadn't helped me at all. He just stood and watched along with everyone else. What had I been thinking? He wasn't the best thing I'd found since arriving in Grimsmead. He was the worst.

Faint, but brimming with anger, Rachel's voice filtered from above. "Aylward Thornton, you return to us immediately."

"Go," I growled. "Go back to your stupid family."

I hit the entrance hall running, wrenched open the front door and ran out into the darkness.

"A goodbye would be nice!" shouted Doormat.

I would have thrown her across the verandah if I'd had time.

As I bounded down the steps, the scent of flowers drifted on the humid night air. Freesias and jonquils.

A tiny olive-green, two-door car fit for a toddler hovered inches from the ground, a chain tethering it to a sturdy oak tree. No one sat in the driver's seat, but a bunch of freesias, jonquils and daffodils poked above the passenger's side door.

Dalford Hrimm? What's he doing here? I slid to a stop as he waddled out of the shadows toward the car. Smiling, he picked up his flowers, tweaked the huge purple ribbon so it sat perfectly, and trundled toward me. He seemed pleased with himself. Smug. What had he been up to in the forest?

"How's Ploggit?" The words choked past the knot in my throat. I wiped my eyes and streaming nose with the back of my hand. Not ladylike, but I didn't care.

"Sleeping soundly."

"So, he's better?"

"We had a few rough moments, but I got them under control."

"And Meeks?"

"Snoring up a storm. Probably got sick of waiting. Why are you so upset?"

"An emotional reunion with an old relative."

"Can't choose your family, can you, eh?"

"Hot date?" I nodded at his flowers.

"Here's hoping!" he said brightly.

"I see you've jazzed them up since I saw them last."

"It's a birthday gift." He had arranged fragrant herbs and thin, nobby sticks tipped with crystals in amongst the flowers since I'd seen the bouquet at the Apothecarium. I had to admit, I would have loved to receive such a stunning gift. Who would have thought that a smart-mouthed gnome could be so romantic?

"What's her name?" I needed to leave, but I didn't

know how to end the conversation without seeming rude or suspicious.

"No one *you'd* know."

"Then what's the harm in telling me?"

"Aurelia Thornton."

Thorn's mother? I smiled, but I knew the friendliness didn't reach my eyes. "Seems the Thornton women have a thing for gnomes."

"So you know about Rachel and Galivonn." Dalford pulled an unkind face. "My second cousin. Unfortunately. Totally smitten with that sour puss, Rachel."

"I noticed."

"Hard not to." Dalford grunted goodbye and headed for the entrance porch. He trundled up the steps, the light sparkling off the crystals within his fancy bouquet.

"A bit late for schmoozing," Doormat said, all snooty and condescending. "What? I'm not worth walking on? I don't know why I bother. I try to be a pleasant welcome mat, always smiling and helpful. Never say an unkind word to folks with manners …"

"Stupid doormat!" I muttered.

The crunch of leaves drew my attention to where Dalford had appeared from the forest. A shadowy cloaked figure tinged with cobalt blue faced me.

The shapeshifter! What was she doing here? Had Dalford Hrimm been consorting with her? Planning some-thing? Or had he just relieved himself behind a bush and that's why he'd been so pleased with himself? All my faith and trust in people had eroded over the last few days. So this is what it was like to be truly vulnerable and alone?

"Hey!" I called, waving to the shapeshifter. "Can I talk to you for a moment?"

"No! But I'll visit *you* soon. That's a promise." Her voice was deep, velvety and sultry.

"Don't you mean a threat?"

"Ah, you brave little fool!" She laughed and fled back into the trees.

"Ding!"

I glanced back at the verandah. Thorn stood there, backlit by light spilling through the open doors. He lifted his arms in a 'what are you doing?' gesture. My options were low. Face whatever hid in the forest and head for the pink flying cart. Or face Thorn and his rotten old cronies. I chose the forest. I took comfort in knowing that the shapeshifter had me in a holding pattern for later, so I was likely safe from her for the moment. And, if things got really scary I could dive into the ground, fly through the dirt and come out far from here. I'd done it before. I could do it again.

I found the paved path Harvey and I had taken earlier. I sprinted along the herringbone pavers, hoping I was headed towards the flying pinkmobile. Everything looked different in the darkness, and my tears made everything smudge together. I dragged the back of one hand across my eyes. A little clearer. But not much.

Cold, pale moonlight broke through the forest canopy, slashing the forest floor. Insects chirruped and buzzed. Frogs croaked and ber-rerped. Night birds whipped and hooted. And then silence. It was as though someone had flipped a switch.

Not good!

Someone or something heavy pounded through the underbrush, the sound growing louder until it kept pace with me off to my left. Whoever they were, they were quick. Faster than me. I risked a glance. It wasn't the cloaked shapeshifter. This was a satyr. Not as big as Cael had been, but still way taller than me.

Knola? Cael's wife?

I looked again, praying I didn't trip over a rock or tree root. Moonlight glinted in a thin, silvery line along the edge of a blade, flashing as the satyr thundered through the underbrush. I remembered the blood smeared on the sheets in Cael's bedroom. Someone had wiped a dagger or knife clean on the quilt cover.

Cripes! I clutched Knola's journal, dashing blindly along the path. She had to know I'd 'borrowed' it. Why else would she be after me? If it was her? But who else would she be? A part of me wanted to chuck away the journal, but I couldn't risk losing it.

Puffing, my side cramping, I kept running. I had to reach the pinkmobile. Then I could fly away, over the forest and back home to the mausoleum. But that wasn't truly home for me. There was no comfort. No feelings of security and cozy relief. And I'd have to face Harvey.

The satyr angled toward me, moonlight flashing off the blade as she ran.

Lake Mead stretched out beyond the tree line.

Yes!

Moonlight reflected off the water, riding gentle ripples to shore. I burst from the forest, and there was the pink croquet cart right where we'd left it.

I sprinted for the cart, my side burning with pain, my breathing ragged. Arms outstretched, I rammed into the side of the cart and shoved Knola's journal under the front seat, hoping she hadn't noticed.

I shot a look over my shoulder, checking if I was safe, and screamed. A hairy wall of muscle and heat knocked me flying, and I tumbled into the lake. I gasped, sucking in cold water. Flailing, choking, I found my feet, my boots sliding on the lake's slimy bottom.

"Stay away from me!" I shouted in between coughs and gasps.

Knola crouched on the shore, blood soaking her cleaner's uniform. Had she been going to work? Or leaving? She could have been in her uniform for days. A long gash sliced up the inside of her left arm, three smaller wounds injured her right. They were similar to Cael's wounds. Perhaps they had fought? Or had they been attacked?

Panting, her heavy-browed face grimacing, she staggered to her hooves, clutching the blood-smeared dagger. She didn't wade into the shallows, shuffling left and right, her wild gaze on the dark water rather than me.

"I know about you and my grandmother," I screamed, stumbling through the thigh-high water. "How you manipulated her."

A spit of forested land jutted into the lake about one hundred paces away. The Finger! Issy had mentioned it earlier. Told us that some of the protestors camped there. I had to reach it. Then I'd be out of Knola's line of sight. She wouldn't know which direction I'd taken once I'd reached the trees, and I'd find help. It wasn't a good plan, but it was all I had.

I looked back. Knola paced the lakeshore but didn't come close enough for the water to lap her hooves. Maybe she couldn't swim?

"I don't mean you any harm," Knola called, her voice deep, almost masculine.

"Says she with the bloody dagger!" I bellowed back.

"I need your help. Just come back to shore. I won't hurt you. I promise."

"I'm not falling for that." I sloshed through the water as fast as I could, my skirt floating about my legs. Seriously, what idiot played detective in a flouncy dress? I really needed to rethink my wardrobe.

Cracking branches, rustling leaves and rapid footsteps

overrode the soft lapping of waves. Someone else was coming.

Please don't let them be Knola's gang!

"Ding!" Thorn shouted. "Get out of the lake!"

"No way!" I waded faster, my boots catching on weed and slippery rocks. My skirt tangled around one leg and I stumbled, falling face first into the water. I scrambled to my feet, my hair clinging to my face like wet seaweed. I dragged back my hair with as much haughty dignity as I could. "I like it just fine in here."

"I mean it!" Thorn yelled. "It's not safe in there."

"Not too safe on shore either. I'll take my chances in the water." Puffing, I ploughed through the water, my thighs aching, my boots slipping and my pride somewhere back on planet Earth. This had to be the worst adventure ever.

A golden light bloomed, bleeding across the night sky, accompanied by harsh roaring. The Hours doing their cuckoo clock thing. One after another, eight times. Eight moments of precious light allowing me to make out my position.

The Finger lay about thirty paces away. I caught the smell of wood smoke. A campfire. Probably the protestor's! My mood lifted. I scanned the trees crowding the narrow stretch of land. Shadows hung thick and black beneath the dense canopy. But, there was hope, a glitter of gold between the trunks and bushes, a flutter of flame.

Yes!

Now I knew where to head. I splashed and floundered toward the pebbled shore, slipping and sliding on hidden stones, my arms windmilling, determination my only ally.

A huge ogre-shaped figure passed between the tree trunks, heading for the campfire. One of the protestors, no doubt.

"Hey!" I shouted, waving madly. "Over here! I need your help!"

The figure ducked under a branch and stood on the pebbles.

I froze.

Hywell Rowlands grinned at me, beckoning, his shoulder horns gleaming in the moonlight, his furs making him far larger than he was. What if he really was Rebecca's murderer? A lot of the evidence arrowed right at him. *And* he worked with the Thornton sisters. Now I saw him again, looming in the darkness, I decided he definitely would torture Ploggit for information. The ogre knew I suspected him. If I got within arm's length, he could break me like a pretzel. Even if he wasn't Rebecca's killer, he was up to something unsavory. No one hikes for pleasure at this time of night. And, why was he so close to the protestors? Definitely something dodgy going on.

What if he was working with Knola? I scanned the shoreline. She sat huddled on the ground. Thorn was edging his way along the water's edge, keeping pace with me.

"Ding," Thorn called. "You have to trust me! Please come out of the water. The merfolk don't like us invading their territory without permission."

"Sure, they don't."

As if on cue, something caught my boot. I pulled back, shaking my foot, trying to break free. Something yanked on my leg. I stumbled, peering at the dark water, searching for movement.

Nothing.

It's only a tree branch!

But after Thorn's warning... And what were merfolk anyway? Were they like mermaids? Beautiful, hair-brushing singers in clamshell-bras that dreamed of being human? What if they were colossal, multi-armed squid-like creatures that could drag down a ship and all its crew?

A chill ran through me. I wrenched backwards writhing, thrashing against whatever held my foot. I slipped, twisting my knee. White-hot pain exploded through my leg. I gasped. The urge to plough through the lake's slimy, stony bottom into the ground beneath and travelling to safety somewhere far away overwhelmed me.

Lights sizzled across my vision.

"Ding!" Thorn shouted, his words muffled, slow, drawn out. And tight with fear.

Blinding pain radiated through my injured knee. My body felt thick and uncomfortable as though I had a huge sack of bricks strapped to my shoulders. I recognised the cumbersome sensation. The dizziness and difficulty in hearing. I'd felt all of that when I escaped Walker Kane's stupid test.

The dark, chilly water shimmered. Water? I was surrounded by a whole lake of the stuff. How far did it seep into the ground? Would I drown if I bulldozed through the soil and stone beneath?

My heartbeat raced, a drum-roll of panic.

No!

I couldn't risk escaping through the lake-floor. As if someone had flipped a switch, I could hear normally again. I felt like me again. In pain and trapped by something I could not see.

A curtain of bubbles encircled me, crawling and bursting along my skin. I yelped, flailed, fighting to free my foot. Blinding pain burst through my knee. The lake's surface gleamed in the moonlight, dancing on the bubbles. Two of those bubbles looked at me with wide, snake-like eyes and blinked.

I screamed and smashed my fist between those cruel

eyes, my hand slipping across something cold and slippery, something with thick coarse, matted hair.

Ice-cold hands wrapped around my leg, spidering their way up to my knee. They squeezed. Pain shot through my leg like white-hot fire. Starbursts exploded before my eyes. Lightheaded, I retched, vomiting bitter bile down the front of my dress.

The slimy, bone-hard fingers walked their way up my leg.

Over my hips.

And yanked me underwater.

The creature wrapped its snake-like arms around me and dragged me close, its long dark hair floating around us, blending with mine in a red, silver and black cloud. Slippery lake weed drifted about its body. Could have been clothing. Could have been camouflage. Its glowing, green eyes scrutinised me through the moonlit water as though I was some kind of alien creature to be studied. Or eaten. I lashed out, clawing its face and long, thin neck. It screeched, bubbles escaping its wide, frog-like mouth in a rapid stream. I thrashed and flailed, fighting to get to the surface. To breathe. I kicked as hard as I could with my uninjured leg, planting my boot deep into the creature's dolphin-like tail. The mer-thing shuddered. Its grip loosened. I shoved the creature away and lurched upward, breaching the surface like a clumsy seal, and sucked in a shuddering breath.

A tree branch smacked into the water beside me, and I lunged sideways, trying to get clear. Thorn stood close by, pounding the water with the branch. The mer-thing scrabbled at my waist, dragging me underwater again.

"Get away from her!" Thorn shouted, his voice distant and muffled beyond the bubbles and splashing. He caught a fistful of my hair and yanked me upward in a shower of water.

"I warned you!" Thorn threw me over his shoulder and waded toward the shore. "Do you still like it 'fine' in here?"

Every breath I wheezed in and out was glorious. But, the pain in my knee and the wound to my pride left me miserable and frustratingly silent.

CHAPTER TWENTY-EIGHT

"*Y*ou really are a fruitcake," Thorn said. "Look at your knee!"

"I am looking!" I raised my skirt over my knee. It was swollen, already bruising and excruciatingly painful. "Here, help me up. I need to get back to the pinkmobile so I can fly home."

"Not likely," Thorn said. "I'm taking you home and calling our family physician."

"Where's the injured satyr? She might need help, too."

"She chased you with a blade and you want to help her?"

"Doesn't mean she deserves to bleed to death alone in the woods." I thought of Rebecca. I didn't truly believe Knola had killed my sister, but I knew she was involved. Suddenly, torn between compassion and revenge, I added, "She might know something about Rebecca's death. If she bleeds out, that information will die with her."

"That's true, but I didn't see where she went. I was trying to help you."

"And Hywell Rowlands, where's he now?"

"The resort developer?"

"I saw him skulking about on The Finger. He looked like he was headed for the protestors' campsite. I think he might have murdered my sister. And your gardener."

"Are you sure?"

"Well, no, but he seems like a good suspect." *Along with your mother and Aunt Rachel!*

"Have you been playing detective?" Thorn laughed. I loved the sound. I wanted to weave it into a fluffy blanket and carry it with me always.

"What would you say if I said yes?" I offered him a foolish grin.

"I'd say you're in way over your head and to leave it to the professionals."

"A lot of good they are. They haven't mentioned one solid suspect. In fact, they keep arresting me!"

"How uncivilised of them."

"I know!"

"You need to take your dress off." Thorn tugged at my skirt's muddy hem. "It's soaking. I'll wring it out while I check you over."

I frowned at him. "Just because you rescued me, don't think I'm going to swoon like a damsel in distress and let you have your way with me. I have standards. Morals. And, let's not forget how you let me face everyone at Spell Haven. Alone. You didn't lift a finger to help me. And after all our dancing, wood-on-a-tug-rugging in the forest, and taxi-calling."

"I'm sorry. You don't know what my mother and Aunt Rachel are like. It's impossible to go against them."

"It's easy! You stand your ground, plant your hands on your hips and say, 'No!'."

"I wish you were right."

"I am right. Oh, and I'm not taking my dress off. You can put up with me dripping like a wet dog."

"It's not the dripping I'm concerned about."

"Well, that's all you get, buster."

"Fine. But don't come crawling to me when you're too weak to stand because fleeches have sucked the life from you."

"Fleeches? Like leeches?"

"Worse."

Something cold squirmed behind my knee. Tiny sharp pins rasped against my skin and a weird fluttery whirring vibrated against my calf. Another slimy fluttering wriggled across my back.

"Get it off!" I squealed, dragging at my dress. "Get it off. What are you waiting for?"

Thorn peeled off my wet dress, his expression neutral, a mischievous glint in his blue eyes.

"I hate fleeches!" I cringed, flicking at a muddy shape the size of my little finger wiggling in the crook of my knee. It had a mermaid tail, slimy torso and side fins that ended in sharp, tiny fingers. I flicked it again. It raised its hairless, elongated head, glared at me with gleaming bulbous eyes, and hissed.

"Nice teeth." I eyed its tiny fangs, so fine and sharp they could probably gnaw right through a limb.

Another, larger fleech wriggled across my outer thigh, its side fins fluttering like barbed wings, each fanned out with a bracing of needle-thin bones.

"Get them off!" I screeched.

I winced as Thorn grasped the head of the larger fleech, wiggling it side to side, easing it upward and outward. As it popped free, the wound site stung like blazes. That was going to bruise. The fleech lashed about, hanging from Thorn's grip, its fin-wings buzzing like a hummingbirds.

"Go home!" Thorn tossed the fleech skyward. It circled above a few times then shot back to the lake, splashing into the water.

It took a bit, but we eventually found and removed five more fleeches—one of them embarrassingly near the clasp of my lacy white bra.

"Shouldn't we check you over?" I motioned to Thorn. "You went in the water too."

"We Thorntons have a long-running truce with the maranormal folks of Arahn."

I figured Arahn was either the name of the country or the world. I didn't dare ask him because that'd lead to awkward questions, and I didn't want to give my secret life on Earth away.

Something dark and flowing caught my eye. Thorn lurched to his feet, his face pale.

The cloaked stranger flounced towards me, cobalt blue shadows trailing it like a living fog. It stopped a few paces away from Thorn, surveyed him, then me.

"It's the shapeshifter!" I grabbed Thorn's sleeve. Was this the visit she promised? Was this the end of me? I scrambled backwards, pebbles rolling and tumbling under my boots, pain flaring white-hot and scream-worthy through my wounded knee.

"Come on!" Thorn slid one arm under my back, the other under my thighs and lifted me off the ground. "I know a safe place for you."

"My dress!" I shouted. " I can't go around in my undies all night."

He picked up my dress and I grabbed it, tucking it to my chest.

I chewed the side of my hand so I wouldn't cry out in

pain as Thorn ran through the darkness. Moonlight speared the ground through breaks in the canopy, shedding pale, grey puddles of light. Not enough to see clearly, but enough to hold total blackness at bay.

Wings flapped behind us.

"Rork-rork-rork," the shapeshifter called. "You can run, but you can't fly."

Thorn stumbled into a moonlit clearing ringed by the most ancient trees I'd ever seen, their branches gnarled, the bark fissured and thick with moss. Ash trees. I'd never seen any this old and disfigured on Earth. Younger ash trees hugged the clearing, their branches interwoven with the brittle, dying ones. Thorn lowered me to the ground in a cradle of knotted roots and fallen leaves that crackled and crunched as I moved.

He glanced about, growled and muttered something I couldn't make out.

Knola crashed between the trees, staggering into the glade, blood streaming down her arms onto the dagger. Groaning, she slumped to the ground.

"Stay back!" Thorn stepped between the satyr and me.

"Try and stop me," Knola said between rasping breaths. "And don't bother using your powers on me. They won't work. I've learned a thing or two recently."

"What's she talking about?" I peered past Thorn. Knola could barely keep her eyes open. I hated to think how much blood she'd lost. And, she was probably riddled with infection from the state of her swollen, red wounds.

"She's delirious." Thorn grabbed a fallen branch. He adjusted his hold on it, two hands equally spaced along its length.

"He's not who you think he is, girl." Knola struggled to her hooves, holding the dagger out, ready to attack. "You think he'll let you leave this clearing alive?"

"What's she talking about?" I struggled into my dress, crying out as pain shot through my knee.

"Ignore her." Thorn didn't look at me as he matched Knola's lumbering shuffle with light, quick movements. "She's manipulating you."

She slashed the silver-misted air with her dagger. He blocked with the knotted end of his branch, hitting her hard against the temple. Knola crumbled as though all her bones had turned to mush. Thorn darted forward and kicked the dagger clear of her hand. The weapon skid to my left along the grass, knocking up against the base of one of the ash trees.

Thorn ran for the dagger, snatched it up and held it forth, ready to strike.

"I think she's down for the count," I said. "If she lives, she's going to have a whopping headache when she wakes up."

"Which of these old trees is will-born?" Thorn asked, his voice tight and breathless.

"I don't understand."

"Which of these ash trees holds a dryad spirit?" He waved the dagger about, Knola's blood crimson in the moonlight.

"How would I know?"

"Can't you sense them?"

"I don't know. I've never communed with trees before. Why are you acting so weird?"

"The question is simple. Reach out with your mind or something. See if you can detect life within any of the trees around here."

"Are these trees special or something?"

"Look around, Ding. They're all ash trees. Your family, your kin. This is your family's home."

"Could do with some redecorating."

"Why do you have to be so frustrating?"

"Why are you being so mean?"

"I'm sorry, Ding. I really am sorry." Thorn rubbed his eyes with his thumb and forefinger. "We don't have much time. I'm trying to help you here."

"Doesn't feel that way."

"Look, I've endured a lot—more than you know. But I still managed to find your family home. So I could show you. So you can ask them about Rebecca. If anyone knows the truth, it's them. All you need to do is work out which of these trees is will-born and ask them what happened."

"Hang on." I fished Hywell's map from my pocket. It was soggy, the folds stuck together and difficult to open. I was no master map-reader, but from what I could see, we were in the exact spot where Ava had fought with Rebecca. A chill ripped through me.

Oh no! What if Hywell had drawn the map just to get me here?

"What is it?" Thorn crouched and rested one hand on my good leg. "Your knee?"

"I think I'm in danger."

He frowned, licked his lips and glanced around the glade. "What makes you say that?"

"I don't know." I shrugged. "Maybe I'm being para-noid. My knee hurts. Makes it hard to think straight."

"Take a few deep breaths. And try to connect with the trees. They could protect you. I'm sure at least one of your family lives here." Thorn looked at me with such despera-tion an icy knot coiled inside my belly.

Rebecca's message, the one the shapeshifter had passed on to me near Narrows Run, flashed through my mind. 'Guard your heart. Run. Kill if you have to. But guard your heart.' Her last words had been, 'Protect our home'.

Protect it from whom? Thorn? His aunt and mother?

Their groundskeeper and his wife? Hywell Rowlands? The shapeshifter? They could all be in cahoots together. And here I was alone, injured and they were closing in.

I froze, my eyes wide, my gaze fixed on the tip of Knola's dagger. "Thorn, I'd tell you if I could. I really would."

Just at that moment, a black leopard padded into the glade, the cobalt-blue markings in her fur shimmering in the moonlight with every graceful step. Thorn spun to face her with a terrified moan, the dagger held forth, ready to strike.

"You'll not take me," he said through clenched teeth.

"As if *you* could stop me."

Thorn backed into a tree, glanced left and right and then faced the shapeshifter and began to sing, the tune sweet, mournful and in some language I didn't understand.

"Are you kidding me?" The shapeshifter laughed. "It would take an army of sirens just to make me tap my foot and hum a few bars."

"Siren?" I frowned up at Thorn. "You're a siren?"

"Don't say that!" Thorn snarled. "You make it sound dirty."

Every one of his words scraped my mind like broken glass on soft, vulnerable flesh. But was that his siren magic? Or did I feel foolish, gullible and hurt? Had he been controlling me this whole time? Or had he truly liked me? Why hadn't I noticed the power of Thorn's voice earlier? He'd gotten me to dance without worry or embarrassment at his estate. He'd made me melt like warm honey with a few words. He could have manipulated me, and I wouldn't have even realised what was happening. And that would mean his mother and Aunt Rachel were sirens. No wonder they controlled the residents of Spell Haven. Growing up on Earth, where there was no magic or supernatural beings, left me at the mercy of everyone in Grimsmead. I was a baby. A stupid, naïve baby.

"Have you been using me?" Rage stung my heart with every word. "Using your powers on me? To get me here?"

"It's not—I mean—I'm trying to help you before it's too late." Thorn shook his head, lowering his gaze. "You don't understand."

"It's a good job you're a siren," the shapeshifter said. "Because your conversation skills are woeful."

"Why are you here?" Thorn shouted at the shapeshifter.

"I have an appointment. I'm a little early, but I'm happy to wait. Besides, everyone's not here yet."

Knola groaned and struggled up on one elbow. Talk about a tough old girl! She wavered, blinking rapidly as though trying to focus. When her gaze landed on the shapeshifter she recoiled and scrambled backwards until she butted up against a tree.

"Come on out, Hywell," the shapeshifter called. "I know you're skulking about watching."

"Not likely!" I heard the rock ogre, but couldn't see him anywhere.

"And you, verge," the shapeshifter added. "Seems we're having an impromptu party."

Ava Cadwaller stepped into the glade and strode towards me, all business and no fear. She certainly had courage. Everyone else seemed terrified of the shapeshifter.

A man-shaped shadow moved between the trees. Narrowing my eyes, I searched the forest where Ava had been only moments before. All I saw were layers of darkness and the occasional scattering of moonlight hitting leaves as they rustled in the breeze.

"Are you all right?" She knelt down and caught my eye,

looked at Thorn, then the shapeshifter. "Interesting company you keep."

"What can I say," I said. "I'm an equal-opportunity gal."

"You really are a fool," Ava murmured. "Not everyone present is equal, I can tell you that much."

"Isn't this the place you hit my sister? Knocked her to the ground?"

"How do you know about that?"

"I read something in Rebecca's diary. And, Hywell Rowlands said he saw you strike her—he even marked this area on a map to show me where it happened."

"I would have known if Rowlands was spying on us."

"That confident of yourself, are you? Maybe your powers aren't as spiffy as you lead everyone to believe."

"Even if Rowlands saw us, why would he draw you a map? He never does something for nothing."

"We made a trade."

"He led you here—he saw an opportunity and you fell for it. Walked right into danger."

Had Rowlands done that to me? Was I that gullible?

"Are we all here now?" Ava stood and faced the shapeshifter, hands on hips, no fear in her voice.

"Almost," the shapeshifter said. "Still waiting for that snippy little gnome Dalford Hrimm and the Thornton sisters. I can't wait to see their faces when they realise I'm here alongside you, Arabella Black."

"I'm not with you," I said. "Wait! How do you know my surname is Black? Everyone here thinks its Ashmore."

"Lucky guess."

"Who are you?" I felt like wringing the truth out of her. Shock rippled through me. Perhaps I was a dark soul like my father, after all.

"Who are you here for?" Thorn asked.

"Yes!" Despite being terrified, I had to know. "What do you want?"

"What?" the shapeshifter growled, a deep thrum that came from somewhere deep in her feline body. "Tell you and ruin the surprise?"

"You're not meant to make a game of it," Ava said.

"You'd spoil the one bit of fun I get in life?"

"Does your family know you treat your calling as a joke?"

"I tell them at every opportunity."

Muttering, Ava rolled her shoulders and shifted her stance, her feet wide, her arms loose, her hands clenching and unclenching.

"What 'calling'?" I frowned, looking from Ava to the shapeshifter. I really had to find a book on Grimsmead and its inhabitants. Perhaps a *Grims-o-pedia for Dummies*?

The shapeshifter licked her paw. "I have so many talents. Why focus on that one?"

We really needed more allies here. Creatures with enough muscle and magic to keep the shapeshifter in line.

"Where's Agent Kane?" I asked Ava. "Or did you sneak out here alone?"

"If you must know, he was taken off the case because of his relationship with the victim."

"Then how was it he questioned us earlier? He seemed like he was on the case then."

"He thought he could hide his involvement with your sister."

"And I wonder who let the bosses know about their relationship, eh?" I eyed Ava coldly.

"It's a mystery." She shrugged, tilted her head and gave a distant, satisfied smile.

"Of course it is."

"Walker is with your pet mooncat Harvey, looking after the spriggit brownie and that raxx."

"Why? What happened to them?"

"Poisoned."

Sitting there, cradled in dead leaves and twisted roots, I felt small and vulnerable. I struggled to my feet, using the tree trunk for balance and the lower branches as pull-up ropes. Once I was upright, I stood alongside Ava. Who would have thought I'd be standing shoulder to shoulder with her against a shapeshifter, an injured satyr and goodness knows who else lurking in the darkness? But, all things considered, Ava was the one person who had been honest with me. Thorn glanced my way, such pain and sorrow on his face.

"Is Harvey okay?" I tested my knee—as soon as I put weight on it, pain seared through my leg.

"I guess so," Ava replied. "Walker and the mooncat were arguing when I left."

"What about?"

"Nothing. Can you move?" Ava asked me, each word precise and careful, as though I was supposed to glean some hidden meaning.

"Not well." I threw her a confused look, hoping she understood that I didn't understand.

She lowered her gaze, pointing at the forest floor. "Just checking if you can move *freely*."

"Oh! Not sure how far I can go."

"Even a few paces is a good start." Ava indicated the dagger in Thorn's hand with her eyes.

All I had to do was concentrate. When I'd transformed into spirit form last time, I'd been terrified. Here I was surrounded by all the people I'd suspected of murdering my sister. Thorn, sadly, a new one on my list. But I had to set my feelings aside. I had to get the truth and bring

Rebecca's killer to justice. I had to find out where her body was so I could bury her with the honour and respect she deserved. And she did deserve more. She deserved to live and be happy with Walker Kane. Have babies. A cozy home with a dog and two cats. She didn't deserve to die.

The moonlit glade swirled before my eyes. Howls rang through the forest, the soul-chilling shrieks rattling my body. The wails had to be coming from someone or something nearby. Heat speared through the crown of my head, boiling every cell in my body, then shot from my feet as golden lightning crackling across the forest floor. Fallen leaves glowed ember-red and gold, curled, blackened and died. I touched my banshee mask, the leathery skin alive with jittery sparks of energy beneath my fingers. I could only imagine what I looked like.

A low howl rang through the forest. So mournful and chilling, I shivered.

Ava stepped away from me, her face pale, her mouth open in shock.

Everyone stared at me.

At me? And then I realised. I was wailing someone's death. Banner day! Hope I wasn't foretelling my own demise. Could a banshee howl her own death?

Thornton spirits appeared, swimming around me, through the trees, circling Thorn, caressing his face, his shoulders and arms. He stood shivering, a feral gleam in his eyes as he watched my mouth, waiting. I struggled to keep my lips closed, hating the fear in Thorn's face, but the screaming wail bubbled and frothed from my mouth regardless. Thorn cried out, hugged himself and backed away. The long-dead Thorntons echoed my shriek. I led a choir of ghosts. Not how I pictured today going at all.

"I'm sorry!" I shouted, tears catching in my throat, filling my eyes. "I'm so sorry."

Another howl. I clapped a hand over my mouth but it was hopeless. Panting, tears streaming down my banshee mask, peace rolled over me and the wails stopped. I lowered my eyes ashamed and embarrassed. Death littered the ground, a mat of charred leaves and twigs, smoke curling around me like a shroud.

The shapeshifter, still in her leopard form, raised her front paws and clapped. "Excellent show! Bravo!"

Everyone else stood in silence, their faces mirroring my self-loathing and shock. A tiny part of me died in that moment. I would never be the same Arabella Black. That person was somewhere back on Earth, pulling beers and mixing cocktails. I was Arabella Ashmore now.

Knola staggered to her hooves, her movements rigid, her breathing rapid and shallow. She wobbled, her maple-coloured skin draining of all colour. She screeched and buckled, clutching her left arm, patting and hitting it as though trying to kill some poisonous creepy crawly. Crying, breathless, she tore away the shoulder of her uniform, revealing a bulging lump that squirmed and writhed, her skin pale and shiny as it stretched. Blood welled as her skin split, then a shard of wood shot from her shoulder, embedding in the forest floor at my feet.

I don't know why, but I picked it up. Worms of energy raced up my arm. An image flooded my mind. It was my grandmother. Only younger, vibrant and happy. As quickly as the image appeared, it vanished, leaving me confused and questioning my sanity.

I looked at Ava. Then at the shapeshifter. Then at Knola, who had sagged to the ground, holding her bleeding shoulder.

"You feeling all right?" Ava's skin was pale, her facial markings crimson. She remained a safe distance from me. I couldn't blame her.

"Been better." I decided to focus on the scene of my grandmother rather than my screeching and wailing. "I think I had a vision or something."

"Or something," Ava said, the snarky attitude back, armed and ready to fire.

"You going to share with the crowd?" The shapeshifter sat on her haunches and cocked her huge feline head.

"When I touched the bit of wood, I saw my grandmother. I know it was her, but she was full of life and joy."

Ava's eyes widened. "I think I know what that is." She pointed to the blood-smeared shard.

"Don't!" Thorn looked at me. I had never seen such terror on a person's face before. Terror? Or was it guilt? Please don't let it be him that killed Rebecca …

"I'm sorry!" Tears filled his eyes. "I had to." He bolted between two bent and twisted ash trees, ducking under a leafy branch as he vanished into darkness.

Anger throbbed deep in my head, my chest. Red pulsed before my eyes. Then the world went dark. It took a moment to comprehend I'd slipped underground, that I was one with the planet, the trees and nature again. The smell of rich, loamy soil and decaying vegetation tumbled though me. The pain in my knee had vanished. Probably because my dryad spirit had no knees. No flesh, no blood. No need to plod through daily life. Distance meant nothing.

"Arabella!" My name rolled over me, not as sound, but as recognition, as a communion of spirits. A scent of sandalwood, Chantilly musk and amber brought with it memories of Rebecca. Us on our holiday in Germany. Happy and dizzy with excitement and discovery.

"Rebecca?" I coiled around whip-quick, sending my spirit in all directions like ripples from a stone dropped in a pond. My energy crashed up against something cold and dead. A metal of some sort. I could taste it. Not with my tongue because I was pure energy. But, I had no other frame of reference to describe the sensation.

Footsteps pounded around me and I knew who they belonged to. Thorn. I shot upwards, exploding out of the ground a few steps in front of him, earth crumbling off my body, showering the leaf-litter carpeting the forest floor. Pain flared in my knee once more, but it wasn't as severe, and I stood without needing to hold on to anything. This flying through the ground thing had a pretty nifty upside.

Thorn slid to a stop, slashing at me with the dagger. I raised an arm, shielding my face from the blow. An icy, burning sting sliced my forearm. Blood, hot and thick oozed across my skin, dripping onto the roots of a forlorn-looking ash tree.

I gazed at the cut, then stared at Thorn. "I didn't mean to wail at you."

"You can't help who you are." The haunted look in his eyes, the paleness of his skin in the filtered moonlight broke my heart.

We had only moved about twenty paces from the clearing. I was sure I'd shot through the ground for miles. Three mossy boulders clustered nearby, their outline softened by nodding ferns.

I've been here. This was where I'd first exited the ground after escaping from F.C.T. Headquarters. I'd been drawn to my family. To our forest home. And I hadn't even realised it. No wonder I'd felt their recognition, no wonder they'd called to me.

More of my blood trickled from the slash, dripping down my hand and onto the tree roots. The ground surrounding them rolled, grumbling as the blanket of moss tore apart. A root whipped up, wrapped around Thorn's waist and dragged him beneath the surface. He screamed, and as the ground thudded closed Thorn's beleaguered cries vanished. A still, uncomfortable silence followed as I stared at the torn earth.

The shapeshifter emerged in her cloaked form and stood off to the side, watching. "Well, that was impressive. Did you do that?"

"Are you mad? As if I could do that!"

"Well, not with a poor attitude like that."

I stared at the broken, moss clad soil and scattered leaves, my mind spinning.

"You going after the little weasel or what?" the shifter said. "I'd let him rot down there if I was you."

I shook myself, tossed aside the shard of wood and without another thought hurtled underground, reaching out with every part of my essence, searching for Thorn. I couldn't just let him die. I had too many questions. And for some ridiculous reason I still cared for him. I couldn't believe he had willingly killed Rebecca.

Thorn's mortal panic seared through me, like a river of water rushing through a sieve. His heartbeat thudded so fast, so hard I knew I'd hear its echoes for years. My dryad spirit found the feelings curious, interesting. My banshee spirit rang with impending doom. Thorn was going to die, his body reclaimed by the earth he walked upon only minutes earlier. I was bound to the Thorntons. I'd just howled a death. It didn't take much to put the pieces together.

I ploughed towards his frantic thrashing. His ragged choking. I grabbed for him, forgetting I had no hands. As my spirit dragged through his shoulder, his panic tore through me. Thousands of red-hot pins and needles.

"Ding!"

I flipped around, certain the call came from behind.

The scent of Rebecca's perfume hit me. Maybe it was her only way of screaming for help?

"Arabella?" Again, Rebecca's perfume washed through me. Sandalwood, Chantilly musk and amber.

Thorn to my left, Rebecca to my right. And me, torn between the two.

Thorn didn't have long to live. Had I truly howled his death? Was it ethical to both howl a death and be responsible for their demise? I didn't have time to debate the issue. The throb of Thorn's life-force weakened, washing over me in fragile, erratic waves. He no longer thrashed and struggled. The roots tangling around his body tightened their grip. Red-hot rage rippled off them, radiating through me, mindless and implacable. My second encounter with my dryad kin and I was terrified. Not the family reunion I'd imagined.

"Stop it!" I shot the words as though they were bullets, scattering them as wide and as far as I could. "You're killing him!"

I sensed the dryad spirit imprisoning Thorn for the first time. Strong, but hesitant, masculine but defeated, his roots shivered, adjusted their grip but didn't let go. Foggy, confused and embittered, they slid around Thorn's limp body. One tendril snaked towards me and stroked my energy gently. I shuddered and froze. Was this how dryads greeted one another?

"Vanara?" The male dryad sounded shocked.

"No," I responded, projecting my thoughts. "That's my mother's name."

"Rebecca?"

"No." My grief welled like a spring, pouring over the dryad.

"You're the little seedling?"

"I suppose so." *Seedling* seemed apt considering I'd only been five weeks old when I escaped to Earth.

"You shouldn't have come."

"We don't have time for this now! You're killing that man. Let him go!"

"I care not. He's a Thornton."

"Well I do! I need him to help me find Rebecca. I can't do that if he's dead."

"Vanara could. Powerful she was."

"I'm not my mother. I'm only half banshee. My other half is dryad. Like you. Surely you recognise me as one of the Ashmore dryads?"

"I have no family. Not anymore."

"Neither do I. My mother is missing, probably dead. My father ran off after trying to kill Rebecca and me. She's dead too now, and I have no idea where her body is. My grandmother hates me, and her mind is shattered. So, you see? I understand how you feel."

"If I release this siren—" The dryad loosened his grip on Thorn but did not let him go. "Will you remove that nasty iron box? It poisons our home."

"I promise."

As quickly as the dryad had dragged Thorn underground, he discarded him, slinging him upward like a stringless marionette puppet.

"Thank you." I reached out with my spirit and stroked the dryad's gnarled roots. I turned to go.

"I know where your mother is."

"What?" I had almost breached the surface. I knew Thorn needed help, but I couldn't help myself. There was no guarantee this dryad would talk to me again once I left the ground.

"Where's my mother?" I surged around the dryad's roots.

"They tricked her. Imprisoned her. Hateful things."

"My father—Druash, he didn't kill her?"

"I would never harm my love. I tried to save her."

I froze. The words rattled though my mind, brittle things that scraped the surface of hope but refused to sink in. My father? This was my dad?

"And me? Rebecca?" I asked, my question just as fragile as my father's revelation. "Did you try to kill us?"

"My memories of that time are splinters. I may have."

"Why?"

"Seeds of such love would grow into trees of grief and loss. I could not live with that."

CHAPTER THIRTY

I thrashed through the ground and heaved free of the forest floor, soil, mulch and leaf litter cascading down my body, scattering the ground with soft, tumbling thuds and 'pppps'. My father's revelations scoured my brain. He hadn't murdered my mother. But it looked like he had come after Rebecca and me. If it hadn't been for my grandmother–his own mum–I wouldn't be here now. Neither would… but she wasn't. When would I stop saying things like that?

"You just going to stand there, shaking?" The shapeshifter crossed her arms. "You should say your good-byes before he gets all rigid and disgusting."

Thorn lay on his side, his face smeared with mud, blood and drool. I squatted beside him, my knee barely hurting at all. Even the slash on my arm looked better. I'd have a scar, but it was better than an open wound.

I searched Thorn's neck for a pulse. Nothing. I yanked my phone from my boot, rubbed the wet screen on my sleeve and placed it under his nose. No condensation.

Nothing. Cursing softly, I rested my head on his chest, closed my eyes and listened. Nothing.

"That's sweet and all," the shapeshifter said. "But cuddling the weasel won't bring him back."

"You're such a cold hearted—"

"Comedian? Jester? Clown?"

"Not what I was thinking. Give me a hand to roll him on his back."

The shapeshifter threw back her hood, and I saw her face for the first time. No. It wasn't the first time.

"Endraya?"

Snow-white skin, ruby lips and dark, dark eyes framed by long black lashes. Elfin, elegant and beautiful. And alive. Long blue-black hair fell to her waist, a braid tipped with blue beads swinging free as she moved.

"Stunning, aren't I!" She said with no hint of vanity or pride. "I'm going to be a movie star, you know. Didn't I play the part of Endraya famously?"

"Who are you?" I heaved Thorn onto his back. "Really."

"Imalia," she said proudly. "*The* Imalia."

"You say that like I should know who you are."

Imalia sighed. "Can you get a wriggle on, please? Deadlines, you know."

"Sorry to hold you up."

Imalia looked down at Thorn, her head cocked to one side as she regarded him cooly. She puffed up her cheeks and blew out a frustrated breath. "So what? Are you going to use your powers to revive him?"

"I howl death, not life." I straightened Thorn's body and raised his chin, opening his airway. A small glass sphere containing a wooden molar slipped from his pants' pocket, bumping into my knee. I sucked in a sharp breath. The globe was suspended from a frayed, knotted leather thong. The same one Thorn had taken from his pocket to unlock the gate into his estate. Given the state of the leather, it's no wonder he'd lost the tooth-globe. It had probably fallen off during a struggle, or while he was out chopping wood or something. And Rebecca had found it. What was the bet—she knew who it belonged to and was going to give it to Walker.

Obviously, Thorn valued the tooth-globe. Probably a family tradition or talisman, given Aurelia had one too. So he'd broken into the mausoleum, found the tooth and put it on his key ring. And he'd taken the map, which had probably led him here, where he had tortured Ploggit for information.

I sat back on my heels. How could I save someone who had done such horrendous things? I wanted to slap him. Pound on him and scream. But he knew the answers I needed. I swore. Not a nice word, but it suited my mood.

"Why did you do it? Why?" Tears filled my eyes, and I wiped them away. I hurled the glass ball and its manky old tooth into a tree. Tinkling glass filled the darkness.

"Ooh!" Imalia clapped. "He won't like that at all."

"Good!" I tore open his shirt and put two fingers at the tip of his breastbone. I placed the heel of my other hand next to the two fingers, closest to his jaw. Once I was sure I was in the correct position, I used both hands to push up and down on his chest, elbows locked, careful to keep my fingers off his body so I wouldn't break any ribs. Pity. He deserved a few fractures for what he'd done to Ploggit and…

"This is fascinating!" Imalia squatted beside me, her eyes bright as she surveyed every movement. "Is this a torture technique? Because if you're trying to take revenge on his soul, you're bouncing and puffing for nothing. The little skirgal left his body while he was still underground. See. He's wafting about near the boulders."

Who knew what a skirgal was? By Imalia's tone of voice, it was obviously something icky and disgusting.

I glanced up, sweat dripping down my forehead and into my eyes. I couldn't wipe it away even though it stung like crazy. Thorn's soul might have been nearby, but all I could see were blurry shadows.

"Can you make yourself useful and wipe my eyes, please?" I gasped. "They're full of sweat and they hurt."

"That's rather disgusting."

"Please! My arms ache and my back is killing me."

"Oh, this is really ewwwy!" Cringing, Imalia dabbed my face and eyes with the hem of her cloak. The fabric was cold and course, like sack-cloth, and made my skin prickle. I wanted to pull away, but I didn't dare stop working on Thorn, maintaining a steady rhythm.

"Get off my son!" Aurelia Thornton crashed through the undergrowth, flailing between trees and waist-high ferns, her purple gown torn, twigs and dead leaves caught in her flowing sleeves.

Puffing, I stopped and felt Thorn's neck. A weak and thready beat pulsed beneath my fingertips. Not strong, but better than dead.

Oh, thank the heavens above! There was no way Thorn's mother would have let me continue CPR. I glanced at the boulders and Thorn's soul was gone. Presumably back into his body, now his heart was beating.

Aurelia threw herself at me, knocking me backwards. I lay on the ground panting, my shoulders throbbing from the cardiac compressions, ferns quivering above my face.

Imalia laughed. "If I'd known tonight was going to be so entertaining I would have brought popcorn."

Knola staggered through ferns and bushes, collapsing with a groan a few feet away from me. I didn't know whether to cheer for her or prepare to fight. I glanced at Aurelia, cradling Thorn in her arms, her long blonde hair curtaining her face. Had her hair been blonde or grey when I'd seen her last? I know it had been up in some fancy bun, but the details were fuzzy. I shook off the thought. She was occupied, so that only left Knola to contend with.

"What do you want from me?" I shouted at the satyr from my nest of ferns. "I've done nothing to you."

"I don't want anything." Her voice was strained and weak. "That wood splinter is out now. It killed my husband, you know. Thought it was going to kill me too. Thought you could help me. Maybe talk to the bit of wood, coax it out of my body before it did too much damage."

"So, Cael wasn't murdered?" I remembered all the blood, the impression of a blade on the quilt.

"Not by me. I tried to help him. I can still hear his

screams. Him begging me to cut it out. Then he died. Before I could think clearly, the splinter burst from his body and shot into mine."

"Where did it come from?"

"An old jewellery box."

Rebecca's missing jewellery box? It had to have been.

"This is all lovely." Imalia fluttered her hand. "And I'm so entranced by your revelations and all, but we have company."

Ava had her wand out, flicking it left and right, tracking movement. She dragged me upright and pointed to where Aurelia had emerged moments before. Dalford Hrimm waddled into view, sweat beading on his furrowed brow, a freesia tucked behind one ear. Within seconds, Rachel appeared from the darkness like smoke. Not a twig cracked, not a leaf trembled. Who else would turn up? That queen dragon lady? The goblin taxi drivers?

"Everyone remain calm," Ava said. "And no one will get hurt."

"Get up, Aurelia," Rachel snapped. "No one likes a snivelling woman."

"Henley!" Ava shouted, shoving me behind her. "Agent Briggs, get your backside over here, now."

She glared at Rachel. "Lost a few years since we last saw one another."

Rachel Thornton's hair hung to her waist in silky chestnut waves. Not a grey hair or wrinkle in sight. She still wore the ratty crimson gown, but she didn't look any older than me. Where had all those years gone?

Breaking twigs and branches drew everyone's attention to the other side of the clearing. Ava spun, her wand raised. A squat shape trudged towards us, slapping ferns out of its path, muttering and puffing. Dalford Hrimm appeared. Again. Though this one held a sad-looking bouquet of daisies. Not a nobby twig, herb or crystal to be seen.

"How delightful!" Imalia clapped her hands. "We have two of the snippy little blighters, now."

Aurelia looked up from Thorn, scraped her hair from her face and stared at one Dalford to the other, her mouth agape, her eyes wide. Her skin was as smooth and clear as her sister's. If these were the results of the *As You Wish Beauty Spa*, I was impressed.

"Briggs!" Ava bellowed. "Anytime soon would be nice."

A man with short black hair and a long coat ran into the clearing, his wand out ready. He skidded to a stop beside Ava. "Had to secure that ogre Rowlands. I need to work on my fitness." He nodded a greeting to me. "Crashed any flying croquet carts into defenceless bushes lately?"

"Henley Briggs?" I frowned. "You're the one who's been skulking about following us?"

"Surveilling." He shrugged. "Has a more professional ring to it."

The Dalford Hrimm who'd arrived with Rachel shimmered, golden iridescent sparkles expanding into a fountain of light. When it faded, Harvey sat in the gnome's place.

Howling, Rachel dashed towards her sister and stood at her back. "You!" She screamed at Harvey. "You little weasel of a slave! How dare you deceive us!" A glow bug buzzed around her and she swatted it away, sending it spiralling to the ground.

Harvey shimmered, her feline body swelling and expanding, shapeshifting into a griffin. With a lion's body and eagle's head, she'd taken on the last shape I'd seen before she'd abandoned me at Spell Haven. She scooped up the glow bug with one talon and dropped it at my feet.

"One of Rachel's spies. Please check if the poor thing's still alive."

I picked up the bug by one wing, its glow pale as I dropped it in my other hand. It was a fairy half the size of my little finger. I recalled the buzzy glow insect that had bothered me while I hid in the bushes beneath the cleaners' window. It hadn't been a bug at all. It had been spying on me. No wonder Rachel had known where I was.

I tapped the fairy's chest. "You alive?"

Her iridescent wings shuddered against my palm, flipping the tiny fairy over onto her belly. She curled into a ball, her wings forming a shell about her body. Not knowing what else to do with her, I dropped the fairy into my ball locket and snapped it closed. Hopefully, she wouldn't unroll and bust the whole thing apart.

Rachel faced Harvey, hands on hips, her chin jutting high with arrogant disdain. "Kill the banshee before she causes any more trouble."

"I can't." Harvey said, a deep growl purring through her throat.

"Of course you can. You've done worse before." Rachel kneed her sister in the back. "Get up and help me bring this shapeshifter to her knees. Seems her time away from this world has bolstered her bravado."

I frowned. How had she known about that?

Aurelia looked from Thorn's unconscious body to Harvey and up at Rachel. She lowered her son gently to the ground and stood with fluid grace, not one arthritic bone cracked, not one hesitation. Aurelia lifted her head and sung what sounded like a lullaby. Rachel joined in, her voice sweeter, more mellow than her sister's darker, deeper tone. The song really was quite beautiful. I yawned, my eyelids fluttering closed. I wrenched them open, shaking my head.

"No!" Harvey roared and pounced on the sisters, batting them in opposite directions with her huge paws.

Rachel tumbled into the boulders, wailed and staggered to her feet. Three bloody gashes from Harvey's claws cut her cheek. She wavered, but didn't fall. "My face!" She shrieked, touching the wounds. "My beautiful young face!"

Aurelia lay stunned at the base of an ash tree. Blood welled from a slash on her neck.

"Aurelia!" Rachel screamed. "Get up. On your feet. Now."

The real Dalford Hrimm tossed aside his bouquet of daisies, raced over to Aurelia and dropped to his knees, stroking her forehead. "Stay down, my sweet. I'll protect you."

He clambered upright and stood in front of his love, arms wide, glaring at anyone who moved. Aurelia groaned, rolled over and began crawling towards Thorn, still bleeding heavily. She wiped away blood with her sleeve and crouched by Thorn, using her body as a shield.

"Traitor!" Rachel screamed at Aurelia. "You're all traitors."

With the boulders at her back, Rachel dropped into a guarded crouch, her eyes narrowed, slewing back and forth, watching. She shifted her stance, widening her feet. She yelped and dragged up the hem of her long skirt. A root had coiled around her ankle. Howling, she kicked and tried to wrench her foot away, but the root held firm.

Ava directed her wand at Rachel, the crystal alive with ribbons of iridescent green and pink light. Pretty but probably deadly. I didn't dare move in case she slung some killing spell my way.

Aurelia shrieked, gathered up her skirts and hurtled towards her sister. Rachel clawed at the coiled root, howling and cursing as the root creaked and snaked further up her leg .

"My sweetness!' Dalford screeched. "Aurelia! What are you doing? Come back before the tree attacks you, too!"

Aurelia threw the gnome an apologetic look, but didn't stop. Dalford dashed toward her, waving his arms. An explosion of light, the smell of seared flesh and hair hit me. I dropped to my knees. Better to be a small target than a dead one. As the smoke cleared, a faint waft of freesias drifted around us. And the little gnome lay dead at Aurelia's feet.

"You killed him!" Aurelia cried, snarling at Ava.

"He shouldn't have got in the way." Ava said softly. "I'm sorry."

"He took the full brunt of your spell," Aurelia screamed. "His sweet little body!" She lurched toward Ava, arms outstretched, her fingers clawed, ready to attack.

A burst of fiery light sizzled over my head, punching into Aurelia's chest, hurling her backward. She sagged to the ground, her eyes wide with shock. I spun to see Walker Kane, his stumpy wand still crackling with red light and power.

"My little love!" Gasping, Aurelia dragged herself across the ground collapsing with one hand resting on Dalford's lifeless body, the other outstretched toward Thorn. She whispered, stroking Dalford's cheek. "We thought it was you who'd brought us the will-born wands Cael stole. The crystals for our spell... we were tricked." She coughed and blood frothed between her lips. "I wanted to be beautiful again. To remember things. My son. For you. I thought it was you..."

Aurelia coughed, her breathing laboured and gurgling. She sagged to the ground with a final cry of panic and fear.

CHAPTER THIRTY-TWO

malia opened her cloak with a dramatic flourish. A chill wind gathered up leaf litter, rattled nearby branches and whipped my hair and skirt against my body, drawing anything loose towards the blossoming pure white vortex within her cloak's embrace. She produced a seven-foot-long scythe from the folds of her cloak and twirled it like a marching girl.

Ava muttered, shook her head and looked away.

Walker said nothing, his jaw set tight, his eyes haunted and filled with pain. Henley Briggs shoved his hands into his coat pockets and kicked at fallen leaves sending them fluttering on the unearthly wind. I seemed to be the only one watching. I had howled a Thornton's death, just not the one I'd thought.

Two translucent, glowing souls floated above Dalford Hrimm's and Aurelia Thornton's bodies. Aurelia's soul shot towards the light, merging into it without hesitation. Feelings of overwhelming joy and love washed over me. Dalford's soul recoiled from the Light, and vanished into the forest.

Rachel wailed, rocking on the ground as she watched her sister leave.

Walker Kane hurried passed me, his stumpy wand held ready, his eyes fixed on Rachel and Harvey.

"Seems your plan worked, shapeshifter." Walker nodded his approval at Harvey.

"You doubted me?" Harvey morphed back into her Maine Coon form and licked her paw.

"Too bad I have to arrest you."

"I knew that when I devised the plan."

"You're arresting Harvey?" I glared at Walker.

"It's the law." Briggs shrugged. "But she'll get a fair hearing."

I pulled a grumpy face.

Briggs chuckled. "Snappy, aren't you!"

"Are Meeks and Ploggit really all right?" I asked Harvey. "Are they safe?"

"Ploggit is healing and Meeks refuses to leave his side."

"So they weren't poisoned?"

"After I left you at Spell Haven," Harvey said. "I flew back to check on Meeks and Ploggit. Sorry, I abandoned you, by the way. I had to leave after I saw Henley Briggs snooping about asking questions."

"It's okay. I'll get you back later. So what happened when you got back to the Apothecarium?"

"I surprised Dalford as he was trying to murder Meeks. Would you believe it? Had a cord wrapped about poor Meek's throat and was tugging the life out of him. When I got Hrimm tied up, I calmed Meeks down and then called Walker—told him everything. About Imalia finding me on Earth, and the two of us formulating a plan to entrap the Thornton sisters. I had thought I'd have to break into Hrimm's lockbox in the treatment room for the will-born wands he'd stolen from Cael—"

"After Cael had stolen them from the Thorntons to pay off a gambling debt," Walker added.

"But Hrimm." Harvey chortled. "Had already arranged them ever-so-wonderfully in his birthday gift for Aurelia."

"And then we searched Hrimm's grimoire library," Walker continued. "For the youth spell. The rest you saw."

"Good plan." Ava nodded to Harvey. "You had to catch the sisters using illegal wands in order to arrest them."

"I shapeshifted to look like Dalford," Harvey said. "Brought Aurelia the wands, crystals and herbs all magnificently arranged with the flowers. And the sisters did exactly as we'd hoped. I recorded everything. I must say, it was a wonderful show."

"Details! Give me details!" I bounced on the balls of my feet. "How did they get all young again?"

"As soon as I found the sisters at Spell Haven," Harvey said. "Rachel snatched the magical bouquet, grabbed Aurelia and ordered me–thinking I was Dalford–and Galivonn Smargett follow them from the dance." Harvey paced back and forth, standing on her hind legs now and then, gesturing with her front paws.

"That was mean!" I scowled at Rachel. "Those flowers were for your sister."

"No interruptions!" Ava flapped her hand at me. "Go on, Harvey."

"Galivonn led us down to the old tunnels beneath *As You Wish Beauty Spa*–the ones dug during the Dragon Wars. I thought they'd been sealed up and enchanted with locking spells after the earthquake—you know the one hundreds of years ago, where a class of student witches on the history excursion were all killed—but Galivonn knew of an entrance the town council missed when they went on that rampage locking *every* stone in place. Overkill, to put it mildly!"

I had never seen Harvey this animated or excited. Her golden eyes shone in the moonlight, bright with enthusiasm as she regaled us with her blow-by-blow story.

"I remember." Walker shook his head. "The Council's ridiculous stone-locking spells stuffed up the Hours time-keeping for years."

"Anyway," Harvey continued. "We had to break into *As You Wish*, pull up a few floorboards and head down into this mucky basement. Crawling with turgills, it was. And would you believe it! We had no fire to scare them off. If it wasn't for the sisters' siren powers, we'd all be wrapped in webs and packed away in turgill burrows for winter."

"I hate turgills." Ava shuddered. "Nothing should have that many legs."

"Or eyes!" Harvey wrinkled her furry nose. "Anyway, we followed the tunnels for a bit. Turn, turn and more turns. I had no clue where we were."

"How did you see down there?" I jumped in. "Do you have magical glowing orbs?"

"Not if I can help it." Harvey flapped a dismissive paw. "Let me finish."

"Yes!" Ava poked me in the shoulder. "Let her finish the story."

"We used a nifty little jar of wists–glow-fairies, Ding–to light the way. Giving them a shake every now and then to rile them up and keep them all shiny."

"Sounds mean," I whispered.

"Don't worry, Ding." Harvey raised her head, all noble and self-assured. "I let them go as soon as I escaped."

"Get to the youth spell!" Henley Briggs grinned, his eyes wide with excitement.

"So, to jump ahead." Harvey plonked her backside on

the ground and glowered at Henley. "The sisters reefed the bouquet out of its basket, lining everything up to take stock of their illegal goods. Rachel laughed all the time, patting her sister's shoulder and marvelling at the will-born wands. Chuckling and tittering about how wonderful it will be to be young again. No more backaches. How wonderful to see clearly again. To eat whatever they liked and not feel ill afterwards. They went on and on."

"Sort of like you are." Ava arched an eyebrow.

"I am endeavouring to give you every detail so you can experience the moment as I did. Spell-me-rotten for trying to give you all the facts!"

"Go on, Harvey." I nodded encouragement. "Regale us some more."

"Aurelia found a rolled up paper in the bottom of the basket." Harvey paced back and forth again. "The youth spell. Along with a bag of dried twigs and a small cauldron —about the size of a tea cup. The strangest thing was a jade vial of some sweet smelling liquid: like honey, roses and fresh-cut grass. Last was a silver athame no bigger than your thumb. That's when things got a little sticky. Rachel asked me if the liquid went into the cauldron before or after their blood. As if I knew the intricacies of the spell! Luckily Aurelia found a scribbled note at the bottom of the page that said the liquid went in the cauldron following the crushed herbs and a thimble each of their blood."

"What about the crystals?" I asked.

"Laid out in alignment with the cardinal directions and elements around the cauldron. Malachite-Earth-North, tourmaline-Air-East, garnet-Fire-South, emerald-Water-West. They heated the cauldron with those dried up twigs. Aurelia crushed the herbs and put them in the cauldron. Then they both cut a finger with the athame and squeezed their blood onto the herbs. Smelled quite tasty, what with the herbs and all. Galivonn swooned a bit." Harvey rolled her eyes. "But didn't pass out. He had a sit down, took off his stomping boots and felt much better."

"And the will-born wands?" Walker looked at me, swallowed hard and lowered his gaze.

"Added to the fire." Harvey's voice broke. "As soon as the fire took hold…" She breathed deep a few times. "As soon as the fire took hold, the screams started. They didn't quieten until the wands crumbled to charcoal."

"Why didn't the dryad souls leave the wands?" I frowned. It didn't make sense. "Why would the dryads allow themselves to be tortured like that?"

"Will-born wood - in this case the wands - only hold a portion of dryads' spirits." Harvey said. "My guess is those threads of spirit didn't have the wherewithal to leave. I can't be sure though."

"What happened when they added the jade vial's liquid?" Ava motioned for Harvey to hurry up.

"Who knew such a tiny bottle could hold so much!" Harvey marvelled. "As soon as Rachel uncorked the vial, a feather of purple light floated free, twining around the sisters like some long lost friend. Brushing them. Caressing them. Made me a bit ill, to tell you the truth."

"What was it?" Walker and I said together.

"You'll never believe it!" Harvey looked at us all one by one, prolonging the suspense. "It was the soul of Rachel's long dead baby—murdered centuries ago, her life essence trapped and bottled like a cask of mead."

"I never knew she had a child!" Walker glanced at Rachel.

Rachel sneered and refused to meet his eye. "Not something you speak of to strangers."

"Who killed your child?" Ava's usual snarky tone softened.

Rachel pointed at me. "Her grandmother."

A sharp weight dropped in my gut. "No! Meduil?"

"No. Your mother's mother."

"But she's a banshee," Walker said. "Shrieking a death is not the same as murder."

"And if the banshee commits both?"

"Shriek and then murder the person?" I couldn't believe what I was hearing. "Why would they do that?"

"I will not speak of it." Rachel snarled. "Especially to you!"

"You captured your baby's soul. Didn't you?" Walker stood straight, his shoulder's rigid. "After her death?"

"That was Aurelia. She thought it would comfort me some."

"And then you chose to use the child's life essence to make yourselves young?" Ava scoffed. "*How maternal.*"

"You come back and talk to me when your life nears its end." Rachel turned her back on us, her shoulders shuddering, her sobs heart-wrenching.

"Do you want to hear the rest of the youth spell story?" Harvey said, her voice barely above a purr.

"Maybe keep it brief for now.' Walker fondly rumpled up Harvey's fur. "You can make a full statement later."

"When I'm arrested." Harvey sighed.

"Sorry, old thing." Walker stroked her head. "You broke the law."

"The plan was the only thing I could think of to escape the sirens' thrall for good, help Arabella and save Rebecca." Harvey looked from Walker to me. "But I was too late."

We all stood in silence for a while, Rachel's sobs an

uncomfortable counterpoint to the rustling of leaves and the distant waves of Lake Mead.

"Did they drink the potion?" I said in an attempt to divert everyone. "Once they poured in the poor baby's soul?"

"No." Harvey sighed. "After the purple meet-and-greet, the sisters poured the remaining contents of the vial into the cauldron and stirred it with a wand, both holding the wood as they recited the incantation. The smoke from the will-born wands and the baby's soul merged, boiling around us in a scintillating aurora. Quite stunning, despite the slight stinging at the back of my throat. There was a whole lot of groaning and writhing from the sisters and when the lights faded and the smoke cleared, they were young again. The part that will stay with me forever, is hearing a child's voice crying for her mother throughout the whole enchantment."

I looked at Rachel, my heart heavy and bewildered. I didn't know what to feel. I wanted to hug her, but I also wanted her to rot in prison for all she'd done. Especially what she'd done to Rebecca. My sister.

Crying, confused, lost and angry, I forced myself to think of something else. Something that had been bothering me.

"How did Imalia cross to Earth without a magical jewellery box?" I wiped away my tears. "And why did she visit Rebecca in the first place? How did she even know about Rebecca and me?"

"Death is everywhere," Harvey said. "Time and space mean nothing."

Suddenly everything clicked into place.

I whirled to face Imalia. "So you're Death?" My mouth dropped open. "*The* Death! A Grim Reaper?"

"Oh!" Imalia rested a hand on her chest. "Finally, we

can get back to me. Imalia Grimm at your service. One of the best reapers Arahn has to offer."

Ava snorted. "Most annoying reapers, you mean."

"You wait until I come for you, verge," Imalia whipped her cloak open revealing an ink-black catsuit. "I'll enjoy that day immensely. Death always wins."

"Arabella, go check Thorn." Walker's voice broke as he wiped away a tear. "See if he's still breathing."

"I think he killed Rebecca," I said.

"Not willingly." Ava pointed her wand at Rachel. "Using your powers on your own kin. How typical."

Rachel hissed. She pressed one hand to her clawed face, blood oozing between her fingers. She gently brushed a few strands of hair from Aurelia's face. "I'm sorry. Not the birthday gift I had planned for you," she whispered, clasping her sister's limp hand. "At least you got to remember your son's life for a little while. You're so lovely. No wonder so many sailors drowned trying to glimpse your beauty."

Rachel tugged a chain from beneath her crimson gown and held up a globe containing a wooden molar. "I shall honour your death forever." She scooped Aurelia's matching globe from the ground and secured it around her neck with her own.

"Did you know Briggs took down Hywell Rowlands?" Ava said to Walker. "That ogre is involved with all this somehow. Where is he now?"

"Iron-bound by shackles to a dirty great tree and guarded by many cheerful protestors. Reckon we got him on falsifying environmental impact studies, bribery and corruption, and accessory to using restricted magic on innocent citizens. And that's before you add resisting arrest."

"You'll be sore tomorrow." Walker said to Briggs. "Taking on an ogre alone."

"Reckon I'll need a vacation. And a bonus. And a pay rise."

"We'll get paperwork," Walker said. "Like always."

CHAPTER THIRTY-THREE

I slumped to the ground and sucked in a deep, ragged breath. Harvey padded over to me and rested a paw on my leg.

"So, you're not a mooncat?" I sighed. "You're the shapeshifter? I thought Imalia Grimm was—the way she morphed into a raven and a leopard."

"Guilty," Harvey said.

"I don't understand. Why didn't you set me straight?"

"The Thorntons blackmailed me into service long before you were born. They kidnapped my fiancé—I tried to find him. When I thought I'd found where they'd locked him up, they used their siren powers on me. It's hard enough to defend your free will from one siren, but three, that's impossible."

"Did you have anything to do with my mother's disappearance? And Rebecca's?"

"You have to understand." Harvey dropped her gaze. "I was controlled by the sirens, but I never laid a paw on your family. When the Thorntons found out that your grandmother had sacrificed her heart-wood and made those two magical jewellery boxes to open a portal to Earth, they compelled me to take the real mooncat's position as chaperone with Ploggit."

Ava, Briggs and Walker stood nearby listening, all three taking magical notes.

"You realise they're recording all this?" I stroked Harvey's soft coat, scratching her behind one ear.

"Yes. I know."

"What happened to the real mooncat?"

"Dead I'm afraid. At least that's what I was led to believe."

I was terrified to ask, but did anyway. "And what were your orders? When we got to Earth?"

"To kill you and Rebecca." Harvey sighed. "And Ploggit."

"What changed your mind? Rebecca was a child. I was a tiny baby—we would have been easy targets."

"The sisters' power lost its grip when we reached Earth. I knew if I returned to Grimsmead, the Thorntons would control me again. I couldn't live with that. So I stayed and did all I could to protect you."

"Why choose to be cats? Surely an adult human would've been a better protector on a planet like Earth."

"I had limited power—no true magic to draw upon, you see. All I could manage were various versions of the same form."

"What were the sisters' orders about the jewellery boxes?" Walker asked. "I'm sure the Thorntons would've tried to steal them before they enlisted you to go to Earth with the girls. Seems pointless to let you go to a whole other world, kill Becca and Arabella, and then bring the boxes home to Grimsmead."

"Oh, they tried to steal them—all that will-born magic

just waiting to be used almost drove them wild. Especially Rachel."

"Almost?" I lifted an eyebrow, staring at Rachel, iron-cuffed and weeping beside her sister's body. Rachel didn't flinch as the metal shackles pressed against her skin. Either she was too distraught to notice or sirens were immune.

"After your mother and father went missing," Harvey explained. "Suspicion fell on the Thorntons. Their estate was the last place your mother had been seen, so the Thorntons were under close scrutiny by the F.C.T. The sisters had to come up with an alternate plan. Their Plan B still suited their agenda even if it was time-consuming. They would have been rid of the last banshees bound to their bloodline, and they'd get the will-born wood when I returned from Earth."

"Why did they want the boxes?" I knew they were magical, but there had to be a specific reason. "Did they want to travel to other worlds?"

"The boxes only work as a portal between Arahn and Earth—where the Thorntons would have no power or influence. That was the last thing they wanted."

"Is that the jewellery boxes only power?"

"The will-born wood, on Arahn is very magical," Harvey said. "Once the Thornton sisters heard about the power of heart-wood, especially heart-wood infused with the dryad's spirit—will-born wood was all they could think of. It's powerful magic—brimming with the planet's very life-force."

"There are so many other sources of magic here on Arahn," Ava said. "Why were they so obsessed with will-born wood?"

"It's the only magic to stave off old age." Harvey slumped to the ground, her chin resting on her front paws.

"They did all this!" Ava laughed bitterly. "Because they

didn't want to get old? Wasn't a few thousand years enough for them?"

"Seems not," I said. "I suppose anyone will fight for life when they feel death looming."

Ava, Walker and Briggs all looked at Imalia perched on the largest of the three boulders.

"She most certainly looms." Ava glared at Imalia.

"I'm confused." I shook my head. "Did the Thorntons kill my mother? And Rebecca?"

"You're banshees," Harvey said. "Your family is bound to the Thorntons. You howl their death, and one of them dies."

"Seriously!" I said. "Killing the messenger wouldn't save their lives. That's just stupid."

"According to legend," Thorn said, his voice trembling as he struggled to sit up. "Neutralising your family banshee staves off death. Will-born wood maintains youth. While my aunt and mother waited for the shapeshifter to return, we searched the forest for will-born trees, harvesting parts to make wands for their stupid youth spell."

Everyone looked at Imalia.

"Is that true?" I asked. "Did my mother and sister die so the Thornton sisters could live?"

"Your mother isn't dead," Imalia said with a flourish. "Just trapped somewhere."

"Where?" everyone said.

"What am I? A map to lost souls or something?"

I looked at Harvey. Then Walker. So my dad was right. "My mum is out there somewhere?"

"And what of Rebecca?" Walker grabbed Imalia's shoulder. "Is she trapped somewhere, too?"

"You're standing on her."

CHAPTER THIRTY-FOUR

"What?" I stared at the ground. "In that iron box?"

Walker and I fell to our knees and began digging. Tears ran, splashing my hands as I gouged away the soil. Harvey, Briggs and Ava joined us. It wasn't long before my fingers, raw and bleeding scraped over cold iron, my hands stinging, the pain shooting up my arms.

"Is it bespelled?" I shook my hands, clenching and unclenching my fingers.

"Iron is like poison to fey folk," Ava said.

I nodded, now understanding why my father wanted me to remove the iron box from our family home.

"Hang on a minute!" I remembered how the verge interrogation room was iron. "How did you do your verge-thing in a room of iron?"

"I'm not your usual fey. I'm special."

"Says you!" Despite the pain in my fingers, I swept away the loose soil. Between Ava, Briggs, Walker, and I, we raised an iron trunk strapped closed with metal bands etched with magical symbols. Three massive padlocks sealed the trunk shut. I grabbed one and pulled, but it didn't budge.

"Come on," I cried. "Someone help me open them."

Ava dragged in a sharp breath and looked at my boots. I glanced down. A tree root snaked up and over the trunk, coiling around the lock closest to me. It had to be my father. Was he trying to save her? Or keep us from opening the trunk? Surely the iron was hurting him?

"But you wanted us to remove it from our home," I shouted.

"No!" A male said. It wasn't Walker or Briggs, and it wasn't Thorn.

A hand rested on my shoulder, and I jumped. I spun around to see a tall, slim man with fissured bark for skin, ash leaves growing through his sandy hair, roots where his feet should have been.

Ava, Briggs and Walker raised their wands, aiming them at the dryad.

"It's okay." I signalled them to lower their wands. I faced the dryad. "Are you Druash?"

"I am."

"Rebecca's in the iron chest," I said. "She could be alive. Please let us open it."

"After all this time, I doubt it," Ava said, no sarcasm in her tone or her expression. The symbols covering her skin shifted restlessly, merging, coiling and glowing a pale blue. I didn't know her well enough to understand the nuances of her verge powers. I glanced at Walker to gauge his reaction. His eyes were dark, his lips tight, his brows furrowed. I couldn't work out if he was angry, stressed or grieving. Probably all three. He rested his hands on his head and looked skyward. I couldn't see, but I was sure he was fighting back tears.

"Leave your sister rest, Seedling," my father said

quietly. "Her soul is broken, her body long dead. You need to find your mother."

"How do you know Rebecca's dead?" I rattled one of the locks. "She might be in a coma. Or some magical sleep."

"He knows she's dead." Walker choked on the words. "She's already transforming."

I shuffled around the trunk with Ava and Harvey following me. A fragile tree root, so young and new it was translucent-white grew out of a tiny hole where a screw had once secured an iron strap to the trunk.

"Ding!" Rebecca's voice drifted upward, a hollow, haunted sound that dug into my heart. Tears welled, and my throat tightened so hard I couldn't breathe.

"Let me rest. I'm tired. I'm sorry I left so suddenly and didn't tell you where I was going. I thought I was keeping you safe. Someone called Endraya came to me on Earth."

I glared at Imalia.

Imalia smiled and took a bow. "I knew she'd be a wonderful friend for me."

"Don't expect me to shout 'Encore' anytime soon!" I turned my attention back to Rebecca. "It's all right, sweetling."

"Endraya said bad people were harvesting heart-wood from our family and using it to make illegal wands. She said they were harassing our grandmother. She didn't deserve such treatment. Not after sacrificing her heart-wood to keep us safe. It broke her mind, giving up her powers like that. Give them to her, Ding. Give the jewellery boxes back to her. Maybe they'll help her recover."

"I don't know where yours is. I'm sorry, Becca."

"It's in here with me," Rebecca said. "Along with Lisk."

"Her mobile stone fairy." Ava brushed soil off the trunk's lid. "We wondered what happened to her."

"She's dying." Rebecca's voice faded. "Too much iron. And the merfolk spines Thorn used to drug me are noxious—poisoning her."

"I didn't mean for Rebecca to die!" Thorn's eyebrows pinched together. "The spines should have just made her groggy, compliant. If she'd just told us if these were will-born trees—if this was the Ashmore grove. But she refused to talk. And then…" He trailed off into silence.

"From what I can see." I indicated the ash trees and the hole in the forest floor where we'd dug up the trunk. "You found my family's home. Why did you steal the map if you already knew?"

"We had to be sure."

"You knew who I was the moment you saw me, didn't you? I bet I confirmed your suspicions about this grove—another Ashmore playing in the dirt. I might as well have drawn a giant X to mark the spot."

Thorn paled. He licked his lips and lowered his gaze. "I figured you were an Ashmore."

"You charmed me into going to your estate. Why didn't you grab me then? Tie me up with a fancy ribbon and hand me to your aunt?"

"She didn't want to take the risk. Not after what we went through when Rebecca went missing so close to home."

"What your family went through?" Walker's nostrils flared, and he shoved Thorn.

Thorn stumbled backward, grasping his chest, wincing. Probably tender from the chest compressions I'd done to save his life. His miserable, rotten life.

"The old bat said nothing about taking risks! She ranted about banshees and—" I rushed Thorn, my arms outstretched, fingers clawed.

Walker grabbed me from behind, and hauled me away,

my legs peddling, my breathing harsh and ragged as I struggled to escape.

"Not to you, she didn't." Thorn rested a finger on his temple. "I heard her. I always hear her."

"So you plotted all this?" Ava's top lip curled.

"Aunt Rachel and mother plotted. I did as they said. Like I've always done."

"Did they tell you to bury Rebecca to hide your crimes?" Ava crossed her arms, glaring at Thorn.

He lowered his gaze and shook his head. "That was my idea."

"You realise once the Maranormal fey know what you did," Walker released me with a stern look. He glowered at Thorn. "The truce between you will be broken?"

"That's why he buried the evidence." Harvey tapped the trunk. "If the evidence is gone, there's no crime."

"Too bad you didn't check the trunk for holes," Walker said.

"There were none," Thorn said. "Not one. I checked it over a dozen times."

"I bet Rebecca found a loose screw," Harvey said.

"And with her last breath she managed to remove it and call for help," Walker said with pride.

He reached over the trunk and squeezed my hand. "I'll get her body out of this cursed iron and bury her here with your family."

I nodded, unable to say anything.

My father rested a bark hand on my shoulder, his body creaking, his leaves rustling. "She will be reborn into a tree. Grow strong and beautiful, a dryad free of death and darkness now her two souls are unbound."

"What happened to her banshee soul?" I looked around the glade, half expecting it to swoop in and join us.

"Oh!" Imalia waved. "Already taken care of. Sent it on

its way after Rebecca visited you all creepy and confused in her bedroom when you first arrived in Grimsmead."

"I came as soon as I heard you needed me." I stroked the trunk, barely feeling the sting of iron. "I tried to find…"

"What I don't understand," Briggs said suddenly, "is why you hid the jewellery box in the trunk when you knew your mother and aunt were so desperate for will-born wood?"

"Exactly," Thorn said. "I couldn't let them have that much power. I gave the illegal will-born wands to Cael—thought they'd help him pay off the bookies. But Dalford Hrimm got hold of them." Thorn sighed. "Cael never stole anything from us, and my aunt treated him like a personal puppet, doing all her dirty work. You don't know how strong she is. Keeping the will-born wands and jewellery boxes from her was all I could do."

"That would have taken all your will power," Harvey said. "To go against them like that."

"You have no idea. Once I saw that shard of will-born wood splinter from Rebecca's jewellery box and burrow into Cael, I knew I had to bury the box. *It* knew Rebecca was in danger. It *knew*."

Thorn cast a hesitant glance my way. "I saw your jewellery box on a mound of things in the Forest Room at the mausoleum. I hid it in amongst the ferns. I just needed my talisman back."

"And a map," I snarled. "Right to my family."

Thorn had the decency to blush and look away. Why did I ever think he was so special? It was all a spell to get me where he needed me. Make me trust him so I'd unwittingly betray my family. I hoped he rotted in prison. Him and his rotten aunt.

"You beat up an innocent spriggit brownie." I spat the

words like venom.

"I didn't want to! My aunt turned up. Probably to make sure I was following orders. The next thing I knew, the spriggit brownie was battered and bleeding at my feet."

"Why? What did she want so badly?"

"You. Your jewellery box. My talisman and the map to Ashmore land. I tried to stop her."

"Oh!" I lowered my eyes.

"Maybe if you read up on sirens, Ding." Harvey said. "You'll understand."

"Are you excusing him?" I turned on Harvey.

"No. What I'm saying is you don't know this world—all the magic, the species. It might do you good to spend some time at Grimsmead Academy."

"Pfft!" I crossed my arms. "Not likely."

An awkward silence descended, and we all stood looking at anything but one another. I kneeled by the trunk, resting my cheek on the iron. It stung, but compared to the grief in my heart, it was nothing.

"We will see each other again, Becca," I whispered, patting the trunk. "I promise."

"We'll visit her, Arabella, every chance we can," Walker said. "Perhaps one day, when she's a fully grown dryad, you will go travelling again." He looked at the trunk and a single tear fell, splashing on the iron prison.

So much heartache and death surrounded us, I wondered if this grove of ash trees, my family home, would ever recover. No, I couldn't think like that. I would give my grandmother the two jewellery boxes, and with Nature's Grace and my love, the heart-wood in those boxes would help her, and we could tend our home together.

I touched the fragile root growing out of the hole. My skin tingled and the faint smell of sandalwood, Chantilly musk and amber drifted around me.

*W*alker and I sat on either side of a mound of soil, raking fertiliser into the moist, crumbly earth with our fingers. We worked in silence, the sounds of birds and whispering leaves echoing through the dappled forest. I patted the soil down and brushed my hands together, but mud still smeared my palms and stained my fingernails. Perfect for a dryad. Well, half dryad.

"Do you think she likes her new home?" Walker added a sprinkle of water to the mound, watching it trickle down the sides in tiny rivers.

"I think Becca loves it," I said. "She's surrounded by family. And she's safe from harm."

Walker watched my grandmother dancing around the trees, a sheer gown of spider-silk and spun silver floating about her sinewy body, her long, flowing hair threaded with moss and leaves. "Now Meduil has her heart-wood back with her tree, and her soul is in one piece—not three—she's more like her old self."

"Urdula Pring reckons my grandmother will never be

one hundred percent." I scooped soil into my hand and let it rain between my fingers.

"At least she doesn't need to be in Spell Haven anymore. She'll watch over Rebecca. And the others."

"But not my father."

"No. He's long gone. Probably afraid he'd be arrested for trying to murder you and Rebecca."

"Or he's looking for my mother."

Walker inclined his head. "Or that."

"I went back to the Apothecarium, you know," I said. "After Ava caught Dalford Hrimm's soul."

"What for?"

"Just following a hunch about my mother."

"You think Hrimm had something to do with her disappearance?"

"Maybe. Who knows?"

"What made you go looking?"

"When we were getting Ploggit medical help, I saw a rusty can-like-thing floating above Dalford's cages. Crimson light shone through these rough-punched holes. I thought maybe my mother was trapped inside."

"But she wasn't."

"The cage was gone. I looked everywhere."

"Strange."

"That's what I thought."

"I'll file a report," Walker said. "See if we can't track it down."

"How's Harvey?"

"Missing you. And Ploggit."

"I should visit her."

"But, you're finding it hard to face her?"

"Yeah. But I will. Soon."

"I spoke at her trial, you know."

"Me too," I said. "I don't know what good I did, though."

"The Elders agreed Harvey was under the sirens' thrall. And that she protected you even though she could have left you and Rebecca on Earth and snuck home. They also took Harvey's unorthodox plan to counter the Thornton sisters into consideration."

"Are they are letting her off the charges?"

"No. Her shapeshifting powers are to be bound. She will remain a cat for the next thousand years. She'll have to do community service twice a week."

"Wow! For a thousand years? I'll bet she's not happy about that."

"It was better than the alternative." Walker grinned, his hazel eyes bright with mischief. "You should have seen the court when Imalia Grimm took the stand and said the plan was all her idea because she'd wanted a best friend. She thought warning Becca about the Thorntons' plot to harvest will-born trees would make them instant best buddies. That was the word she used. Buddies. And when that plan failed, she figured you would be a great replacement buddy. The court erupted with laughter. The Elders muttered and frowned. I'm not sure if she helped Harvey's case or hindered it."

"How did Imalia know about Rebecca? Seems a long way to go to find a friend."

"She's Death. The Reapers keep meticulous records of where everyone is at all times."

"I'm glad I'm not a records clerk for them."

"I'm sure they have a system. Goodness knows what it is." I bowed my head, my cheeks warming. "And Thorn?"

"Undergoing reprogramming at the psych hospital."

"That sounds scary."

"Maybe, but it's necessary. He's been controlled and manipulated his whole life. As was Aurelia. Rachel really is a nasty, self-serving piece of work. She's at the F.C.T. locked in the deepest, darkest and most soundproof dungeon we have. Anyone who deals with her wears noise-cancelling ear-muffs."

"Good!"

"Oh! I forgot." Walker dug in his shirt pocket and pulled out my golden-orb locket. "Here. The fairy you tucked in here was most helpful at the trial—gave away lots of Rachel's secrets and schemes in exchange for immunity."

I looped the chain around my fingers. "It's still glowing."

"Boo likes it in there. I think she's grateful to you. Hope you don't mind."

I held the filigree ball up and peered inside. Two peridot-green eyes stared through one of the swirly gaps.

"I guess it's okay. She's sort of like a nightlight. Hello, Boo!" I waved my pinkie finger at her.

The glow from the orb radiated bright and golden, and I slipped the chain around my neck.

As I tucked it beneath my shirt, I remembered the glass globes with wooden molars.

"Why do the Thorntons carry those old teeth around as if they're something precious?"

"They are precious to them—to all sirens."

"Seems odd to me."

"You're not a siren. Look at them as a badge of honour—a token from a rite of passage."

Chills crept along my spine. "A rite of passage?" I didn't want him to elaborate, but I couldn't help myself. "What rite?"

"When a siren reaches sixteen years old, they're taken

out to a rocky island in the Smoking Sea. They're left with basic supplies, a single rescue flare and the hopes of their family."

"They're left alone? At sixteen?"

Walker nodded. "They must use their siren call to lure a passing ship to a stretch of water that hides submerged rocks.

"I guess it's dangerous on these rocks?"

"Deadly. The young siren has to enthral any surviving sailors—make them retrieve drowned crewman and extract a back molar."

"The tooth isn't wooden!"

"Let me finish." Walker chuckled. "But, the ship's wheel is. The siren has to make the crew fetch the wheel from the wreck, and carve a molar from the timber. An exact replica of the drowned sail's extracted tooth."

"Then the young siren fires the rescue flare?"

"All the while, keeping the ship's crew enthralled."

"And some sirens don't survive this rite."

"No."

I understood now why those tokens were so valuable to the Thorntons, even if they were disgusting.

My grandmother leaped and spun around Rebecca's little mound of soil, humming and smiling.

"Join me, Seedling," she called. "I'm helping Rebecca grow."

"It's okay," I said. "I don't know the steps. I'll probably grow weeds instead."

"Nonsense! You have dryad blood."

I looked at Walker. "Save me!" I whispered.

He smiled and waved me on. "Go! Dance."

Dance like no one is watching. I had a poster with that saying on my bedroom wall when I was a teenager. Who knew I'd need that very advice in a whole new world?

I swayed left and right, my floaty green skirt swirling about my army boots.

"Take them off!" my grandmother shouted. "You need to feel the soil, be one with the planet. Shoes are for plodding."

I unlaced my boots and kicked them across the ground. Yanked off my socks and hurled them away. I wiggled my feet into the cool earth, felt the raw energy coil up through my body like liquid lightning. My sways became swirls, my arms reaching for the sunny sky high above the forest canopy.

My grandmother laughed, twirling around me.

"She's sprouting!" Walker jumped up and ran to me, grabbing my hands.

All three of us dashed back to the mound of earth, dropped to our knees, staring in amazement. A fragile shoot crowned the soil, a single trembling leaf reaching for the sky.

And I danced like no one was watching.

The End
Brooms Away
Book One in the Arabella Black Magical Cozy Mysteries

Turn the page for a sneak peak at Book 2
Sequins of Events

Chapter One

Hooray for Death

The apothecary gnome, Dalford Hrimm, had been a know-it-all grump in life. Dying hadn't improved his manners at all. And now that he was my official shackled ghost, he oozed misery and animosity like a squashed frog.

He wafted above Magic and Mystree's serving counter, clanking his translucent chains through wax-sealed jars, neatly stacked candles and a triangular display of jars, each stuffed with seventy-six troll hairs–our current Special of the Day. Dressed in undertaker-esque garb, he followed my every move with a sullen scowl and much muttering. His groans and glares made my day brighter. And every grin I flashed him made him scowl all the more. It was a win-win affair for me.

"Arabella Black, you have no clue what you're doing." Dalford's hollow, echoing voice sent chills along my arms, but at least I didn't shudder any more. The icy wind still rolled across my skin whenever he got too close, but a cup of coffee, a scarf and a thick jacket took the edge off.

"Say that one more time." I wagged my finger. "And you'll spend the next month in your box." Mumbling, Dalford crossed his arms and turned away.

I loved 'The Box'. It had taken five summary incarcerations in the rickety iron-bound chest before he'd learned that my word was law. Last time he'd annoyed me, I'd spent a gleeful afternoon playing Jack-in-the-box with him. Now I only had to glance at the box for him to behave.

The bell above the front door tinkled as someone pushed it open. My first customer. Ever. I fashioned the best, most welcoming smile I could and prepared to greet them.

"I told you I'd come for you." A cloaked and hooded figure loomed in the doorway for a moment, then flounced into the store, weaving around tables of pre-packed fairy-skulls, dried fungus gnats, and auto-gnashing teeth (All toothy sets secured by regulation Red-String and a warding rune–didn't want them eating the customers).

The cloaked figure, backlit by the store's diamond-paned window, bumped into a display stacked with garden gnome party-hats and bottles of a liquid I couldn't pronounce. I was doing my best to learn the store's inventory, jotting notes each time Dalford Hrimm rattled off some medicinal herb or magical device, but some items had ridiculous names with way too many letters.

The cloaked customer poked the party hats. Several of them tumbled to the floorboards, squeaked 'Hooray!' shot up a fountain of streamers and confetti, and wobbled back to the display stand. With tiny puffs of glitter squirting from their points, the hats started climbing up the stand's black skirting. Laughing, the cloaked customer threw back her hood. Five feet ten (at least) athletic and slim, she was stunning, ethereal, but not fragile. She'd changed her hair since I'd last seen her, so it fell a few inches below her shoulders in soft waves. She'd kept her colour theme though, her inky locks streaked with cobalt blue.

"Imalia! What are you doing here?" I grabbed an athamé from a shelf behind the serving counter and unsheathed the silver blade from its scabbard.

"You are so funny!" Imalia clapped. "Waving a shiny dagger at Death." She whipped her seven-foot-long reaper scythe from the folds of her cloak and twirled it like a baton, swiping more gnome hats off the display. They tumbled into the hats struggling up the black skirting, knocking them to the ground. New hats shouted, "Surprise!" Old hats shouted, "Hooray!" More confetti, streamers and glitter. Dalford was going to love sweeping up this evening. I slid the athamé behind the troll hair jars, keeping it unsheathed just in case. Nothing stupid happening here.

"I knew you'd be like your sister." Imalia Grimm shoved her scythe back into some mysterious pocket in her cloak and strode toward me, grinning. "Growing up on another world really sharpened your humour, Arabella."

"Yeah," I said. "I'm a hoot. What do you want?"

"Friendship."

"Seriously?"

"No one likes me on Arahn."

"No one likes you on any planet."

"That's not very nice."

"You're Death. *The* Death. The Grim Reaper."

"I've taken a sabbatical."

"You can't go on leave."

"That's what my mother said."

Dalford floated from the shadows, glowering at the confetti, streamers and party hats struggling up the display stand. He cocked his head, eyeing Imalia hopefully.

"I've changed my mind. I shouldn't have run when I died. I'd like you to send me into The Light now."

"You shouldn't have done a lot of things," I snapped.

"Too late now, buddy." Imalia prodded him in the chest, sending Dalford careening through a potted palm. "I learned the word 'buddy' from Rebecca," Imalia said. "Did I use it correctly? I'm fact hunting. It's called a hobby."

I didn't answer for a moment. Hearing Imalia speak my sister's name aloud brought back too many distressing memories. "I can't have got it that wrong." She frowned. "I've been practicing all morning. You should have seen my father's face when I said, 'Buddy, I'm off to my friend's place. She's going to help me become a movie star.'"

"Are you still going on about that?" I re-sheathed the athamé. Now Imalia and I were 'buddies', the dagger seemed overkill. I kept it close, though. I wasn't that naïve.

"You sound like my mother." Imalia paced the floorboards, gesticulating madly. "'Mali,' mother says, 'You have a perfectly perfect vocation. Why do you insist on this 'acting' thing?' And I say, 'Why do you insist on insisting?'"

"What acting opportunities do you have?" I hadn't heard of any movies or TV shows here in Grimsmead, but I'd only been on the planet for a short time. "Is there a glitzy movie city here on Arahn like we have on Earth? A place where they make big-budget films?"

"Not yet, but we do have the Grimsmead Live Players."

"As opposed to the Dead Players?"

"Rivals, especially during the holiday seasons when it's

pantomime time. I can technically join both, but I prefer the Live Players. It's the ever-present stink you see—the dead do waft a bit. You see my dilemma?"

"Clearly." What I needed was a customer. Someone interesting to distract Death from waffling on. The shop door remained closed. Maybe the townsfolk thought the Magic and Mystree shop was still closed for refurbishment.

"The Live Players have a show coming up in a few months and their calling for auditions." Imalia grinned. You'd think Death smiling at you would be terrifying, but taking a sabbatical must have dulled down her grimness.

"And you want to try out for a role?" Imalia nodded, her blue eyes bright with enthusiasm. "It's a murder mystery. I want to play the murderer. Very exciting, wouldn't you say?"

"Very. Do you have some sort of resume? Reviews of your acting prowess?"

"Well, I played Endraya fabulously. You had no idea I was acting the part of a dead girl. I call that a rousing success."

"Not exactly the words I'd use." Imalia Grimm had pretended to be the ghost of Endraya, breaching time and space to find me on Earth and get me to return to Arahn to help find my missing sister Rebecca. But we'd been too late. And Becca had died. Sort of. It's a long story.

"Why do you look so glum?" Imalia said. "Come! We need to audition before the murderer role goes to some ugly shlob." She grabbed my hand, her cool skin sending prickly shivers up my arm. "Have you studied the role?" I asked. "Practiced the lines? Got inside the head of a cold-hearted killer?"

"Ooh! I should do that, shouldn't I?"

"If you want to wow the director, you should."

"Hmm, I need to murder someone. Really understand what it feels to kill."

"That's not what I meant!" The bell above the shop door jangled. As the door opened, a wedge of sunlight illuminated the Magic and Mystree Store's gloomy interior. Funny how that never happened when Death swooped in.

❧

I WOULD LOVE it if you joined my V.I.P Club. I've written a short story about Rebecca and Walker Kane especially for you. If that sounds enticing, tap the link below.

Ooh! Join Me Up!

OR, if this is a print book, head over to my website. You will find the download link waiting for you.

https://dakellyauthor.com/

LAKE MEAD
THE HOURS
AS YOU WISH
ASHMORE HOME
THORNTON ESTATE
SPELL HAVEN
F.C.T. HEADQUARTERS
MAUSOLEUM
GRIMSMEAD TOWN
SHOWGROUNDS
NARROWS RUN

F.C.F. HEADQUARTERS
THEATRE
TOWN COUNCIL
PARK MARKETS
MUSEUM
CALL CENTRE
GRIMEMEAD TOWN CENTRE
EXHIBITION BUILDING
SYMATREE

ACKNOWLEDGMENTS

There are so many wonderful people to thank.

I'll start with my partner Darren. You're unwavering support and belief over the years is why I'm here now writing this. Without you, this book would never have been written. Love you Big Lots. And more lots. I'd draw my signature smiley face, but there's not enough room for my wild hair. XXX

My kids, Daniel, Kaela, Jayke, Callum and Jeb, yes your mum is nuts, but now I add my nuts to the page. Mostly.

Cameron, Jacci, Nick and Trinity. See I was doing something in my office.

The list of people who have been there for me is vast so I think I'll list them rather than waffle on.

Kellie Croft - best friend and lovely lady. Thank you for being you.

The Springfield Writer's Group, including Neen, Pamela, Caroline Ann, Annie, Meg, Lynne, Jem and especially Aarjaun.

Jacqui and Kev, Craig, Kate and Pam Dunstan for having to put up with me and my scatterbrain.

Ally Blake, thanks for never giving up on me.

Tabitha and Damian Herde for support, laughs and wine.

Jason, Paul, Mark, Shel, Chris and especially Nea - who I miss terribly. Louise Cusack, Jack Dann, Sean Williams, Rowena Cory Daniels, Annabel Blay and Robert Hood.

My cheerleaders across the ocean, especially Cailin Fili, Jane, Ileana, Nadine, Meg, Jenna, Petra, Maria, Catherine, Candice, Nancy, Theresa, Brandi, Marsha, Marcie, Lousie, Stephanie, Andrene, Victoria, Tracy, Jeannie, Lily, Betsy, Cheryl and Wendy.

My fellow Aussie cosy authors, Dionne Lister, Kelly Ethan and Morgana Best. Morgana, thanks for the formatting help. And Jane Hinchey for helping me with my Newsletter. Jen for helping with fiddly stuff. Cat for your patience and support helping me behind the scenes.

Mark Leslie Lefebvre for being there when I needed guidance.

My wonderful, patient and understanding editor, Rebecca Grubb, you are a pleasure to work with.

And lastly the lovely readers in my ARC team. Thank you for joining Arabella in the Ark. Your comments made me cry, not in sadness, but with relief.

Deb

ABOUT THE AUTHOR

D. A. Kelly is a writer and delighter in all things magic. Her stories are relentless, spellbinding mysteries stuffed full of quirky characters, wicked humour and magical murder.

Sparkles are the best thing ever. If it's shiny she stops everything to look at. Cake and chocolate turn her head. Mainly so she can get them in her mouth.

She lives in Queensland, Australia with her much-loved partner Darren and a hoard of boomerang kids. Seriously, she needs a revolving door built in her house.

She'd like nothing better than to have a cosy witchy hovel built in her backyard to use as her office. Hint, hint, Darren.

You can find out more about D. A. Kelly at:
www.dakellyauthor.com